A Bloody Road

The Iron Teeth: Book Three

Scott Straughan

ISBN: 978-1-7750029-7-0

This book is dedicated to my family. Although it must have vexed them, they put up with me and all my flaws. This story never would have gotten written without their patient support.

THE NORTHERN EDGE
N
COROULIS
THE IRON TEETH
SHELTER
BRACKENMOUNT
DAGGERPOINT
WESTWATCH
HERAD'S CAMP
ATTERVALE
RIVERRUN
HULGARON
GREENTILT
ROMESCA
HIGHFIELDS
ELORIA
ILHDA
WHISPERING LAKE

Part One:
Rolling the Dice

Chapter 1

The creaking of the wagon's wheels was somewhat muted by the frequent thud of footsteps on the dusty road. The only other sound to be heard was the rustling of leaves as the wind blew through the trees.

Blacknail the hobgoblin looked up from where he'd been absentmindedly inspecting a set of tracks next to the road, near a thick clump of coned reeds. The footprints had caught his interest, but they were just from wolves. The forests of the North contained many things much more dangerous than wild dogs.

On the road, a dozen men and women walked alongside a wagon piled high with goods. Their clothing was mostly tough-looking leather, and every one of them was armed. This wasn't surprising, since they were bandits who had robbed a traveling merchant and were taking their spoils back to their base.

"What's the hobgoblin doing over there?" a nearby blond man nervously asked the scarred woman walking next to him.

"He's plotting to kill us in painful and humiliating ways," the woman replied sarcastically. "Why are you bloody asking me? Why do you even care? He probably smelled a rabbit or something."

The outlaws had gotten some great loot. Blacknail knew this because he'd been happily robbing the merchant caravan alongside them. The bandits were his comrades, and together, they served under the outlaw chieftain Herad the Black Snake. You could tell she was important because she had a sweet nickname.

Even though they were allies, not all the human bandits liked Blacknail. Some of them were jealous of his good looks and superior murder skills. Happily, a few demonstrations of those skills had silenced the hobgoblin's most vocal critics. Permanently.

Recently, Herad had ordered her minions to charge tolls instead of outright robbing people, which meant they didn't do much looting anymore. However, the bandits' last target had been trying to sneak through her territory without paying. That meant they had to be made an example of, and so the hobgoblin and his companions had gotten to murder them and take their stuff. That was Blacknail's favorite part of being an outlaw.

As soon as most of the merchants were dead, the hobgoblin had sniffed out the best loot and taken it for himself. After he'd done some hissing and snarling to scare away the other bandits, five wheels of cheese, a pretty red cloak, two plucked ducks, and a bag of shiny stones were all his. He couldn't wait to get home and show Saeter. The old ranger was the one who had trained him and taken him in when he'd been just a little goblin.

"What have you got there?" a cloaked man asked politely as he walked over.

The man was one of two scouts on the mission. Blacknail was the other one. They were there to track down the target and to keep watch on the forest. Most of Herad's scouts were friendly toward the hobgoblin and greatly respected his master, Saeter. The old ranger was the best scout in Herad's band.

"Nothing-ss, just wolf prints," Blacknail replied happily.

"Ah, there's probably nothing to worry about then," Wyre the scout said.

"Dunno. Forest doggies aren't that dangerous, but-ss a bunch of people are watching us from the trees behind-ss me," the hobgoblin told him.

"What? How do you know?" the man asked as he jerked in alarm.

"I smell their trail all along the road. They were just on-ss it, but they ran off in that direction when we got close."

The hobgoblin's master Saeter would have been able to detect the watchers by observing the flight of birds or something. Blacknail didn't need to do that because most humans smelled like a pile of shit on legs. They were hard to miss.

Wyre frowned thoughtfully and took a few seconds to process the hobgoblin's words. "How many of them are there, and what can you tell me about them?"

"There are three men-ss, all in good health, and they were waiting here for a while before we arrived," Blacknail answered with a shrug.

"Hells, they're probably not friendly then. I can't think of a good reason for a small group like that to be hanging out here in the middle of nowhere. I have the unpleasant suspicion that they were waiting for us."

Blacknail nodded. As a general rule, everything in the forest was dangerous and hostile. Humans were also a very violent race. They started fights over the weirdest things, instead of for all the right reasons like hobgoblins did.

"What are they planning though? Three men aren't a threat to us," the scout mused.

"Let's go ask them. I like asking people questions!" Blacknail was good at it too, and rarely had to actually start cutting people.

After a brief talk with the other bandits, Wyre agreed with the hobgoblin's plan, and they slipped into the bushes at the side of the road. Together, they stalked into the shadowy woods that bordered the road. They moved slowly and approached their targets from the side to conceal themselves, but it soon became obvious their stealth was unnecessary.

"They all left," Blacknail mused as he examined a muddy boot print beside a bush. The forest was still damp from the spring melt. The mud made it easier to track their quarry, but it also meant a lot of annoying insects were flying around.

"That way leads back to the road. They must have slipped ahead of us," Wyre pointed out as he swatted at an insect. "That's not something an innocent passerby would do. It would be much safer to hide and wait until we were gone."

"They were waiting-ss for us, and now they've gone to tell someone that they've found us," Blacknail suggested as he slapped a bug that had landed on the tip of his nose.

"Damn, I think you're right. We've got an ambush waiting ahead of us. It's the only thing that makes sense. They have to be out here for us."

Blacknail got up and moved back toward the road.

"Where are you going?" his companion asked.

"I'm going to follow them. You stay here. I'll be right back," the hobgoblin answered as he broke into a run.

If those humans were going to meet up with their friends so they could all attack at once, the solution was simple. He would run them down and kill them before that happened. It would be easy. Humans were fat and slow, while he was not only a hobgoblin but a magic one.

Blacknail's cloak billowed behind him as he raced through the trees. He crushed broad-leaved plants beneath his boots and smashed through the slight branches that tried to block his path. The hobgoblin felt the Elixir in his blood simmer as he unconsciously tapped into it to boost his speed. The ability to use Elixir to strengthen himself was what made him a Vessel, and magic.

A shallow woodland stream appeared in front of Blacknail. It was flooded with water from the spring melt. Without stopping, Blacknail jumped across and landed on the other side. Wyre was already out of sight behind him. The human scout couldn't keep up with Blacknail.

A second later, Blacknail burst out of the forest and came to halt in the middle of the dirt road. There, he took a second to sniff the air and listen. He could no longer hear the creak of the wagon his tribe had stolen. His companions were far behind him, but he could smell the men he was tracking. The scent was old enough that he knew they were ahead of him by a fair bit. With a gleeful hiss of anticipation, Blacknail kicked off the ground and ran down the road after his prey. At a full sprint, it didn't take him long to catch up. The hobgoblin heard the pounding of their footsteps before he saw them. His long, pointy ears weren't just for show.

A curve in the path ahead blocked Blacknail's sight, so he slowed down and glanced around it. Three men were in front of him, running down the dirt road at a steady pace. For a second, Blacknail almost mistook them for members of his own tribe. Their clothes were the same worn-looking mix of leather and rugged cloth. They also carried themselves the same way, as though they were used to fighting for what was theirs.

The hobgoblin didn't recognize any of them or their scent though. They were strangers. Who were they? They were enemies, but of what kind? Blacknail licked his lips as the urge to hunt flowed through him. It didn't really matter who they were, as long as they were acceptable prey, and Blacknail was certain they were. Also, the prey might soon reach their destination. It was time to strike.

The hobgoblin dashed off the road and back into the forest, where he was harder to see. Blacknail moved quickly, and that meant he made a fair bit of noise as he trampled through the brush. Even puny, pink human ears would be able to hear him. Pink was a silly color…

"What was that?" the smallest of the men asked as he glanced in Blacknail's general direction.

"It was probably a deer or something," one of his companions replied dismissively.

"Just keep moving. I want to put more distance between us and Herad's men," the last man added.

With long strides, Blacknail passed the running men. When he had a fair lead on them, he turned and moved back toward the road. From the shadows, the hobgoblin watched the three unsuspecting men approach. As he waited, Blacknail reached into his coat and pulled out a vial of liquid. The Elixir in the vial tasted unpleasant as it hit his tongue, like dirty water with a hint of sour fruit, but soon, a familiar warmth spread throughout Blacknail's body, from his toes to the top of his head. It was accompanied by a rush of energy that mingled with his desire to hunt and drove it to new heights. His teeth ached with need. It was time to attack.

As the three men passed through an area where the forest encroached upon the road, Blacknail drew his sword and launched himself out of the bushes. There were only a few feet between him and the closest man.

The rustling of leaves alerted Blacknail's prey, but they didn't have enough time to respond. The closest man's eyes widened in horror as the hobgoblin charged straight at him. He fumbled for the blade at his hip, but before he could draw it, Blacknail's sword sank into his chest. The hobgoblin didn't even try to pull it free, but instead drew two long knives and whirled to the side.

The man to the hobgoblin's left raised a sword and stepped forward. Blacknail reacted faster. Before his enemy's boot was firmly planted on the ground, the hobgoblin kicked his foot out from under him.

"Arrh, fuck," the man wheezed as he landed hard on his side.

A silver sword sliced through the air toward the hobgoblin's head as the third man attacked. Blacknail dove under the swing, and he slashed at the man's arms as they went by. His dagger cut through the man's sleeves and drew blood. The wounded man stepped back, but Blacknail stuck with him. The man's slow block didn't stop the hobgoblin from sliding to the side and slashing at his arms again. Blacknail sniggered as he kept up the pressure. He dodged the man's increasingly frantic swings and attacked again and again. Soon, the man's arms were covered in bleeding cuts. Blacknail was having fun.

The second man climbed to his feet and charged the hobgoblin with his sword held high. Blacknail stepped back from his current opponent and spun out of the new attacker's way. Combat stopped for a second as everyone faced each other. Blacknail gave his two playmates a wide grin that showed off his sharp teeth and long tongue.

The wounded enemy's face went white from terror. "What the fuck is that? It's not human!"

"I don't know, just kill it!" the other responded as he raised his sword with shaking hands.

Blacknail giggled merrily. That was so not going to happen. The scent of blood was thick in the air, and he had to suppress a shiver of excitement. Beneath the blood, he smelled the fear that was starting to undermine his prey. It would destroy their resolve and leave them weak.

The hobgoblin dove forward. One of his opponents countered with wide defensive swing, but the other jumped back in fear. Blacknail's move had been a feint though. He bounced backward out of the way of the sword, leaving the man overextended. With careful precision, the hobgoblin stepped forward and knocked the sword down with one dagger. There was a hollow gasp of pain as the other dagger sank into the man's side. The short steel blade parted flesh and slipped in under ribs as it cut into vital organs.

"You're dead," Blacknail whispered gleefully into his opponent's ear as the man collapsed.

The only remaining enemy's eyes went wide with fear. He stuttered as he tried to raise his sword into a defensive stance. However, his cut up arms shook and quickly lost strength. With a moan of despair, the man dropped the sword. Blood flowed down his mangled arms and dripped from his fingertips. Defenseless, the whimpering man turned and ran. Blacknail laughed then hummed cheerfully to himself as he pursued at a leisurely pace. His prey had no chance of escaping now. He had been hobbled and was leaving a trail of blood.

The terrified man was dashing madly away from the hobgoblin, but he didn't get far. Soon enough, he tripped over his own feet. Blacknail laughed again when the man's attempt to catch himself failed. His arms gave out a second time and the man's face hit the dirt with a loud thud. He was whimpering as Blacknail walked over. It was a shame, but it seemed the hunt was already over. His quarry had been no match for his Elixir-powered speed and hobgoblin cunning. He was just too amazing!

Blacknail crouched and poked the fallen fighter in the shoulder. "I think-ss I'm supposed to ask you questions now."

"Don't kill me! Oh, gods. Please don't kill me," the man sobbed weakly.

"No problem, just answer my questions. Who are you and why-ss are you waiting for me and my friends?" Blacknail replied cheerfully. The man's request was a simple one and more than worth the reward. Now that the hunt was over, Blacknail's bloodlust was waning. He felt no need to kill this man.

"You have friends?" the man asked in disbelief.

Blacknail scowled and poked the man again. This human was kind of rude. His long fingernail jabbed into an open wound and the man spasmed in pain.

"The men from earlier. The ones you were watching," the hobgoblin hissed.

"Sorry, I'm sorry." The man moaned. "We were sent to watch the road in case any of Herad's men came by. We were headed back to tell the rest of our squad you were coming."

The hobgoblin took a second to think that over and to lick his finger clean. It sounded a lot like an ambush. Who would be stupid enough to fight Herad's men in her own territory though? His chieftain had a lot of warriors and was a dangerous Vessel as well.

"How many of you-ss are there, and who do you work for?" Blacknail asked.

"Please, don't eat me. There are thirty men at the camp. You can eat them! They're just an hour down the road, and we work for Werrick," the man quickly answered as the hobgoblin stared at him.

Blacknail shifted in surprise. He knew that name. When he'd gone to the human city of Daggerpoint with Herad, it had been mentioned a lot. A lot of the groups of bandits and human warriors they had fought in the city had been working for him. Werrick was someone Herad really wanted dead, and the feeling was mutual. He was a bandit lord just like Herad, which explained why the men seemed somewhat familiar.

"I'm not-ss going to eat you. I said I wouldn't already. Now tell me, what does Werrick want?"

"To kill Herad," the captive replied nervously. "We're just the tip of the spear. He's coming here himself and bringing all his men with him, hundreds of them. He intends to destroy the Black Snake, and he has more than enough swords to do it."

The man tensed as if expecting to be poked again. Blacknail smiled instead. It sounded like there was a war coming. What fun! The hobgoblin knew his chieftain. There was no way she would be taken down easily. Blacknail had watched her slaughter foes who outnumbered her before. This time would be no different.

Although before he joined back up with her and his master, he had to escape the ambush waiting for him. He had almost forgotten about that…

Chapter 2

It took several minutes for Wyre to catch up, and a few more after that for the wagon to arrive. By then, Blacknail was seated on a rock at the edge of the forest. The hobgoblin hummed cheerfully as he watched them come down the road. When his slow human comrades were close enough, he hopped off the rock and walked over to them. Wyre and the others warily drew to a stop as Blacknail came toward them.

"I see you've been busy," Wyre remarked as he took in the bodies littering the ground. "Are any of them still alive?"

"Yep, that one there," Blacknail replied as he pointed. "I'm not stupid. I asked him a lot of important questions."

"Oh, what did you learn?"

"They don't-ss have any cheese," Blacknail answered with a grunt of disappointment.

Wyre gave Blacknail an annoyed glare. "Anything else?"

"Yep, these guys brought-ss a lot of friends. They're camped up ahead of us."

Scowls and various looks of displeasure appeared on everyone's faces. A pair of bandits scanned the road up ahead as if they expected attackers to appear at any second.

"Good thing you stopped them then," one of the bandits remarked.

"Yes, nice job, Blacknail. Did your captive happen to mention why they want us dead and who they are?" Wyre inquired.

The hobgoblin smiled. He had done a good job! He was such an amazing scout and ranger! "Yep, I asked that! They're all-ss part of the army Werrick sent to kill us all."

There was a shocked silence as everyone took that in. The hobgoblin gave the humans a few seconds so that their slow brains could catch up. Sometimes watching humans think was like waiting for someone to light a fire by striking two rocks together. It took a lot of time and effort to get a good spark.

"Ah, that would certainly make sense," Wyre eventually mused.

"What? Bloody hells, I hope that's some sort of weird hobgoblin joke!" one of the other bandits exclaimed in shock.

"If it is, then it's not bloody funny," another added.

"My jokes are funny, but that wasn't one." Blacknail didn't make a lot of jokes, but when he did, people laughed. He was fairly sure they were laughing with him…

"Maybe he's making this up! Are we going to trust his word?" another scared-sounding bandit added.

"Why wouldn't we?" Wyre replied sternly. "He has no reason to lie about this."

"I'm not a liar," Blacknail hissed as he gave his captive a kick.

The man on the ground grunted. "He's telling the truth."

Blacknail gave the bandit who had questioned him a mean stare. Everyone else looked at the captive. They had forgotten he was still alive, because he certainly didn't look like it. The man was lying on his stomach with his wounded arms out beside him. His face was turned away from them and pressed against the dusty ground.

"See, you're being paranoid," Wyre told the blond man.

"Bah, why are you defending a bloody hobgoblin? That thing kills everyone around him!" the blond man exclaimed.

"I don't kill everybody!" Blacknail countered reproachfully. "That would-ss be pointless and a lot of work! Look, I left this captive alive. We're even friends now."

"You're friends?" Wyre asked skeptically.

The scout looked at the prone man Blacknail had chased down. The cuts on his arms had mostly stopped bleeding, but the long scarlet gashes and the trails of blood they had created across the dusty road were still visible. Even the slight rising and falling of his chest as he breathed looked painful.

"Yep, we're definitely friends now," Blacknail announced as he gave the man on the ground another light kick. "I saved his life. From myself."

"We're… the best of friends." The man on the ground coughed painfully a second later.

"I'd hate to see his enemies," someone muttered.

Wyre grunted. "I'm pretty sure that's not how that works. You can't save him from yourself."

"Then I saved him from you. If you had-ss caught him, would you have left him alive?" Blacknail asked with undeterred enthusiasm.

"Probably not," Wyre reluctantly agreed.

"See, I promised to let-ss him live and everything!" Blacknail added to support his argument. He had kind of forgotten where he was going with this… but that wasn't going to stop him.

"And that's actually a promise you intend to keep?" Wyre asked with morbid curiosity.

"Why not? I have no reason to kill him. I'm-ss a nice person. Also, Saeter said lying was bad-ss. If you're good and never lie, then people will start to believe everything you say. That sounds amazing!"

Wyre blinked in surprise and stared at the hobgoblin for several seconds. The scout's face was completely blank and revealed nothing as the hobgoblin beamed at him.

"Ah, words of wisdom if I ever heard them," he remarked deadpan. After a few moments, Wyre walked over to the prisoner. He crouched over the man and asked him questions of his own. When he was done, he turned back to Blacknail. “Let’s get going. Apparently we have a hostile army to avoid. Do you plan on leaving this guy here?”

Blacknail hadn’t really thought about it. He wasn’t against Wyre’s suggestion though. It certainly sounded like the least amount of work. “Sure, he can-ss stay here. He won’t be able to catch up to us and no one-ss should find him for a while.”

“Something will probably eat him, like wolves… or a hobgoblin,” one of the other bandits muttered.

Blacknail ignored the comment and turned back to the man on the ground. “When you do get back to your comrades, remember to tell them how-ss scary I am!”

“I will do that,” the man replied dryly as he stared in fascinated horror at the hobgoblin.

Blacknail liked how his new friend was absolutely terrified of him. He should probably encourage this behavior in others.

“Also, I’m going-ss to come back here soon and kill everyone in their sleep,” Blacknail cheerfully said to his captive. “I’ve been told I’m good at that! Make sure you tell-ss everyone that. I’ll let you live again though, because we’re friends.”

“Thanks, I think,” the man replied quietly. He sounded somewhat delirious and out of it.

Blacknail gave him an encouraging pat on the head to cheer him up.

“Come on, leave him be,” Wyre told the hobgoblin. “We need to go. The longer we stay here, the more likely it is they’ll send someone to check up on their lookouts.”

With a sigh of resignation, Blacknail nodded and got up. Altogether, the bandits started down the road again. One of them maneuvered the creaking wagon around the bodies of the fallen. The horse pulling it seemed more worried about keeping an eye on Blacknail than anything else.

However, his patience was soon rewarded. Blacknail heard a rustling sound then a murmur of voices. The hobgoblin's long green ears perked up. The noise was clearly coming from atop the hill. There were definitely people up there.

"Grab my bag when you go," someone out of sight said. "If I'm going to be stuck here, I want it. And don't take too long. There's supposed to be two of us here."

Someone muttered a reply, and Blacknail watched intently from behind a thick tree trunk as a rough-looking man with brown hair made his way down the hill. This was perfect! Carefully, the hobgoblin drew his sling and loaded it with a rock. A second later, the unsuspecting man collapsed after a rock ricocheted off his head. Smiling smugly, the hobgoblin dragged his victim's body out of sight. Blacknail then walked up the slope. At first, he moved silently, but then the last sentry's back came into sight and Blacknail sped up. The man was preoccupied with watching the road and not looking his way.

"Do you have my stuff?" the sentry asked without turning around.

"Nope," Blacknail replied as he bashed the man in the back of the head with a rock.

The hobgoblin then waited a few minutes for the wagon to roll into sight. From atop the tree-covered hill, he watched it make its way across the road. When it was safely past the lookout spot, he jumped down the hill and ran to catch up with the others.

"You're back. Murder anyone while you were gone?" the leading bandit asked Blacknail when he stepped out of the forest.

"Just two," Blacknail replied as he held up a pair of fingers. "I found the enemy sentries."

"Good, did you find the camp?" the man asked.

"Nope, I didn't see it-ss. Maybe it's on Wyre's side of the road," Blacknail answered.

"It is, and we need to move faster," the aforementioned scout announced as he stepped out of the woods. "There were no sentries watching the road on my side, but they had a few around the camp. I only got a quick look, but it's not small or unorganized. It looks like a military camp and they have at least a few horses."

"You think they'll notice their sentries are missing and send riders after us?" the female bandit asked.

"Of course. The gods never miss a chance to mess with us mere mortals," Wyre replied. "We're simply going to have to move as fast as possible. It's all we can do."

"What if they just ride us down?" someone who sounded nervous asked.

Blacknail sympathized. Being chased by a bunch of horses with people on them didn't sound like much fun to him either. From experience, he knew it didn't usually end well for the person without a horse.

"Depends. If there are only a few of them, then we'll fight. If there are too many for us to handle, then we'll make for the woods. They'll have to dismount to follow us," the short scout explained.

There were a quick series of acknowledgements from everyone present, and they all picked up the pace. Wyre gave the chestnut horse pulling the wagon a slap on its flank. The beast snorted disdainfully and gave the man an annoyed look, but it moved faster as well. Blacknail did his best to ignore the stupid creature as he jogged alongside the others.

"Can't you humans go any faster? This is very slow," Blacknail remarked after a while.

"We have to keep this pace up all day if we want to make it back to camp," one of the bandits replied angrily.

"So? It's still really slow. Stop being so lazy and go faster," the hobgoblin told him.

"I'm not bloody lazy! This is as fast as we can go. We're not all hobgoblins, Vessels, or batshit insane like you!" the man shot back.

"Huh, I guess," Blacknail replied as he ran. After a moment of thought, he dropped back to talk to Wyre.

"What do you want?" the scout asked.

"We need to run faster."

"Unless you know magic—or at least an incredibly inspiring running song—that's not going to happen."

"No, but I do have a plan! I could go to the back and poke the slowest runner with a sharp stick until they go faster," Blacknail explained.

"Tempting, but no. I'm going to have to pass on that." Wyre chuckled.

"Ugh, fine." The hobgoblin sighed. With such slow idiots for companions, there was no way the group could outrun anyone. If they got chased down, he planned on being at the front where it was safer. All the slow humans could take the brunt of the attack. Maybe that would motivate them to move faster…

The running continued for quite a while. As they moved, the sun slipped behind a cover of thick white clouds and its light dimmed. The creaking of wooden wheels and heavy wheezing from the nearby humans filled the hobgoblin's ears. Up ahead of him, the road made a sudden turn. A particularly tall tree stood on the very corner of the bend. Its long trunk had grown on a slant and its drooping branches hung over the road. Blacknail was watching it out of the corner of his eye when he saw movement. As he focused, a figure stepped out from under the tree and froze in surprise. Several other people quickly appeared around him and pointed toward the hobgoblin's group. Uh, oh. That wasn't good.

"There are men ahead-ss of us," Blacknail hissed in alarm as he skidded to a stop.

"Shit, I see them too." Wyre swore.

The rest of their party stopped. The horse neighed when one of the bandits pulled on its reins to stop it, and there was tension in the air as everyone stared at the new arrivals.

"There shouldn't be anyone from Herad's camp out this way," Wyre commented darkly.

“Whoever they are, they’ve got us cut off,” someone added.

More and more people came into sight up ahead. There were at least as many of them as there were bandits in Blacknail’s group, and who knew how many more were still out of sight. The hobgoblin heard one of the unknown men shout, and blades appeared in their hands.

“Draw your weapons and get ready for a fight,” Wyre commanded everyone.

Blacknail drew his blade and threw a worried glance at the wagon. It had finally happened… they had come for his cheese.

Chapter 3

Blacknail snarled as the unidentified humans on the road in front of him drew closer. They had weapons in hand and looked ready for a fight. Well, if it was a fight they wanted, then that was what they would get. No stupid humans would get their dirty hands on his tasty cheese without a fight!

"We must defend the loot!" Blacknail growled loudly to his companions.

Behind the hobgoblin, those of his fellow bandits who hadn't already taken out their weapons did so. Wyre pulled out a bow and hurriedly strung it. It wasn't a particular long bow, but next to his short stature, it looked large.

"Why are we listening to the bloody hobgoblin?" one of the bandits whined with an edge of panic in his voice. "When did that start to make sense? They're murderous savages! Maybe the horse has some tactics it would like to share as well?"

"We're not listening to the hobgoblin. We're doing what Herad ordered us to, which is bring this wagon back to base," Wyre responded in a harsh, commanding voice.

"We should leave the wagon and head into the forest. This must be a trap! There are probably more of them coming up behind us," the scared bandit said as he threw a nervous look backward down the road.

Blacknail growled. If the coward was allowed to run, then the others would follow, and that was no good. The humans had to stay and fight to protect his cheese! "I don't hear anyone behind us. How could it be a trap, you stupid human?"

"What does a beast like you know? We need to run!" the man shot back.

Blacknail growled in annoyance and stepped up beside the man. "If you run-ss, you'll never make it. Something terrifying out in the woods will kill you slowly and painfully. Me!"

The bandit paled and stepped back from the hobgoblin, then threw a nervous look toward Wyre. The scout was too far away to have heard Blacknail, but he noticed the other man's reaction.

"Stand your ground, both of you," Wyre ordered. "There's no need to run yet. Blacknail is right. I see no sign of us being encircled, and they seem just as surprised as us to have run into company."

Blacknail did as he was told. Not because Wyre was his boss—he wasn't—but because it was what he wanted to do anyway. Up ahead, one of the unidentified people detached from the rest and walked forward. His hand was raised to shield the sun from his eyes, and he appeared to be trying to get a good look at Blacknail and the bandits.

"Hey, I think that's Boots!" the female bandit standing next to Wyre exclaimed. "They're not enemies at all; they're from Herad's camp. We've got reinforcements!"

Blacknail turned and squinted at the approaching man but could only make out the blurry outline of a face. Well, most humans looked alike anyway.

Wyre walked forward. "It seems we hit a spot of good luck after all. Come on, get the wagon moving. Let's see what brings our fellows out this way. Not that I'm complaining."

There was a loud neigh and the creaking of straining wood as the horse hitched to the wagon moved again. Blacknail and several other bandits put away their blades and followed Wyre. Most of the tension from earlier had already faded away. Now everyone seemed relieved and excited.

Soon, the other group came into focus, and it became obvious they were from Herad's camp. Blacknail recognized several of them, even if he had never bothered to learn most their names. Most bandits with less status than him weren't that important. Blacknail recognized the man leading the other group though. It was his master, Saeter. The hobgoblin perked up and smiled. Now he could brag about all the amazing things he had done on this mission! His master was sure to be proud of him!

"You're early. Did you forget to pack enough food or something?" Saeter yelled. He was a grizzled old ranger with grey hair.

"And you're not supposed to be out here at all. We almost ended up charging you!" Wyre shot back. "Did Herad finally kick you out, or did you just miss us?"

"Bah, more likely you were about to piss yourselves and run, and who would miss your faces? Blacknail's the best looking out of all of you," Saeter replied. "No, one of the patrols ran across some signs of movement, so we're checking it out."

Blacknail grinned smugly after hearing his master's words. He was an amazingly handsome hobgoblin after all. Obviously none of the humans could match the beauty of his long pointy nose. It was the perfect length and shape.

"We—" Wyre started to say before Blacknail cut him off.

"I'm right here, master," the hobgoblin shouted as he waved enthusiastically. "I saved everyone's lives, like, twice! I also killed some enemies, snuck around a lot, and found some cheese!"

"I'm glad you had fun," the old scout replied as he rolled his eyes and signaled for Wyre to speak up.

Blacknail's feelings were a bit hurt, but he would have plenty of time later to talk to his master.

"As I was saying, on our way back, we ran into some unexpected company, which would explain the signs of activity you found. It seems Werrick is on his way here," the other scout explained.

Saeter frowned as he and Wyre met in the middle of the road. The pair talked, comparing notes, and soon, neither of them looked happy. Blacknail found their talk boring. He already knew all that stuff. As he idled away the time, the hobgoblin saw a hint of something that might be a berry bush off to one side of the forest. All the walking had made him hungry, so he decided to investigate.

"Stay here," Saeter commanded the hobgoblin after only a brief glance his way.

Blacknail sighed in annoyance but did as he was told. He spun around and made his way back to the wagon. He had some snacks tucked away on it. No one could complain if he ate those now. A few minutes later, after Blacknail had finished shoving half a loaf of bread down his throat, Saeter and Wyre decided on a course of action. The pair of scouts called all the other bandits over.

"There's no point sticking around," Saeter told everyone. "We have no idea how many men Werrick has. That camp may not be the only one, and we need to get the wagon back to base."

"Later, I'm sure Herad will want to send a few squads out to watch and harass the enemy, but that's not our job right now," Wyre added.

No one argued. All the other bandits simply nodded or didn't respond at all. Most of them were deserters, and they hadn't left the army because it didn't fight enough. After a bit more instruction, everyone got moving again. The two groups of bandits melded seamlessly into one and started back down the road toward camp.

Saeter had a rearguard to protect the wagon, but no one attacked them. The only sign of the enemy was a single horseman off in the distance that appeared and observed them for a while before disappearing. It was rather disappointing to Blacknail, really.

The walls of thick bushes and trees that flanked the road eventually widened to reveal a barricade of tall, lashed-together stakes. Blacknail gave the men guarding the barricade a friendly wave—they were also part of Herad's tribe. Behind the crude wall lay Blacknail's home, the camp of the bandit chieftain Herad. The barrier was pulled aside and the captured wagon rolled in, along with all the men and women accompanying it.

Saeter and Blacknail took a minute to unpack their gear and settle down after the trip. The hobgoblin had to make sure all his prizes and tasty treats were hidden away where he'd left them.

"You're all back early," Red Dog commented as he walked over. "Should I be concerned?"

Blacknail looked over from where he was prying open one of the sacks on the wagon. Red Dog was the lieutenant whom Herad had left in charge of the camp when she went to Daggerpoint last fall, and he'd been very disappointed to see Blacknail return with her. Red Dog had probably been hoping that Blacknail would run off into the wild, never to be heard of again except in unsettling campfire stories.

Saeter snorted. "We need to talk to Herad. Things are moving quickly, and not in a good way. It looks like some of Werrick's men are moving into our territory."

"So I should be concerned," Red Dog replied with a sigh. "Damnation, I was hoping for another easy spring of robbery and lying about. Shit like you're talking about is how honest bandits like myself get themselves killed."

"Honest bandits?" Wyre asked in amusement.

"I don't pretend to be anything else," Red Dog replied with a shrug.

"And here I thought you were without virtue," Saeter commented. "But enough chitchat. We need to report to Herad."

"I'll let you talk to her," Wyre added. "She seems to like you best."

The older scout gave the younger one an annoyed glare but didn't say anything. Instead, he turned back to Red Dog. "Where is she?"

"The boss is at Vorscha's cabin right now. They're talking about supplies and stuff," Red Dog answered. "I might as well go with you. It sounds like this is going to throw all our plans up in the air."

"Come along then," Saeter grunted as he started off toward Vorscha's cabin.

Blacknail followed his master through the camp. Crudely constructed wooden cabins of various sizes littered the clearing. They had all been built last year as shelter from the winter that had just passed. Many of them were large barracks-like structures that housed groups of bandits.

The grass that had once dominated the clearing had long since been trampled into dirt that was dusty in dry weather and muddy after the rain. In the center of the camp stood the old farmhouse Herad had taken as her own. Along the edges of the camp, the tall trees of the northern forest loomed, reminding everyone that they were far from true civilization here.

Herad was indeed talking to Vorscha out front of Vorscha's cabin. Of the two women, Herad was very much the smaller one. She was only of average size.

Herad scowled at the new arrivals. "What brings all you lazy bastards back so quickly? I hope for your own sake that you actually followed my orders."

"I certainly did, as always. However, the men you sent with Blacknail ran into some trouble after taking their spoils and hurried back here with news," Saeter explained in a carefully neutral tone.

By the time he had finished explaining what had happened, a cold look had appeared on Herad's face. Well, colder than usual. Herad always looked as if she was one step away from violence. Blacknail tried to attract her attention as little as possible, unless he had something to brag about.

The bandit chieftain ran her fingers through her short black hair as she considered Saeter's words. Her dark eyes stood out from her pale skin and were narrowed in thought. "Well, this isn't completely unexpected. We thought it likely that Werrick, and the fucking bloody bastards backing him, would move against us."

"They're moving quickly though. Faster than we thought they would," Vorscha pointed out with a hint of concern in her voice. The large brunette was wearing a loose cloth shirt, and crossed her arms in a way that highlighted both her lean muscles and her ample chest.

"Doesn't matter," Herad responded. "The longer he waits, the more men and equipment Werrick can rally. Having him move this early is to our benefit, not his. The impatient fool is underestimating me."

"You're right, and that has me worried. Why is Werrick moving so quickly? He knows you won't be easy to beat in your own territory. He must be confident for some reason," Saeter pointed out.

"I'd be confident too if I had the kind of backing he did," Vorscha countered. "With those crooked merchants behind him, he can probably afford to lose his entire army and then just buy a new one. Manpower isn't hard to come by out here, with all the deserters fleeing the southern wars."

"True, in Daggerpoint his lieutenant Zelena used mercenaries. I would be shocked if Werrick hasn't hired a few more," Saeter added.

"If he relies on outside forces too much, the other bands will never accept him," Herad replied with a disdainful sneer. "He can't just buy himself an army and use it to control the North. That would make him too much like a conquering outsider out to crush all banditry."

"That won't do us much good if we're dead," Red Dog muttered.

"If Werrick does come against me with a mercenary host, then I'll retreat and wait," Herad replied as she drew one of the many daggers she had tucked around her person. Idly, the bandit chieftain toyed with it as she spoke. "He'll have to leave eventually to deal with other bands, and then we'll raid the forces he leaves behind. He won't be able to conquer the North with strength of arms alone. He needs to convince the other bands to follow him, and to do that, he has to convince them he's one of them."

Saeter nodded, and a flash of annoyance gleamed in Herad's eyes for a second. The old scout's approval always seemed to anger her for some reason.

"Most of the outlaws I've worked with came North to escape the rule of kings," Saeter explained. "They wouldn't fall to their knees and accept Werrick as their master if he looked like a southern puppet out to destroy their livelihood and freedom."

"Which means we just have to worry about Werrick's band and maybe a little outside support. He must have left some men behind, but he undoubtedly still has more than us," Vorscha pointed out skeptically.

"I'm not too worried if that's all he brings to the table," Herad said. "We have the defensive advantage. We know the terrain, have fortifications up, and are building more. I've outmaneuvered him before. This time will be no different."

Vorscha looked thoughtful. "We need to be prepared. We should speed up construction, double our patrols, and cancel all leave. Every man in camp should be assigned to a job until Werrick is defeated."

"Practical as always, Vorscha," Herad responded approvingly. "I'll leave organizing that up to you."

Off to one side, Red Dog sighed regretfully and grimaced. Blacknail took a not-so-casual step behind Saeter, where he was harder to notice. He wanted to avoid being given a job.

The talk lasted for a few more minutes before Herad dismissed everyone. Saeter and Blacknail were given the rest of the day off, and they headed back toward their campsite. They lived in a pair of tents off to one side of the encampment, near the forest, instead of in one of the larger buildings. Both of them had spent the winter in Daggerpoint and liked to live simply. Everything Saeter owned could be packed up in a few minutes.

As soon as they arrived, Blacknail ran over to his tent. All the yummy snacks, shiny trinkets, and hard-won loot he'd acquired from his last mission had to be put away. If he left it out, then a despicable thief would probably steal it! Some people were just savages.

The hobgoblin took off his cloak and outer garments, flipped open the door to his tent, and crawled inside. The interior was small, but once inside, Blacknail's body heat heated up the place. Beneath him, a small collection of blankets carpeted the floor, and his familiar scent filled the air. The hobgoblin gave out an unexpected yawn and collapsed onto the ground. He leisurely shifted the blankets beneath himself as he closed his eyes and smiled. It was so comfy and warm here. If it wasn't for the need to eat and drink, he would never leave.

Blacknail gathered up a clump of blankets and rested his head on them like a pillow. One of the sheets was little more than a beat-up rag, but that rag was his favorite by far. It had been given to him by his master when Blacknail had been nothing more than a little goblin. His memories from way back then were blurry and confused, but when he held the blanket close and smelled it, he was overcome by a sense of security and… something else. Was it comfort and appreciation? It was a nice feeling anyway. It made him feel warm inside.

A few seconds later, Blacknail let out a deep breath and opened his eyes. He wanted to rest some more, but he had things to do. Reluctantly, he reached into his pockets and removed the best of his new acquisitions. A small metal figurine was placed off to one side. The tiny warrior's bronze surface was dull, but it still had a slight shine to it. Next, a glass eye was put down beside it. Blacknail snickered as he remembered how he'd gotten that. Fun times!

Oh, there was also a little bit of biscuit in there. Blacknail pulled the chunk out of his pocket and shoved it into his mouth. He chewed on it as he slipped out of his tent. Up in the sky, the sun was a fair bit past its midday peak. Small fluffy clouds were scattered around, but they didn't block its light. With a thoughtful expression, the hobgoblin studied the human dwellings. The first thing that had to be done was chores, so Blacknail went to find the person he'd told to do them all.

Chapter 4

Blacknail threw on his cloak and went to find Elyias. Before he'd left to go on his last mission, the hobgoblin had given his minion a list of chores to complete. Blacknail had saved Elyias's life, or something, back in Daggerpoint. He'd forgotten the details, but the important bit was that he'd taken the man in as his minion. All the other important bandits had minions, so Blacknail needed at least one too.

Eventually, Blacknail found Elyias outside one of the barracks. The blond young man was standing several feet from a group of men playing dice. A small crowd was watching the players, and Elyias was at the very back.

"What are you-ss doing?" the hobgoblin asked as he stepped up right behind the young man.

Elyias hadn't seen him coming, and he rose almost half a foot into the air as he twitched in fear. A look of unrestrained terror appeared on his face for a split second before he got control of himself. Then he saw Blacknail and was terrified all over again. "Ah, what the hells? You! You're not supposed to be back yet."

Several other bandits noticed Blacknail and gave him wary looks, but they soon turned back to the game. They were used to him.

"Some enemies showed up, so we came back quickly," Blacknail explained cheerfully.

"Damnation, what's with my luck? I can't ever catch a break," Elyias muttered in a muted manner that Blacknail could totally hear.

"Have you been a good-ss minion and done the jobs I gave you?" Blacknail knew it was important to keep one's minions occupied. His master had certainly made sure he had been busy all the time. You had to be firm but fair with minions.

"Err, ya, I did, Blacknail," the young man answered. "Your firewood has been replaced, and I made sure no one went near your tent."

"What about all the traps? You emptied-ss them?" Blacknail asked coldly as he stared into the man's eyes.

"Ah, no… I was going to, but when I got out there, something had torn most of them apart," Elyias replied uncertainly.

Blacknail scowled at the man and stared him down. He was disappointed in his minion. The young bandit wilted under his gaze.

"Then you fix them-ss!" Blacknail hissed angrily. "I know you can make the string and set up the traps!"

The hobgoblin's long tongue wormed its way out from between his teeth as he spoke. Elyias paled and furtively glanced around for anything that would help him or distract the hobgoblin. He didn't find it. Meanwhile, Blacknail had to suppress a smirk. He wasn't actually that angry. He'd been the one who had destroyed the traps, and he'd known Elyias wouldn't fix them. It was all part of the teaching process.

"I'll get right on it, I swear," the blond young man exclaimed fearfully. "Just let me grab my gear."

"Fine, but I'm checking the snares-ss tonight and if they're not done…" Blacknail snorted disdainfully and stomped away with overexaggerated anger. He felt Elyias watching him leave.

A few seconds later, the hobgoblin walked around the corner of a building. Once he was out of sight, Blacknail stopped and turned back around. He then peeked back at the group of people around Elyias and listened in. He was pretty sure Elyias was going to be bad and slack off.

"There's got to be some way I can give that creature the slip," the young man complained to the bandit next to him.

His compatriot was a tall man with a pot belly and long black beard. He was dressed in rough furs. Unlike Elyias, he had been part of Herad's band since before Blacknail had joined. "I wouldn't try it if I were you. Just do what he says and don't piss him off. Let me tell you, some extra work is nothing. Fresh meat like you usually goes through much worse."

"That's right," a bald woman with a vicious scar across her face added. "I've seen pretty boys like you forced to do all sorts of things. Although maybe you're the type who wouldn't mind having a big strong guy to look after you and keep you warm at night."

"No, thanks," Elyias responded as he grimaced in distaste.

The bearded bandit laughed. "Then get to work."

"I will, right after this round is finished. I want to see who wins so I know who to play with when I join in later," Elyias replied as he watched the gamblers.

There was a clatter of wooden dice and murmurs of appreciation from the crowd as one of the players got a good roll.

"You'd be much better off not playing. Even if you somehow ended up winning, that would be worse than losing for you," the bearded bandit told him.

Elyias muttered vaguely and stepped closer to get a better look at the players. He seemed too focused on the game to pay the other man much attention. From his hiding spot, Blacknail sighed and shook his head. Elyias was going to get himself into trouble. He obviously wasn't that smart. It was a good thing he had Blacknail to look out for him!

Well, that was a problem—or entertainment—for later. Blacknail didn't feel like harassing Elyias anymore right now. It would be more educational—and amusing—to punish him later when he didn't fix the snares in time.

The hobgoblin headed back to his tent. It had been over an hour since he'd last eaten a full meal, so he was hungry again. Time sure went by quickly when you were having fun!

On the way, Blacknail passed by Vorscha's home. Herad and Vorscha were both long gone, but the large woman's minion and mate, Geralhd, was outside now. The skinny human was leaning against the building's entrance while talking with Red Dog and another man. Red Dog's hands were moving energetically as he spoke to Geralhd, and their conversation was loud and boisterous enough that it drew Blacknail's attention. Maybe something important was going on?

"Fuck, and I was planning on going to town soon. I guess I won't be getting roaring drunk and visiting the brothels after all," Red Dog said.

"Get yourself a lover in camp. It's cheaper and you won't spend so many cold nights alone," Geralhd told him.

"No thanks. I prefer my women to be… less dirty and not so well armed. Give me a flower-scented whore over the women in this camp any day," Red Dog replied with a wince.

"I find that comment more than a little insulting," Geralhd replied as his face took on an affronted expression.

"Ha, who cares? Everyone knows you only shack up with Vorscha for protection. Although I wouldn't mind feeling up those big tits of hers once or twice myself," the third bandit interjected with a laugh and some rude hand gestures. He was a man of average height, but he looked to weigh a fair bit. His arms and legs were thick, if somewhat soft looking instead of muscled. His round face was covered by a short, patchy brown beard.

Geralhd glared at the bandit angrily. They were about the same height, but Geralhd was much lighter and his face was clean-shaven. He was one of the few bandits in camp who bothered with shaving regularly. "I'll have you take that back, Urick. You shouldn't talk like that about Vorscha or me."

"Are you going to make me, pretty boy? Because I don't think you can," Urick replied with disdainful sneer.

From where he was watching, Blacknail sighed and rolled his eyes. Why did Geralhd keep picking fights with people bigger than him? It was stupid. He should just stab them from behind.

"Don't start a fight, Urick. I'll be pissed if you make me intervene," Red Dog told the other man.

"Bah, I haven't started anything," Urick spat. "Pretty boy here is the one getting too big for his boots."

"If he doesn't apologize, then we're going to have a problem," Geralhd told Red Dog.

The bandit lieutenant looked amused as a smirk appeared on his lips. "It's not my job to make people say sorry. If you want a nice flowery apology, then that's your business. I'm not too worried about it, or Urick."

"Hear that? This is your problem, pretty boy," Urick announced cockily. "You don't realize that, besides the gal you're shacking up with, no one likes you or has any use for you."

Soundlessly, the hobgoblin walked up behind Urick and put a hand on his shoulder. His touch made the big man flinch in surprise and turn his head to see who it was.

"I like Geralhd. He feeds me so that I don't get hungry," Blacknail interjected meaningfully as he stared into Urick's eyes and grinned toothily.

The unwashed man's green eyes widened in fear. Then his mouth dropped open as he stared uncomprehendingly at Blacknail.

While Urick's brain was trying to catch up, the hobgoblin flashed Red Dog a grin. "Hello!"

"Apologize, Urick," Red Dog said grimly as he narrowed his eyes and scowled at Blacknail.

Urick looked stubborn. "I don't want—"

"Shut your trap and apologize!" Red Dog hissed.

The bandit hesitated for a second and threw Red Dog a confused look. Blacknail just kept on smiling.

"I take back what I said," Urick muttered grudgingly.

"Your apology is accepted," Geralhd replied as he grinned. He seemed genuinely happy to have the conflict resolved.

Blacknail smiled and patted Urick's shoulder in a friendly matter. They were all friends here for now! The bandit just looked confused. He still hadn't managed to completely close his mouth.

"Come on, let's go," Red Dog told Urick as he pulled the other man away.

"See you around," Geralhd told them.

"See, we can all get along if we try!" Blacknail announced.

"I don't know how that idiot has survived this long. He must be the luckiest fool in all the North," Red Dog muttered as he walked away. Blacknail thought that was kind of mean. Red Dog needed to relax more.

"Why did you make me apologize?" Urick asked the other man peevishly. The big man looked annoyed and his hands were balled into tight fists.

Red Dog gave him cold glare. "Geralhd's harmless, but you shouldn't give the hobgoblin a reason to dislike you. That monster will kill you for giggles and you won't see it coming. It would also get away with it just fine. It's smart enough not to leave proof, and to make itself useful to Herad."

The hobgoblin couldn't hear any more of their quite interesting conversation, because a beaming Geralhd stepped down from the doorway and spoke up. "Thanks for the support, Blacknail. It was nice of you to stick up for me and show Urick that I have lots of friends."

"No problem," the hobgoblin replied as he waited.

"Here, have a treat," Geralhd announced as he reached into a pocket. The man withdrew a piece of candied meat and tossed it to Blacknail.

"Thanks." The hobgoblin smiled smugly and caught it. He had been pretty sure Geralhd would have a treat on him and that showing up would earn him it. He had the man well trained, so there was no way he was going to let some big stupid human injure him.

"Urick is such an asshole. I don't know how Red Dog can stomach being around him. Someone should stick a knife in his back," Geralhd muttered.

"Sure," Blacknail replied distractedly as he chewed. Urick was now on the list, which meant the hobgoblin would get to him eventually. It was a long list. Blacknail didn't mind killing the man, but why was Geralhd so bloodthirsty? Whatever, humans were weird.

"Since you're here, do you mind running an errand for me?" Geralhd asked. "I have some letters I need delivered. Mahedium is constantly sending out packets, so could you give him mine?"

"No problem," Blacknail answered as he finished chewing and wiped his hands on his shirt. A chore like this was sure to earn him another treat, and it would only take a second. The hobgoblin grinned as he was handed several pieces of folded paper. "What are these for?"

Blacknail had never really understood the point of writing. Remembering things and sending people with messages worked fine for him. Humans must have terrible memories if they felt the need to write so much down.

"I keep in contact with some of my family. I may be in exile, but I hope to one day return when my bounty expires. Who knew killing a twat in a fair duel could get someone in so much trouble?" Geralhd explained with a frown. "Also, I left some of my clothes and other stuff with my friends. I have to keep reminding them I'm still alive so they don't sell them."

That sounded complicated. Why hadn't Geralhd just buried his stuff somewhere no one would find it?

"All right, I'll give these to Mahedium," the hobgoblin told the young bandit. If he let Geralhd talk too much, the man would never stop.

"See you soon," Geralhd replied as he waved Blacknail goodbye and stepped back into his home.

Happy to be helpful and fed, Blacknail wandered through the camp and toward Mahedium's lab. The log cabin stood apart from all the others, and most of the bandits avoided it. Many of the humans were superstitious and wary of the mage. There were a lot of rumors about the dark sorcery that went on in his cabin, but mostly they avoided the area because of all the explosions. The roof of Mahedium's lab had caught fire three times already.

After listening at the door to make sure Mahedium wasn't doing any dangerous experiments, Blacknail entered the cabin. If he knocked, it might disturb the mage, so he just stepped inside. The first room was the rectangular living quarters with a scattering of furniture. A bed, a table, and a bookshelf dominated the room. Loose papers and open books lay on all the surfaces. Blacknail ignored it and walked over to the door on the opposite wall from where he'd come in. That was where Mahedium would be—in his lab. As he moved, a familiar yet unexpected scent reached his nose.

The smell didn't belong. Blacknail grimaced and his fingers curled up slightly as he contemplated the smell. Quickly, the hobgoblin entered the lab. It looked like it usually did. Only a few items had been rearranged inside.

Tables and shelves full of equipment filled the room. Glass beakers, metal tubing, and crystals were everywhere. There were no windows. Light was provided by glowing mana crystals hanging from the ceiling or set in tabletop lamps. The mage was leaning over a table and staring at a glass jar full of bubbling liquid. Beneath the beaker, a small fire was burning steadily. The hobgoblin ignored all that and continued looking around for the source of the smell. A quick look from the door didn't work, so he took several steps into the room.

Mahedium stood up and removed the spectacles he had been wearing. "Blacknail, what are you doing here?"

The mage blinked several times and looked confused to see the hobgoblin. He was an average-looking man with short brown hair. Mahedium didn't even seem particularly old or young, just average. He was dressed in heavy trousers, a tan shirt with long sleeves, and a thick leather apron. The apron was covered in burn marks and several unidentifiable stains of various colors. Blacknail handed Geralhd's letters to the mage, who briefly looked them over.

"From Geralhd," Blacknail explained distractedly. The hobgoblin then peered past the mage and continued to scan for his target.

"Ah, of course. I had mentioned to him that I was going to send a bunch of letters out to Daggerpoint and other places, and he said he might slip a few of his in with my own," Mahedium explained.

Blacknail ignored him and kept peering around the room.

The mage noticed his odd behavior and frowned. "Are you looking for something?"

"Yes, I smell it," Blacknail replied grimly as he sniffed the air again.

A look of comprehension appeared on Mahedium's face. He turned away from Blacknail and glanced toward one corner of the room. The hobgoblin followed his gaze and noticed a small cage on a table.

"Ah, I had Varhs capture one for me," Mahedium told the hobgoblin. "I wanted to run some experiments on Scamp, but he wouldn't let me. So I had Varhs trap some wild ones and test them for the mage gift."

Blacknail peered into the darkness that concealed the contents of the cage. There was ashuffling sound from within as something moved. As the hobgoblin's eyes adjusted to the darkness, the form of a small creature became visible. It was a goblin!

This was unacceptable! Why did people keep bringing goblins into camp without asking him? It was incredibly rude! How would they like it if he brought in a bunch of random humans, let them wander around, and let them pee everywhere?

Chapter 5

Blacknail stared at the goblin in the cage. The creature was hard to see in the shadowy corner of the lab. The only light came from the magic crystals across the room.

Beside him, Mahedium continued talking casually. "I keep it locked up most the time. I was afraid I was going to have to drug it, but that hasn't been necessary. For some reason, it seems mostly content as long as I keep it up high where it can see most of what's going on."

The small creature in the cage was thin for a male goblin, but not unhealthily so. Its lanky form was hunched over as it regarded the hobgoblin. Its eyes were what drew Blacknail's attention. Not only were they bright red, but they shone with something more than animal cunning—patient intelligence. Blacknail didn't like that one bit.

As the two stared at each other, a smug grin appeared on the goblin's lips. Blacknail growled softly. How dare this pipsqueak smirk at him! Blacknail was, like, three times his size! A second later, the goblin turned away and lay down in the far corner of the cage. The hobgoblin frowned at the unexpected action. Was that a sign of submission? Was it just crazy? Blacknail wasn't sure…

Anyway, why had Mahedium brought this weird goblin here? This was Blacknail's territory. Humans shouldn't bring goblins into camp without asking him! He wanted to yell at the stupid human, but he tried to keep his calm. He had seen the mage blow up buildings and set dozens of men aflame. There was no telling what type of mana crystals the mage had tucked away on him, and Blacknail didn't want to find out the hard way. It would be better to keep things polite.

"Stupid human! Why do you need a goblin? There are enough goblins here!" Blacknail hissed. Apparently, he wasn't good at being polite.

"Red Dog would agree with you." Mahedium chuckled. "Don't worry, I only take it out for short walks and experiments. I have to keep it healthy if I want to draw blood from it. It's very convenient to have another source of mage blood and not have to constantly cut myself. Maybe I should get an apprentice? Anyway, my fingertips haven't been this smooth in years!"

Blacknail glanced at the lock on the cage door. It was a double latch. There was no way the goblin didn't know how to open it! The only reason it was still in the cage was because it wanted to be!

"It just watches you do magic-ss and stuff?" Blacknail asked doubtfully.

"I guess. It's a feral goblin though, so it probably doesn't even know what magic is. It probably just likes the fire and flashing colors," the mage replied with an indifferent shrug.

Blacknail threw a glance over his shoulder, back toward the cage. The goblin within was staring intensely at Mahedium's bubbling glass jar and the crystal inside it, but it looked away when it noticed the hobgoblin's attention. The complete fascination and intelligence in that gaze unnerved Blacknail. The hobgoblin was more than willing to bet that the goblin understood a lot more than Mahedium thought it did. Stupid humans! How could they be so blind?

"It even responds to one or two basic commands," the mage added.

"I see," Blacknail replied. This goblin was deeply suspicious! Goblins didn't normally act like that! The hobgoblin squeezed his fist shut as he tried to rein in his anger. "I don't like it. Can I kill it?"

"What? There's no need for that. Here I'll show you," the surprised mage replied. Mahedium then unlatched the cage.

The door swung open with a creak, but the goblin didn't attempt to leave. Instead, it gave Mahedium an inquisitive look.

"Out. Heel," the mage ordered.

The little goblin stepped out of the cage and scampered over to Mahedium's side. It looked up at him with a dutiful expression, which didn't fool Blacknail for a second. Suspicious! Much to the hobgoblin's surprise, the goblin then raised a green arm and offered it to the mage. Mahedium just shook his head though.

"Hmm, I don't need to draw a blood sample today. Good boy, back into your cage now," the mage said as he pointed toward the pen.

Sure enough, the goblin hustled back into the enclosure it had come out of. It kept its eyes downcast in a sign of submission to both Blacknail and the mage the entire time.

"See, the little thing is remarkably well-behaved and incredibly beneficial to my research, including the production of your Elixir," Mahedium told the hobgoblin proudly.

Blacknail sighed in annoyance. The new goblin was a lot more obedient and useful than Scamp. Of course, Blacknail couldn't shake the feeling that it was bidding its time until it could murder everyone in their sleep. No one was perfect though. Besides, the goblin was more of a prisoner than a member of the tribe, no matter how well it behaved, so Blacknail didn't feel the need to beat the snot out of it so it understood the hierarchy. He would just have to keep an eye on the creepy little thing.

Anyway, he'd delivered the letters, so he didn't see any reason to stay around. Blacknail eyed the bubbling liquid on the table warily. Something might explode, and not in a fun way, but more likely in a burning-liquid-in-your-eyes kind of way.

"Fine, it's your problem-ss. I'm leaving," Blacknail told the mage.

The hobgoblin threw the little goblin an annoyed grimace and stalked out of the room. It was getting late, so he decided to look for Saeter. His master should be cooking supper soon.

By the time Blacknail arrived at his tent, he'd somehow managed to pick up a few new interesting trinkets, including a small coin pouch. It was weird how people just left them lying around everywhere…

Saeter was seated next to his campfire. The old scout was stirring the contents of a big iron pot with a wooden spoon. The smell that rose from the pot as it cooked above the flames was heavenly. The hobgoblin's mouth watered.

"You're making stew!" Blacknail exclaimed. The hobgoblin loved his master's cooking! Usually he had to make his own food, and it was never as good as the stuff Saeter could cook.

"We've done a fair bit of walking recently, so I thought we should put some weight back on our bones," the old scout replied.

Blacknail eyed the big iron pot. It was almost full. That was a lot of food! It was time to stuff himself silly. However, his delicious thoughts were interrupted by the sound of people approaching. Blacknail had to fight a sudden urge to spin around and hiss threateningly. It was his food! Whoever was coming would have to fight him for it!

Instead, Blacknail looked over his shoulder and scowled at the newcomers. It was Geralhd and Vorscha. What did they want? Vorscha was his sword instructor, so he knew fighting her would end badly for him. Geralhd also had to be handled carefully. The man kept Blacknail well supplied with snacks. Blacknail didn't want to scare him away. Hopefully neither of them was after his food.

"What are you two doing here?" Saeter asked suspiciously as he looked up from the pot.

"Do we need a reason to visit a good friend such as you?" Geralhd countered courteously.

"Yes," Saeter grunted. "You weren't invited."

"It's too nice of an afternoon for anyone to be spending it alone. We just felt like stopping by and enjoying the pleasure of your company," the younger man explained with a smile.

"Plus, you make really good stew, and I'm hungry," Vorscha added. "We could smell it from across the camp."

"Too bad," Saeter told them. "Leave."

"Blacknail wants us to stay," Geralhd told the old scout.

The hobgoblin frowned. He didn't want any such thing.

"I doubt that," Saeter replied.

"Do you?" Vorscha asked as she grinned and winked at Geralhd.

"Blacknail, we brought cheese scones!" her lover announced.

The hobgoblin's ears perked up and oriented themselves toward Geralhd. The rest of his head quickly followed. Then his eyes locked onto the bundle of cloth the younger man had just taken out from behind his back.

"They can-ss stay!" Blacknail declared.

Saeter glowered at both visitors, highlighting the lines of his weathered face. He looked as if he was trying to think of some way to get rid of them. He sighed in defeat a few seconds later. "Ugh, fine."

"Yeah, scones!" Blacknail giggled. This meal was going to be so great, maybe even the best ever! Rabbit stew with cheese scones! He couldn't wait.

Vorscha smiled, and Geralhd placed the rolled up cloth on a rock next to the fire. The pair grinned at each other as they settled down on the other side of the campfire from Blacknail and his master. Saeter's fire pit was quite large, even if it was just a shallow hole in the ground surrounded by a ring of round stones. Two nearby flat rocks could be used as chairs, and there was also a nearby collection of cut-up logs for people to sit on. Wait, why did his master have so many seats around his campfire if he didn't want visitors? Blacknail couldn't figure that out. Was the old scout going to use them for something?

"Bah, I suppose I cooked enough food to share." Saeter grunted as he stirred the stew again. "It goes bad quickly anyway."

His master's speech, and the intense stare Blacknail was directing toward the yet-to-be-unwrapped scones, distracted the hobgoblin enough that the voice from behind him was a surprise.

"What's going on here?"

"No!" Blacknail hissed in alarm as he realized who it was and spun around.

It was Khita! She had probably come to steal some of his delicious scones and stew. Well, he wasn't going to let her! She was useless.

"There you are," Vorscha announced as Khita walked closer. "Take a seat."

"I didn't say she could-ss come," Blacknail whined.

"She's with us," Vorscha replied as she gave the hobgoblin a flat stare.

Blacknail froze under her gaze. Good-natured or not, there was a steely edge there. She clearly wasn't going to accept any complaints from him. Why was the big woman always sticking up for Khita? She was useless.

"What's one more mouth to feed? She may as well join us," Saeter remarked sarcastically as he sat down on his favorite stump.

"Thanks, your stew usually tastes nice," the young woman remarked.

Saeter frowned at Khita and pursed his lips. Clearly, he was insulted. "Nice…" He huffed as he shook his head. "I've been perfecting this recipe since before you were a fire in your father's loins."

"It's the nectar of the gods itself, if that's what you want to hear," Vorscha told the old scout as she rolled her eyes.

Khita smiled and sat next to Blacknail. The hobgoblin groaned and shuffled away. The cheese scones had better be bloody delicious!

"Hey, Blacknail! How did your last mission go?" Khita asked. "Herad and Vorscha never let me go on any important missions. I'm either stuck here in camp or Vorscha is watching my every movement."

"It was all right. I snuck around, met a new friend, and killed a bunch of people," Blacknail remarked offhand as he waited for stew. He didn't mention the food he'd looted from the wagon. He wouldn't put it past Khita to steal it, like the thief she was.

"Sharp! That's what I'm talking about," the young woman exclaimed happily. "I want to go on a mission like that!"

"I don't think killing people is a good measure of success," Geralhd interjected.

"It is if you're a hobgoblin," Saeter said.

"Is the food ready? The smell is making me hungry," Khita asked.

"Close enough," Saeter replied as he got up.

The old scout reached into a sack and pulled out a bunch of wooden bowls. One by one, he filled them with stew and passed them out. While he was doing that, Geralhd finally unwrapped the cloth bundle to reveal the scones within. It only took a few seconds for him to toss them around. Blacknail grinned as he caught his and took a bite. It was delicious, so cheesy and yet so smooth and rich.

Up in the sky, the sun was setting behind the western clouds. The clouds glowed a deep red as darkness set in. All around, the shadows grew thicker as flickering firelight filled the camp.

There was silence as everyone ate, if you didn't count the hobgoblin's smacking. Blacknail thought that this was fine, but Geralhd apparently found it awkward. The young man looked around at everyone else seated by the fire. "So, Saeter. What do you think of our current situation? From what I hear, Werrick is coming and he's bringing more than a few men."

"I think there is going to be a fight," Saeter replied.

"Ugh, I don't want to discuss fighting right now," Vorscha interjected. "Here we are enjoying a great meal among friends! Why bring up violence?"

"Imagine what will happen if Herad wins though," Gerald pointed out. "She'll basically hold dominion over all the North! All its wealth will be at her fingertips and part of that will be ours!"

"That's a good point," Vorscha remarked as she smiled. "Retiring from the bandit life with a chest full of gold sounds great to me. I could really use a nice mansion full of servants."

"That does sound nice," Geralhd mused.

"It would have to be in Daggerpoint, or somewhere else beyond the king's writ, but it would still be much nicer than my current cabin. Especially if you were there with me," Vorscha told her lover.

He looked uneasy and smiled sadly. "That does sound wonderful. Unfortunately, as you know, I need to be heading home as soon as possible. My parents and sister need me back down south."

"You're still a wanted man," Vorscha pointed out.

"The warrant for my arrest will eventually expire, especially if I get my hands on enough coin to grease the right hands. Bribes are the only reason I was ever charged in the first place. All I did was win a fair duel!" the young man complained.

"And kill a man," Vorscha added dryly.

"There are duels all the time where I come from, back in Eloria proper. Some of them are even to the death, yet rarely is anyone arrested and sentenced to life imprisonment," Geralhd exclaimed.

"Ha, you're all lazy or cowards. I don't plan on retiring ever! I'm going to work my way up to becoming Herad's most trusted lieutenant, and maybe even eventually be her successor!" Khita bragged.

There was a lot of eye rolling and skeptical looks from everyone else present. Blacknail tried to picture Khita as the leader of anything and failed. How could anyone ever be stupid enough to accept her as their chieftain?

"I don't think Herad trusts anyone, especially not her lieutenants," Saeter grumbled as he got up and refilled his bowl.

"I don't think that's very likely. Everyone retires eventually," Vorscha told Khita. "You really should be trying to figure out how to escape the criminal life."

"It will be an adventure!" Khita replied. "Besides, I won't be alone. Blacknail won't be retiring to some stuffy mansion. He's a hobgoblin, and they know how to have fun!"

Blacknail looked up from where he was eating the last of his scone. Bits of crumbs fell off his chin. "I'll go where Master Saeter goes."

That made everyone look Saeter's way. The old scout frowned and sat back down.

"Bah, having dreams like yours is just a good way to be disappointed. Only fools believe in happy endings. You're better off accepting things the way they are," he told the others.

Blacknail put his empty bowl down and gave his master a questioning look. He seemed to remember Saeter saying something else a while ago. "I thought you wanted-ss to make Herad Queen of the North and kick the southern king person in the balls. Didn't you say that? I think-ss you did…"

Geralhd snorted in amusement, and a huge grin appeared on Vorscha's face.

For some reason, Saeter's face grew noticeably redder. The old scout winced and looked off to the side. "I never said anything like that! Stop lying, Blacknail. You're imagining things, you stupid hobgoblin."

"Ambitious, but I like it," Vorscha remarked.

"Ha, so much for not having any dreams!" Geralhd laughed. "I should have known you had a reason for sticking around here."

"I wouldn't mind kicking a king or two in the nuts," Khita mused as she smirked. "Those fancy bastards have never done anything for me."

"That was just something I said once as a joke," Saeter protested.

"Of course it was. Don't worry, Saeter. We all know you didn't mean it," Vorscha joked.

As Saeter glowered, Blacknail looked around at everyone's smirks. He didn't get it. What was so funny?

It grew dark as the bandits talked and laughed. Soon, the only light came from their campfire or those of other nearby bandit groups. However, by the time Saeter's guests left, almost everyone else in the camp had turned in for the night.

With a happy yawn, Blacknail went to bed. An owl hooted off in the trees as he walked over to his tent and crawled inside. Feeling comfortable, Blacknail curled up and fell asleep.

However, his rest was disturbed by unpleasant dreams, and Blacknail tossed and turned in his sleep. A green maze of twisted trees surrounded him, and there was only a single path through it. Skulls and swords littered the ground. Coins slipped from his fingers no matter how hard he tried to hold them, and eventually he was all alone in the darkness. The hobgoblin looked up and saw a white light shining down the forest path in front of him. He reached toward it…

Chapter 6

Blacknail smiled as his knife opened the helpless man's throat. Blood poured out of the jagged wound and spilled down his chest. The man's body jerked and twitched, but the hobgoblin held it still. A few seconds later, he went limp and Blacknail let the body fall.

With an annoyed sigh, the hobgoblin rolled the corpse into a nearby clump of bushes, where it would be hidden. When that was done, he scuffed the dirt with his boot to conceal the blood trail. Cleaning up after himself was such a pain. This was the second sentry he'd taken out today, and it was probably far from the last. There were undoubtedly a few more around the perimeter of the enemy camp. A lot of humans seemed to think that if they simply had lots of guards everywhere, it would make up for the fact that they were all incompetent. It didn't work that way.

The forest around Blacknail was full of thick green vegetation, and small hills lay scattered in every direction. That made spotting people difficult and hiding easy. To keep one step ahead of his prey, the hobgoblin needed a better view.

Quickly, Blacknail pulled off his boots and socks. He took a second to wiggle his toes and flex his fingers before sinking his claws into the bark of a nearby tree. Then, he climbed up into the higher branches to find a good vantage point. The tree swayed ever so slightly in the wind once he got higher, but that didn't bother him. His flexible and light body gave him excellent balance. Up among the leaves, Blacknail made himself comfortable and looked around.

Herad, Blacknail's great and deadly chieftain, had ordered the hobgoblin to scout around the base Werrick's men had set up out in the Green. The other bandit chieftain's encroachment on her territory would be met with blood and fire.

Blacknail had spent two days skulking around the forest by himself to get all the information his mistress wanted. He'd been told to avoid being seen at all costs, and he hadn't even been allowed to kill anyone! This was the North. Who would notice one or two missing humans? There were hundreds of ways they could have gotten themselves killed or vanished. Most humans were so dumb, Blacknail was constantly surprised they lived long enough to breed. Not his humans though. They were remarkably intelligent—almost hobgoblin-like really. Of course, Blacknail had only ever met one other hobgoblin, and he'd stabbed him to death several minutes after their first meeting. Still, that meant half the hobgoblins he'd ever encountered had been incredibly smart and handsome. He could not say the same thing about humans.

Well, that was the past. He certainly had permission to kill now. The time for scouting was over. Herad's attack was underway.

Blacknail balanced on a long branch as he studied the terrain. From his high perch, he saw the steep hill that concealed the enemy camp. It looked as though the way there was clear. However, a pair of Werrick's men stood off some distance to his left.

"Hmm, difficult," Blacknail mused.

It was practically impossible for someone to take down two sentries by himself without making any noise, and that meant it was sort of difficult even for Blacknail. The hobgoblin preferred easier targets. Why work hard?

With this in mind, Blacknail swung below the branch he was sitting on and climbed back down the tree. Once on the ground, he brought his fingers to his lips and whistled. The sharp cry of a bird echoed through the forest as he blew. A few moments later, an answering bird call rang out from the wild greenery. Blacknail smiled as Saeter slipped out of the forest and walked over. The old scout was dressed in brown leathers with a dirty green cloak. He held a bow, and there was a full quiver on his back.

"We're all clear here?" Saeter asked.

"Yes-ss, there are no enemies around until we get closer to their camp," Blacknail replied.

"Good, then let's go together in case we run into a larger group," his master suggested.

Blacknail opened his mouth to agree, but he was interrupted by the sound of another bird whistle. His mouth snapped shut in surprise. That was their signal!

"What? It's not the right season for real grey warblers to make that cry," Saeter remarked. "And no one else could possibly know we were using it."

"I don't know," Blacknail replied nervously. "Maybe-ss it's an ambush."

Together, the pair peered off into the forest in the direction the sound had come from. Slowly, Saeter drew an arrow and strung it on his bow. Nothing moved up ahead. Instead, there was a fluttering noise behind them. Blacknail flinched in surprise and jumped around, pulling his long knife free in one smooth motion. Beside him, Saeter moved as well.

The hobgoblin's heart pounded as he scanned the forest for the cause of the noise. There was nothing there, or at least he didn't see anything. Something had made the noise though. Suddenly, a flash of movement made Blacknail look up into the trees. Perched there was a harpy. Its human-like face looked at Blacknail and Saeter with amusement. It flashed them a toothy smile, then a familiar bird cry issued from it lips. The foul thing had mimicked their signal!

"Shoot it," Blacknail hissed in alarm.

Harpies were dangerous. The large bird-like creatures had long talons on their feet and the tips of their wings. They were also cunning.

Saeter raised his bow to take the shot. Before he could do anything though, there was another flutter from the direction they had just turned away from.

"Shoot it," someone or something said.

Blacknail's head whipped around, and he raised his dagger defensively. A second harpy was standing on a tree branch not too far away.

"There's another harpy behind us, isn't there?" Saeter asked. The old scout hadn't turned around. He kept his arrow aimed straight at the first harpy.

"Yes, but two harpies aren't much of threat-ss. I'll take one and you can take the other," Blacknail replied as he stepped toward the second creature.

However, before he could get near it, the beast let out a muted screech and flapped its wings. Blacknail froze. They were still near the enemy camp. Raising a commotion would draw attention, and that would be bad.

"Don't let it make so much noise!" Saeter hissed.

"Fine, you shoot both of them," Blacknail replied. What did his master expect him to do? The hideous creatures could fly!

Saeter grunted in annoyance. "I can't get both of them at the same time."

"So much noise!" squawked the first harpy merrily.

"You shut the hells up," Saeter told it.

"Ya, no one asked you," Blacknail added angrily.

Saeter and Blacknail stood there silently for a few seconds as they contemplated their next step. The hobgoblin scratched his nose as he warily eyed the harpies. They didn't appear to be doing anything…

"What should we do?" Blacknail asked his master.

"I don't know. The fucking things are probably just messing with us. I don't think they'll risk a real attack," Saeter replied.

The first harpy, who still had Saeter's arrow pointed at it, hopped down from the tree. It landed on the ground and eyed the hobgoblin and his master. Blacknail thought it looked smug.

"I want to kick it in-ss the face," the hobgoblin muttered.

The harpy ignored him and crawled across the ground using the claws on its wings as another set of legs. Its motions were smooth and purposeful as it headed toward a familiar set of bushes.

"Oh," Blacknail remarked in surprise.

The harpy slipped into the bushes, and there was a tearing sound as it ripped into the corpse within them. Saeter's eyes widened as he realized what the beast was doing. He spun and pointed his arrow toward the second harpy, which was still sitting in the tree.

"In the face!" The beast laughed merrily as it licked its wing feathers. It didn't seem concerned about the bow and arrow at all. Instead, it continued cleaning itself while studying them out of the corner of its eye.

"The bloody fuckers!" Saeter growled as he realized what was happening.

Blacknail's eyes narrowed as he came to the same understanding as his master. The creatures were extorting them! The harpies wanted the human corpses Blacknail had left in his wake, and if he tried to stop them, they would create enough noise to raise the alarm. The hobgoblin grimaced and flexed his clawed fingers. Human corpses were worthless to him, but he didn't like the idea of being outsmarted and bullied by a bunch of bird brains!

"Let's kill them!" he hissed.

"No, stop, Blacknail," Saeter commanded. "Leave them be. They're no threat to us and we have a job to do."

The hobgoblin stared at the grey-feathered creature up in the tree. It seemed to have completely dismissed them as threats and was busy cleaning itself.

"Ugh, fine. Let's get out of here," Blacknail replied.

Saeter nodded, and the pair cautiously made their way away from the feasting harpies. The old scout kept his bow nocked, but he let the string go loose.

"Job to do!" a shrill voice whispered mockingly as they walked away.

Blacknail clenched his fist but kept on walking. He'd killed harpies before and he would do it again. Next time, he would enjoy every moment of it though.

Soon, they were away from the flying pests. Blacknail and his master scanned the forest for further threats. While the harpies hadn't made too much noise, it was possible they might have alerted someone. The pair of sentries he had seen from the tree might not be the only ones around.

"We're good," Saeter remarked quietly a few moments later as he motioned Blacknail forward.

The hobgoblin ground his teeth as he stalked through the forest. The base Werrick's men had built lay before him, and he fully intended to take his frustration out on its occupants. Oh yes, there would be blood! He might even booby-trap the corpses as a surprise for greedy harpies.

Blacknail stepped up to an old thick tree that sat atop a hill. Its branches hid him, and he could look down on the enemy camp. Saeter joined him a second later. The base was nestled in a large clearing. The tall dark trees of the forest surrounded it on all sides. The ground was slightly sloped toward a small creek that ran through the middle of the clearing before disappearing into the forest. The camp itself was a massive collection of blue tents. They filled the center of the glade. Off to one side lay a hitch post where dozens of horses were tied up, and men could be seen walking everywhere.

"Hmm, it's weird how they have all those tents. They look new. Did Werrick buy them all just for this attack?" Saeter mused.

"Does it matter? Let's just find-ss the sentries and kill them," Blacknail hissed. It wasn't the hobgoblin's job to worry about such things. Herad could deal with it later. He just wanted to work out his bad mood.

Saeter gave Blacknail a critical look. "Keep your emotions under control or you'll fuck this up and we will be the ones getting killed."

"Fine, sorry," Blacknail grunted. The hobgoblin knew he was letting his rage slip out of control. Having the harpies steal his trophies was infuriating. It didn't matter that he hadn't actually wanted a bunch of human bodies. They were still his!

"There is a sentry over by that log," Saeter remarked as he pointed down below.

"I'll go take him out so we can slip closer," Blacknail whispered.

The hobgoblin mentally worked through a few basic sword forms to calm himself as he turned toward his destination. Discipline had been beaten into him by his master during his sword training. Suddenly, and without warning, there was an outcry from below that made the hobgoblin flinch.

"Intruders! To arms! We're under attack!" someone in the camp yelled.

A chorus of answering shouts soon joined it. As Blacknail watched in dismay, the enemy camp came alive and dozens of men emerged from tents. The sentry below was reinforced by a fully armed squad of bandits, and together, they disappeared into the forest. Uh oh, this wasn't good.

"We need to leave. Let's get to the fallback route," Saeter announced as he spun around.

"What? No! They couldn't have seen us!" Blacknail whined. He wanted to hunt! This wasn't fair. What had just happened?

"Less moaning, more running," Saeter replied.

Blacknail growled in frustration before following his master into the forest. As the pair ran through the woods, Blacknail managed to get his emotions under control.

"What's going-ss on? How do they know we are here?" Blacknail asked.

"They probably don't. We aren't the only ones here, remember?" Saeter huffed as he ran.

Oh, right. Blacknail had actually forgotten that. Herad had sent several teams of scouts, but Blacknail had sort of assumed they would all hang back while he and Saeter did the real work.

Shouting could be heard behind them as Blacknail and his master ran back to their rendezvous point. The hobgoblin's long pointy ears also detected some closer voices.

"This is all your fault!" a female voice whispered off to Blacknail's left.

"Me? How could it be mine? I'm the scout here, not you!" a deeper male voice answered.

Blacknail sighed when he recognized the voices. He now knew why the enemy had been put on alert—incompetent people.

Saeter apparently heard the sound of nearby people trudging through the forest but not their voices because he turned to the hobgoblin. "Who is it? Enemies?"

Blacknail grimaced in distaste. He wanted to say yes. "No, they're… allies."

Saeter nodded then dodged left. Blacknail jumped over a fallen tree and followed him as they both veered toward the newcomers. A few seconds later, the pair slipped out of the greenery and met up with their comrades. Running out in front was the scout Varhs. His pet goblin, Scamp, was scrambling alongside him, and trailing them was the young redhead Khita. Varhs looked shocked for a second as Saeter and Blacknail appeared, but he calmed down when he recognized them.

"Ah, Saeter! Don't surprise me like that," the younger scout exclaimed as he kept moving.

"Oh, the boss is here," Scamp commented excitedly. The little goblin had obviously heard them coming.

Blacknail squinted at the three running figures. He was pretty sure he knew who to blame for this mess. Varhs was a good ranger and at home in the forest. Scamp was annoying, but he could at least stay hidden, especially if there was work to do. That left Khita, the most useless one.

"Why are you here? You're not a scout," Blacknail asked her.

"I convinced Varhs to let me come," Khita replied. "Staying around camp was boring."

The hobgoblin threw Varhs a questioning look. He was disappointed in him. Varhs seemed like a half decent ranger, but he kept surrounding himself with idiots.

"She said she could keep up," Varhs muttered.

Saeter gave the other scout a cold glare. "Next time, don't let a pretty face sway you. For now though, keep running and follow me. It sounds like there are people right on your tail."

Sure enough, Blacknail heard the sounds of pursuit. Several people were yelling and crashing through the underbrush behind them. The hobgoblin made sure he was running near his master at the front, where it would be safest.

"Where are we going?" Khita asked.

"The rendezvous point. Just slow down for a second," Saeter replied as he gulped down air. The old scout looked worn out. His pace had slowed, and he was wheezing.

Blacknail frowned in concern. They hadn't been running all that fast…

"Is that a good idea with this many people chasing us?" Varhs asked as he looked back over his shoulder.

"Don't worry, I have a plan. A good ranger always has an escape route prepared," Saeter explained. "Just make sure you follow my steps exactly."

Up ahead, the forest opened up to reveal a sunny clearing. The old scout headed straight toward it.

"Oh, this plan…" Blacknail remarked uncomfortably. He remembered this plan. It was terrible. He really hoped his master knew what he was doing…

"Did you place traps here or something?" Khita asked as she ran up beside Blacknail. The young woman was studying the long grass ahead of them suspiciously. They'd reach it and be out of the forest within a few seconds.

"Or something-ss," the hobgoblin hissed. He was too busy running to answer her more clearly and didn't really care anyway. Although if she wandered off the trail, she would ruin everything… even more than she already had. "Stay close behind me and you'll be fine."

"All right, thanks," the young woman replied.

The mismatched group charged out of the forest. Blacknail pushed a leafy branch away from his face and winced as the light from the sun hit him. Saeter was ahead of him and already stomping through the grass. Blacknail frowned and looked around nervously as he followed his master. Behind him came Khita. Much to the hobgoblin's annoyance, she seemed to be making a game of only stepping in his footprints. Holding up the rear was Varhs and Scamp. The other scout didn't question Saeter's plan, but he had drawn his bow and was watching carefully for pursuers. Scamp was scampering along beside his master. The goblin looked more than a little spooked and hesitant to enter the clearing.

"Danger everywhere!" he moaned as he looked over his shoulder.

Together, the group worked their way into the clearing. They were surrounded by long green grass and thick plants. Clumps of taller bushes and small trees spotted the glade, but Saeter led them away from those.

They had barely made it halfway through the clearing when their enemy caught up. There was shouting as over two dozen men burst out of the forest and stepped into the grass.

The leader instantly spotted Blacknail's group. "There they are. The grass is slowing them down. There's no way they can escape!"

Unfortunately, Blacknail had to agree. The hobgoblin felt his stomach twist nervously. Saeter wasn’t moving fast enough. Theywouldn't be able toget away without a fight.

Chapter 7

Enemy troops spilled out of the bushes at the edge of the forest and into the clearing. Like Herad's own men, they wore a rough collection of leather armor. Hatred-filled eyes glared toward Saeter's party from unshaven faces framed by long, messy hair. Those few who didn't already have weapons in hand drew them. Swords hissed free from sheaths, and one of them pulled a war axe from off his back.

"Don't let the bloody vermin get away! Charge!" their leader ordered his minions.

Varhs raised his bow to pick off the man, but Saeter put a hand on his shoulder and stopped him. "Hold your fire until they get closer. I don't want them to scatter just yet."

Varhs did as he was told, but he gave Saeter a doubtful look. The front ranks of the enemy contained over a dozen men and were closing in on them. They only had a few minutes until Werrick's men caught up, and there were only four people in Saeter's group—four and a half if you included Scamp. If you didn't count Khita as a full person, then you only had like three and a half or something… counting wasn't Blacknail's strongest skill.

Scamp was sticking close to his master's heels, and he looked terrified. His normally large eyes were huge as he gazed around nervously. He looked as if he was going to run at the slightest provocation.

"Fine, but I hope your plan is a good one," Varhs grunted at Saeter.

"So do I," the grey-haired scout replied.

That didn't make anyone feel better. Khita just looked puzzled, but Blacknail groaned and Varhs looked as though someone had slapped him across the face.

"Running away would be a lot safer than this," the hobgoblin muttered. Sure, not all of them would survive if they ran, but he would. He was the fastest runner by far. Also, killing everyone else would probably slow the enemy down enough for Saeter to escape.

"Hey, they've got bows of their own," Khita interjected.

Everyone looked over to see three of the enemies nocking arrows. The archers stood back as the rest of their group advanced. The enemy fighters were getting uncomfortably close. The tall man with the war axe was leading the way with a wicked grin on his face.

"Perfect. This way," Saeter told them as he turned away.

"Perfect? How is this situation anywhere near perfect?" Varhs remarked in exasperation.

Saeter didn't reply. He led the others toward a clump of tall bushes off to one side. Before they reached it though, there was a whistling sound and three arrows tore through the air toward them. The first one was aimed too high, but the others were more on target. One arrow zoomed a few feet wide of Varhs's chest. The other flew through the group and passed right by Khita's face before slamming into the ground with a thud.

The young redhead went completely still when she realized what had happened. Slowly, the color drained from her face. She lifted a hand up to wipe her cheek, and drops of blood appeared on her fingers. She stared in shock. The arrow had grazed her. If it had been an inch to the left, she would have died.

"Don't stand there. Get down, you idiot!" Varhs growled as he pulled her toward the bushes.

Within seconds, they were all behind cover. Blacknail peered suspiciously at the nearby bushes and the tree in the middle of them. When he didn't detect anything off, his healthy paranoia focused on all the men with swords coming to kill him.

However, Blacknail's concentration was broken when Khita pressed her back up against his side. What was she doing? He turned around and saw the young woman trembling slightly. She still looked more than a little pale. As he watched, she shuffled even closer up against him and accidently jabbed him with her elbow. Blacknail winced as his ribs throbbed. Ow, she was sure was bony.

Saeter noticed the young redhead's behavior and the hobgoblin's confusion. "She's in shock. Comfort her!"

"Why?" Blacknail asked. That didn't sound like something he'd do.

"Because I said so," his master hissed back. "And she might slow us down."

"I don't mind doing it," Varhs interjected.

The scout was crouched next to Blacknail on the opposite side from Khita. He had been keeping watch on the advancing bandits. Now he was staring at Khita with a thoughtful expression though.

Saeter gave Varhs a hard look that was completely devoid of amusement. "Keep watch! You wanting to show off is what got us into this mess!"

Varhs looked reluctant and glowered at Blacknail for a second, but he turned back around. Blacknail had no idea why the man was angry at him! What had he done? This was obviously Khita's fault!

"How do you comfort people?" the hobgoblin asked his master.

"Tell her she's safe," Saeter answered.

"Would slapping her work?" That would be quicker.

His master gave him an angry glare. "No!"

Blacknail sighed in annoyance and turned toward Khita again. She was huddled up next to him. Gently, he reached around to hold her shoulder.

"You're safe-ss now," he told her as he patted her head reassuringly. A good pat on the head always made him feel better. In fact, he kind of wanted one now. Why had he become the person who gave out pats instead of receiving them? When had that happened?

"Thanks, but I just needed to catch my breath. That's all," Khita replied with a forced smile. "Ha, I guess I'm lucky those arrows missed me." Her shivering had stopped, but she still looked pale. Well, that was good enough.

Blacknail withdrew and stepped back from her. "Your idea-ss of luck is different from mine. If I was lucky, I wouldn't be here with you."

For some reason, that totally truthful statement earned him a glare from Saeter, but Khita smiled. Her eyes looked a little wet.

"Ha, you remind me of my brother," she told him. "You joke around just like him. You also look after people."

"I bet I'm better-looking though." The hobgoblin had obviously never met her dead brother, but that didn't matter. Humans were pink after all, and that was a really stupid color to be. Green was a much better color all around.

The nearby bushes shook, and everyone flinched and ducked low. A pair of arrows tore through the plants and slammed into the ground. Leaves were knocked loose and rained down over Blacknail and the others. After making sure he hadn't been shot, Blacknail gave Scamp a kick. The startled goblin had tried to squeeze between him and Varhs so he could use them as a meat shield.

"Why are we still sitting here?" Varhs asked. "They're almost upon us."

Saeter got up and looked toward the mass of angry bandits stomping toward their hiding spot. He scrutinized them carefully as he pulled out his bow and nocked an arrow to it. "All right, now!" he ordered the other man. "Aim right toward their center."

Both scouts rose and loosed their arrows. The shots skimmed through the air above the grass and slammed into the approaching enemies. Two of the men fell with shafts sticking from their chests. Blacknail had pulled out his sling as well, so that he could help. He spun it, and his stone projectile was launched into the air a second later. It hit the arm of an advancing enemy and made him drop his sword.

"Bloody hells!" the man screamed hoarsely.

A tall blond bandit who had been standing near the back pushed his way to the front of the enemy ranks. "Get to cover but keep advancing. Spread out and surround them!"

The enemy bandits followed his orders. The mass of armed and dangerous-looking men split up into smaller groups. A few of them kept coming forward, but most headed off to the sides where they could find cover behind the nearby clumps of trees and bushes. Before Saeter and Varhs could get off another shot, the enemy archers opened fire. The two scouts had to duck back out of sight as the arrows flew over their heads.

"Now what? They're circling around," Varhs asked as he crouched.

"Now we wait for a reaction."

"They are reacting! They're running everywhere," Varhs pointed out.

Saeter shook his head. "I'm not talking about the men."

A sharp crashing noise filled the clearing. Something snapped, and there was a hollow thud. Khita flinched, and beside her, Blacknail jumped slightly. However, the hobgoblin grinned as screams of surprise and pain filled the air. It was music to his ears. Saeter's plan had actually worked! They most likely weren't all going to die! The enemies who had headed into the thickets to find cover were under attack by the bushes themselves. The tallest of the nearby trees had slashed at several bandits.

Familiar angry hissing reached Blacknail's ears as the trees transformed into mimics. They looked angry too. The giant, spindly, insect-like creatures tore into the bandits with their many long claws.

Werrick's men were too surprised to put up much of a fight. Even the bandits well away from the fighting had stopped moving and were gaping at their distressed allies. They didn't seem to know what to do. A few of the enemy soldiers retaliated, but their blades either missed the mimics' flailing limps entirely or bounced off their hard carapaces. One of the tree creatures grabbed a man and tossed him aside. Leaves cascaded down as the mimic moved to smash aside a new target.

"All right, now it's time to run again," Saeter informed his companions.

None of them argued. Almost instantly, they were all on their feet and headed away from the fight. The end of the clearing and the way back into the forest loomed ahead of them.

"What in all the hells are those?" Khita asked. "Did you bring those trees to life?"

The young woman kept as close as possible to Blacknail as she ran. Which annoyed the hobgoblin. Her eyes were wide with surprise and more than a little excitement.

"No, they're just beasts, mimics," Saeter replied as he ran.

"How did you know they were there?"

"Obviously I scouted this path out in advance," the old scout told her.

"How did you know—"

"Stop asking me such stupid questions and run," Saeter growled at her.

Behind them, the sounds of battle continued. Someone screamed, and there was a thrashing sound, like branches colliding. Blacknail risked a look over his shoulder. None of the enemies were giving chase, and no arrows were flying their way. The surviving thugs were backing away from the mimics, and the creatures were letting them. Unmolested, Saeter's party reached the far edge of the clearing. A wall of bushes and younger trees blocked their way.

"Are you sure there are no mimics here?" Varhs asked Saeter.

"There weren't yesterday," the old scout grumbled before pushing his way through.

After a few tentative steps, everyone else followed him back into the woods. The barrier of thin branches and greenery gave way to reveal a dark expanse of tree trunks under a shadowy canopy.

"Are we safe now?" Khita asked when they were all out of sight of the battle behind them.

"No, they're not bloody idiots, girl," Saeter told her scornfully. "They will have sent men around to cut us off."

"Oh."

"But you have a plan, right?" Varhs asked. "Preferably something better than sitting in the middle of a bunch of mimics and hoping the enemy walks into them before we do!"

Saeter nodded. "Yes, we keep running."

Blacknail hadn't stopped. The hobgoblin ducked under a low branch as he jogged through the forest. He wasn't stupid enough to think they were out of danger even for a second. The others were right behind him. It wasn't like he was slowing his pace to keep an eye on them or anything. He just knew it would be dangerous to run ahead alone…

Rows of trees surrounded them on all sides. The ground was almost completely bare of anything but dark earth. Only a few short, leafy plants and small ferns grew around the base of the thick tree trunks, and the group was silent as they ran between the trees.

"Um, there's a…" Khita mumbled.

"Save your breath," Varhs huffed from beside her.

"But there's a dead guy right over there!" Khita shot back angrily.

Varhs's eyes widened as he turned in the direction Khita was pointing. Saeter's and Blacknail's gazes quickly followed. A body lay strewn over a tangle of roots at the base of a tree. The cause of death was obvious. An arrow jutted out from his back, and his brown scout's cloak was red with blood. It was undoubtedly one of Herad's men, although without getting a better smell, Blacknail wasn't sure exactly which.

Saeter swore. "They're ahead of us."

Both scout's cloaks swished as they turned to survey the surrounding woods. Blacknail's gaze lingered on the corpse for a moment. Maybe he should go through his pockets, in case there were any clues there?

"Incoming! Get down!" Varhs yelled.

There was a shrill whipping sound. Instantly, Blacknail was lying face-first on the ground with his arms shielding his head. He didn't have to be told twice. Stopping to think could get you killed!

Arrows hissed through the air where he had been standing a second ago. There was a dull crack as one embedded itself into a nearby tree trunk, and Blacknail flinched in pain as the sound stabbed into his ears. Ah, that was too close!

The hobgoblin didn't take any chances. From on the ground, he lurched sideways and rolled toward the base of a tree where the roots would shield him. When he didn't hear any more arrows, Blacknail peeked out from behind his hands. His companions were on the ground around him, and none of them seemed to have feathered shafts sprouting from uncomfortable places. That was good. Even better, Scamp was nowhere to be seen. The cowardly goblin had been running behind Varhs but had disappeared after Saeter had yelled. With luck, something had already eaten him. More likely though, he had run off somewhere.

The next thing Blacknail noticed was the squad of enemy archers stomping through the woods toward him. Several of them were already reaching for new arrows.

"We need to get to the road!" Saeter yelled as he jumped to his feet.

The old scout dashed forward and placed a wide tree trunk between himself and the archers. Blacknail scrambled up and ran after his master. Varhs and Khita sprinted for cover together, sort of. It looked as if both of them were trying to outrun the other so that they could use each other as human shields. Blacknail easily kept ahead of both of them. Losers!

Another arrow flew past and cut through the forest. It didn't come close to hitting anyone, so everyone kept running. Then a ledge came into view up ahead. Past a few trees, the ground fell away. Down below, the road could be seen on the other side of some bushes.

"Damnation, I meant to go around this," Saeter growled.

The fall couldn't have been more than ten feet, but it would still be an uncomfortable jump. They didn't have a lot of choices though. Blacknail put on a burst of speed and raced ahead. A second later, he jumped off the edge and plummeted. He felt his bones shake as he landed in a crouch. The hobgoblin ignored the feeling. He quickly stood and glanced backward at the ledge.

Khita and Varhs were right behind him. The pair jumped over the ledge, and they seemed to hang in the air for a moment before plummeting back to earth. Both of them landed feet-first and rolled straight past the hobgoblin. However, Saeter hesitated. Sensing a problem, Blacknail gritted his teeth and reached down inside himself to burn any Elixir left in his system. There wasn't a lot, but it would have to do.

"Jump and I'll catch you," he told his master.

"What? You don't need to do that," Saeter grumbled.

Blacknail gave his master an annoyed glare, but before he could say anything, shouting broke out on top of the ledge. It sounded as though the enemy was very close. Saeter threw a look over his shoulder and jumped. The hobgoblin froze for a split second, then he spun to the side and reached out to scoop up his master's legs. As Saeter's weight descended, Blacknail cushioned it. Then he lost his balance. The impact knocked him backward, and Saeter landed on top of him.

“Ack, toad piss.” Blacknail coughed painfully as he lay flat on his back. His master had landed right on his chest, and the impact had squeezed his ribs and knocked the air out of him. Ouch. His lungs burned painfully when he tried to draw a breath.

Saeter got up, brushed himself off, and ran toward the road again. It was only a few dozen feet away. “Hurry up, Blacknail! Don’t just lay there like a log!”

The hobgoblin coughed again, pulled himself to his feet, and ran. As he picked up speed, he glared hostilely at his master’s back.

“Some thanks-ss would nice!” he hissed to himself.

When they got back to camp, Blacknail was going to make sure Saeter paid him back! If he didn’t, then the hobgoblin was sure Vorscha and Geralhd would find the story amusing. Yes, he was definitely going to get something tasty or shiny…

Khita and Varhs were already pushing through the bushes. Saeter was right behind them. Blacknail brought his hand up to shield his face as he stepped through the brush and out of the forest again.

“Your plan sucks,” Khita remarked as she looked around the empty road.

“What now?” Varhs asked. “Do we make a break for the other side?”

Saeter scowled as he studied the surroundings. The wide dirt road was empty. It cut through the forest, but there was nothing to see in either direction. The bushes down the road shook as several enemies stepped out. They raised their weapons.

“Shit, we’re right back where we started,” Varhs said.

Chapter 8

More enemies stepped out of the bushes, until Blacknail counted ten of them. The hostile bandits marched onto the road and eyed Saeter's group. All of them were armed with swords and looked dangerous, like hardened killers.

"Capture some of them alive!" their leader ordered the rest. "We need to interrogate them."

Blacknail weighed the odds. He had some Elixir on him, but he wasn't sure he could fight this many people and protect Saeter at the same time. The old scout looked worn out, and Khita wouldn't be any help. She was useless. That left most of the work up to him and Varhs.

Unfortunately, he couldn't sneak his master away from the others, so it wasn't like he had a choice. The hobgoblin drew his blade and reached into his pocket for his vial of Elixir. Varhs and Khita both took out their own short swords.

"Are we fighting?" Khita asked Saeter.

The old scout didn't reply. He was frowning and seemed to be staring straight at the enemy, but Blacknail could tell he was scanning their surroundings out of the corners of his eyes. He was looking for something.

"That one looks like a girl!" one of the larger enemies said as he grinned at Khita. "I'm taking her."

"Just make sure they don't get away," the leader responded.

The big brute raised his sword and stepped forward—just as an arrow took him in the chest. Blood sprayed from his mouth as he collapsed limply. A hail of arrows quickly followed the first.

They slammed into the enemy bandits until most of them had fallen.

"Fucking hells, an ambush!" the leader cursed as he backed up and raised his sword defensively.

A new group of humans rose from where they had been hiding in the ditch along the road, but these were Herad's men. There was the sound of shaking leaves as more of them, including Red Dog, stepped out of the forest behind the ditch. The bandit lieutenant scanned the remaining enemies.

"Swordsmen forward, take them down!" Red Dog bellowed.

At his command, the men from the ditch drew their blades and jumped onto the road. They charged and engaged the now vastly outnumbered and injured enemies.

"Thank the gods!" Varhs exclaimed as several of Herad's men ran past him.

Blacknail let his sword drop. It didn't seem like his help would be necessary.

"We didn't really need their help. I could have taken the big guy," Khita remarked, "and Blacknail could have taken the rest."

The hobgoblin gave her a skeptical look. How could she possibly believe that? Blacknail had seen Khita fight. She wasn't that good at it! Also, why did he have to do most of the work?

There was the sound of blades clashing as Red Dog's men fought. Only a few of Werrick's men were left standing, and they were quickly surrounded. Seconds later, they were all cut down. No prisoners were taken.

"Is that all of them or are there more hiding in the trees?" Red Dog asked as he walked over to Saeter.

"That's all the ones that were chasing us," the old scout answered. "I was beginning to think you had gotten lost and missed the rendezvous point."

"I had to wait until they were all out in the open," Red Dog replied with an indifferent shrug. "It wouldn't have been a very good ambush if I didn't get them all."

Varhs scowled. "But the ambush would have worked fine if we all died? What if they had used bows?"

"Did you get your job done?" Red Dog asked Saeter as he ignored Varhs.

"I certainly did my part, and Blacknail did his," the old scout replied. "We took out quite a few sentries before being discovered and led several more right to you. I'm not sure about Varhs though. He let himself get distracted."

"I can see that," Red Dog said as he eyed Khita disdainfully.

Varhs coughed and looked away. There was an embarrassed flush to his cheeks.

"Hey, I did more than you!" Khita interjected as she glared at Red Dog. "I was out there fighting and risking my life. All you did was stand here and order other people to fight for you."

"That's the burden of command," the bandit lieutenant replied.

"Burden my ass. You're just lazy," Khita told him.

Saeter swatted the side of her head. "Don't argue with the commander in the field. There will be plenty of time later to tell Vorscha all about how he put you in danger."

Red Dog frowned at the old scout's words. He looked nervous for a second, then he just scowled in annoyance. It was quick, but Saeter grinned for a second.

"Since you feel so hard done by, let me escort you the rest of the way," Red Dog said as he motioned toward one of his men. "You there, make sure the small redhead stays safe. She might trip in a pothole and hurt herself. Also, you should watch out for squirrels."

The man in question froze and stared in confusion as Red Dog and Khita glared at each other. He didn't know how seriously he should take the order. Either option could backfire on him.

"So we're moving on then?" Saeter asked to break the tension.

"Since you seem to have drawn the enemy sentries out of position so well, we should go join up with Herad. The main attack has probably already begun," Red Dog replied.

"What about the rest of the scouts sent out with us?"

"Most of them have already returned. I'll leave a few men here in case more show up, but I'm not going to risk sending men into the forest after them," Red Dog explained.

As soon as he was done talking, Red Dog led the group down the road toward the enemy's camp. A wedge of sword-wielding bandits went first. Behind them came the archers, and in the middle were Blacknail and his companions. They arrived at their destination within a few minutes. The once-hidden path that led from the road to the enemy camp was now plainly obvious. Corpses littered the ground, and boot prints were everywhere. The bushes on either side of the trail had been hacked down to create a gaping hole that led into the dark forest.

"I'm not a scout, but I think we should go that way," Khita announced as she pointed toward the mess.

That earned her more than a few glares. However, no one stepped toward the looming entrance. The group came to a stop and took a moment to study the scene. Blacknail heard the sounds of battle down the path, although the forest canopy muted the noise. He scanned the nearby bodies. Most seemed to be enemies, but he did recognize one of the fallen men. There was definitely a fight going on. He hoped his side was winning.

"I don't suppose you'd mind taking a look around?" Red Dog asked Saeter and Varhs. "That brush would be an excellent spot for an ambush."

Saeter shook his head. "I think we've done enough of that today, don't you?"

Sighing, Red Dog motioned his men forward. The lead bandits carefully made their way down the path. When they weren't ambushed, attacked by wild animals, or maimed by traps, everyone else was quick to follow.

"And we're back into the woods," Varhs commented as he stepped into the shadows. "I hope Scamp catches up with us soon."

The path itself was narrow, but moving through the forest was easy. The ground was sparse and mostly bare from the lack of light. The only real obstacles were the trees, and they were easy enough to go around. Blacknail followed the members of his tribe up the shallow hill. Shouting and screams could be heard on the other side of it, so that was probably where Herad was. She enjoyed that sort of thing.

When they reached the top of the hill, Red Dog and Blacknail stopped and looked down. A lot had changed since the hobgoblin had seen the enemy's camp. It was in shambles. The mass of blue tents were still there, but many of them had been flattened. Several were on fire.

Herad was leading a push through the center of the camp. Close to a hundred of her men fought beside her as she cut in deeper. The enemies' resistance was scattered and failing. Her sword flashed through the air, and bandit after bandit fell before her.

"Damned fools, they're getting crushed," Red Dog remarked. "They let their sentries get pulled out of position, then their rear was assaulted."

"This fight was already over once Herad got past the chokepoint behind us," Saeter added. "They should have defended it better."

"Doesn't seem like there's much left for us to do," Varhs observed without a trace of disappointment.

Red Dog nodded. Across the valley, an enemy captain appeared to be trying to rally the defenders. He waved his sword above his head as he shouted orders.

"We'll stay here and pick off any stragglers who try to make it back to the road," Red Dog told everyone.

The enemy captain didn't manage to assemble much of a force before Herad reached him. There was a brief struggle as he was overwhelmed by Herad and her minions. With him dead, there was no organized resistance left. The remaining enemies lost all will to fight and fled. Herad screamed something that sounded both bloodthirsty and triumphant as her organized formation split up to pursue them. Bandits streamed throughout the camp in every direction and slaughtered each other. From so far away, it was hard to tell who was who, especially since most humans looked the same to Blacknail.

"What about our share of the loot?" one of Red Dog's men asked. "How are we supposed to get it from up here?"

"You'll get it, don't worry. I certainly plan on getting my cut," Red Dog answered as he stared at the carnage below.

Blacknail frowned in disappointment. He wanted to be down there with Herad. It looked like everyone there was having fun, and that was where the best loot was. He didn't trust most of the humans in his tribe. They would squirrel away all the good stuff and keep it for themselves!

"Ha, if all of Werrick's men are this soft, then winning this war will be easier than pinching a fat man's purse!" Khita chuckled.

"Do you remember-ss being chased through the woods?" Blacknail asked her. "I do! It was just a few minutes ago!"

"That wasn't so bad," the young woman replied. "They fell into our trap."

Varhs stepped closer to Khita and smiled her way. "Yep, I had the situation completely under control. Rabble like the men chasing us were no match for me."

"The hells?" Blacknail exclaimed in disbelief. They had almost died several times! What were these morons saying? Khita was an idiot, and he had no idea what was wrong with Varhs! The scout didn't usually act this stupid. Maybe Khita was infectious…

As Blacknail watched, a small group of Werrick's men broke away from the camp and headed his way. They had been hiding in some of the tents off to one side.

"It looks like we're going to have company," Varhs observed.

Red Dog gave the approaching men a disgusted look. He didn't seem too concerned. There were less than a dozen of them, and several of them didn't even appear to be armed.

"Idiots. Even if they made it to the road unmolested, how do they think they are going to survive in the woods without any gear? There isn't any shelter nearby," Saeter remarked condescendingly.

"They're cowards. What do you expect?" Red Dog answered.

Blacknail smiled and hummed to himself. These humans seemed to be acting pretty normally to him. Fear did strange things to men's heads, but it almost always made them easy targets. "Sharp!"

The hobgoblin purred happily as he watched the fleeing enemies draw closer. He had been worried for a second, but it looked as though the loot was coming to him! How lucky.

Blacknail's group was waiting for the cowards when they crested the hill. After a brief struggle, Red Dog's men put them down. Taken by surprise and unarmed, they didn't put up much of a fight. The hobgoblin killed two without even bothering to use Elixir. He'd made sure he was right at the front when the fighting started. That gave him an excuse to loot the bodies.

Sometime after the hobgoblin had finished increasing the size of his bauble collection, the entire group of bandits he was with headed down to rendezvous with the others. The battle had ended a while ago and things seemed to have settled down.

Blacknail led the way down the hill and through the trees. When he stepped into the clearing, one of the first people he saw was Vorscha. Several other people were nearby as well, including Geralhd. The female warrior was seated on a crate someone had left next to a tent. Her armor was covered with mud and several bloodstains, but she looked unharmed. She had obviously seen combat, but instead of resting, she was busy cleaning her gear. A large long sword was balanced on her knees, and she seemed focused on wiping it down with a cloth. Geralhd was standing next to her and inspecting a pair of daggers. Unlike his lover's, his armor looked perfectly clean.

"Hail the camp," Red Dog announced as he stepped out behind Blacknail.

At the sound of his voice, Vorscha looked up and smiled. "There you are. I was wondering how long you were all going to hang out up on that hill."

"Just as long as we needed to," Red Dog replied with a shrug.

The rest of his men and Saeter walked up as well. Khita was directly behind the old scout, and Varhs was holding the rear.

"It's good to see you're all alive. I was a little worried when Khita disappeared," Vorscha told them.

"And I was worried when she showed up," Red Dog added dryly.

"I can take care of myself," Khita interjected in an irritated tone.

"Maybe," Vorscha replied doubtfully.

Red Dog ignored the exchange and turned to his men. "You can all stay here. I need to find the boss and make a report."

"I don't really need them. I have sentries out, and everything else has been wrapped up already. They can go where they want," Vorscha replied.

Immediately, most the men either found somewhere to sit down or wandered off. Blacknail moved to leave too. There had to be something nearby worth eating.

"Not you," Saeter told the hobgoblin. "Stay here. I still remember all the trouble you got into last time you wandered off in a place like this."

The hobgoblin froze and scowled. He wanted to go look around, but his master seemed determined that he stay here. That was no fun!

"Stupid naked lady!" the hobgoblin muttered irritably. It wasn't like he was going to run into another one. That sort of thing wasn't common, was it?

"So did you see any action? We had quite a bit here," Geralhd asked Saeter politely.

"You could say that," the old scout huffed.

"We got chased through the woods, shot at, and attacked by a bunch of trees," Khita bragged.

"Is that right?" Vorscha asked Saeter with an annoyed glare.

Saeter shrugged. "I didn't ask her to come."

His words made Vorscha sigh and turn back to her blade. After a few more wipes, she resheathed it. "Well, thanks for bringing her back in one piece."

"You need to stop worrying about other people. You're not responsible for every hopeless case that wanders by. The girl needs to take care of herself," Saeter told her.

"Ya, stop," Blacknail added irately. It was annoying how Vorscha kept forcing Blacknail to look after Khita. The girl was constantly getting herself into trouble and she never learned from her mistakes! Why did he need to be involved? That wasn't fair.

"Ya, stop," Khita said in imitation of the hobgoblin. "I can take care of myself."

Everyone ignored her.

Geralhd coughed and politely changed the topic. "I must say, this is quite the victory for us and our capable leader. I hope the rest of this little backwoods war ends like this battle did."

"It was foolish of Werrick to leave this force unsupported. We cut it to pieces like a hog on a slab," Saeter told him.

"Maybe he didn't plan on us finding them, or maybe he just didn't care," Geralhd guessed.

"Logistics is a bitch," Vorscha explained. "Werrick has to move quite a few men from several different places. It can't be easy to do all that at the same time, as he can only be in one place at a time. Most likely he made a mistake, or one of his subordinates did. It's not like he's an experienced general, and the man in command here didn't seem all that smart."

"Still, that's another advantage Herad has. She's already emplaced and doesn't have to worry about being picked off in detail," Geralhd added.

Vorscha shook her head. "We're going to need every advantage we can get. We've won this battle but not the war. Even after losing this many men, Werrick will still outnumber us. He can afford a mistake or two, but all he needs to do is win one major battle and Herad's position will be shattered."

There was a grim silence as everyone considered her words. However, Blacknail wasn't too worried. Herad had one other advantage that no one had mentioned. She had him! He was the greatest killer in the North, if not the world! Let the human named Werrick come. Death was waiting for him.

Part Two:

Comes the Wolf

Chapter 9

Blacknail watched the enemy march down the road toward him. There were hundreds of them. The impact from their boots hitting the hard earth filled the air with a thudding sound and caused dust to billow up. The savage-looking fighters formed a long serpentine line of moving bodies. More and more of them came into sight as they marched past a bend in the road and out from behind a mass of greenery. The lead elements of the army drew to a stop out of bowshot. They were plainly visible under the noonday sun because a gentle wind carried all the dust away and over the forest. Werrick's main force had arrived.

Blacknail watched from the forest nearby as their commanders ordered them to stop and rest their feet. Herad had sent the hobgoblin and Saeter out to keep an eye on the invaders.

"So many pathetic cowards," the hobgoblin hissed angrily.

He was perched atop an old dead tree trunk that had fallen over in the forest. It lay on an angle so that the end Blacknail was seated on was several feet above the ground. Saeter was standing beside him. Together, the pair peered out past the edge of the woods at the enemy on the road.

"They're not doing anything. How can they be cowards?" Saeter remarked uncertainly.

"It's because they aren't doing anything!" Blacknail answered. "They should-ss attack already. There are so many of them, but they are just sitting there. It's boring!"

Saeter chuckled. "It would be nice if they were that stupid."

"Ah, I have so many things to do!" Blacknail whined as he glared at the humans who had entered his territory uninvited.

"But I need to stay here and watch them! They might try something tricky-ss if I leave."

Saeter was dressed in his forest greens. The wrinkles on his weathered face were plainly visible as he eyed the hobgoblin critically. As usual, he was clean-shaven and his grey hair was kept practically short. "You don't need to watch them, and besides, what is it you want to do so badly? If I didn't get you moving in the morning, you'd sit around all day like a pig in the mud."

"Stuff. Important stuff, that is what I need to do," Blacknail responded as he fidgeted.

Usually he did a daily round of the camp to make sure nothing had changed, but he hadn't had time today. There were also a few items that he had hidden away, and he liked to check on them every once in a while. Being unable to do that was making his brain itch. What if a thief found them and hid them somewhere?

"Stupid humans," Blacknail hissed as he continued to stare at the enemy troops.

"What was that?" his master asked.

"Nothing-ss," the hobgoblin responded. His master would probably misunderstand the comment. Sometimes Blacknail forgot that Saeter was technically a human. He was a lot smarter and sneakier than most men.

"I think I've seen enough. Let's head back," Saeter told the hobgoblin. "I don't see any signs that they're planning on leaving the road or circling the camp."

"Sure, sure," Blacknail murmured. But the hobgoblin didn't budge. He remained perched on a log at the edge of the forest where he had a good view of the road. He knew that any second now, the enemy humans were going to do something important, and he didn't want to miss it.

"Come on, Blacknail. If that army moves, then you'll bloody know, trust me. Someone will raise the alarm. You don't have to watch everything yourself," Saeter said as he walked into the forest.

The hobgoblin wasn't so sure. His personal experience was that human sentries were completely useless. He sneaked by them all the time. It wasn't even that hard. He didn't think it unlikely that they could miss an army or two.

"It's about time for lunch anyway," Saeter remarked as he ducked under a low tree branch.

With a sigh, the hobgoblin got up and followed his master. Watching the enemy was important, but there was no way he was going to skip a meal. Together, the pair slipped through the forest back toward their camp. Saeter whistled a signal before stepping out onto the road in front of the gate. The entrance to their band's camp was heavily guarded these days.

Herad had received plenty of warning of the enemy's arrival and had used that time to build up her defenses. The barrier of long wooden spikes that had run along the side of the camp facing the road had been expanded to encircle the entire base, and raised platforms had been set up for archers. Trenches had also been dug around the road to slow invaders.

Saeter and Blacknail carefully made their way to the entrance. A dozen bandits were guarding the narrow gap in the wall. The closest one gave the pair a nod when he recognized them and signaled them forward. On the other side of the wall, several more squads of bandits were waiting, ready to reinforce the gate in case of an attack. They were armed and armored more heavily than usual. The sunlight glinted off shields, helmets, and bits of armor. Off to one side, Herad stood at the base of a watchtower. She was issuing orders to several other bandits. Tension and the acrid smell of human sweat was thick in the air as Saeter headed over to talk to her. Everyone was waiting for the attack they knew was coming.

"I just came back from taking a look around," Saeter told the bandit chieftain when she noticed his approach.

"Oh, did you see anything important?" Herad asked derisively. "You must have if you're bothering me about it. I'm very busy right now."

"It's what I didn't see that matters," Saeter replied. "I see no sign of Werrick being here yet. The enemy appears to be waiting for him."

"You're probably right about that." Herad huffed. "If he was here, we would know about it. Werrick is an arrogant braggart. He would announce himself with all thesubtletyof a charging ogre."

"I also haven't seen any sign of mercenaries or anything unexpected," Saeter told her. "It seems like they are planning on treating this like a straight-up brawl."

Herad frowned. "And that bothers you? Why? They could be with Werrick or on their way."

"Maybe, but something isn't sitting right in my gut." The old scout grimaced. "This whole campaign feels slapdash. We took out that exposed first group too easily, and this next attack is too straightforward. It's like Werrick isn't even trying."

"I think you're overestimating Werrick."

"He could do better than this," the old scout responded.

"I can't afford to be jumping at shadows now, old man," the bandit chieftain said as she rolled her eyes. "If you do find something, then feel free to inform me. If not, then keep out of my way and stop wasting my time with useless conjecture."

"Very well. As you wish," Saeter grumbled before he turned and walked off.

"Are we going to have lunch now?" Blacknail asked his master as he followed.

Saeter grunted irritably. "Yes, because we bloody well earned it."

"Are you going to cook something?" the hobgoblin asked. When he cooked or ate rations, it was never nearly as good as the fare Saeter made. For instance, the worm stew Blacknail had made yesterday should have tasted a lot better than it had…

"No," the old scout answered as he looked around the camp. A few seconds later, he stomped over toward Vorscha's cabin. She and Geralhd were seated out in front of it. "It's someone else's turn to whip up some grub."

The hobgoblin and his master circled around a large group of bandits resting next to a pile of crates.

When they got to the other side, Vorscha noticed them and smiled. "Oh, Saeter! Geralhd and I were just sitting down to eat. Care to join us?"

"Is Khita going to appear out of nowhere?" Saeter asked.

"Not likely. She's apparently fooling around with Varhs right now. The little vixen has that man wrapped around her little finger," the muscular woman replied with a knowing wink. "I taught her how to do that."

Saeter blinked for a second before replying. "I'll accept your invitation and join you then. I hope you aren't having rations or such shit."

Vorscha smiled at him and Blacknail. A delicious meaty aroma came from their fire pit as something roasted over the flames on a spit. It obviously wasn't any kind of trail ration.

"All we have is a bit of venison and some fairly fresh bread, but you're welcome to it. You may have even brought the meat in yourself," Geralhd explained as he gestured toward the fire.

"It smells great." Blacknail sniffed the air and licked his lips.

"What do you think of this mess we're in?" Saeter asked Vorscha as he sat down across from her.

"The fight with Werrick you mean?" she asked.

"Of course, what else could I mean?"

"I think I'm tired and want to rest for a bit. It's important to keep rested up before a battle."

"This is important. Things have been too easy. Herad doesn't see any problems, but my instincts are telling me something is wrong," Saeter told her.

“It might be because a large army is a few hundred feet that way and everyone in it is intent on killing us. That bothers me!” Geralhd commented dryly.

“Then you should go do something about it,” Saeter said sarcastically.

That made Blacknail giggle. The image of Geralhd trying to fight off an army, or even more than one person, was hilarious.

“It’s not like we’ve been winning every battle,” Vorscha pointed out. “Werrick has pushed us back all the way here. I’m still sore from the fight at the river.”

“That’s just weight of numbers,” Saeter told her. “Herad wasn’t seriously planning on stopping him before he got here. Those fights went exactly the way Herad wanted them to.”

“We could have held the river for quite a while if that mage hadn’t frozen it. It would have been nice to have done a bit more damage there,” Vorscha countered as she grimaced.

Blacknail remembered the fight at the river. It had just been a few days ago. Mostly, he had stood back and shot a few arrows at the enemy. Not that he had been counting, but he’d managed to hit two enemies. He had even been aiming for one of them! Vorscha had led a large group and tried to stop the enemy from crossing the river. At first, picking off anyone trying to make the crossing had been easy. However, when the river froze over, they had been forced to retreat.

Saeter shook his head. “Even that was a victory for Herad. She drew that mage out into the open, and now she has a better idea of the tricks at his disposal.”

“I think your logic is a little flawed there,” Geralhd interjected. “It sounds to me like you’re trying to twist things to fit your argument.”

“It’s a good thing I don’t care then,” Saeter commented before turning back to Vorscha. “The thing is, we both know things are going too smoothly. It doesn’t seem like Werrick is really trying! Hells, he hasn’t even bothered to show up yet!”

"Maybe he just likes to sleep in. If I was the boss, I'd sleep in all the time," Blacknail contributed. How great would it be to sleep in to noon every day? He could stay curled up in his blankets and minions would bring him breakfast…

Vorscha frowned and poked the fire with a stick. There was a crack as a hot coal shifted and a small shower of sparks rose into the air. "It does seem like he is doing exactly what we expect him to. That's not something I would anticipate from a man of his reputation. He hasn't become the most powerful bandit chief in the North by being so predictable."

"Exactly! He's basically just throwing bodies at us!" Saeter announced. "We've bled him quite a bit so far by making him fight for every choke point on the way here, but what if he doesn't care? What if it's not only Herad's plan that is going perfectly but his as well?"

Vorscha made a sour face. "I don't like that idea, but it makes a lot of sense. It would explain why we haven't seen much from the man himself. There has been no need for him to change his plans or get involved."

"But that would mean he wants to fight us here?" Geralhd remarked with a voice full of doubt. "I can't see the logic in that. We have all the advantages here! He doesn't outnumber us all that much, and we have a solid defensive position. How does he expect to get through our walls?"

"I don't know what he's planning. My gut is just telling me he has a plan and that we won't like it," Saeter told him.

"You sure know how to ruin someone's appetite," Vorscha remarked. "No wonder you don't get invited over to eat by many people."

Blacknail nodded. Even he got invited over more than his master, and he was far from the most popular member of Herad's band. It was probably because Saeter was so grumpy and because hobgoblins were so handsome.

"Werrick doesn't need to have some sort of complex machinations in the works," Geralhd added. "Maybe he thinks he has the blades and mages to swamp us. He is known to be quite the arrogant ruffian."

"Just right. We have a few tricks up our sleeves as well," Vorscha commented as she raised a fist and grinned. "The enemy isn't going to get inside our walls without a hell of a fight."

"I should just stab this Werrick man," the hobgoblin mused. "All this waiting for battle is getting annoying."

A leader as powerful as Werrick probably also had a lot of great stuff to loot. Blacknail wouldn't be able to get his hands on it during a battle, but if he was the one who killed Werrick, then things would be very different.

"It's probably best if you don't try that," Geralhd told Blacknail. "Werrick is a skilled Vessel. They say he has killed hundreds of men."

"I've killed Vessels before," Blacknail said without concern as he shrugged. It hadn't even been that hard. Everyone needed to sleep, and human guards were usually lazy. The trick was to stab them in the back a few times.

"Not like the Wolf, you haven't," Saeter interjected. "If skilled assassins could get anywhere near him, then he would already be dead. Also, he will have heard of you and won't be taking any chances. You weren't exactly subtle back in Daggerpoint."

"I was the sneakiest! No one saw me coming," Blacknail bragged as his master rolled his eyes.

"Maybe, but they sure noticed the bloody carnage you left in your wake. You went through Daggerpoint like a troll through a barn," the old scout replied.

The sound of trumpets blared from the other side of the walls, and Geralhd and Blacknail jumped in surprise. The hobgoblin dropped the bit of bread he had been holding, but he quickly picked it off the ground and shoved it into his mouth. The dirt didn't even make it taste any worse. It was almost a seasoning, really.

Shouting followed the sound of instruments, from both outside the camp and within it. Bandits all around the camp moved.

"Vorscha, get over here! I need you at the wall," Herad called out of the din.

The tall woman was on her feet, grabbing the long sword that had been lying at her side, and ran toward Herad's voice. The others were quick to follow. Men and women were rushing around everywhere, but Blacknail's group managed to find a way through the crowds. Together, they ran to the closest stretch of wall and peeked through the gaps in the posts. The lookout platforms above them were already crowded.

It was obvious what had raised the alarm. Werrick's army was moving. As the trumpets blared, banners rose above the enemy host. A white wolf's head flew on a black field.

With a chorus of shouting, the lead elements of the enemy army marched toward Herad's base, and the sound of their footsteps echoed off the trees. Before the advancing forces got into bow range, shields were hoisted to form a protective barrier of steel and wood. The attack had begun. There could be no doubt the Wolf himself had finally arrived.

Chapter 10

The enemy shield wall drew inexorably closer to Herad's barricades. The formation contained hundreds of men and spanned the road from one side to the other. The approaching mass of soldiers only ended at the edges of the forest.

"First rank, fire!" Herad yelled.

A swarm of buzzing arrows leapt into the air. They rose from all along the wall and descended upon Werrick's men. The sounds of the arrows hitting the enemy's shields was almost like the patter of raindrops on a roof, only with more screaming in the background. Unfortunately, while some of Werrick's men fell as arrows slipped through the gaps in their defensive barrier, most of the enemies remained unharmed. They continued marching toward the wooden barricade Herad had erected to block their way.

"Second rank, fire!" Herad yelled.

Another cloud of arrows hit the enemy, with much the same effect.

"Should we do something?" Geralhd asked Saeter as he stared at the enemy in shock.

Blacknail was standing with them at the wall, peeking between the crude wooden posts that composed most of its length.

"Feel free to run out there if you want," Saeter replied sarcastically. "I plan on staying right here unless I'm ordered to move."

Blacknail nodded. "I think-ss I should go scout something out in the woods. Just in case the enemy attacks… somewhere else." The hobgoblin's guts felt a little watery as he stared at the approaching army. Standing in its way didn't seem like a great idea.

"You're staying right next to me," Saeter ordered Blacknail with a level stare.

The hobgoblin grinned nervously but nodded. He would have to wait until things got more chaotic before making a break for it.

"Do you think he will want to parley?" Geralhd asked.

"Who, Werrick? What would be the point?" Saeter answered condescendingly.

"To settle his differences with Herad without getting hundreds of people killed?" the other man asked with uncertain hope.

"Ha, neither of them will give ground. They have nothing to talk about. This is a fight to the death," Saeter replied.

"Why are we even fighting again?" Geralhd asked. "I know Herad and Werrick hate each other, but how does Werrick profit from a huge fight like this? Shouldn't he be more concerned with robbing people and other bandit activities?"

"Feelings have little to do with this," Saeter told the other man. "Things in the North are changing, and there isn't room for two top dogs."

"Wait, I thought the boss was protecting our territory from intrusion. She never said she wanted to rule over any of the other bands!" Geralhd remarked in surprise.

"You don't know Herad well," Saeter said. "Holding this patch of land and setting herself up as its ruler was always but the first step. With a firm footing here, she can quickly expand all through the North."

"That's just great," Geralhd remarked sarcastically before sighing deeply.

"Yep, if you can conquer more land, why would you ever stop?" Blacknail exclaimed excitedly. He had always assumed

Herad was going to kill all her rivals. What was the other option?

"So that you don't get killed in a stupid battle in the middle of nowhere?" Geralhd countered as he frowned at the hobgoblin.

Blacknail shrugged. "Everyone dies, but not everyone gets the pick of all the best loot."

Geralhd sighed and looked back at the wall. He didn't seem convinced. In the background, another volley of arrows flew into the air at Herad's command. "This is an enlightening conversation, but perhaps we should focus on the battle. I'm still not sure what I should be doing right now."

Saeter huffed. "If Vorscha didn't order you to do anything, then stay back. You can join one of the reserve units if you want, but it's not like you're even properly equipped."

Geralhd gave the old scout an annoyed glare. The younger man was dressed in lighter clothes than most of the nearby bandits. Instead of armor, he wore a long cloth shirt and a thin leather vest. Even the leather jackets Blacknail and Saeter wore offered much more protection.

"I like being able to move freely, and I don't see you manning the walls," Geralhd remarked.

"Not my job," Saeter countered. "I just got back from a scouting mission. I'm not a grunt."

"I'm not a grunt either," Geralhd replied.

"Oh, then what are you? A camp follower?" the old scout joked as he grinned with obvious amusement.

The younger man stared at Saeter coldly. It looked as though he wanted to say something, but he bit his tongue instead. After a few seconds, he turned to look at the approaching army. "Why doesn't Herad just have Mahedium blast their formation? They are all tightly packed together."

"Do you think Werrick doesn't know we have a mage? This entire attack could be bait," Saeter told him. "If Mahedium shows himself, then Werrick's mages will bombard him with everything they have."

“Oh, I had forgotten about them. Why is Werrick even bothering with an assault? His mages could just blast our barricade to smithereens,” Geralhd asked.

Blacknail looked at the wooden wall that was a mere three feet from him. He could easily picture it exploding into a hail of deadly splinters. “Why are we standing here? This seems like a bad idea.”

Ignoring Blacknail, Saeter rolled his eyes at Geralhd. “He doesn’t want to lose his own mages. Herad probably has Mahedium lying in wait, ready to drop a ton of war magic on Werrick’s mages the second they try to assault our barricades. The first side to reveal its magic users is at a disadvantage in a fight like this.”

“So Herad and Werrick are holding back in hopes of forcing the enemy to commit their mages?” Geralhd mused.

“Or whatever other tricks they have tucked away,” Saeter confirmed.

“Obviously,” Blacknail added smugly as he took several large steps away from the wall, just in case it exploded.

A squad of Herad’s men ran up beside the hobgoblin’s group. The enemy was only a few seconds from the wall now. Herad could be heard yelling for reinforcements at the gate. Blacknail and Geralhd turned to look at Saeter for guidance. He was the only one who knew what was going on. However, the old scout seemed content to stand there.

There was a furious roar from outside, and Blacknail winced and instinctively covered his head. In front of him, Werrick’s men hit the wall. Their formation seemed to ripple as the wall halted their advance.

“What are they—” Geralhd started to ask before he was interrupted by a chopping sound. He flinched as an axe blade hit the wall before him. It was swiftly followed by many more blows as the enemy chopped their way through the barrier. At the same time, ladders appeared from out of the mass of enemies and were thrown up against the wall.

Arrows continued to fall on Werrick's troops, but men with shields stopped most of the deadly projectiles. Several bandits near Blacknail used spears to push down ladders or to stab through the wall at the axemen, but most of Herad's minions didn't seem to know what to do. They could only wait for the enemy to make their way through or over the wall.

More intense fighting was happening at the entrance to the camp. A mass of enemy troops was trying to force through the gap in the wall there. However, that was also where Herad had most of her troops. Friends and foes were pressed closely together as the wall channeled Werrick's troops toward the gate. Bandits hacked and slashed at each other as they fought for space. There, Herad was watching and yelling orders as her minions fought to push back the enemy.

Blacknail stepped back as an axe-head burst through the wall near him. As a pair of bandits stepped forward to deal with it, the hobgoblin noticed the top of a ladder appear above the barricade. It shook as someone climbed it. His first instinct was to let someone else deal with the problem, but then an amusing idea occurred to him. After a quick look around, Blacknail jumped onto the wall and climbed. His claws had no problem gripping the wooden posts, and they easily supported his weight. Once he got to the top, Blacknail waited a few seconds.

Soon enough, a man's head popped up and looked around. He froze when he noticed the hobgoblin staring at him from only few inches away. Blacknail smiled and sliced one of the man's hands. His knife cut cleanly through several fingers, and the man yelped in pain. His face was an agonized red and his eyes were wide with terror as Blacknail pushed over the ladder he was standing on. The hobgoblin smiled as the man crashed into his fellows below. With that done, Blacknail scampered back down the wall to safety. He'd had his fun, and hanging around up there would be dangerous.

Saeter and Geralhd were still standing in the same spot, so Blacknail walked back to them. The hobgoblin gave his master a happy smile. Saeter rolled his eyes.

"Unless either of you feel like joining the defense here, I see no reason to stay," Saeter said before striding away. "I want to get a better view, and right now I can't see the forest for the trees."

"I don't think I'd be much help here. Lead the way," Geralhd replied as he threw a nervous glance at the fighting going on near the wall. The young man then hurried after the old scout.

Blacknail didn't feel the need to stick around either, so he joined them. Saeter led the way to a small hill that lay closer to the camp's entrance. The old scout stepped up onto one of the crates there and looked around. At the gate, something was happening. The fighting slowed down as the front rank of the enemy split. A man with a chainmail shirt and a steel helmet that covered his face stepped forward. Wielding a long sword in one hand and large round shield in the other, he cut down all of Herad's men within reach. The effortless way he swung his heavy weapon seemed to indicate he was a Vessel. The forces Herad had guarding the entrance to the camp hesitated. As the Vessel stepped forward, none of them went to meet him; instead they held back.

"Cowards, all of you!" the Vessel bellowed. "Will none of you face me? Not even your useless bitch of a leader, Herad?"

The bandit chieftain didn't budge. She glowered at the enemy without answering. After a few moments, she yelled new orders.

"Is that Werrick?" Blacknail asked. Maybe things were finally coming to a head!

"No, Werrick is taller and would never expose himself so early," his master explained.

"Ah, Herad should just go kill that human." Blacknail frowned in disappointment. "He doesn't look so tough and she's scary strong."

"That's what Werrick wants, you green idiot," Saeter countered. "What do you think will happen if Herad steps out onto the front line?"

"Er, something bad?" the hobgoblin replied.

The old scout smacked the side of the hobgoblin's head. "She will be roasted like a feast day duck! Werrick will bombard her with all the magic at his disposal and that will be the end of us."

"Okay, she shouldn't do that then," Blacknail replied sheepishly as he rubbed his sore head.

When no one appeared to challenge him, the enemy Vessel charged. His sword slammed into the neck of a bandit, then he stabbed the chest of another. He wasn't alone either; a squad of heavily armed soldiers protected his flanks.

"I hope Werrick doesn't have many more Vessels at his disposal," Geralhd remarked. "We only have Herad and um… Blacknail."

Saeter grimaced. "Herad has trust issues when it comes to other Vessels, but it seems like the Wolf doesn't."

"Except for me, because I'm so loyal and handsome. I'm the boss's favorite!" Blacknail added cheerfully.

Herad's minions seemed incapable of stopping the enemy Vessel's advance. As the flow of the battle turned against her, Herad yelled a new series of orders. Suddenly, the center of the bandit formation defending the gate pulled back.

Werrick's men surged forward unopposed, especially the Vessel and those around him. Rather than fight him, Herad's minions retreated. The Vessel lunged forward to attack, but his sword smashed harmlessly into the shield of a defender. The bandits nearby raised shields and stuck together as they fell back.

"Cowards!" the Vessel roared.

However, he didn't chase them farther. He was already too far ahead of most of his companions. Only a few of Werrick's men had kept up with him. The Vessel raised his shield and banged his sword hilt against it as he held his position and waited for reinforcements.

Before that could happen though, Herad yelled another order and a flight of arrows descended upon him. Most of the projectiles missed as the Vessel dove to the side and raised his shield defensively. His companions weren't all so lucky; several of them fell with bloody wounds. However, the rest of the arrows bounced ineffectively off the Vessel's shield and armor. For a moment, he hesitated, unsure of whether to advance or retreat.

Herad ordered another volley, and the man made up his mind. He roared a challenge and charged forward. A horde of Werrick's men raced after him toward the defenders. They stepped through the gap in the wall and into the bandits' camp. Before they could steady themselves, more of Herad's troops emerged from both sides and slammed into the attackers.

A fierce melee erupted at the entrance of the camp as the defenders attempted to encircle the Vessel and the men near him. More attackers poured through the gate in an attempt to stop them until the fight was a chaotic mess. In the center of it all, the sword-wielding Vessel continued to batter Herad's men. It seemed as though he would hold his ground long enough to create a hole in Herad's defenses and allow the attackers to gain a foothold in the camp.

That was when Herad joined the fight. She drew her sword and charged toward the melee, her bodyguards at her back. Her minions quickly got out of the way as she raced forward.

The enemy Vessel was fighting hard to hold his ground. He bashed one of Herad's men aside with his shield and slashed at another. His sword smashed into a helm and sent it flying as the owner fell. That was when Herad dashed out from behind a group of her minions and struck. Her blade lashed toward the enemy's neck with viper-like speed.

The Vessel managed to step back and block the first blow, but Herad smoothly launched a barrage of lighting-fast attacks. He could only stumble backward and try to hold his shield up in front of himself. As Herad kept the Vessel busy, two of her bodyguards charged in from the side. They were big men in dark leather armor and they held long spears, which they stabbed toward the enemy's chest. The Vessel had no option but to try to block this new attack, and Herad took full advantage. She ducked under a swing of his sword and slashed his groin. Crimson blood splashed onto the ground, and the enemy stumbled.

Herad tripped the stunned warrior, and he hit the ground with a metallic crash. She then drew a knife from a sheath on her belt. Its oddly thin blade glinted in the sun as she stabbed it through his chainmail shirt and into his heart.

"She did it!" Geralhd observed happily.

Saeter grunted. "Of course she did. That was the easy part."

Without wasting a second or reclaiming the dirk, Herad turned and ran away. Her bodyguards were right behind her.

From somewhere at the back of the enemy formation, several dozen feet outside the camp, a ball of energy appeared. It hung in the air and glowed with an odd green light. Then without warning, it arced off toward where Herad had been fighting. The crackling orb flew over the heads of fighters from both sides before hitting the ground a few feet from the fallen Vessel's body. A second later, it exploded into green flame. Dozens of men were thrown off their feet, and the smell of burning flesh filled the air. Herad was well out of the blast zone though, and most of the victims were Werrick's own men.

From atop one of the archer platforms behind the wall, a blast of fire descended at the origin of the magic. Mahedium had revealed himself. The scarlet flame flew toward the location of the enemy mage, only to be stopped by an invisible barrier. However, the flame didn't completely disappear. Tongues of fire slid off the barrier and rained down on the men below. More screams of pain and horror filled the air.

Immediately, Mahedium launched another attack. This time, there was a screeching sound as a blast of energy hit the ground beneath the barrier. The earth beneath the target burst open. Jagged shards of rock flew into the air as the ground tore itself apart in a violent eruption. All the nearby troops were thrown off their feet. There was no way to tell if the enemy mage had been hit or not, but no more obvious magic was cast, so Mahedium stopped his attacks. Blacknail saw the mage jump down from the platform and hurry away.

More magic wasn't necessary though. The enemy's advance halted. They had managed to cut their way into Herad's camp, but they had lost their Vessel and been hit by several damaging magical blasts. Herad's troops redoubled their efforts and pushed back the intruders. The enemy's morale had been crushed.

Someone else had noticed the attackers' poor position as well. Trumpets called out from across the battlefield. It was the signal to retreat, and Werrick's men disengaged from the fighting. The first day of fighting was over, but there would be more. Off in the distance, the wolf's head banner flew above a still-intact hostile army.

Chapter 11

"Well, that's all over," Saeter remarked. "I'm going to go sit down."

"You didn't do anything," Geralhd pointed out. "We just stood here and watched the battle."

"Wrong. I was out scouting before the fight. That's my job," the old scout replied. "You're the only one here who didn't do anything."

"I fought one enemy," Blacknail added proudly. "He won't be climbing the wall again without-ss the fingers I cut off."

Geralhd didn't have anything to say to that. He sighed in dissatisfaction before looking at the retreating enemy. Blacknail thought Geralhd should have been used to being useless by now.

The hobgoblin also took a second to look over the battlefield. It hadn't been the first human battle he'd ever seen, but he had been impressed by it nonetheless. Not only had there been more fighters than he could count, but the way they'd fought together was overwhelming. Also, the magic was scary. What could a normal hobgoblin do against that sort of power? Goblins would be climbing all over each other if they had been packed that tightly, and that was only if they didn't start fighting among themselves. Even if they did stay loyal, they would have most likely forgotten which side they were supposed to be on.

Below them, Mahedium was still moving away from the wall, in case the enemy retaliated against him for his earlier magic, but he'd slowed his pace. The mage noticed Saeter and the others atop the hill and headed their way.

"Can you see what's going on from there?" Mahedium asked as he approached.

"Most of it. The enemy is retreating." Saeter looked annoyed at this new interruption. He had been about to leave before Mahedium called out to him.

"That was some spectacular magic and a great improvement over your earlier works," Geralhd told the mage. "You certainly put some fear into the enemy."

"Thank you, that means something coming from an educated man such as yourself," Mahedium replied. "I am always striving to advance my craft."

"I've seen both better and much worse," Saeter noted.

"I imagine you have, and I'll take that as a compliment," Mahedium replied graciously as he glanced at the old scout.

Blacknail was fairly sure his master's words hadn't been a compliment. Saeter didn't give out a lot of those. "I liked the explosions. You should blow people up more often. It's hilarious. I wish I could do that!"

The hobgoblin waved one hand dramatically toward the enemy and made a fake-sounding explosion noise. There was an uneasy silence from the humans. Judging by the pained look on his face, Mahedium found the idea of Blacknail gaining such an ability particularly unsettling.

"Anyway… do you think you got that enemy mage?" Geralhd asked Mahedium.

"I don't know. Things were very chaotic at the end. He was too far away for me to see clearly."

"Hopefully you got him. You certainly blasted everything around him beyond dust and death," Geralhd replied happily.

"Herad's plan was effective. I'm simply grateful she knew what she was doing and that she obviously values me," Mahedium commented. "If she had been less worried about my safety and had ordered me to attack first, I might not have survived that fight."

"Oh, she won't throw away someone so useful," Saeter said as he grinned unkindly at the mage.

"Ah, yes. I've heard that battles where both sides have mages can be complicated and dangerous," Geralhd interjected.

"Indeed. The key to hostile exchanges between mages is twofold," Mahedium explained. "Firstly, you have to hit hard and fast. It is easier to attack than defend. Secondly, if that fails, you need to analyze your opponent's defenses and find a way around them. Having a multitude of attack spells is important."

All of Mahedium's long-winded chatting didn't interest Blacknail. He glanced away and observed the activity around them. Maybe there was something interesting going on, or free food. There were certainly a lot of human corpses littering the ground. It was a shame that humans didn't approve of their dead being made into snacks. Well, they didn't taste all that good anyway.

Outside the walls, Werrick's troops had come to stop. They were well out of bow range and had returned to their encampment, which was swarming with activity. The fight might be over for now, but wounds had to be tended and order had to be restored. That was certainly what Herad was doing. The bandit chieftain was yelling orders as she stomped up and down the length of the wall.

"Let's move, it's windy here," Blacknail suggested to the others as he watched her. Standing on the hill made them very visible, and the hobgoblin didn't want to catch Herad's attention. She might give him work.

"Good idea," Saeter replied as he started down the hill.

Geralhd and Blacknail followed the scout toward his campsite, but Mahedium hesitated. He remained where he was and glanced toward his cabin.

"I should talk to Herad, then get back to my lab," the mage announced.

"Good, you do that," Saeter grunted as Blacknail waved goodbye.

Without further interruption, the two men and the hobgoblin walked the short distance to Blacknail and Saeter's tents. The camp was oddly empty. No one was near the cabins or tents at the back of the clearing. Almost everyone was still over by the wall.

"Why did you follow us? I didn't actually invite you," Saeter asked Geralhd as he took a seat on a chair by the fire pit.

"I don't really have anywhere to go," Geralhd replied as he shrugged. "Vorscha is probably busy doing something important, and I don't want to get in the way."

Blacknail smiled. It was obvious the thin human had grown used to Saeter's grumpiness and was ignoring it. That was fine with Blacknail; he enjoyed having Geralhd around. It usually meant more food for him.

The hobgoblin and Geralhd took seats near Saeter. The old scout ignored them, grabbed a large sack, and went through its contents.

"I don't suppose you want to play some dice to help spend our time more quickly?" Geralhd asked Saeter.

"No," Saeter grunted without turning away from the bag he was rummaging in.

"I suppose I could teach Blacknail to play…" the young man mused as Blacknail's ears perked up.

Before the hobgoblin could reply though, someone yelled in their direction. They all turned to see who it was and saw Varhs approaching. The other scout was dressed in his leather armor and wearing his forester cloak. Behind him, Scamp plodded along happily. The goblin was wearing a pair of human-sized brown trousers that had been cut short and secured with a rope.

"It's good to see you all intact." Varhs grinned and waved cheerfully in their direction. "Although I never doubted for moment that you were fine, Saeter. If mere mortal blades could pierce your old hide, it would have happened years ago."

Geralhd smiled at the joke. Blacknail glared at Scamp. The little goblin had disappeared for a while during a fight with some of Werrick's men out in the forest. Since then, the hobgoblin had been sure that he had smelled traces of him around, but he had never laid eyes on Scamp until now. Obviously, the goblin had been avoiding him. Saeter saw the other scout, frowned, then did a quick double-take. He glanced behind the man and seemed relieved that there was no one behind him except Scamp.

"You're alone, right?" Saeter asked. "That red-haired pest isn't following you?"

"What? No, Khita had some stuff to wrap up," Varhs remarked in surprise. "She seems to go wherever she wants."

The younger scout looked a little troubled when he talked about Khita. Maybe they had gotten into a fight, or maybe he'd finally realized that being around her was making him stupid. Blacknail hoped she was dead. Khita was useless and annoying.

"As long as she isn't *here*," Saeter replied. "I see your goblin came back."

That comment seemed to cheer up Varhs. His frown quickly became a self-satisfied smile. "Scamp came back the very next day. He's a great companion and well trained. He just got lost in the forest after that chase."

"Trained by me, not you," Blacknail muttered.

Scamp was an undisciplined nuisance! Blacknail had no idea why the scout had gone out of his way to find and train a goblin. Varhs let Scamp do whatever he wanted, and he had never taught the goblin how to behave. When Scamp had caused a huge mess a while back, he had almost been executed by Herad and had only survived because Blacknail had promised to help train him. Thus, the hobgoblin had selflessly tried to beat some sense into Scamp in exchange for the occasional snack. However, Blacknail had grown too busy to continue the training. The snacks hadn't been very good either. Also, Blacknail had more important things to do, like keep an eye on Elyias, his new minion. Wait… he had forgotten about Elyias.

"Oops," Blacknail muttered. He hoped his minion hadn't managed to get himself killed. That would be inconvenient. The man was amusing.

"So are you here for a reason, or are you just trying make a nuisance out of yourself?" Saeter asked as he scowled at the younger scout.

"I just got back from watching the forest paths," Varhs replied. "Herad told me to check in on you and make sure you were going back out soon."

"There are plenty of other scouts who can do that job. Why do I need to go out?" Saeter asked.

"I'm not the one you need to convince. Go argue with Herad and see how that works," Varhs replied. "I can only guess that the boss values your skills and Blacknail's nose."

"It is very nice-looking," Blacknail bragged as he wiggled his nose.

There was a chuckle from Varhs and Geralhd. Even Saeter grinned. Blacknail took that to mean they agreed with him. He was an undeniably handsome hobgoblin.

"I have some chores to finish before I head back out. I'm not leaving right away," Saeter told Varhs as he scowled in annoyance.

"Again, it's not me you have to worry about. I'm just the messenger," the scout replied with a shrug.

"Then she should be here telling me herself," Saeter muttered.

Blacknail frowned. He was fairly certain that wasn't how the chieftain-and-subordinate relationship worked. His master was getting dangerously grumpy. Blacknail took it upon himself to prevent any conflict between Herad and his master. Saeter was usually wise, but when it came to the chieftain, he was stupider than Scamp after he'd been kicked in the head a few times.

"Let's just go out. It's quieter out there anyway. You like the forest," Blacknail interjected.

"Fine. I have some stuff to do first though. I need a few minutes," Saeter replied reluctantly.

While everyone else had been talking, Scamp had wandered over to Geralhd. The bandit noticed the goblin and reached into one of his pockets. A second later, he pulled out a bit of dried meat.

"There you go," Geralhd said as he handed the morsel to the little goblin.

"Traitor!" Blacknail gasped as his mouth fell open in shock. Geralhd was supposed to give treats to him! Scamp didn't deserve tasty things! Even if Scamp was behaving himself, it was only because Blacknail kept him in line. Scamp was so going to get a good kicking later, and the next time Geralhd needed help, he was on his own! They had betrayed his trust!

"Hm, what was that, Blacknail? I bet you want a treat too," Geralhd commented as he turned toward him.

The man pulled something out of his pocket and tossed it to the hobgoblin. Blacknail snatched the gift out of the air and studied it. Was it… candied fruit! Joy!

"Yummy, thank you!" Blacknail exclaimed before he shoved the treat into his mouth and chewed.

"Of course, I have something for you, my favorite hobgoblin," Geralhd told him.

As he scarfed down the treat, the hobgoblin smirked and eyed Scamp. The goblin was staring at Blacknail with obvious jealousy as he chewed on his pathetic piece of meat. That cheered up the hobgoblin completely. Fine, he would forgive Geralhd and Scamp this one time. Scamp could keep his tiny morsel. Blacknail knew how to make dried meat anyway. He was practically throwing out the stuff. Candied fruit was so much better than meat, just like how he was superior to Scamp!

"I need to go get back a dagger I lent someone. You can wait here, Blacknail," Saeter announced as he got to his feet.

Blacknail was too busy chewing to do more than nod as his master walked away. Geralhd invited Varhs to play a round of dice, and the scout agreed. Varhs took a seat, and the pair started a game. Apparently Geralhd had been carrying the dice in his pocket throughout the entire battle.

Instead of watching, Blacknail took advantage of the humans' preoccupation to sneak up behind Scamp and place a hand on his shoulder. When the goblin turned around, Blacknail smiled toothily at him.

"Hey, boss," Scamp nervously addressed the hobgoblin. He had flinched at Blacknail's touch and didn't seem happy to have his attention. That was fine with Blacknail.

"So you've been getting tasty treats from Geralhd," the hobgoblin mused. He wasn't upset at the goblin anymore, not really, but a certain pecking order had to be enforced. Blacknail was at the top. "Have you been avoiding me? Maybe because you did something bad?"

"No, boss!" Scamp whined. "I, um… was looking for stuff to give you!"

"Really?" the hobgoblin replied skeptically.

"Ya, look," the goblin said as he rummaged through the pockets of his pants.

After a few seconds of searching, the goblin withdrew a collection of small items and held them up to Blacknail. The hobgoblin studied them. He saw a few coins, some shiny rocks, a mouse skull, and a twisted bit of metal.

"All right, fine. I believe you," Blacknail told Scamp reluctantly, even though he knew the goblin was lying through his crooked little teeth.

It was useless junk and no good to Blacknail at all, but the act of giving was important. It showed who was in charge, even if the hobgoblin already had much shinier rocks.

"Is this everything?" Blacknail asked Scamp.

The goblin froze before looking off to the side thoughtfully and scratching his head. He seemed to remember something after a moment, because he reached back into his pockets. "I did meet that goblin in the mage's house."

Blacknail's eyes narrowed in suspicion. The goblins were conspiring behind his back to overthrow him! He had to do something. The hobgoblin's claws inched toward Scamp's neck.

However, his murderous intent was delayed when Scamp withdrew a thin shard of black crystal from his pocket. Its murky surface looked oily and seemed to shift as Blacknail stared at it in fascination.

"You haven't been stealing from Mahedium again, have you?" the hobgoblin asked.

Stealing a crystal was what had gotten Scamp into so much trouble before. The goblin could apparently set them off, because he had been born so annoying that he was magical.

"No, boss! This was given to me, to give to you, from the goblin in the mage's house. It's tribute from him. He said no one would be missing it," Scamp explained in an excited burst. "Or at least I think so. He doesn't speak good; I think he's stupid."

Blacknail took a second to mull over this new development. Maybe he had misjudged the goblin Mahedium had captured. If he was willing to pay Blacknail his respects in such a way, then he might not be so bad after all, even if he was a creepy little thing. It was a rather nice-looking piece of crystal, and it didn't look like the kind that exploded. Yes, if the goblin was offering tribute, then he would be allowed to stay. Organizing the goblins in Herad's tribe would be useful…

"Fine, I accept his gift. He is now one of my minions, like-ss you," the hobgoblin announced as he took the crystal from Scamp. "You both have to keep paying tribute though. Just don't steal from the mage."

"Sure thing, boss," the goblin replied enthusiastically. "Finding good stuff is easy. The humans forget things everywhere, and if you beg, they give you stuff!"

After cursing a bad roll of the dice, Geralhd looked at Blacknail and Scamp. Varhs was laughing in delight.

"Hmm, what are you two up to?" Geralhd asked.

"Nothing," Blacknail hurriedly replied. "We were just… talking about candy."

"Yum, candy!" Scamp added as he forced an awkward smile.

With a distracted frown, Geralhd turned back to his game. Blacknail uncurled his claws and let Scamp go. Good, the humans suspected nothing…

Chapter 12

It only took a few minutes for Saeter to come back. After shooing Geralhd and Varhs away from his campsite, the old scout led Blacknail off into the bush again. Herad wanted them to watch the enemy and make sure they didn't circle around them, so that was what they would do.

The hobgoblin and his master took the path at the back of the camp then circled around through the woods toward Werrick's flank. They moved stealthily through the trees. With the enemy so close, the green maze was even more dangerous than usual.

"It's not just enemy scouts or war parties we need to worry about. All this human activity and blood will have scared away some creature but attracted others," Saeter told Blacknail as they stopped at a lookout point.

Below the rocky overhang at their feet, a vista brimming with thick vegetation stretched out before them. Studying the trees, neither of them saw any movement, so they moved on. As they scouted through the dense forest, it became apparent that the enemy seemed to have little interest in moving off the road. They only ran into a single scout who had ventured into the forest. They trailed him carefully for a few minutes as he circled his own camp, but he never approached Herad's base. Other than that one man, they only discovered a few sentries positioned around Werrick's army to warn them of attack. All and all, the enemy seemed more concerned with Herad's band attacking them than entering the forest themselves.

"Let's get a closer look at their encampment before we head back," Saeter announced.

The pair were crouched behind a fallen tree. A gully lay before them, and it wound through the forest toward the road. They had just watched from concealment as a pair of sentries made their way along the gully and back to camp. Many of Werrick's men were obviously using the gully as a path, because its banks were covered in muddy footprints.

"There will be people watching," Blacknail pointed out.

"You will just have to deal with them," Saeter replied.

"Good! Sounds like fun," Blacknail exclaimed as he grinned and rubbed his hands together. That was the answer he'd been hoping for.

Eagerly, the hobgoblin popped out of hiding and looked around. He didn't see or hear anything, so he crept over to the path Werrick's men had trampled. Saeter was right behind him, and together, they headed toward the road.

It was a few minutes before they spotted any sentries. Blacknail noticed them first. A woman with short, curly brown hair and a black-haired man were standing next to a large rock. Blacknail signaled to Saeter then slid up next to a tree. He peeked out from behind it. The enemy sentries had a good view of the surroundings. It would be difficult to sneak past them without having to circle quite a distance around.

"I'll take care of them," Blacknail said as he stepped forward.

"No bodies," Saeter ordered sternly.

A sigh of disappointment escaped Blacknail's lips. That made things more complicated, but he still had an idea that could work. Why was his master so against having fun?

The hobgoblin made sure no one was looking in his direction before dashing over to a clump of nearby bushes. He withdrew a stone from one of his pouches and threw it toward the sentries. The small rock arced silently over the enemies' heads and hit the bushes on the other side of them. The resulting rustling drew the sentries' attention. While they were distracted, Blacknail slipped around to the side and behind another tree.

"Huh, it was probably just a bird," one of the sentries told the other.

While they were still looking in the opposite direction, Blacknail threw another stone. This one hit the woman in the back of the head.

"Ow, did you just hit me with a rock?" she exclaimed at the man as she rubbed the back of her head.

"What, no?" he replied in surprise.

"You're the only one here," she pointed out as she scowled at him.

The man glared back. "I didn't hit you. I have no idea what you're talking about."

"Fine, forget about it," the woman huffed as she turned back to survey the forest.

The man did likewise. A few moments later, they both happened to look away from Blacknail's hiding spot again. The hobgoblin threw another rock. This time it hit the man in the back of the head.

"Ow, shit. You hit me!" he growled at his companion. "I told you that I didn't touch you! Don't fucking hit me for no reason, bitch!"

The woman stiffened then whirled toward the man. Her face was red with anger as she shoved a finger in his face. "I didn't do anything to you. You're the one who hit me!"

"I didn't hit you, stop lying," the man replied as he straightened up and glared at her.

As the two stupid humans argued, Blacknail signaled for Saeter to move. The old scout swiftly made his way over to the hobgoblin. Neither of the sentries so much as glanced in his direction.

Once out of sight, Saeter led the way up the hill until the forest ended abruptly at the top of it. A stretch of bushes and a shallow ditch was all that lay between them, the road, and Werrick's army. Carefully, Blacknail stalked over to a thick bit of brush that would conceal him. Then he nudged aside a branch and peeked out. Saeter moved up beside him.

Werrick's men were everywhere. Some of them were only a dozen feet away. Troops stomped around as they performed their duties. A maze of blue tents filled the road and all the clear ground around it, until they stretched out of sight. There were hundreds of them.

Saeter tapped Blacknail to get his attention and pointed out a group of wagons. Half a dozen of them stood off to one side of the camp. Next to them, a line of horses were tied up. Blacknail eyed them suspiciously for a few seconds before moving on.

The next thing Blacknail saw that stood out was a huge pavilion. Its peaked tip towered over the other tents, and it looked wide enough to hold over a dozen men. It was common sense that the biggest and fanciest quarters belonged to the chieftain, so the tent was probably Werrick's. The huge wolf's head banner that flapped in the wind above it was also a clue. There was no sign of anyone who fit Werrick's description though. Blacknail frowned. He'd wanted to catch a glimpse of the enemy chieftain he had heard so much about.

Another tap from Saeter drew the hobgoblin's attention. This time, the old scout pointed back the way they had come, so without wasting another moment, the pair withdrew. They slipped past the still-arguing sentries and headed back to Herad to report. Before they got halfway back, Blacknail caught an unsettling scent and froze in shock.

His master noticed his reaction and reached for his sword, but he stopped short of drawing it. "What is it?"

"I smell a troll," Blacknail answered just as quietly.

"How recent?"

The hobgoblin sniffed the air again and took a moment to mull it over. The forest was full of animal and plant smells that he had to sort. "A few hours."

"It was probably attracted by the blood earlier. There's no real need to worry, but let's hurry back," Saeter explained.

Blacknail nodded. There was a new urgency in both his and Saeter's steps as they walked, and they watched the forest around them more intently. At their quicker pace, it didn't take them long to make their way back to Herad's base. After greeting their own sentries, the pair headed directly to talk to their chieftain. Blacknail wanted to take a nap, but his master was in a hurry for some reason.

Herad was resting in her cabin after the battle. As usual, two large guards stood outside the door.

They recognized Saeter and greeted him. "She knows you're here and will be out soon."

Saeter nodded as Blacknail took a seat on the ground. He didn't feel like standing. Herad might be a while. Before too long, the door of the cabin swung open with a creak and Herad stepped out. She was wearing a loose white shirt that was obviously fresh, and her dark eyes looked tired as she glanced their way.

"What is it, old man? This had better be important," she asked crankily.

"While out scouting, I got a good look at Werrick's camp," Saeter explained.

"Oh?" Herad remarked with obvious interest.

"He has most of his supplies loaded onto several wagons that are parked next to each other. They're only a few dozen feet from the edge of the forest. Obviously his lookouts are sloppy too, since Blacknail and I got so close," Saeter told her.

"You want to hit them." The bandit chieftain seemed intrigued by the idea but not convinced.

"I can lead a group through the forest before it gets dark. We'll hit the wagons and set them ablaze before high-tailing it out of there. They won't have time to react," Saeter explained.

Herad considered the old scout's words carefully. "I can give you twenty or thirty men, of which only half a dozen can be woodsmen."

"That will be fine. Blacknail and I can clear the way," he replied.

"Do you need anything else?"

"It would be nice to have some magic on this raid," Saeter suggested. "There is no better or faster way to get things burning."

"No, I'm not risking Mahedium," Herad replied. "It's not worth any of the possible gains."

"Things will be a lot slower if we have to depend on torches and fire arrows. We might lose more men," Saeter pointed out.

"Then that's what will happen," Herad said coldly as she leveled a heavy gaze his way.

Saeter sighed but nodded. Herad relaxed a little in response to his submission, and her expression softened slightly. Blacknail smiled. His master was actually doing the right thing for once!

"Let's just bring Scamp then," the hobgoblin said.

"What?" Saeter and Herad replied in surprise at the same time. They threw each other a quick glance before turning back to the hobgoblin.

"Scamp can use magic. We could just take him," Blacknail explained.

"The goblin can set things off. That doesn't make him a mage," Herad replied.

"All he needs to do is make some-ss crystals explode. We can throw him at the wagons. It worked against the big mutant snake from before." Blacknail was careful not to challenge her in any way or give her an excuse to take offence. Herad was both violent and quite dangerous.

"We probably don't need to actually throw the goblin," Saeter pointed out.

"No, but it would be more fun," Blacknail countered.

"Don't remind me about that," Herad said as her eyes narrowed. "If you want to consider this, Saeter, then feel free, as long as Mahedium agrees. You can run the mission your way. I don't want to hear anything more about exploding goblins."

"As you wish," Saeter quickly replied.

"Exactly. Now is there anything else you want to bother me about?" she asked.

"No, that's everything," the old scout responded.

"Good. Talk to Vorscha about getting the gear you need. I'll make sure she knows to give it to you," Herad said as she dismissed them with a wave. The bandit chieftain then turned around, walked through her cabin's door, and slammed it in everyone's faces.

The guards to either side flinched at the unexpected noise.

"Well, that went a lot better than I thought it would," Saeter told them.

The hobgoblin and his master then went to talk to Mahedium. It didn't take much to convince him. He was more than willing to give them some crystals, so long as he didn't have to go anywhere near combat.

After that, they met with Varhs. He had no problem with Scamp joining their raid and wanted to come as well. That was probably for the best, and Saeter readily agreed to it. Finally, they talked to Vorscha about rounding up men and equipment. That wasn't a simple or quick process, so Blacknail left it to Saeter. He went to find something to eat instead.

An hour or so later, the raid was about to begin, but Blacknail had one more task to complete. The now-sated hobgoblin sniffed around, looking for his lost minion. It didn't take him long to pick up a trail, even though Elyias seemed to wander around the camp a lot for some reason. The hobgoblin followed his scent to a cluster of small, ramshackle buildings. Behind them, Elyias was having a conversation with three other men. It didn't look as though he was having fun.

"We would like our money," the first man said menacingly. He was the tallest and most physically imposing of the group. His posture was both confident and aggressive, and the two men beside him were obviously following his lead.

“Come on, fellows! It was just a few friendly games of dice!” Elyias replied nervously as he backed away. “You shouldn’t take it so seriously.”

“The money now!” The man’s voice was cold and completely without camaraderie.

Elyias’s grin stiffened, and he paled. “Just calm down, fellows. There’s an army attacking us right now! What good would money do you? You can’t spend it until we win, and then I’ll get paid and have more than enough to pay you back. There will be plenty of spoils for everyone!”

“You owe us now, not later. If you don’t have the metal, then you can pay us back with labor. If we ask around, I’m sure someone can find some way for you to work off your debts,” the large man replied with a dark chuckle as he gave Elyias an appraising look.

Elyias clearly found the attention uncomfortable, and he gulped in fear. Sensing weakness, the large man reached for him, but he stopped at an unexpected noise.

“He’s busy,” Blacknail explained with a pleasant smile.

His agreeable demeanor was somewhat ruined by the fact that he was standing less than a foot behind the leader of the trio, and they hadn’t heard him approach. All three men jumped in shock and whirled around. They flinched again when they took in the hobgoblin’s toothy grin.

“Hells, it’s the hobgoblin!” one of the men said.

“What do we do?” another asked.

However, the leader regained his composure. His look of surprise became an angry glare that he leveled at Blacknail. The hobgoblin could tell that this human considered himself to be an alpha, and he was unlikely to back down. Joy!

“Listen, we’re going to get our money—” His speech was interrupted by a high-pitched squeak that whistled forth from his own lips.

Blacknail continued smiling as he stared into the man's wide, trembling eyes. No one spoke. After a few tense moments, the hobgoblin loosened his grip on the man's groin. His sharp claws slid free from flesh as he relaxed them slightly.

"Mine," Blacknail explained as he pointed toward Elyias. "Go away. Or would-ss you rather lose all the little bits of meat I can take without killing you?"

Blacknail let completely go of the man's privates. A moment later, all three men were flat-out running away. The hobgoblin watched them for a second before turning to his minion.

"Ha, thanks, I guess," Elyias said as he smiled in relief. "That was just a small misunderstanding."

"Come with me," Blacknail replied.

His minion frowned and bit his lip. It didn't look as though he wanted to come, but he wasn't stupid enough to believe he had a choice either. "What are we doing?"

"A mission," the hobgoblin replied pleasantly.

With his minion in tow, Blacknail walked over to the corner of the camp where Saeter was preparing to leave. The old scout had over twenty men around him, and they were all armed and ready for a fight. Dusk was falling, so the nearby forest was dark and ominous.

"Why is a greenhorn following you around?" Saeter asked as Blacknail approached.

"I volunteer him for the mission. He should be at the front," Blacknail told his master.

"Sure," Saeter replied indifferently as he faced Elyias. "Try not to die, lad."

"I will do that…" Elyias replied with obvious trepidation.

No one was listening though. Saeter and Blacknail had already otherwise preoccupied themselves. Elyias groaned and threw longing look back toward the way he had come. He stayed put though, reluctantly.

"Where are we going?" Elyias asked.

It took a few seconds for one of the bandits to reply. "We're launching an attack on the enemy."

Elyias paled. He looked around again and counted the nearby bandits. It didn't take him long, although he paused for a second when he noticed Scamp sitting next to Varhs. "By ourselves?"

Chapter 13

As evening gave way to night, Saeter led the raiding party out into the forest. One after the other, the bandits slipped into the heavy shadows cast by the trees. It was too late in the day for bird song, so they moved in almost complete silence. Only the occasional sound of a snapping twig or rustle of movement could be heard. Even Scamp was perfectly quiet.

Soon, they reached the span of the forest where they had seen Werrick's sentries. Saeter signaled for everyone to stop then motioned Blacknail over to his side.

"You know what to do," he told the hobgoblin.

Excitedly, Blacknail smiled and nodded before spinning around and creeping into the forest. His hunting instincts were already urging him on. This was a game he both loved and excelled at. He had been born to hunt, and men were among his favorite prey. The bushes around the hobgoblin were thick and dark. However, he had no problem seeing. His eyes shone with hunger as they pierced the shadows with ease.

Blacknail stalked silently toward the spot where he and Saeter had seen the sentries earlier. There was no light or noise to indicate anyone was nearby, but Blacknail smelled their scent on the wind and felt the presence of prey in his bones. Yes, there they were. Two humans were standing next to the same stone as before. They were hidden by the shadows, but Blacknail knew where to look. Closer inspection revealed that it wasn't the same two people as before. Their builds were different. However, these new lookouts weren't any better at their jobs than the last ones.

Against a human enemy, they probably would have been able to raise an alarm long before being detected, but against a hobgoblin, they were outmatched. Blacknail easily circled around until he was in their blind spots, then he crept their way through the bushes. The darkness was his ally, not theirs. They were only human.

Moments later, Blacknail's thin, cloaked form stood only a few feet behind the sentries, and they were none the wiser. This delighted the hobgoblin, and he had to suppress a grim chuckle.

The pair of humans stared off into the darkness as he observed them. The only sound they made was of gentle, relaxed breathing, while Blacknail made none at all. One of the sentries started to turn around, but before he could finish, Blacknail was beside him, his dagger drawn. The unseen blade lashed out through the night air and tore open the unlucky sentry's throat.

As the first man fell with a faint gagging noise, the second reacted. He spun around, only to see nothing but his comrade's body and an empty black forest. His mouth opened to raise the alarm, and Blacknail's knife slid in under his ribs. The hobgoblin had dashed in under the man's vision and gotten behind him unseen. Both sentries silently bled onto the forest floor until the light went out of their terrified eyes.

With his task done, Blacknail took a second to hum a happy little tune while he cleaned his daggers. He hadn't even needed to burn any of the Elixir he had taken a few minutes ago. When his blades were clean, the hobgoblin headed back to his master to report in. He had done such a good job!

After whistling the prearranged bird call to announce his arrival, Blacknail walked out of the shadows. Everyone looked his way, but they didn't otherwise react. In the middle of the group, Elyias was glancing fretfully about and seemed ready to bolt. The dark forest that lay in every direction and loomed above clearly unnerved him.

"Are you done?" Saeter asked in a whisper.

"Yep, all done," Blacknail replied smugly.

"Then let's get going," Saeter said as he motioned the group forward again. "We don't have time to waste."

The raiders immediately headed past the fallen sentries and toward the road. Soon, the flickering light of campfires could be seen ahead of them through the trees. The raiding party stopped at the edge of the forest. Saeter gazed out at the scene as his subordinates drew their weapons. Out on the road, Werrick's troops were tucking in for the night.

The tents were all still there, but there wasn't nearly as much movement as before. Only a few shadowy figures were walking about. Others could be seen around campfires, but most seemed to have gone to sleep in their tents. The wagons the raid was targeting were still in the same place, only a few rows of tents away, but getting to them wouldn't be easy. A fair number of armed guards had been posted to watch the trees. They stood with the fires of the camp behind them so they didn't lose their night vision. It also made them great targets. If that wasn't bad enough, the road was too close to the forest for them to have a good view. With the sentries in the forest already gone, they would only have a few seconds of warning. Blacknail could do a lot with a few seconds.

"We make for the wagons there," Saeter told everyone as they huddled near him in the gloom. "Archers will take out as many lookouts as possible, then we will charge. Varhs, make sure Scamp throws his stones well away from allies. The rest of you should sow chaos, set things aflame, and then retreat back this way."

There were nods as everyone readied themselves. Elyias raised his hand as if to ask a question, but Saeter stared him down until he sheepishly lowered it. Then the old scout signaled, and everyone sprang into action.

A dozen cloaked archers stepped out of the bushes and let loose a volley of arrows. The nearby lookouts went down before any one of them could raise the alarm. The rest of Saeter's men burst out of the forest and dashed toward the wagons. That was when some of Werrick's bandits noticed that something abnormal was going on. Cries of surprise rose into the air as men lurched to their feet. However, the fastest members of the raiding party, including Blacknail, had already reached the closest campfires.

The hobgoblin slashed at a startled man who was trying to back away from him. His blade caught the man's arm and sliced deeply into it. Even as the man fell, the hobgoblin was already running past. There was much to do, and it had to be done fast.

Similar scenes played out nearby. Werrick's men had been caught off guard, and they were being cut down before they had a chance to organize or even draw their weapons. Well, almost all of them. One squad of half a dozen men seemed to appear out of nowhere. They were armored, and they drew their blades as they charged toward the raiders.

Varhs saw them coming. He quickly passed something to Scamp and pointed toward them. The goblin tossed the object at the charging enemy. It flickered with orange light as it sailed through the air, before exploding with a thunderous bang. The cluster of enemies was violently blasted backward and scattered.

Blacknail raced past tents as he closed in on the wagons. That was when he encountered the first bit of resistance. A pair of enemies ran out of the darkness to cut him off. Both of them already had their swords out and up in defensive guards. However, instead of slowing down, Blacknail sped up. He grinned as he burned Elixir and felt its effects wash through him. The power tingled as it boosted his body.

The hobgoblin's move caught the enemy off guard. Before they could react, he had already batted aside one sword and flanked his opponents. The closest man was off balance, so Blacknail stabbed at his chest. With his Elixir-driven strength, the hobgoblin's blow punched through the armor and into the soft flesh beneath. Blacknail quickly kicked his victim's chest so that he could tug out his sword easier. It came loose with a loud sucking noise, and the man's body flopped over backward.

The other defender lunged forward past his comrade's body to strike at Blacknail, but the hobgoblin was too fast for him. Blacknail stepped back out of the way then dodged another strike by jumping to the side. Before the defender could try for a third blow, Blacknail launched a series of attacks. The lightning-fast slashes pushed the man back until the last caught him in the shoulder. The hobgoblin's foe screamed in pain and dropped his blade. His voice was silenced a second later when Blacknail's sword cut deep into his neck.

Several of Blacknail's comrades raced past him toward the wagons. Two of them had stopped to light torches, and they hurled them into the backs of the wagons. The contents of the carts almost instantly burst into flame. As the fire spread, it frightened the horses tied up nearby. The beasts screamed harshly and stomped around in a panic. It was music to Blacknail's long, pointy ears. The hobgoblin grinned madly as he grabbed a flaming piece of wood and threw it toward them. He hoped the vicious beasts burned! This was great!

Now, the wagons were completely ablaze. Flames roared above them and crackled madly, illuminating the camp for hundreds of feet. The sounds of both human and animal screams filled the night, and Blacknail basked in it all. Energy surged through him in incredible amounts. He was truly alive. The hobgoblin took a moment to let out a loud, hysterical laugh as another explosion went off somewhere behind him. He was having so much fun!

"Everyone, back!" Saeter roared from somewhere nearby.

Shaking off his crazed euphoria, Blacknail leapt to obey his master—mostly. Instead of heading straight back the way he had come, the hobgoblin took a slight detour. He picked up a flaming torch someone had dropped and dashed into a thick cluster of tents. The cloaked hobgoblin ran through the camp, dragging fire and death behind him. He pressed the torch against the fabric of the tents as he moved, setting them ablaze. Whenever someone lurched into his path, he cut them down mercilessly. They seemed to move in slow motion compared to his Elixir-boosted hobgoblin speed.

Werrick's men started running away from Blacknail instead of trying to face him. The hobgoblin laughed in vicious delight as panicked men and women fled before him through the darkness. The raging fires that surrounded him blinded as much as they illuminated. His blade reflected the flames as he cut down a fleeing man, and he laughed harder as joy overtook him. The sound of his high-pitched voice rose above the flames. Its eerie cadence sounded nothing at all like a human's.

The rows of tents eventually came to end though, and Blacknail found himself standing not too far from the edge of the forest. He threw a quick look back at the chaos, then he dashed into the bushes and shadows with a smug smile on his lips.

Back in the forest, he heard people running through it in front of him. It was probably Saeter and the others, so he headed their way. It didn't take him long to catch up. Most of the raiding party, including Varhs and Scamp, had made it out safely. Saeter was leading the group.

As Blacknail approached, the old scout turned to him. "Is anyone following us?"

Blacknail took a second to listen. He could still hear shouting and mayhem from Werrick's camp and someone in the forest stumbling around behind them. He focused on the closer sound and recognized a familiar, terrified mumbling.

"Just a straggler. I'll go get him!" the hobgoblin told his master. Before Saeter could reply, Blacknail was already dashing off into the trees.

"Oh, gods! I'm going to die here, all alone in this accursed dark forest. I can't see anything!" Elyias whimpered as he staggered in the dark. The young bandit clearly had no idea where he was going. He was stumbling around in circles.

"You're fine; I'm here," Blacknail announced as he stepped out of the shadows.

Instead of being comforted, Elyias sucked down a breath to let loose a scream. Before he could though, Blacknail kicked him in the stomach. The young man coughed and gagged as the impact knocked the wind from him.

"Don't do that, silly," Blacknail explained cheerfully. "You need to be quiet. Now, come with me." As Elyias tried to right himself, the hobgoblin patted him reassuringly on the shoulder. "You'll do better next time."

Blacknail dragged him toward the others. Elyias seemed too stunned to resist, so it didn't take them long to catch up. Most the humans were having trouble moving in the dark, and that slowed them down. Night had truly fallen now, and there was little light to see by. The slow pace meant it took them a while to get back to Herad's base. Eventually though, they slipped in through a side entrance and make it back to safety. They were greeted quite jovially by the guards, although Blacknail got a few uneasy glances. Apparently, he was absolutely covered in human blood.

Elyias took the opportunity to collapse against the wall. He sat on the ground and rocked back and forth as he muttered softly to himself. He was such a funny human! Blacknail really looked forward to bringing him on the next mission.

Herad showed up, along with Vorscha and Red Dog, before the rest of the raiding party had a chance to sit down and relax. All of them had excited grins, even if Herad's was a lot more bloodthirsty than the others.

"You can see the flames from here!" Herad bragged. "I bet this knocks the wind out of Werrick's sails."

"The wind also carried the screams and laughter here," one of the guards remarked. "Hearing that probably sent shivers down more than a few spines. I know it scared the crap out of me."

There were a few murmurs of agreement and looks directed toward Blacknail, which made the hobgoblin feel quite good about himself. He was feared!

"We got the job done," Saeter told his chief. "The wagons were destroyed, and we did more than a little damage besides that."

"Did you get the information I wanted?" Herad asked.

"Yes, the chaos gave me enough time to find someone to ask some pointed questions," Saeter replied. "I'll give you the full report later."

Herad nodded as her eyes glinted excitedly. She obviously wanted to hear his report, but she was being uncharacteristically patient about it.

"They should have cut back the forest." Vorscha shook her head in disapproval. "Camping next to it is just asking to be taken by surprise."

"Ha, these are bandits, not a real army. I'm surprised Werrick has managed to get them as organized as they are," Red Dog replied scornfully.

"Well, they might make it a priority now," Vorscha mused.

"Only if Werrick doesn't pack up and leave," Red Dog countered. "That light you see over the trees is their main supply cache going up in smoke. They'll probably start running out of food before too long, and it'll be hard to get more all the way out here safely."

"Not to mention their morale has to be down in the drags. They have no reason to believe we can't pull this off every night," Vorscha added.

"We probably can," Saeter said. "I wouldn't want to strike them again quite so hard, but we could certainly hit them around the edges and see what gets knocked loose."

As the others talked, Herad's grin widened. The bandit chieftain looked positively delighted. It was more than a little unsettling. "Werrick can't afford to retreat, but this is still a huge blow against him. I bet the rude bastard is fuming and cursing himself sick right now."

"I think I deserve a treat, great mistress," Blacknail interjected hopefully. He had been very useful, and all the killing and setting things on fire had made him more than a little peckish. Also, everyone was smiling, so this was probably a good time to ask.

"You deserve many more than just one," Herad replied as she placed a hand on the hobgoblin's shoulder.

Blacknail's eyes widened from shock and he shuddered slightly. The chieftain was touching him! It was terrifying! What should he do?

"I'll have someone whip you all up a feast," Herad told the raiding party. She withdrew her hand from Blacknail's shoulder, which made him feel a lot better.

All the nearby bandits smiled, and several of them cheered. More than a few conversations broke out as people bragged. The hobgoblin slipped away while the others were busy. The humans were being too chatty for him, and he wanted some space. They almost never discussed things that interested him. He'd come back when the food was ready.

Blacknail shivered as he walked. The hot remnants of battle lust were still working their way through his system. He felt in his muscles the urge to run and fight. As a gust of wind blew by, Blacknail wandered toward the wall. He picked out an empty expanse and climbed it. Once perched atop the barrier of stakes, he stared into the darkness.

The road was dark and empty for quite a distance until it reached Werrick's camp. The flames there illuminated the treetops on either side of the road as they swayed in the wind. Only a few of the fires Blacknail and his tribe had set were still burning, and they were reduced in size. There were quite a few campfires to see by though, and Blacknail saw the small shadowy figures of people moving everywhere. Werrick's camp was still a hive of frantic human activity.

Blacknail watched them scurry about for a while. He kind of wanted to go back and hunt a few more of them, but that would be a terrible idea. It had gotten too dark for even him to see properly, and going out alone was dangerous. No, he would just have to wait until tomorrow.

Chapter 14

Cries of alarm woke Blacknail. His ears twitched as he heard excited yelling outside his tent. It was probably nothing though. Humans were prone to meaningless fear and could get themselves worked up over nothing. Blacknail sniffed and pulled his blanket up higher.

A minute passed, and the noise failed to fade away. Groaning, the hobgoblin got up and stuck his head out of his tent, although it took a moment to clear the sleep from his eyes by blinking. Outside, it was so early that it was still dark out. The tip of the sun was barely visible on the horizon, and the trees blocked most of its light. What could possibly be going on so early in the morning? If there wasn't a good reason for all this commotion, then Blacknail was going to track down the person responsible and make his displeasure known. It didn't seem like a false alarm though. All around Herad's base, there was an unusually high amount of activity. The bandit chieftain's minions were all running around with far more enthusiasm than they usually mustered this early in the day.

"To arms, the enemy is coming!" someone off in the distance yelled.

An annoyed hiss escaped Blacknail's lips. He had a feeling this wouldn't be one of his favorite days. Any morning that started hours before breakfast was bound to be terrible.

There was a rustle from the nearby tent where his master slept, then Saeter stepped out. The old scout was only partly dressed, but he was quickly slipping on the rest of his clothes. "Come on, what are you waiting for? Let's go."

Blacknail grunted sourly before disappearing back inside his tent. After making sure his shirt wasn't on backward again, he finished dressing himself and stepped outside. "This is bloody annoying. Why is the enemy attacking so early?"

"They probably wanted to move before we could catch them napping, like last night," Saeter replied.

That made sense to Blacknail. The enemy should fear his awesome martial prowess. They would be fools not to. In this case though, it would have been nice if they had feared him a little less so that he could get a good night's sleep.

The pair headed off to talk to the nearest group of bandits so that they could figure out what was going on. However, before they got halfway there, someone called out to them.

"Saeter and Blacknail, over here!" Vorscha yelled as she waved and stomped toward them.

The muscular woman looked both aggravated and distracted. Khita trailed behind her, and the redhead looked excited. Saeter kept walking as if he hadn't heard anyone call his name, so Blacknail poked him in the shoulder and pointed their way.

When she saw Saeter looking in her direction, Vorscha turned to make sure Khita was still behind her and then dragged her over to them.

"I need you to watch this ruffian," the warrior woman told them when they got close.

Blacknail and Saeter scowled in distaste.

"I can take care of myself," an affronted Khita declared.

Vorscha rolled her eyes and pushed her toward Saeter. The much smaller woman stumbled but managed to catch herself.

"If that's an order, then I guess I have no choice. More importantly, what's going on?" the old scout asked Vorscha.

"Werrick's men are marching toward the wall right now. It looks like he's throwing everything he's got into the assault this time. I think your raid last night really pissed him off," Vorscha explained.

"You should have told me about that sneak attack! I would have gone with you," Khita exclaimed.

Blacknail wouldn't have minded taking Khita along for the raid. Unfortunately, if he had invited her, then he would have also taken the blame when she got herself killed. A much more subtle way of getting rid of the annoying pest was required.

"I just got up. What are the plans for the defense?" Saeter asked.

"We were up late burning important things," Blacknail added grumpily.

"I don't have time to fill you in. I really need to get back to the gate before the fighting starts," Vorscha explained. "If you're looking for a place to be, then you should just do what you did last time. Hang back and reinforce any spots that look stressed."

"Sounds like fun," Blacknail replied. It also sounded easy and like a great way to keep an eye out for good looting opportunities.

"Which, conveniently enough, will allow us to keep Khita back away from most the danger," Saeter remarked.

Vorscha leveled a heavy glare at Saeter. Khita's face was red with anger and her fists were clenched tightly. She looked as if she wanted to punch someone. Blacknail took a small step away from her.

"Are you complaining about something? Do you want to join the front line or something?" Vorscha asked the old scout.

"No, it sounds like a great plan," Saeter replied with sudden indifference. "I was just thinking aloud."

Blacknail threw Khita a speculative look. Was it possible that Khita's uselessness was actually proving useful right now? No, he must be misunderstanding something.

Suddenly, there was a loud twang as a volley of arrows tore through the air. The enemy had entered within bowshot. Vorscha flinched at the noise and turned to Saeter.

"Then shut up, old man," Vorscha growled with uncharacteristic vehemence.

Everyone stepped back from her in surprise. Even Saeter had been caught off guard by her temper.

"I need to go," she told them. "But before I do, I have one last thing to say. Blacknail, I'm holding you responsible for Khita. Watch her like a hawk or I'll gut you like fish."

With that said, Vorscha turned and hurried toward the entrance to the camp and the break in the wall there. No one said anything for a moment, but off in the distance, the now-familiar sound of an army marching could be heard.

"Fine, follow me," Saeter told his two companions.

The old scout led the way toward the same hill they had watched the battle from before. Still somewhat off balance, Khita and Blacknail followed him silently. Before they could get to their destination, a wave of hot air slammed into them as the sound of splintering wood filled their ears. Something had exploded.

Blacknail ducked low to regain his balance. He shielded his head as he turned to look in the direction the blast had come from. There was a huge gaping hole in the wall between him and Werrick's army, and flames danced around the edges of the new opening. The nearby bandits had been thrown aside and scattered. Some of them were picking themselves off their feet, while others weren't so lucky. Shrapnel from the explosion had crippled and killed.

"Well, all hells and damnation. I think we found a spot that looks stressed and needs reinforcing," Saeter remarked sourly as he surveyed the damage.

Blacknail nodded. There was a lot of damage to survey. A dozen men could have stepped through the gaping hole that had been blown in the wooden barrier protecting the camp.

"Fucking magic," Blacknail muttered. He hated mages when they weren't on his side. It didn't seem fair.

"Wow, that doesn't seem fair," Khita remarked in an awed tone as she gazed at the blast zone.

Blacknail glared at the redhead. She wasn't allowed to agree with him. It made him seem dumb…

"Very little is fair about war," Saeter remarked. "What I want to know is why Mahedium isn't firing back."

"He's over there," Blacknail pointed out.

The other two turned in the direction the hobgoblin indicated. They could clearly see Mahedium running toward the wall from his workshop. The mage was carrying a long staff.

"That's another reason they struck so early," Saeter commented. "Werrick knew Mahedium couldn't always be on guard. He's not nearly as dumb as Herad likes to say he is."

Before the mage reached his destination, the sound of shouting intensified and there was a series of metallic screeches. The enemy had reached the wall. A wave of enemy bandits was fighting toward the front entrance, and a large mass of Herad's troops were blocking their way and pushing them back. Unfortunately, a second group of foes was headed toward the hole the enemy mage had blown in the wall. There, Herad's troops were still recovering and badly outnumbered. Only a few of them fought back when the front rank of enemy bandits reached the break and began trying to force their way inside the camp.

"We need to help out," Saeter said as he pulled his bow off his back. "They can't be allowed to get a foothold inside."

The old scout nocked an arrow, aimed, and let it loose. The arrow took flight and slammed into the chest of a bandit who had just stepped up to attack one of Herad's troops.

Blacknail was already running after the arrow. He pulled out a vial and downed it as he dashed down the hill. It took him only a few seconds to run past Herad's nearby minions and reach the fighting. The invigorating rush of Elixir being burned washed through him as he drew his blade, and the hobgoblin aimed its silver edge at the nearest enemy. There was no point in holding back. The hobgoblin wasn't going to dive into a melee full of armed humans without taking every advantage he could get.

Humans might be dumb and slow, but they were also big and tough.

Around Blacknail, about a dozen disorganized bandits were desperately trying to block what seemed to be hundreds of enemies from slipping through the break in the wall. Their resistance seemed pointless. Then the hobgoblin's blade cut down the first attacker. Everyone barely had time to register his presence before Blacknail moved on to a second. Relying on pure Elixir-driven speed, he slipped around the attackers and cut them down, one after the other. Half a dozen of them fell before they could react to this new, unexpected threat. When they realized what was happening, the enemy recoiled in fear as shouts of surprise escaped their lips.

"Gods' sweet mercy, it's a monster," someone shrieked in terror.

Blacknail grinned as their sweet fear made his heart flutter with joy, then he launched himself forward with renewed energy. Instinct guided Blacknail as he attacked his enemies' weak points. A familiar bloodlust rose within him and drove him forward. His blade sliced through soft flesh as he easily sidestepped a counterattack. However, for every one of Werrick's men he killed, another soon took its place. The mass of attacking enemies didn't seem to be shrinking at all.

Suddenly, the enemy stopped coming. They lined up just out of reach, and Blacknail had to stop himself from leaping forward after them. Fury and hunger burned within him. He wanted to fight! As he warily watched the enemy, Blacknail took a careful step back. An enemy officer screamed something, then the entire enemy line marched forward together. Now there was no space between them that Blacknail could use or slip through. They were a solid mass of furious-looking humans bearing down on him.

"Shit," one of Blacknail's allies swore.

"Double shit," the hobgoblin added in agreement. His bloodlust was giving ground to his love of running away from danger.

The enemy approached, and Blacknail glanced over his shoulder. Herad's forces were still greatly outnumbered; there were only a little more than ten of them still standing. Those weren't odds the hobgoblin liked. Saeter and Khita stood off to one side. They had apparently followed Blacknail without him noticing. Both of them had swords in their hands and looked tired from fighting.

The front rank of the enemy reached the wall. Instead of fighting them, Herad's scattered forces retreated, giving the enemy a foothold inside the camp. Even Blacknail didn't like the idea of trying to fight that many humans back to back. Running would probably be a better option, especially if he could get his master away but leave Khita behind.

"Don't let those rutting bastards take a single step forward!" a familiar voice yelled.

Everyone turned to see dozens of bandits charging toward the fight, Vorscha leading them. The warrior woman had taken the time to get armored up. She had a steel breastplate and was wearing a chainmail shirt underneath that. A long sword was raised above her head as she ran past Blacknail and joined the defense.

Right behind her ran other bandits, including Geralhd. The laid-back man had finally bothered to throw on some real armor, including a steel cap that looked somewhat ridiculous over his long hair. However, he used the short sword skillfully.

The defenders were invigorated by the reinforcements and threw themselves alongside Vorscha in an attempt to push the enemy out of the camp. Overextended and flanked, Werrick's troops were quickly forced back. The entire time, Vorscha was in the middle of the fighting, wielding her long sword with skill and power as she urged on her troops.

"Push the damned bastards all the way back. Don't leave a single one alive!" she yelled as she cut down an enemy.

There was a ragged cheer from her comrades as they pressed forward. Even Blacknail found himself rejoining the fighting. The urge to fight alongside Vorscha's counterstrike was just too great to resist. He liked being on the winning side.

Soon, the enemy was in full retreat and Vorscha had secured the break in the wall. Once her troops had formed up to block further entry by Werrick's men, she looked back the way she had come. A pair of horses was pulling one of the supply wagons toward her.

Vorscha saw it and motioned toward the drivers. "Get that bloody thing in the gap right fucking now!"

The drivers nodded and jumped off the wagon. Then they unharnessed the horses and led them aside as Vorscha led a small team over to the cart. As the defenders of the wall jumped aside, the bandits pushed the wagon into the break and swung it around. The wooden sides of the wagon filled most the space, even if there were gaps.

Almost immediately, enemy troops attempted to scale it or slip around it. They were quickly fought off by the reinforcements Vorscha had brought.

The warrior woman backed away from the fighting and turned to Saeter. "That's one crisis averted for now. I wish I could say that would be the last."

"How are things going at the gate?" Saeter asked as he sheathed his sword.

"We're holding for now. I can't say much more than that."

"Things aren't going badly, but they aren't great either," Geralhd added as he wandered over.

Vorscha's lover was smiling cockily as he flourished his blade. Blacknail wasn't sure why Geralhd was so proud. The man had fought alongside everyone else, but he hadn't really distinguished himself.

"It's still early in the day. Werrick might be trying to wear us down with his superior numbers," Vorscha explained. "That damn opening magic barrage of his widened the battle line and has forced us to commit most our reserve already."

Before anyone could respond, a chorus of blaring trumpets split the air. It was almost immediately followed by the steady beating of drums. The energetic refrain was clearly coming from near the front gate. Everyone turned to look that way. However, the press of bodies around the gate was too thick. All they could see was the back of Herad's forces.

"Damnation, what in all the hells is going on now?" Vorscha asked.

This terrible view didn't satisfy Blacknail. He dashed toward the wall to get a higher position, but instead of climbing to the top, where he would be an easy target for every enemy with a bow, he peeked over.

Hundreds of enemy soldiers were trying to push through the gap in the wall where the camp's front entrance was. However, there wasn't nearly enough space for them to attack all at the same time, so Herad's forces were holding them off. Above the fighting floated the wolf's head banner, and it was steadily moving closer to the front line. Right below the symbol was a small group of people. The enemy soldiers moved out of their way and gave them space as they advanced toward the front.

One tall figure stood out from all the others and strode confidently through the ranks. He was dressed in heavy armor made of overlapping steel bands, and he wore a steel helmet shaped like a wolf's head. A thick mane of grey hair jutted out from the back of the helmet and cascaded down the man's back.

The large armored warrior could only be Werrick. The Wolf had finally shown himself, and he was now personally leading his forces in an all-or-nothing assault. A shiver of fear seemed to run through the ranks of Herad's outlaws as they recognized him. Something terrible was about to happen.

Chapter 15

"Don't just hang there, you green idiot! Tell us what you see!" Saeter ordered the hobgoblin.

Blacknail suppressed his irritation at being addressed so rudely, then he explained to the others what was happening. A force led by Werrick himself was headed straight toward the gate that Herad was trying to defend. None of his companions seemed to think that was good news. Nervousness and fear were plain on their faces. Their reactions surprised the hobgoblin. A battle between chiefs sounded exciting to him!

"Showing himself now makes no bloody sense!" Vorscha cursed. "He's got the advantage in numbers, so he should be wearing us down, not leading a charge."

Without warning, a sizzling ball of flame shot toward the group of people beneath the wolf banner. Mahedium had revealed himself in a display of fiery power.

Before the flaming orb could reach its target, a lanky figure beside Werrick raised a hand. A shimmering wall of force sprang into existence and smashed into the fireball. The flames were batted aside before disintegrating into a brilliant rain of sparks. The shower of tiny lights fell over the battlefield without any noticeable effect.

Werrick's advance continued unimpeded. The huge armored figure reached the front line, and his troops cheered as they stepped aside for him. The sound of bandits screaming in exhilaration drowned out everything else.

"The Wolf has come! Forward to victory!" they roared as they redoubled their attack on Herad's camp.

Their annoying voices hurt Blacknail's sensitive ears. Now he really wanted to kill them, if only to shut them up. Also, their cheer was stupid.

"We need to get closer," Saeter exclaimed in frustration.

There was a small lookout platform halfway down the wall in Herad's direction. There was no way to get through the press of bodies at the front lines, so Saeter headed over to it. Vorscha and Geralhd were quick to follow. Blacknail gave them all a head start before racing ahead. They were just humans, so he was much faster. He barely had to try.

"Down now," Vorscha ordered the archers in the tower. "We need to see what's going on."

After they'd climbed down to obey her, Saeter made his way up the rickety ladder. It was little more than a bunch of branches tied together by rope, and the platform itself was little better. Vorscha and Geralhd followed him. There was only room for about three people on the crude wooden platform, so Blacknail climbed up the wall again.

From their new vantage point, they saw Werrick and his elite join the melee. His banner flapped loudly as the Wolf waded into combat. The huge warrior had a shield in one hand and a long sword in the other. His heavy steel armor and ornate helmet shaped like a wolf's head made him easy to pick out of the crowd.

With seemingly unstoppable momentum, Werrick cut down Herad's forces. They broke before him like the tide hitting a rock as his blade cleaved and knocked them aside. None of her men so much as slowed him down, and they fell back away from him in fear. Thus, the tide of battle shifted and the attackers steadily gained ground.

Herad didn't take the challenge lying down. She screamed out a series of orders from where she stood at the back of the battle. Instantly, her bodyguards and Mahedium rushed to her side. With the bandit chieftain at the lead, they formed a solid wedge that moved to intercept Werrick's advance.

"Why aren't the mages calling up any magic?" Geralhd asked as he squinted in Mahedium's direction and leaned over a wooden rail.

"They're too close for that now." Vorscha cursed. "I doubt our comrades would appreciate Mahedium dropping a ball of fire on their heads while they're fighting."

"They also need to keep their defenses ready in case of surprise attacks," Saeter added. "That close to the melee, they need to be careful, and the first thing on a mage's mind is always their own safety."

As Blacknail's group watched, the two bandit chieftains converged on each other. Without needing to be told, fighters from both sides moved out of the way and gave them space. Soon, only a few feet separated the two leaders' parties. They stared ferociously at each other, and the fury of all the nearby combatants ebbed slightly as they noticed what was about to take place among them. Everyone knew that if Herad and Werrick fought, the outcome would determine the course of the battle. Even if they were fighting for their life, no one wanted to miss this.

"Shit, she's going to fight him herself!" Saeter said. "I need to get over there."

Before he could take more than a single step, Vorscha placed a hand on his shoulder to restrain him. He stopped and glared at her. The wrinkles around his eyes seemed deeper than usual.

"There's nothing you can do. You'll never cross the field safely, and what could you even accomplish if you did? You're just going to have to trust the boss. She knows what she is doing," Vorscha told him.

"Damnation! I should be there, but I never guessed this would happen." The old scout didn't make another move to climb down the lookout platform though. He gazed toward the center of the battle and bit his bottom lip nervously.

Geralhd and Vorscha also looked worried as Herad came face to face with her nemesis. Huh, Blacknail didn't know what to think. The mood of his human friends bothered him, but he couldn't see Herad losing. She was the most dangerous and ruthless human he had ever met! He doubted Werrick could beat her in a stabbing contest.

"So you've decided to show yourself at last, coward," Herad yelled in Werrick's direction.

The other man didn't reply. There was quiet lull as he gazed in her direction, though his steel helm hid his face and concealed what he was thinking. Both bandit chieftains stood just out of striking range with their raised weapons in front of them. Violence could erupt without warning at any second.

"I have nothing to fear from the likes of you," Werrick eventually announced. His voice was deep and serene, without the smallest hint of fear or worry. Like Herad, he had a natural commanding presence.

Both bandit chiefs were still in a way that suggested restrained power. As people fought and died around them, they remained motionless and sized each other up.

Herad moved first. She lunged forward, and the quiet that had overtaken the field ended. Werrick blocked her blade with a casual raise of his own, but before he could counterattack, Herad had already slipped out of his range.

The bodyguards and companions of the band leaders rushed forward to support their bosses. They encircled their chiefs as they fought each other, but they didn't get too close. A bubble of space developed around the fighting Vessels. Beyond the bodyguards, the other bandits were still fighting. Screams of pain and rage filled the air as violence was done and lives were ended.

As the masses fought around them, Herad and Werrick dueled. Under his heavy armor, Werrick moved slower than his opponent. Herad ducked in and out of his range while launching a series of feints. However, the larger man easily kept her away from his vital points by holding his shield high and with the occasional lazy swing of his sword. He might have been slower, but his fluid movements betrayed no lack of skill.

Again and again, the pair of Vessels crossed blades. They moved with superhuman speed, and their ferocity was unrelenting. Herad seemed unable to hurt Werrick, but the advance of his troops had come to a complete halt.

From off to the side, a pair of wrestling bandits stumbled between the two chieftains. They were too preoccupied with fighting and too off balance to stay out of the way. Herad saw them coming, lunged to the side, and kicked the closer man's back, sending them both careening straight toward Werrick. He, with a mighty swing of his shield, batted them out of his way. There was a crunching sound as they hit the ground and rolled. Neither of them got up.

Herad took advantage of this momentary distraction to dash in from the other side and strike. Werrick's blade slashed through the air to block her advance, but she ducked under it and stabbed toward his armpit.

The tip of Herad's sword accelerated toward a gap between two steel plates under Werrick's arm. All Werrick could do was take a frantic step back and turn away from the blow, but it was enough. Instead of hitting flesh, the blade impacted steel and slid away without drawing blood. The heavy shield on Werrick's other arm swung around, and Herad had to dodge back out of the way. The two combatants separated and watched each other warily. Neither of them dropped their guard, and their respective bodyguards stepped forward to protect them.

"You can't defeat me like this. You aren't my equal, Black Snake," Werrick shouted haughtily.

"This isn't a duel, cur," Herad replied. "I don't need to beat you in a fancy fencing match."

As she finished speaking, the bandit chieftain raised a hand and signaled someone. Two volleys of arrows rose into the air. Two groups of a dozen archers had stepped out from behind the wall on either side of the opening and shot a swarm of projectiles that descended upon Werrick's party from opposite directions.

Only one arrow sped toward Werrick though, and he easily blocked it with his shield. A few more ripped through the banner that one of the Wolf's men was holding aloft, but most the buzzing projectiles were aimed at the nearby mage.

"See, the boss has a plan," Vorscha observed with more than little relief.

No one answered her. They were fixated on the events unfolding before them.

The mage hurriedly raised an amulet. A rippling wave of force smashed into all the arrows coming at him from one direction and smashed them harmlessly aside. He quickly turned to block the ones from the other side as well, but he was too late. His second blast hit the other flight of arrows and batted some of them away, but a lot of them had been too close. Two of the mage's bodyguards fell as arrows pierced their bodies, but the others raised shields and blocked the rest of the projectiles. But the staff-wielding mage laughed triumphantly. He was completely unharmed.

"That could have gone better," Geralhd remarked unhappily.

That was when a lance of yellow energy slammed into the enemy mage from the front and hurled him off his feet. The men all around him were knocked aside as well; their bodies spasmed for several seconds before going still.

Mahedium stood off to the side of Herad. The staff in his hands was still glowing faintly yellow. Several of Herad's bodyguards surrounded him. They had been keeping the fighting safely away from him. As Mahedium leveled the staff in Werrick's direction, Herad laughed triumphantly.

She pointed her blade toward Werrick as a mocking grin appeared on her lips. "Victory is mine, you arrogant son of a whore! I'm going to enjoy destroying you."

The enemy chieftain stepped backward. It was hard to see under his armor, but Werrick looked tense and anxious. He glanced back and forth between Herad and Mahedium as the troops behind him froze in fear. They knew that the tide of battle had made a sudden and dramatic turn against them.

"She's got him!" Vorscha exclaimed breathlessly from the lookout platform. "We've got this in the bag!"

"It… definitely seems like it," Saeter said skeptically. As usual, the old scout refused to give in to optimism or the equally repugnant feeling of happiness.

"There's no way even a Vessel could dodge war magic at that range," Geralhd remarked. "Vorscha's right. We've won. Werrick is finished."

"Mahedium may have him cornered, but I won't be counting the Wolf down until he's actually dead," Saeter replied. "If he escapes, then he can just come back with a new mage and reinforcements."

The fighting between both sides didn't stop, but it slowed a little as people noticed what had happened. Blacknail smirked from his perch atop the wall. He had known Herad would win. She always did. That was why she was the chief!

Leisurely, Mahedium strolled forward. Everyone except for his guards backed away from him. Without the other mage around to check his power, Mahedium was free to let loose against anyone who threatened him, and he had already demonstrated the lethal power he had at his disposal. The mage kept his staff leveled directly at Werrick, and its tip crackled with yellow energy. He avoided getting too close to anyone else as he moved toward the enemy leader.

"Are you going to try to run?" Herad taunted her opponent. "You might be able to make it." A wide grin was plastered across her face. It made her seem almost mad, or at least madder than usual. Her dark eyes blazed with excitement as she watched her cornered enemy.

"I don't think that would accomplish anything," Werrick replied tonelessly as he gazed at Mahedium.

"Take off that helmet," Herad commanded. "I want to see your face."

Werrick hesitated for a second, then removed his steel helm. He tossed it aside, and it rolled across the ground. His face was stern looking but handsome. The grey mane had been part of his wolf helmet, but he had fairly long brown hair of his own. He looked neither particularly young nor all that old. However, there was a defiant glint in his eyes as he met Herad's glare. She noticed it, but it made her chuckle. She liked breaking peoples' pride.

From his perch on the wall, Blacknail studied Werrick. He frowned as he realized the man didn't seem all that scared. The hobgoblin considered himself an expert on human behavior, especially their fears, and this man was too calm. Despite himself, Blacknail was intimidated, and he didn't like that at all.

"For years you've claimed to be the biggest and baddest bandit in all the North. Now look at you!" Herad gloated. "In the end, you fell right into my trap!"

"Trap?" Werrick asked skeptically. "You were simply fortunate enough to take out my mage, and I'm not defeated yet."

"As you made your way here, I tested your forces several times and interrogated a few captives," Herad explained smugly. "I learned that you only had two mages with you, and during your first attack on these walls, my mage defeated one of yours."

"That's far from any sort of grand strategy. It's just basic intelligence," Werrick remarked with noteworthy calm.

Blacknail studied the enemy leader closely and licked his lips uncertainly. He knew his humans. They were simple creatures at their core, and he sensed that something was off about this one. What was it?

"I knew you would eventually have no choice but to join the attack yourself and that you would need to bring your mage,"

Herad explained. "I knew that without him guarding your back, you would be an easy target, and I was right. Here we are."

"That certainly sounds like something a second-rate backstreet thug like you would come up with," Werrick replied coldly. "It's as cowardly as it is simple."

"Petty insults will do you no good, Wolfy. Everything that was yours is about to become mine! I want you to reflect on that before I kill you," Herad gloated.

"You have no idea what I possess, Black Snake. It's sad that you think that killing me would elevate yourself," Werrick replied. "You are as blind and ignorant as always, a mindless killer with delusions of greatness. You aren't worthy of walking in my shadow."

"We'll see about that," Herad replied.

"Enough useless talk. Are you just going to stand there, or am I going to have to make you use that thing?" Werrick asked as he turned toward Mahedium and leveled his sword at the mage.

"As you wish," Mahedium remarked coolly as the energy around his staff grew more violent.

The air was thick with tension as everyone waited to see what was about to happen. Werrick didn't flinch as Mahedium moved. The mage swung his staff around and blasted the guards behind him. They went down as yellow energy arced between them.

"What?" Herad gasped as her eyes went wide with shock.

She froze in surprise, which gave Mahedium more than enough time to point his staff in her direction. At the last moment, her survival instinct kicked in and she tried to dodge as Mahedium unleashed a bolt of magic in her direction, but it clipped her side. A cry of pain and complete disbelief escaped Herad's lips as the energy hit her. A tremor worked its way through her body, then she collapsed bonelessly onto the ground. She didn't get back up.

Werrick laughed. There was a mocking tone to it as his deep, booming voice echoed over the battlefield.

Chapter 16

There were gasps of horror from the people on the platform near Blacknail. It was swiftly followed by swearing.

"King's blood! What just happened?" Geralhd whispered.

"He's turned traitor!" Saeter roared. "That treacherous rat, I'm going to kill him!"

The old scout dropped and climbed down the ladder. His movements shocked his nearby companions out of their own paralysis.

"What do you plan on doing?" Vorscha asked him. "You'll never get there in time."

"I'm going to do whatever I have to!" Saeter spat as he jumped down the final length of the ladder and ran.

Vorscha threw out a few more colorful curses then turned to Blacknail. The hobgoblin was still in shock. What was going on? Was his glorious leader dead? That didn't make sense!

"Don't just hang there! Go watch his back!" Vorscha ordered Blacknail.

It took a moment for her words to penetrate the haze of uncertainty that had filled the hobgoblin's mind. However, when her meaning became clear, he nodded and dropped down onto the ground. As soon as he hit dirt, he ran.

His master was headed toward the fighting all by himself. That was dangerous! Why was his master always doing such dumb things? Why did Blacknail always follow him?

A mob of tightly packed enemies and allies stood between Saeter and Herad's fallen form. Blacknail couldn't even see her from ground level. However, he could still see Werrick's head. He was much taller than most humans.

Most of Herad's fighters hadn't seen her fall, and even if they had, they were still stuck in the melee. Blacknail caught up with Saeter before he reached the fighting.

"What are you-ss doing?" Blacknail asked the old scout. "Do you have a plan?"

His master barely registered the hobgoblin's presence. He spared Blacknail a brief glance before facing forward again. "I'm going to get Herad out of there!"

A wave of exasperation and anguish hit Blacknail and made him groan. That was a terrible plan! What did his master think he was doing? "We should wait for help or find somebody else to do it. Red Dog must be around here somewhere. This sound-ss like something he should do."

Unfortunately, the hobgoblin got no reply. Blacknail seriously considered clubbing his master over the head and dragging him away. That was probably unnecessary though, because the way forward was blocked by a wall of their allies. There was no way Saeter could press through it.

Up ahead, Werrick was talking to Mahedium, and he made a sweeping gesture in the direction of the thickest fighting. With a nod, Mahedium turned and shot bolts of magic at those of Herad's minions who were still fighting. The battle turned against them as the yellow blasts of crackling energy thinned their ranks.

With cries of despair, the force of bandits protecting the camp's gate collapsed. Their leader was down, and they had no protection from Mahedium's magic. Overcome with fear and hopelessness, the remaining defenders broke. Large groups of bandits turned to run. Roaring in triumph, Werrick's troops eagerly gave chase. Many of Herad's forces were cut down as they fled. Other, more organized squads of defenders tried to keep fighting and were swiftly surrounded and cut down as their allies deserted them. A few lucky groups managed to hold their attackers back as they retreated.

The battle at the gates swiftly degenerated into a dozen smaller fights as Herad's forces fled deeper into camp. It was into this mess that Saeter dove. Blacknail groaned and followed him. The dissolution of the battle and the resulting chaos was allowing Saeter to advance. Fortune seemed to favor the stupid.

There was little organized resistance to Saeter's dash into enemy lines, much to Blacknail's annoyance. Why was no one stopping them? Even if the fighting had moved on, there were still more than a few scattered enemies around. Well, it wasn't like Herad or Werrick's minions wore uniforms, and most of the enemies were confused by the fact Saeter and Blacknail were running toward them instead of away. Others were more concerned with settling grudges or looting.

A few enemies did try to intercept Saeter, but Blacknail leapt ahead and cut them down without mercy. The hobgoblin was adept at taking advantage of chaos, and he still had a lot of Elixir burning through his system. As Blacknail's blade gutted a man wearing particularly shoddy armor, Saeter ran ahead. They were only a few dozen feet from Herad now, and well out of what was left of the fighting. Those groups of bandits still resisting Werrick had already retreated deeper into camp.

However, before the old scout could reach his destination, Mahedium noticed him. The mage was standing guard over Herad's prone form. The fallen bandit chieftain's chest rose and fell as she drew breath and her fingers were twitching. She was still alive!

"Oh, it's you two. I was wondering when you would show up," the mage remarked as he leveled his staff in their direction.

"Die, you traitorous filth!" Saeter spat as he lunged forward with his blade held high.

A frown appeared on Mahedium's lips as yellow energy once again burst from his staff and slammed into Saeter. The old scout stumbled and collapsed. The sight of his master falling enraged Blacknail. Mahedium would pay for this! He would feast on the man's eyes!

With an angry hiss and a new burst of speed, Blacknail dodged a blast aimed his way. He rolled across the ground for a second before jumping to his feet and leaping at his magic-wielding opponent.

"Hmm, you're frighteningly fast," the mage remarked as he grabbed an amulet on his chest.

When he touched the amulet, an invisible wall of air slammed into Blacknail. It whipped up clouds of dust as it raced across the ground, and its impact threw the hobgoblin backward. He soared quite a distance before smashing into a pile of crates. Pain ripped through the hobgoblin's back, and his ribs felt as if every single one of them had cracked. He whimpered, and his jaw hurt.

Even though he was having trouble even breathing, Blacknail fought off the pain and tried to pick himself off the ground. Fury and adrenaline rose within him to drown out all other concerns. This wasn't the time to be sitting around! He had to save his master and the chief! He was Blacknail! It would take more than a treacherous mage and a big fat human Vessel to defeat him! He was an invincible killer and they would taste his blade!

The hobgoblin hissed and managed to get back on his feet. He shook his head to clear it and tried to think up a plan. He was good at sneaking, so maybe he could get behind Mahedium and…

Another beam of energy slammed into the hobgoblin. Blacknail lost all control over his body, convulsing. His spasming limbs sent crates flying and snagged a tarp. By the time the convulsions stopped, he was back on the ground and thoroughly wrapped up in the tough fabric.

Stunned, Blacknail groaned in pain. Every muscle in his body was aflame, and all his joints felt out of place. He phased in and out of consciousness for a few seconds as he tried to figure out what had happened. He remembered it was bad…

Blacknail opened his eyes, which hurt in ways he hadn't thought possible, and saw his master lying on the ground a fair distance away. Several unfamiliar and unfriendly-looking bandits stood around Saeter. The hobgoblin tried to reach out in his master's direction, but his hands wouldn't move.

"Just the man I was looking for!" a tall armored man announced as he walked over the fallen scout. "You're right on time to see me kill Herad."

It was Werrick! Blacknail recognized him now. The enemy leader smiled broadly as he looked at the old scout. Behind him, corpses littered the battlefield and the shattered remains of the camp's walls loomed. Pillars of black smoke rose into the sky in the distance.

Saeter was laid out on the ground where he had fallen after being hit by Mahedium's magic. He slowly turned his head to glare at Werrick. No one had touched him, but he still seemed incapable of making large movements. A dozen of Werrick's troops surrounded their leader as he looked at the old scout. There wasn't a friendly face in sight, unless you counted some of the corpses that littered the ground. A lot of bandits had died in the fight for the gates.

"I've been wanting to talk to you for a while, White Raven," Werrick told Saeter.

"Go fuck a pig," Saeter spat vehemently. He was apparently able to talk now, although the old scout sounded winded and like he was in pain.

As Saeter wheezed, the man he had insulted grinned. "I suppose I deserve that. I did just have you blasted by magic. It looks like it hurts a lot."

"It's only a brief stunning effect. There is no lasting harm done," Mahedium interjected. "But it certainly keeps people down long enough for more permanent solutions to be achieved, although both Vessels and mages resist it. The length varies, but Herad won't be up for—"

With a wave, Werrick silenced the rambling mage. The victorious bandit chieftain turned back to Saeter. "Your old leader has been defeated and will soon meet her end at my hand. However, I'm willing to show you mercy if you pledge your allegiance to me, and I will also to extend that kindness to others you choose. I've always been an admirer of yours, and having the White Raven under my command would be useful."

"No," Saeter replied as he glared defiantly at his captor.

"I see I'm going to have to strengthen my argument." With an exasperated sigh, the bandit leader turned and strode over to Herad. She was still breathing but appeared to be unconscious.

"I don't suppose your offer extends to her?" Saeter asked scornfully. There were hints of fear and concern concealed behind his veneer of contempt though. The old scout's stubborn resolve seemed to grow weaker as Werrick got closer to Herad.

"No, she's too stupid to ever learn her place. Honestly, I don't know why you would even ask. Look at her," Werrick replied contemptuously. When he reached her, the large man gave her a solid kick to the ribs.

She flinched as the pain of the blow woke her, then again when she saw the man looming over her. Herad gasped as she tried to sit up. "What?"

"It's rather simple actually. You're the one who fell into my trap, not the other way around," Werrick explained. "I've defeated your pathetic band, and now I just need to deal with you."

Herad coughed and looked around. Sometime after she had fallen, someone had stripped her weapons from her. Her sword was gone, and after checking her clothes, she didn't find any daggers. Her actions didn't seem to concern Werrick.

"I made a deal with your mage. He agreed to switch sides if I presented him with a perfect opportunity," Werrick continued as he held his arms out wide to emphasize his surroundings. "And here we are. You led him right to me and set yourself up."

"You cursed faithless coward. I hope demons drag you down to the deepest hells beyond the sight of the gods," Herad swore as she glared at Mahedium.

The mage shrugged without concern. He didn't seem insulted. "I simply did what was in my best interest. Just like when I first joined up with your band. Werrick has resources and connections that you would never be able to give me. Everything I do is to advance my work, and the Broken Wheel knows the true value of my knowledge and skills. There's absolutely no reason for me to stay in your dirty little camp anymore."

"Can you really blame him for betraying you? Just look at the mess you've made of things and how pathetic your strategy was," Werrick remarked. "Luring me forward? Again? Really? That was how you dealt with the Vessel I sent to test you."

"So what are you waiting for? Kill me, you coward," Herad growled as she collected herself. Her cloak was torn and her leather armor was covered in dirt and grime. Her fall had even smeared dust over her face. She looked tired and defeated, although her eyes still burned with anger.

"I'm the coward? You're the one who tried to use magic to subdue me! I simply turned your own ploy against you," Werrick replied dismissively.

Herad opened her mouth to reply, but then she noticed Saeter. Her eyes flickered with recognition, and she hesitated. "What are you doing here?"

"I came to see your victory parade. It could use some work," Saeter replied sarcastically.

"And I'm currently trying to recruit him," Werrick added in a smug, taunting tone.

"I hope you're both very happy together," Herad remarked bitterly as anger flashed in her eyes.

"I haven't decided on anything yet, although it's definitely sounding like a better idea all of a sudden," Saeter shot back.

As the pair glared at each other, Werrick looked momentarily taken aback. "He's far less likely to run into obvious traps under me," Werrick rebuked Herad. "Did you really think I would charge into your base unprepared? How pathetic of you."

Herad glared at her opponent.

"I suppose I'm being uncharitable," Werrick told her. "It's not like you're anything more than a petty bandit. I knew exactly what you were thinking every step of the way. I timed my attack so that you would have no chance to question your strategy or come up with a new one."

"Enough with the pompous bragging, you bloody ass. Why am I still alive?" Herad asked. "I'd rather be dead than listen to you expel such rot."

"You're here because I don't fear you in the slightest. You're beneath me, and I want there to be no misunderstandings about that left in your head, or those of your minions, when you die," Werrick answered as he smiled.

As he finished speaking, a new group of enemies walked his way, escorting a nervous-looking Red Dog. The bandit lieutenant had been disarmed, and a gash above his eye was bleeding. His face was inscrutable as he took in the scene before him. When they got to Werrick, one of the men kicked the back of one of Red Dog's knees. With a huff, the bandit lieutenant landed in a kneeling position.

"He surrendered as soon as he learned you wanted to talk to him," one of the guards told their master.

Werrick nodded and motioned for the newcomers to step back.

"What do you want from me?" Red Dog asked. His voice was full of fear, but it was also edged with hope.

"While most of the bandits you find in the North are nothing more than deserters and riffraff too incompetent or stupid to stay in the army, there are a few exceptions. It would be a waste to kill such men when they could be of use to me," Werrick told him.

"So you want me to join up with you?" Red Dog inquired optimistically.

"Perhaps. First, there will be a demonstration, and then I shall test your loyalty."

As everyone warily watched him, the tall Vessel gestured, and one of his minions tossed him a sheathed sword. Herad flinched as her enemy drew the blade, but instead of attacking her, he tossed it onto the ground and took several large steps backward.

"What in all the hells are you doing?" she asked him.

"Proving a point. Pick up the sword and let's have another fight. You can even have a few minutes to rest if you want. It doesn't matter; you're no threat to me and you never were," Werrick replied as he drew his own blade.

Herad hesitantly picked up the blade and climbed to her feet. When Werrick didn't react, she brushed her black hair from her face and raised the sword defensively.

A ring of enemy soldiers surrounded her and Werrick. Saeter and Red Dog were dragged out of the way by some of them so that there would be enough room for the fight. However, neither of them was allowed to stand, and an armed guard stood behind them.

Nothing happened for a few seconds. Herad seemed to be taking her time to collect herself. Then Herad lunged. Her eyes blazed with hate and she snarled as she slashed at her opponent's head. However, Werrick wasn't caught off guard. He parried her attack, and his front foot caught Herad's leg. As she stumbled, Werrick's sword came around and stabbed her in the stomach.

"No!" Saeter gasped.

Herad's eyes went wide with shock as she collapsed onto her knees. She landed in a kneeling position with her forehead against the ground. A savage wound on her back matched the one on her front, and both of them bled profusely. Werrick's blade had gone right through her.

A moment later, the bleeding stopped as thick black scales appeared. They sealed the wound and replaced her torn armor.

However, Herad groaned and drew a wheezing breath. Her face was still pressed against the dirt. Her internal injuries hadn't disappeared; they had only been patched over.

"That's a convenient power, but it won't save you this time," Werrick said as he raised his blade again.

"You damned butcher!" Saeter cursed him.

"It was a fair fight, or close enough," the Vessel remarked with a shrug.

He kicked Herad's blade from her hands. She barely reacted, except to hiss in pain and pull her hands in close to her chest. A second later, she coughed and splotches of blood hit the ground.

There was an unexpected clang as Werrick dropped the blade he was holding next to Herad. Red Dog and Saeter stared at it uncomprehendingly.

"Now you have both seen me defeat Herad in terms of strategy and in personal combat. I am clearly the better master for you to serve," Werrick told his captives.

Red Dog glanced at Herad's fallen form and winced. He turned to the enemy leader. "I'll take you up on your offer. I see no point in dying here."

"It's not quite that simple. First you must prove yourself," Werrick replied. "Pick up that sword and finish off your old boss. Only when her corpse lies before me will you be allowed to serve."

There was silence for several long seconds as his words sank in.

"And if we refuse to bloody our hands and darken our souls on your behalf?" Saeter asked.

"Then you and everyone else in this band will die," Werrick answered.

Chapter 17

Saeter didn't say anything for several long moments. He just stared at Herad. She was still stooped over in the dirt. Her breathing was labored, and she didn't seem aware of what was going on.

"No, I won't do it. She is my leader, and she has my loyalty," he told Werrick. "I'm too old and tired to throw everything away again. I've done that too many times already."

The enemy bandit chieftain stood in front of Saeter. The old scout was still sitting on the ground, and Werrick's huge presence loomed over him.

"Are you sure about that? If you don't join me, then I will kill every last member of this band. Surely there are some among them that you wish to see saved?" Werrick asked. "You may choose a few to keep as your subordinates."

Saeter frowned, and wrinkles formed under his eyes. He looked unsure of himself as the Wolf continued his speech.

"There is the goblin you took in, for instance. I saw your loyal pet at your side but a few moments ago. Mahedium may have swatted him aside, but he still lives," Werrick said as he pointed toward where Blacknail lay. "If you refuse me, then I will have no choice but to kill him as well."

There was another moment of silence as Saeter glanced in Blacknail's direction. His face was blank, and it was impossible to guess what he was thinking.

"No? If self-interest isn't enough, then perhaps you need a cause to call your own?" Werrick inquired. "Join me and I shall create a new kingdom, greater than all the others! Together we will usher in a new age where men's actions count for more than their blood!"

"You're nothing but the puppet of a gaggle of corrupt Southern merchants. I know you work for the Broken Wheel Company," Saeter accused the bandit chieftain.

"I don't work for anyone. The Broken Wheel's backing is simply convenient for now. When they try to undermine me, I will be ready," Werrick replied. "I am the one using them."

"That's what every pawn and tool ever born believes," Saeter replied.

"Join me and see for yourself." Werrick countered. "The White Raven fought for Northern independence and was the first bandit chief in the North. I intend to be the last. I shall raise a new kingdom in these untamed lands, one greater than all the others. We dream of the same thing, old man. I fight for what you fought for."

"You expect me to believe that when you revel in torture and misery?" Saeter accused Werrick. "You obviously don't fight for anyone but yourself and your own sick enjoyment."

"I am never cruel without a reason," Werrick replied evenly. "We both know Herad did far worse to others. Her minions killed, raped, and robbed their way across the North. Countless lives were destroyed by her actions, and you supported her. Don't pretend you're better than this."

"Oh, then why did you set up this sick show?" Saeter's voice seethed with anger.

"To show you that she wasn't worth your loyalty," Werrick explained. "Here in the North, it is natural for the strong to rule the weak, and I am far stronger than her. I'm simply making this clear to you."

"That doesn't explain why you are making us finish her off," Saeter countered.

"That's simply so I know if you can be trusted," Werrick replied. "If you refuse to strike down your old leader, I know you remain loyal to her and will work against me. If you do finish her off, then you'll be just as responsible for her death as I am. I find this is an effective test of character."

Saeter had been slouching, but after hearing Werrick's words, he straightened and met the man's eyes. "No, I refuse. You're going to have to kill me. I've done enough evil for one lifetime and this is a line I refuse to cross."

Werrick frowned and turned to Red Dog. "Well, what about you then?"

"I'll do it," the other man answered with a voice full of reluctance and guilt.

Slowly, the bandit lieutenant got up and reached for the fallen sword. He picked it up then froze. For several seconds, he stared at Herad and bit his lip.

Werrick waited patiently. Even though he was unarmed and within Red Dog's striking distance, he didn't seem concerned. An aura of self-confidence around the bandit lord weighed on his surroundings. It was hard to imagine things not going his way.

"I'll be doing her a favor at this point," Red Dog muttered.

"You'll be saving your own skin by betraying her," Saeter rebuked him.

"He promised to spare some of my men as well. They're more important than one woman who is already dead, even if she used to be the boss," Red Dog shot back. "It's not like she would risk herself for us anyway. She's always been a selfish bitch."

The bandit lieutenant stepped toward Herad and raised the sword above his head. His old boss didn't respond. She appeared to have lost consciousness.

"Stop!" Saeter ordered Red Dog.

As his captors watched, the old scout rose to his feet. Red Dog froze as Saeter took the sword from his hands.

"What are you doing?" Werrick asked.

"Let me do it. I'll be the one to take her life," Saeter answered. "I just need to tell her something first."

One of Werrick's eyebrows rose in a surprised look, but he didn't say anything.

"Goodbye, Herad. You've always been an arrogant snake without a shred of decency and look at where it has led you," Saeter told his fallen chief. "You should have taken your ill-gotten riches and retired."

The old scout then stuck the blade he had taken from Red Dog into the earth and knelt at her side. He placed a hand on her shoulder and shook her slightly. She turned to look in his direction. Her face was clouded by pain and hate, but she was conscious as Saeter leaned in close and whispered something to her. Too quiet for anyone to overhear, he spoke as a weight seemed to disappear from his shoulders.

"Fuck you, old man." Herad coughed as she glared at him. A few seconds later, she coughed again and rolled onto her back. Her eyes were clenched shut and her face was tight with suffering.

Stony-faced, the old scout drew a dagger from his side. A moment later, he stabbed Herad up under her ribs then pulled the blade back out.

As everyone watched, the defeated bandit chieftain let out a deep breath and went still. All the fatigue and anxiety disappeared from her bearing as she died. Saeter placed a hand on her face and muttered a quick prayer.

"There, she's dead," the old scout said as he turned back toward his captors and pulled the sword he had sheathed in the ground.

There was a frown on Werrick's face as he examined the old scout and Herad's corpse. He then turned toward Red Dog. "You still need to do your part. The bitch is already dead or dying, so you'd better get your blow in quickly."

"Right," Red Dog acknowledged nervously as he gestured for Saeter to hand him the sword.

The old scout nodded, stepped forward, and ran Red Dog through with the blade.

"What?" he croaked in disbelief as he looked Saeter in the eyes.

"I never really liked you, coward," Saeter explained before he pulled out the blade and spun toward Werrick.

The ranger brought his sword around and stabbed at the bandit chief's chest. Werrick was caught off guard and a look of shock appeared on his face, but he jerked his body to the side and dodged the blow.

Instantly, his guards drew their own weapons and readied themselves to take down Saeter. They had the old scout completely surrounded.

However, before they could act, Werrick raised a hand and stopped them. "No, I'll do this myself."

Saeter slashed at him again, but Werrick easily stepped back out of the way. With a disappointed look, Werrick glared at the old scout. The Vessel dashed to the side, and one of his men passed him a sword. He started to say something, but another attack by Saeter forced him to stop and concentrate on blocking the blow.

Before Saeter could strike again, Werrick took the offensive. There was a slick metallic noise as Werrick pushed Saeter back and their swords slid against each other. The Vessel's inhuman strength knocked the scout back, and he stumbled. Werrick followed up with a slash that slammed into Saeter's side.

"Damnation," Saeter cursed as he fell.

Blood poured from a great gash in Saeter's side as he collapsed onto his back. However, a smug grimace appeared on his lips. It was clearly a fatal wound, but the old scout didn't seem afraid or angry.

"What was the point of that? Why were you loyal to her?" Werrick asked. "She didn't deserve it, and I had hoped for more from you."

If Saeter was capable of mustering a reply, he didn't have time. There was a distant bang before a thick column of black smoke rose into the air. Everyone turned to look at this new distraction.

"That came from my lab!" Mahedium shouted.

"I left specific orders that no one was to enter that building," Werrick replied with obvious frustration.

"I need to go see what has happened. The materials and papers there are irreplaceable!" the mage whined.

"Then go see what happened," Werrick told him coldly. "You're not needed here."

The bandit chieftain ordered several of his men to accompany the mage. With his escort in tow, Mahedium hurried toward the explosion and whatever remained of his lab. Amid the nearby rubble, Blacknail watched in dismay. Shock and confusion had overwhelmed the hobgoblin. His head was numb and hazy, and thinking about the events he had just seen caused pain to stab through his mind. Nonetheless, his self-preservation instinct was strong. He wasn't about to lie down and die. He could figure things out later. Right now, he just had to live. There was no way his master was really dead. He could still be saved somehow…

Despite his will, Blacknail was unable to muster the strength to get up. He barely managed to move his legs. As two new enemies, a man and woman, approached Werrick, he settled back down so that he wouldn't be noticed.

"The remains of the Black Snake's forces are scattered and fleeing, sir," the man told his boss as he gave a proper salute. He was wearing a distinctive steel breastplate over leather armor, and he had a goatee and short black hair that had been greased back. There was a grim cast to his face and a cold look in his eyes.

Werrick gave the man a polite nod, and he dropped his salute. The woman behind him gave a quick bow. She didn't look as if she belonged on the battlefield. She had long blond hair and an elegant manner. A fur-trimmed cloak hid the rest of her clothes.

"Well done, Orvito. I would expect nothing else from a former knight," Werrick told the man. "I'm putting you in charge of hunting down any stragglers. I want to send a message, so I don't want too many of Herad's troops surviving. Crush them before they get away."

"As you wish, lord. I will organize hunting parties right away," Orvito replied before saluting again and turning to head back the way he'd come.

When he was gone, the woman spoke up. "Lord, I watched the mage as you requested. So far, he has done nothing to arouse my suspicion, although I find the timing of this fire suspicious. I had hoped to go through his lab and correspondence."

"I think that fire hurt him far more than it did us, Zelena," Werrick replied. "It also changes nothing. We will simply have to be cautious in case he has struck additional bargains with the Broken Wheel behind our backs."

"I will remain vigilant, my lord," Zelena replied.

"I know you will. It was very reassuring to have you there during the battle. I wouldn't have wanted to actually put myself under that traitor's power," Werrick told her.

"He could not have harmed you. I had defenses ready to neutralize anything he could have cast," Zelena explained as she held up her hands. Her cloak slipped away to reveal a pair of delicate-looking golden gauntlets. They were exquisitely crafted and fit her petite hands snugly. Symbols ordained the metallic surfaces, and large crystals had been set into the palms.

"Oh, I don't doubt your abilities as a mage bodyguard. Mahedium would never have known what had hit him if he had tried to back out on our bargain," Werrick told her confidently.

"We should kill that man now that we no longer need him," Zelena replied as she scowled. "It is dangerous to associate with a dark mage such as him. Nothing good will come of drawing the attention of the guilds. They are ruthless in protecting their secrets."

"You don't think his research will be useful?" Werrick asked. "I would have thought you'd welcome a new source of mana stone."

"I can buy new ones on the black market or from my connections, and his dealings with the Broken Wheel concern me," she replied.

"Perhaps, but I also have plans for our renegade alchemist and the magic he can provide us. The mage guilds are a long way from here and care little about the North," Werrick countered. "If he betrays us, you can kill him though."

There was a disapproving scowl on Zelena's face, but she nodded. Werrick seemed amused by her reaction and smiled.

"I will make sure he has no chance to work against you, lord," she said with complete confidence. "His understanding of magic is deep, but he's a floundering novice when it comes to conspiracy and subtle maneuverings."

"That's what you said about Herad when you went to Daggerpoint, and we both know how that turned out," he replied.

"She had resources and allies I did not suspect," the blonde said defensively. "How was I to know that…"

That was when Blacknail stopped listening. A rustling sound from nearby stirred him from his stunned stupor and reminded him that he had his own problems. Was one of his enemies finally coming to finish him off? Blacknail quietly struggled to rise to his feet again. As he moved, he glanced toward the direction of the noise and saw a familiar face. Khita was leaning around the corner of the nearest building. Her eyes narrowed as she spotted Blacknail, and she raised a finger to her lips to signal silence. Blacknail stared at her blankly as she skulked to his side. What did she want? He didn't have time for her.

"I'm here to help," the young redhead explained as she pulled out a knife and cut him free from the tarp he was tangled up in.

When that was done, Khita grabbed his shoulder and pulled him up. With Blacknail leaning on her shoulder, she walked back over to the building. She was leading him away from his master, but Blacknail couldn't muster up the will to resist. His everything still ached.

No one noticed their escape; none of Werrick's minions glanced in their direction. Half of them had gone with Mahedium, and the half a dozen who remained were all looking at the pillar of smoke winding its way up into the sky.

Khita led Blacknail around the corner of the building she had come from. When they got there, Blacknail was surprised to see several members of his tribe hiding out of sight among a scattering of barrels and other equipment. Vorscha stood out in front of the others. Behind her was Geralhd and a half dozen other bandits. Oddly enough, Scamp was cowering behind Geralhd's legs, but there was no sign of Varhs.

"Here he is. I told you I could do it!" Khita exclaimed as Vorscha took Blacknail from her.

"And I told you not to try! You could have been killed!" the large woman snapped.

"But she succeeded, and we need to worry about our next move now," Geralhd interjected. "You can drum her down later. The explosion won't keep them distracted forever, and the Wolf's men are everywhere."

"There's no chance of getting Saeter?" Vorscha asked Khita with obvious concern.

"No, Werrick's right on top of him and he's been badly wounded," Khita explained.

"Then we need to leave. We've already overstayed our welcome. I was hoping to grab Saeter or another scout, but we will have to make do."

"Finally! I don't know why I followed you idiots. We should have run off into the woods at the first chance we got!" a man behind Geralhd exclaimed nervously.

Several other bandits nodded. They all looked terrified, and more than a few of them kept scanning their surroundings.

Blacknail was reminded of rabbits that had been spooked by a predator.

"Have any of you morons ever traversed the Deep Green?" Vorscha rebuked them. "Without supplies and proper scouts, we wouldn't last a day, and Werrick will have people watching the roads for us. To escape him, we have to hike through the forest for who knows how long."

"Fine, we've got the hobgoblin and the gear, so let's go. Blacknail is supposed to be a holy terror out in the forest," the man replied.

"I have to agree with that. I know we're short on scouts, but I don't think we're going to find any still around," Geralhd added.

"Ugh, it's amazing how fast those bloody bastards disappeared," Vorscha said darkly.

"That's rangers for you. Half of them probably had their gear ready to go, just in case, and I don't blame them," someone else muttered.

While still supporting Blacknail, Vorscha led the squad of bandits off toward the forest. However, the hobgoblin tried to pull away from her.

"My master!" he hissed. "I need to go back."

He was too weak to break free, and Vorscha kept moving. She only threw him a pitying look, deep sadness reflected in her eyes. "You can't save him, little one. You would only be throwing your life away. A good soldier knows when the cause is lost and when to fight another day."

"No! I will sneak up on the man named Werrick and stab him the back. I can kill them all!" Blacknail argued.

"You can barely walk," the woman replied.

The group of fleeing bandits were slipping through the more built area of Herad's camp. They used the buildings and tents for cover as they slipped toward the back of the base and the forest that lay beyond it. Chaos reigned all around them. Most of Werrick's forces seemed to have chased Herad's forces back onto the road. Another large group had been roped into helping fight the fire at Mahedium's cabin. The roof of the building was covered in flames, and black smoke continued to pour out of it.

A few small groups of Werrick's men were around, but they seemed busy looting. None of them wanted to get a close look at Vorscha's party, lest they turn out to be unfriendly.

"I will save my master! Let me go!" the hobgoblin protested.

"I'm not going to let you go. The people here need you, and I won't let you throw their lives away along with your own," Vorscha told him.

Shouting interrupted any reply Blacknail could have made. It rang out from near Werrick's location.

"The hobgoblin, it's missing!" someone yelled.

"Search the area. He can't have gone far!" Werrick shouted.

The bandit chieftain's voice was followed by pained laughter. Blacknail had never heard such a sound before, but he knew without a doubt who was making it. It was Saeter. The noise died a few seconds later, and there was silence.

Dread overpowered Blacknail, and his gut twisted. His heart skipped a beat as he tore himself away from Vorscha. He only made it three steps before collapsing.

No, this couldn't be happening. He could make it in time! There was no way his master was dead. All he had to do was pick himself up and run to his rescue! For the first time, tears welled up in Blacknail's eyes. His claws sank into the ground, and as he clenched them, they tore up the earth. He whimpered in pain. Why did it hurt so much! He didn't understand!

"Get up!" Vorscha grabbed Blacknail and wrapped an arm around his shoulder.

"Come on, Blacknail! Keep moving," Khita begged.

They walked again. Feeling was beginning to return to Blacknail's limbs, and his stride strengthened. However, a new type of weakness plagued him. He felt hollow inside, and he couldn't think straight.

"There they are!" someone shouted from off in the distance.

“Damnation, run for the trees!” Vorscha yelled as she passed Blacknail to Khita.

The warrior woman spun around as a small horde of enemy soldiers bore down on her party. Among them was the man called Orvito. Instantly, most of Vorscha’s companions made a break for the safety of the trees ahead of them. Only Geralhd and Khita hesitated.

“Take the hobgoblin and go! I’ll hold up the rear,” Vorscha ordered.

Geralhd nodded and helped Khita drag Blacknail. Together, they managed to get him moving at a fair pace. The sight of the enemy awoke something in Blacknail. Now that he had a focus, despair gave way to rage. Someone was going to pay for making him feel bad.

“I can run now,” he hissed as he pushed aside his two human helpers.

The hobgoblin broke into a jog. He was still unsteady, but he could keep up with Khita and Geralhd easily enough. Anger burned within him, but he kept it contained by mentally running through sword drills his master had taught him. His master…

As his gait strengthened, Blacknail saw his tent off to one side. He and Saeter had set their campsite up near the forest, and Blacknail veered toward it.

“What are you doing?” Geralhd asked between exhausted breaths.

The hobgoblin didn’t reply. He dashed toward his tent, grabbed his and his master’s backpacks, snatched up one other item, and hurried back to the others. They hadn’t slowed down for him, but it didn’t matter. It took him mere seconds to catch up. The diversion had been more than worth the time. Saeter had always made sure that he and Blacknail kept a bag ready in case they needed to go out on a mission. Their contents would be useful.

The thick bushes that grew at the edge of the forest where the wall ended were only a short dash away. Blacknail headed straight toward them. There were too many enemies to fight. All he could do was run, not think about the bad things, and try to figure out his next move. He wasn't going to throw his life away in a fight he couldn't win, not when there were so many people he needed to kill.

There was a whistling sound and a loud, meaty thud. Blacknail's ears perked up and he ducked low as he recognized the sound of arrows in flight.

"Gods damn it!" Vorscha roared.

Someone had shot an arrow at her, and it had grazed her leg. The warrior woman stopped running. A deep graze bled profusely a few inches below her knee.

"I'll help you. Come on," Geralhd offered as he came to a stop as well.

"No, keep running. I'll hold them off. I'll never make it with a wound like this slowing me down," his lover replied.

"But—"

"Go!" she growled as she drew her sword and turned to face the enemies bearing down on her. "We both knew this was a short-term thing, lover. It was never going to work out."

"Goodbye, and thank you for everything, love," Geralhd replied sorrowfully. After a moment of hesitation, he ran again. Anguish was plain on his face, but he had no choice but to flee.

The sounds of fighting rang out as Blacknail slipped into the bushes at the edge of the forest. Khita had already gone ahead, and Geralhd was right behind him. At the border, the hobgoblin took a moment to peer through the greenery at everything he was leaving behind. Smoke rose above Herad's camp. Somewhere out of sight lay Saeter and Herad's bodies.

Nearby, Vorscha held off the first few enemies with a swing of her long sword. As they encircled her, she lashed out and cut down one enemy, but another bandit took his place. With no other option, Vorscha ferociously swung her blade in wide arcs as she tried to defend herself from the mobs of attackers.

“Enough of this!” Orvito shouted as he pushed two of his men out of the way and stepped into the melee.

The grim warrior slashed at Vorscha, forcing her to block the attack. Vorscha stumbled back as her wounded leg gave out. Without mercy, Orvito pressed his advantage. He unleashed a flurry of attacks, then stabbed Vorscha in the chest. The warrior woman gasped and fell.

There was nothing Blacknail could do. He was helpless. The hobgoblin choked and his eyes watered as he clung to the item he had taken from his tent. It was the first gift his master had ever given him—his raggedy blanket. Without a word, Blacknail slipped away into the Green. He would be back one day…

Part Three: Into the Green

Chapter 18

What was pain? Blacknail contemplated the awful nature of the feeling as he led the way through the forest. Agony coursed through him. His injuries ached from walking, but it was more than that. Something had been taken from him, and he knew he would never get it back.

The absence enraged him. How dare they take what had been his! Herad had been his chieftain and Saeter had been his one and only master! Blacknail wavered slightly as hate boiled through him. Rage filled him to such an extent that it seemed to want to burst from his insides like vomit, and he had to fight the urge to scream and rip apart the nearest bush or human scapegoat.

The survivors of Werrick's attack meekly followed the hobgoblin. There were thirteen of them, but Geralhd and Khita were the only ones Blacknail knew well. Scamp was also following meekly. He didn't count toward the thirteen.

It had only been a few minutes since they had fled their old base. None of the humans were scouts, so they didn't question the path Blacknail had chosen. They reeked of mind-dulling fear and sweaty defeat. Blacknail ignored their weakness and forged on ahead. There didn't seem to be any other option.

"Did you see Varhs?" Scamp asked Blacknail as he ran up to his side.

"No!" Blacknail hissed with barely contained fury.

The little goblin's eyes were huge and shiny with tears. He looked both terrified and sad. Blacknail had to resist the urge to kick him. His pain was so much worse than Scamp's! What did the spoiled little goblin know about suffering?

Herad was dead. His chieftain had seemed invincible, but she had fallen in combat after being betrayed. He had thought her cleverer than that. How could someone so ruthless and powerful die? Very little of her band remained after her demise. Vorscha was probably dead by this point, and so was Saeter. The memory of his master's fallen body enraged Blacknail again. The hobgoblin focused on breathing to keep his rage under control. It was what his master had taught him.

Even Red Dog had died. That wasn't fair! Blacknail had wanted to kill him, and he had been saving him for a special occasion! The hobgoblin snarled and squeezed his fists together. The idea of living without his master was… distressing.

Did he want to stay with this other remnant of his tribe? What would be the point in that? The humans behind him were weak and useless, especially Khita. Most of them had injuries that made them next to useless in a fight. Leaving them would increase Blacknail's odds of survival, but where would he go? Out into the Green alone?

Blacknail had never really understood Saeter. His master's pink head had contained many weird human thoughts, but the hobgoblin had respected him. He had owed the man so much. Saeter had made the hobgoblin who he was.

Vorscha had also been a complete idiot, even if she had been strong. Why sacrifice yourself and look after useless people like Khita? Blacknail didn't get it. It was Herad who Blacknail had understood the best. The bandit chieftain had ruled as a hobgoblin would… just better. It didn't take much imagination for him to know what she would have wanted him to do. Werrick had to die.

Killing the human named Werrick wouldn't be easy though. It was possible a sneak attack might work, but it would be risky and gain Blacknail little. He would still be alone and surrounded by enemies. Other strategies would require he seek out help. The humans he was traveling with right now had been overcome by fear and were useless. It was annoying how cowardly men could be.

He didn't want to travel all by himself though. That sounded really boring! Besides, the clumsy humans had one significant use. They served as a meat shield that would attract any attacking predators. That was important, because out here in the Deep Green, a lot of things liked people-sized meals.

A scent reached Blacknail's nose. The hobgoblin stopped and stared off into the trees for a moment. He recognized it.

"What is it?" Khita asked him nervously.

"Stay here. I'll be right back," Blacknail replied as he stomped off into the bush.

The hobgoblin sniffed the air as he ducked under a branch. After a quick look around, he located the source of the scent. It was coming from a cluster of roots at the base of a nearby tree. The tree itself was huge, and its trunk rose into the canopy, where it blocked out the sun.

"Come out, you idiot. I know you're under there," Blacknail hissed.

There was a shuffling noise, and a second later, a head poked out from the space between two large roots. It was Elyias, and he didn't look all that happy to see Blacknail. What a stupid human.

Elyias looked pale and scared and wouldn't meet Blacknail's eyes. "Oh, it's you. I heard something and was afraid it was some sort of monster… other than you. Is it safe now?"

A frustrated sigh escaped Blacknail lips. What kind of idiot hid in a stupid place like that just because they had heard some sort of noise? Instead of replying, Blacknail grabbed the man's shoulder. With a quick tug, he hauled him out of his hiding place. The young man was too petrified by fear to put up any resistance.

"There are some more people this way. Come with me," Blacknail told him.

"Thank the gods. I was afraid that I was going to be stuck alone or with just… someone else," Elyias whined.

The stupid minion had obviously run off into the forest all by himself as soon as Herad had been defeated. He wouldn't have lasted a day if Blacknail hadn't found him. Elyias owed him another favor now.

Elyias trailed after Blacknail with a relieved expression. They got a few looks as they approached the spot where the hobgoblin had left the others.

"Oh, a straggler. The bastard is lucky you found him," one of the bandits said as he spotted Elyias.

"Ah, he's that kid who kept losing at dice. Why do we want him?" another bandit remarked disdainfully.

"We already have Khita. He won't be any worse than her," Blacknail explained.

The hobgoblin wasn't quite sure why he had bothered going after Elyias. Had it been just out of habit? No, it was because Elyias was his minion. He had lost too many tribesmen today to give up any more. Anyone who tried to take what was his would have to pry it from his clawed hands!

"True enough," the man replied. "I guess he may as well join us."

"Hey!" Khita exclaimed. "I'm a better woodsperson than any of you asses!"

All the survivors talked amongst themselves, but Blacknail took back his position at the front of the group and started walking again. He didn't care about what they said.

"Um, Blacknail, maybe we should stop for a second?" Geralhd told him as he hurried over to the hobgoblin's side.

The hobgoblin turned to look at the man standing right behind Blacknail with a nervous smile. There were mutters of agreement from the other humans as well.

"We need to keep moving," Blacknail hissed.

"I understand that, but we don't even have a plan. Where are we going?" Geralhd asked.

"We're headed away from the people trying to kill us," Blacknail explained condescendingly. That should have been really obvious.

"Yes, but that doesn't tell us where we are headed," Geralhd countered.

Out of morbid curiosity, Blacknail decided to ask and see if any of the humans had something in mind. He stopped walking and turned toward them. "Where do you want to go?"

Geralhd and the others started talking. Unsurprisingly, none of them had any good ideas.

"We should probably head in the same general direction as the road. It's not like there's anywhere else to go," someone commented.

"But if we get too close, someone might stumble onto our trail," another replied. "Werrick probably has a lot of men out looking for us."

This discussion went on for a few minutes before Blacknail lost patience. He grunted in annoyance and started walking again.

"Hey, where are you going?" Geralhd asked the departing hobgoblin.

"There is a place Saeter and I sometimes used as a campsite this way, and it will be dark soon. Follow me if you want. I don't care," Blacknail grunted without stopping.

After a few more seconds of arguing, everyone decided to let him lead the way.

Despite all the dramatic events that had unfolded less than an hour ago, the forest was the same as always. Blacknail was still struggling to hold back the rage he felt, but around him, things were almost tranquil. They were walking a path the hobgoblin had used many times when he'd gone out hunting. Birds sang in the trees off in the distance. Leaves rustled as small animals scampered around out of sight. The canopy overhead was porous on this trail, so the undergrowth was thick.

As Blacknail stepped over a fallen log, a crunching sound reached his ears. It had come from a fair distance down the trail behind him, and it was swiftly followed by a dull snap.

Blacknail's hackles rose and he turned to scan the forest in that direction. He didn't see anything, but he knew something was there.

"What is it?" Khita asked.

The concern in her voice disturbed the hobgoblin. He looked her and the other humans over. Some of them were wounded, and they all looked exhausted.

"I think someone is following us," he told her loud enough that everyone could hear.

Fear appeared on most of the bandits' faces. Several of them twitched and threw nervous glances backward. Blacknail watched them and frowned. It was unlikely they would be useful in a fight. Their retreat had broken their spirit. Human minds were fragile things.

"What do we do?" someone asked with barely concealed panic.

Blacknail provided no immediate answer. He took a few seconds to mull over his options. As he thought, he looked at the sky. It was getting dark. The sun had almost reached the western horizon already.

"I will go back and see who it is. Keep following this trail until you reach the end," Blacknail told everyone. He explained to them how to get to the campsite he had mentioned.

As soon as he was done, most of the humans hurried away. They wanted to be as far away from any form of pursuit as possible.

"Are you sure you don't want help?" Khita asked.

Blacknail snorted disdainfully. Khita was incapable of being helpful. There was no way she could move through the forest unseen. "No, I'm just going to take a look, scout stuff."

The redhead nodded and headed after the others. Blacknail watched her go before stepping off into the bushes at the edge of the trail. Before he could come up with a plan, he needed to find out who was tracking his party. He had only heard one person, but there could easily be many more. Luckily, it was getting dark now. In just a bit, it would be too dark for humans to see properly, but he wouldn't have that problem.

The forest was silent as Blacknail slipped through the trees. He headed away from the trail then moved parallel to it. With great care, he kept to the shadows and out of sight. It was important that he not be seen, but he had to keep an eye on the trail.

Almost immediately, he heard another crack as someone stepped on a twig. The hobgoblin went perfectly still. There was movement along the trail. From his hiding spot behind a fallen log, Blacknail studied the source of the noise. It was a group of humans. Saeter would have found their movements sloppy, but they were much better than most humans. They moved carefully, and only the occasional sound betrayed their presence as they followed the trail and the signs left by the survivors of Herad's band.

The seven enemies were dressed much the same as Herad's rangers had been. Most of them wore hunter's cloaks and dirty leather clothing. Blacknail didn't think they had any scouts out or backup nearby. They wouldn't want to split up in unfamiliar territory. But even without reinforcements, seven was more than Blacknail would usually want to fight. However, this wasn't a normal situation and he really wanted to kill something.

The hobgoblin considered running ahead and getting help from his human allies, but he discarded that idea. They would be too scared and tired to fight properly, and they would only give him away. Alone, there was no way the pursuers would detect him before it was too late. However, the most important consideration was the rage. Every second Blacknail watched the enemy, images of Saeter dying filled his head. He had been helpless before, but this group of foolish humans had left the safety of their pack and entered his domain. There was no one to hold him back from taking his bloody vengeance.

Blacknail headed deeper into the woods. Once safely out of sight, the hobgoblin broke into a run. The trail curved up ahead, so he could cut across the forest to get a lead. There was a good ambush spot down the trail that he wanted to take advantage of.

After whipping through a patch of bushes, Blacknail jumped back onto the trail and kept running until he came to the place he remembered. A huge tree had recently toppled across the trail here. The fall of the towering giant had opened up the canopy, but the undergrowth hadn't had time to thicken yet. Except for two more tall trees, there was no real cover along this part of the path, and one side of the trail was blocked by a rocky ledge that was twice as tall as a man.

Blacknail slipped off his backpacks and hurriedly began his preparations. First, he pulled out some rope. He emptied his backpack, filled it with rocks from the ledge, and tied the rope to it. With that done, he threw one end of the rope over a thick branch overhead and scrambled up the other tree.

He chose a sturdy limb over a dozen feet up and stretched over the path as his hiding spot. The leaves of the tree made him almost impossible to see from below. From there, he made his final preparations and strung his bow.

Nothing happened for several long minutes. With a faint rustling noise, the first scout appeared below Blacknail and carefully walked down the path. He didn't look up. Humans almost never did. It was a weakness of the species.

Soon, the rest of the party followed their leader. The hobgoblin grew excited as he watched them. When they were directly below the trap, Blacknail grinned and cut the rope. The only warning the men got was a slight rasping noise as the rope rubbed against bark. Surprised faces looked up just in time to see the sack of rocks drop on top of them.

Cries of pain were quickly followed by a sickening crunch as the heavy weight smashed into two men standing in the middle of the enemy formation. It knocked one man aside and hit the other dead on, crushing him.

The other humans panicked and threw themselves to the sides, away from the danger. Blacknail didn't give them time to recover or figure out what was happening. He already had his bow drawn back and let loose an arrow that sank into one of the scout's backs. The twang of the bow was muffled by the commotion caused by the first attack. It took several moments for the hobgoblin's enemies to realize another one of their comrades had fallen and how.

"Ambush! To cover!" a hooded scout ordered as he dove off the path and into some bushes.

His fellows were quick to scatter and seek the closest cover as well. None of them seemed to know where they were being attacked from, but they knew the general direction from which the arrow had come.

The man who had been knocked aside by the hobgoblin's trap was trying to get to his feet. He was struggling and had obviously been badly hurt. Blacknail reloaded his bow and shot him in the back. Much to Blacknail's cruel satisfaction, the man flopped onto the ground and went limp. There were no more easy targets, so the hobgoblin dropped his bow and dashed farther out onto the tree limb he had been perched on. Jumping off the branch, he caught another one, then threw himself sideways. He didn't think. His inner predator simply acted.

Branches whirred past Blacknail as he flew through the air and landed on an unsuspecting enemy's back. The hobgoblin had taken off his boots so that he could climb easier. Thus, the long claws on his hands and feet sank into the man's clothes and the flesh beneath. With a shrill scream of pain, the man collapsed under Blacknail's weight. A shock went through the hobgoblin's arms as they both hit the ground, but he caught himself. Without hesitation, Blacknail drew his knife and cut the stunned man's throat.

There were three enemies left, and they were scattered around the ambush site. This was going to be easy! Bloodlust rose within the hobgoblin and tinted his vision red. He almost spasmed with the need to bite and tear into his prey. It was time to make his enemies pay for what they had done!

Chapter 19

Blacknail rose up from atop the corpse of the enemy scout whose throat he had just slit. The salty scent of blood flooded the air as the crimson liquid seeped into the ground. Without a word, he launched himself toward his next victim. There were still three of Werrick's minions scattered around the area. All of them needed to die.

A cracking noise revealed someone moving behind a tree up ahead. As Blacknail dashed across the ground, he drew his sword. It came loose with an eager hiss, as if anticipating the spilling of blood.

A bearded human peeked out from behind the tree. He was an older man with untidy brown hair and a tense look on his face. Instantly, Blacknail leapt forward and slashed at the human. The man's eyes went wide, and he disappeared back behind cover.

A predatory growl escaped Blacknail's lips, but he didn't give chase. Instead, he threw himself the other way. He dashed around the opposite side of the tree trunk, toward the man's back. His claws sank into earth and tree roots as he moved.

"Bloody hells!" the bearded man yelled as he turned and realized what had happened.

His back was exposed. He had drawn his blade, but it was useless since he was facing the wrong direction. His eyes widened in terrified helplessness as the lightning-quick hobgoblin closed the distance and stabbed him in the side. The blade sank deep into flesh before grinding against bone and coming to a halt.

Two humans left. Blacknail laughed as he tugged his sword free, and his voice echoed eerily through the trees. Behind him, the bearded man fell like a puppet whose strings had been cut.

"What in all the hells is going on here? What is this?" a panicked voice shouted from off to one side.

"It's him, the monster!" someone exclaimed. "The reaper of Daggerpoint!"

Their terrified tones sent an excited shiver down Blacknail's spine. He sensed weakness to be exploited. The hobgoblin licked his lips eagerly. He could practically taste their terror, and it was sweet and satisfying. It quenched a need.

The last two humans were on the other side of the path and hiding behind a fallen log. There was no benefit in giving his prey time to think and collect themselves, so Blacknail darted toward them.

Just as he reached the center of the path, a hooded figure rose and aimed a short bow at him. Sunlight reflected off the steel tip of the nocked arrow. It was aimed directly at Blacknail's face, but the hobgoblin ignored it. Unflinchingly, he stared directly into the archer's eyes and kept running straight.

Time flowed slowly as Blacknail moved. His muscles were as taut as a coiled snake's, and his eyes glowed with hunger and hate as they focused completely on the enemy. The archer was a tough-looking woman with short brown hair and a crooked nose. Her eyes shimmered with fear, but they also held steely determination. One well-placed arrow would turn the tide of the fight.

The woman's gaze relaxed, and the tension left her face for a moment as practiced calm took over. The arrow flew free as the archer's fingers let it go, but Blacknail had already dived to the side. He had seen his opponent's expression change and known what it meant. The projectile missed the hobgoblin entirely and shot off into the forest.

"Mine!" Blacknail growled triumphantly as he leapt forward and raised his blade.

The archer jumped back and dropped her bow. She reached for the blade at her side, but she wasn't quick enough. Blacknail's sword cut into his opponent's exposed arm and drew blood. It wasn't a deep cut, but the archer stumbled back and lost her grip on the blade she was drawing. Blacknail swung his sword around again, but his attack was interrupted as, with a rustling of leaves, the last enemy ranger rose from his nearby hiding spot and attacked with a swing of his own blade. The hobgoblin was forced to dodge this new attack and bring his blade up defensively.

There was a loud metallic clang and sparks as the two swords collided. Despite his strength, Blacknail was pushed back by the man's sheer weight. The hobgoblin smiled sourly as he absorbed the force of the blow by jumping backward. He didn't like being pressed back by a human fatty.

"Damnation, it's really him!" the new attacker said as he looked at Blacknail. He was a stocky human male dressed in the same rough clothing as the others. His long blond hair had been gathered up into a ponytail, and he had a patchy looking goatee. There was alarm in his eyes as he studied Blacknail.

As soon as he landed, the hobgoblin brought his sword back up into a defensive posture. He met his opponents' stares and grinned in a way that highlighted his pointy teeth. They flinched, much to his delight. They should fear him! Soon he would tear them apart for daring to raise their weapons against him and his tribe. Saeter would be avenged! Nothing could stop him.

"I'm going to chew your bones," Blacknail hissed.

He wasn't actually going to do anything like that. Humans didn't taste good, especially not their bones, but the idea of being eaten unsettled them in a way that simple death didn't, because they were dumb.

"It's a demon! It talks!" the man stuttered fearfully. "How can it speak?"

His words amused Blacknail. The hobgoblin had spoken before that. This human was aparticularly stupid specimen.

"Shut up and fight," the female hissed as she drew her sword. "That doesn't matter right now."

Blacknail's eyes flickered with interest. Her grab for her weapon had been clumsy, probably because her main hand had been wounded and she was using her weaker one.

The man stepped forward. Blacknail circled around away from him and toward the woman. She was obviously the weaker of the two.

"Cover me," she told her companion as she tried to step back.

However, Blacknail didn't give them the chance to coordinate. He dashed forward and jumped onto a nearby log. It was a massive fallen tree trunk and slippery with moss, but Blacknail's exposed claws gripped the bark without any problems. Before his opponents could react, he sprinted along its length before leaping back onto the ground. His unexpected move placed him on the far side of the woman, out of reach of the man.

"Get back!" the man yelled as he tried to circle around.

He was way too slow. Blacknail launched a flurry of sword slashes at the woman. She desperately tried to block and parry the hobgoblin's blows but was clearly having trouble. Her use of her weaker hand slowed her reactions.

As he crossed blades with the woman, Blacknail kept an eye on the man. Every time he tried to join the fight, the hobgoblin pushed the woman in his way or circled around in the opposite direction. His inability to get near the hobgoblin frustrated the man, and the woman was tiring. Both of them grew red in the face as the fight went on. Suddenly, Blacknail stepped forward. The woman was slightly off balance, and a blow from the hobgoblin knocked her sword aside. She was now completely open to attack.

The woman's face paled as Blacknail raised his sword in one hand. She had no way to block his next strike. The hobgoblin grinned as he stared into the woman's terrified eyes. This was the end! However, before the hobgoblin could attack, the man leapt forward with his sword raised. His blade came down in a mighty blow that batted Blacknail's weapon aside. Instead of resisting, the hobgoblin relaxed and absorbed the force of the strike. As Blacknail spun around, the man's momentum carried him closer. When he staggered past, the hobgoblin casually drew a dagger with his free hand and plunged it into the man's exposed back.

"Humans are so easy," Blacknail purred as he let go of the knife.

In front of him, the man fell and coughed blood onto the ground as he died. The long dagger had sunk deep and cut into his vitals.

The woman squeaked before running away. Blacknail sighed overdramatically. Humans were also slow. She had no chance of getting away. Really, what was she thinking?

Dagger still in hand, the hobgoblin caught the woman's cloak. Instead of trying to pull her down, he simply tugged on it to slow her down and pull himself closer. She glanced over her shoulder, panicked, and tried to backhand him. The blow missed as Blacknail ducked under it. He took the opportunity to tackle her legs, and they both fell in a tangle. As he hit the ground with a thump, the hobgoblin was tempted to burn Elixir so he could quickly overpower his enemy. He resisted the urge though, since he had little left in his system and only one vial in his backpack.

Dirt and debris from the forest floor was thrown into the air as they rolled. Blacknail fought to keep his hold on the enemy scout. With a grunt, he pulled himself up onto her chest and they came to a jarring stop. The woman tried to buck her hips to throw him off, but Blacknail easily held her down. He hissed menacingly as he placed his dagger against her exposed throat, and she went perfectly still.

"Oh gods. Oh gods, no. Please spare me," the woman begged tearfully.

This reaction stumped the hobgoblin. He stared at the now-crying woman's face and hesitated. A flicker of emotion stirred within his chest as he studied her face.

"Why would I do that? It would be stupid," he asked her as he tilted his head.

"Please spare me!" the woman whined.

Blacknail frowned and shook his head disdainfully. "You're trying to kill me, so I need-ss to kill you first. That's how this works, and I hate you. You killed my tribe. Ending your life will make me feel much better."

The suppressed anger he'd unleashed at the start of the fight still roiled within him, but it had mostly been spent. Victory was now his, and with it came smug satisfaction. He wanted to drag out the fun for a little bit, and he was honestly curious about what she was going to say. Did she have something valuable to offer him?

"You can have all our gear and coins!" she told him frantically.

Blacknail scratched the back of his head. That idea didn't work for him. Even bringing it up was stupid. "I can just take your stuff after killing you. Not having you running around is much better for me."

The woman stared at Blacknail for several long seconds without replying. She seemed to have regained some measure of self-control and was studying the hobgoblin carefully now, even though his dagger was still pressed against her neck. "I can offer you pleasure."

Blacknail considered her words. He had no idea what she was talking about, but he noticed her right hand was now behind her back. It looked suspiciously like she was reaching for a concealed weapon. "I already said I would enjoy taking my vengeance."

"But surely laying with a woman would be much more satisfying," she replied confidently.

"Laying with a..." Blacknail mused as he thought over her words.

Suddenly, his eyes opened wide in shock. A stab of pain went through his skull as visions of a certain woman from Daggerpoint flashed through his mind. Even worse than the sight was the phantom smell of perfume. He didn't want to remember that!

Blacknail flinched away from the woman, and his cheeks felt hot. There was no way he was doing anything like that with a human woman ever again! Nope, that wasn't happening. If it hadn't been for that perfume, he would have never let that smirking woman control him like that.

As the hobgoblin was working to repress painful memories, he felt the person beneath him shift. His eyes focused in time to see a dagger plunge toward his side. Blacknail threw himself sideways out of the way of the attack, but the knife cut through Blacknail's shirt and grazed his ribs. The woman took advantage of his movement to throw him aside and scramble back onto her feet. A second later, she was dashing off down the trail that led back toward Herad's old camp.

"No fair," the hobgoblin grumbled as he jumped to his feet. She had almost stabbed him while he had been thinking! Even worse than that, she had made him recall things he had been repressing for months.

Rather than pursue his escaping enemy, Blacknail picked up the bow she had dropped earlier. He grabbed a few arrows off the ground as well, then he leapt atop the huge fallen log. There, he took careful aim and shot the fleeing woman in the back. She crumbled and rolled across the ground until she hit the base of a tree. Blacknail stuck his tongue out at her corpse before turning away. He hadn't felt like chasing her down and tackling her again. Her disturbing offer had totally ruined his vengeful moment!

Why did humans think he wanted to mate with them? Several members of Herad's band had mentioned stories about hobgoblins raping humans. They were so fat and tall and pink! How was that attractive? Blacknail wanted to rant at the woman for suggesting such a thing, but she was already dead. In the hobgoblin's experience, it was human women who came onto him! Not that he wanted them to. They were perverts.

All the enemy scouts who had been following his group were dead now. Blacknail sighed as he looked at their remains. What was left of his fury and outrage was fading away. The killing had sated his bloodlust, but he still felt oddly hollow. The meager vengeance hadn't made him feel any better. Saeter and his other tribemates were still gone and would never come back. The emptiness ached.

If killing half a dozen minions hadn't filled the void within him, then he would have to find something else that would. The answer was simple. Werrick was the one who had taken his tribemates. Nothing would be right until that smug human was dead.

An idea occurred to the hobgoblin. Werrick thought he had won, that the battle was over, but that wasn't the case. Blacknail didn't like the idea of his future prey feeling relaxed and triumphant as he rummaged through the spoils of Herad's camp. He would leave the man a message. An actual written message wouldn't work because Blacknail couldn't read or write, but that didn't matter. The hobgoblin knew more than a few other ways to get his point across. Blacknail grabbed the leg of a nearby human corpse and dragged it.

After a bit of hard work and creative self-expression, he completed his project. Now, the forest path looked much better. There was no way anyone would miss this message or misunderstand what it meant! Three human corpses were hanging from tree branches and creaking as they swayed. The other bodies had been piled in the center of the path nearby.

Several of them were missing their heads. The skulls now decorated spikes that had been driven into the ground.

After looking around and nodding approvingly, Blacknail smiled. It was annoying he didn't have any more time to play, but this would do. It got the point across.

There was a muted cracking noise behind him, so Blacknail glanced over his shoulder. He wasn't too worried. It was unlikely an enemy could have sneaked up on him, and they would have acted already if they had.

For a few moments, he didn't see anything. Then his eyes focused on a large green shape. He stared at it for several long seconds as he stayed perfectly still. It was a troll.

Oh, right. There had been signs of a troll hanging around before the battle. Perhaps staying next to all these bloody corpses had been a stupid idea.

As Blacknail watched, the huge beast stepped onto the path and ambled over to the pile of corpses. With a loud snorting sound, it sniffed them, then in an impressive display of strength, it reached out one muscled arm and picked up one of the bodies.

The troll stared at the body for a few moments, then it took a bite out of it. There was a series of loud crunches and wet smacking noises as it chewed and tore into the now-mangled body. Blood splashed onto the ground as the beast ate.

This troll was noticeably larger than the one Blacknail had seen before. Like the other, it had thick green skin and a mane of dirty brown hair. It's face somewhat resembled a very angry goblin's, but it obviously weighed several times more than a hobgoblin. Heavy muscles seemed to roll under its skin as it moved, and two large tusks jutted out from its mouth.

A minute passed slowly for Blacknail as he watched the massive predator. There was a smile on Blacknail's lips because he didn't dare let his facial expression change, lest even the tiniest movement attract the troll's attention.

After swallowing a particularly large chunk of meat, the troll turned toward the hobgoblin and growled deeply. Blood dripped from its jaws.

Blacknail had been hoping, futilely it turned out, that the beast hadn't seen him. The hobgoblin carefully weighed his options, but none of them seemed to offer him very good chances of survival. He was doomed.

Chapter 20

The troll growled as it glared at Blacknail. The sound was full of raw rage and hunger. A shudder went down the hobgoblin's spine, and he instantly understood what the beast was trying to communicate.

"Yep, you can have those," Blacknail stuttered with false cheer. "Consider the meat a gift!"

He carefully stepped back from the troll and the pile of bodies it had been feeding on. Overcome by terror, he kept his eyes lowered submissively. He didn't plan on trying to assert his right to his own kills. With all that food in front of it, the troll probably wouldn't bother chasing down one scraggly hobgoblin, as long as it didn't get angry. Unfortunately, trolls were famous for getting homicidally enraged over nothing and killing people.

The hobgoblin continued to back away slowly, and the beast turned away from him. It continued eating again. Blacknail reached the edge of a patch of bushes. He stepped backward, and there was a snapping sound as his foot crushed a twig. Blacknail winced at the unexpected sound and his breath caught in his chest. He hoped the unwelcome noise didn't draw the beast's attention.

He wasn't so lucky. The troll looked up, and its furious eyes locked on the hobgoblin. It growled, and its massive green bulk shifted as it stepped toward him.

"Damnation," Blacknail swore under his breath.

With a hiss of rage, the troll lurched forward. Its mouth opened to reveal huge, razor-sharp teeth as it lunged toward the hobgoblin. Blacknail yelped in terror and jumped backward. He twisted around in the air and was already moving when he landed. The terrified hobgoblin sprinted madly toward the closest tree. Its huge trunk might get in the way of the terrible beast and slow it down. It wasn't a great plan, but it was the only one he had.

The sound of claws tearing into the earth and growling closed in on Blacknail's exposed back, but his plan worked. The hobgoblin reached the tree without getting eaten, and he put a hand against its bark as he rushed around it.

Blacknail threw a terrified glance over his shoulder to see the troll's charge slow. It didn't want to collide with the tree trunk at full speed. The hobgoblin would have laughed triumphantly, but he still had nowhere to go and he was probably going to be eaten alive. Could trolls climb trees? The hobgoblin had no idea.

Another menacing growl issued forth from the troll as it approached and its claws tore into the tree bark as it came to a stop. Fury radiated from the beast as it studied the hobgoblin hiding on the other side of the tree.

"Go away… please," Blacknail said as he stared at the unstoppable predator with eyes wide with fear. "I'm just a little hobgoblin. You don't want to eat me; I probably don't taste nearly as nice as a fat juicy human."

He was totally doomed. The hobgoblin whimpered softly and his stomach felt sick. There was no way he was going to survive this. Blacknail had seen how fast trolls could move and how hard they were to kill. It had taken a large squad of specially armed humans to take down the last one. This one was just toying with him, as if he were rabbit or a mouse.

So much for all his plans; Blacknail was never going to kill Werrick. This troll was going to chew him up, then it would finish eating all the humans he'd killed. Werrick wouldn't even get Blacknail's message. It would look as if a troll had killed the scouts. It had all been pointless.

The troll smelled of foul meat and rot. Its muscles flexed as it crouched low and prepared to spring toward Blacknail. The hobgoblin drew his sword. It was a pitiful weapon, but maybe he would get lucky and piss the beast off enough that his death would be quick.

There was a rustling sound as a breeze blew through the forest and shook the branches. For a second, the scent of the troll was replaced by that of leaves and soil. Then the moment ended, and the beast leapt. Its eyes glowed with hunger as its massive jaws opened.

Pure terror overwhelmed Blacknail and his entire body froze solid. Time moved slowly, but the troll was fast and its jaws promised inescapable death. There was no way he could possibly get out of the way.

As the beast lurched through the air toward him, something hit it. The troll was knocked sideways as a long wooden spear slammed into its flank and sank deep. There was a thunderous crash as the beast hit the ground. It roared in fury and pain from the unexpected assault.

Blacknail stood there and watched uncomprehendingly. He twitched slightly but didn't otherwise move. He had no idea what was going on.

With tremendous force, the huge spear was driven deeper into the troll. There was a snapping sound as it pierced right through the green predator and sank into the ground, pinning it there. The troll roared and thrashed, but it was held fast. Four arms held the long spear in place. Each of them was much larger than those of a human. They were also covered in bark. Blacknail had been saved by what looked like a mimic.

A closer look revealed more details. The creature with the spear was undeniably similar to a mimic but also quite different. It had the same shell-like armor that looked like bark, but its tall body was much bulkier and had fewer growths with leaves protruding from its back. The biggest difference was the face. Instead of eye stalks, it had a head that looked almost like a human wearing a polished wooden mask. Its dark eyes shone with intelligence instead of the dumb blackness that filled those of a mimic.

The creature was silent as it held down the troll. No matter how much the troll thrashed and howled, it couldn't get free or reach its attacker. After a few moments, it slowed and eventually went completely still. It was dead.

Nothing happened for a moment. Blacknail watched silently. He didn't want to attract the attention of anything that killed trolls. That would be stupid.

With a quiet creaking noise, the tree-like creature turned to look at Blacknail. The hobgoblin cringed and reluctantly met its gaze. The thing was very tall, and it had a big spear. However, the strange creature simply looked curious as it studied Blacknail. At least, it didn't seem hostile, but it was hard to tell since its face resembled a solid slab of wood.

There was a soft muttering noise from behind Blacknail. He cringed again and glanced over his shoulder. What was it now? Another troll? Hadn't things gotten crazy enough?

Another creature stood behind the hobgoblin. It sort of resembled the spear-holder, but it was much smaller and only had two arms. Like the other, it had a carapace that resembled bark, but pale green flesh was visible in the joints.

Blacknail felt his jaws go slack with surprise. The second creature resembled a human! In particular, it looked like a woman wearing oddly-shaped wooden armor. Instead of hair, a mass of long vine-like tendrils grew from the back of its head. It even had breast-like bumps under its chest carapace!

The female tree monster met Blacknail's gaze. Her face was serene and revealed nothing. The hobgoblin felt as if someone had shaken him until he couldn't stand straight, but he stayed on his feet as the creature opened her mouth and incomprehensible words spilled from between her weirdly human lips. Blacknail stared at her blankly. Her voice was soft and melodic, but he had no idea what she was trying to say. It sounded nothing like the words of humans or goblins. He hoped this wasn't a test.

When Blacknail didn't reply, she turned to her much larger companion and said a few more strange words. He answered in a deeper voice that echoed like sound through a hollow log. When they were done talking, she walked over to the spear-wielder, and he picked up the now dead troll. Together, the pair walked off into the forest.

Blacknail let them go. He wasn't going to question what had just happened. If trees wanted to come alive and save his life, then that was fine with him. Also, he was still so shocked that he'd forgotten how to move. What were those things? Saeter had never mentioned anything like them, and they seemed important!

After a few moments had passed, Blacknail shook himself free of his paralysis. He was glad that he had already repacked his bag and gear before the troll had shown up. It was time to get the hells out of there and meet back up with the others. He would be safer among his human meat shields.

Without a word, the hobgoblin dashed onto the trail. He moved as quickly as his legs would carry him, and he didn't look back. It was getting very dark now. Dusk had passed and the sun was well past the horizon. Even Blacknail's hobgoblin eyes were having trouble seeing through the gloom of night.

The only sound that reverberated through the forest as Blacknail scrambled down the trail was his own heavy breathing and frantic footsteps. That didn't reassure him much. He hadn't heard the strange tree creatures approach at all, and they had been near silent when they left. He simply had to hope they weren't following him or that he could outrun them.

After a few long minutes of running, and almost tripping over unseen stones or branches a few times, Blacknail saw a familiar rock ahead. It was taller than him, and its grey bulk jutted out from the ground beside the path. It was the marker he was looking for. Off the path, the darkness of the forest was almost impenetrable, but Blacknail stepped into it. This was the way to the campsite where he had sent the others.

A lot had happened today. Blacknail had fought a battle, lost comrades, hiked through the forest, gotten into another fight, and seen things he didn't understand. He was too tired and sore to even process it all.

Even if it was too dark now to see footprints or other signs, Blacknail could still follow his comrades' scent. The campsite was just up ahead, and Blacknail would be very angry if there wasn't a hot meal waiting for him. They had no excuses. The hobgoblin didn't care if half of them had fallen into a sink hole or been mangled by a giant boar. None of his human tribesmen could navigate through the forest or help all that much in a fight, so they had better at least have set up a half-decent campsite. If they hadn't, Blacknail was going to give them such a kicking in the morning.

Blacknail stepped out of the forest. Moonlight shone upon the ground in front of him, and up ahead, a rocky hill ended at the base of a cliff. A small fire burned atop the hill, and it cast a host of shadows against the backdrop of the cliff.

The hobgoblin had found the rest of his party. He raised a finger to his lips and whistled shrilly in a way that imitated the call of a particular bird. He didn't want to startle anyone by sneaking up on them unannounced. They might overreact, then he would have to hurt them.

There was no response, so after a few seconds, Blacknail whistled again impatiently. What were they doing? Were the lazy pink fools even listening?

This time he did get a reply. It didn't sound anything like the signal though. It sounded more like a frog being strangled than any sort of bird call. Still, it was close enough. Blacknail grunted in annoyance as he made his way over to light.

The hobgoblin saw a pair of figures near the fire watching him as he climbed the rocky hill. Saeter had used this spot as a campsite because the open ground around the hill and the cliff behind it made it almost impossible to approach without being seen.

When he got closer, Blacknail recognized one of the humans as Geralhd. The thin young man was standing with his back to the fire. The other bandit beside him wasn't important.

"You're back! I was afraid something had happened to you," Geralhd announced happily when Blacknail was close enough to see by firelight.

"Is there hot food?" Blacknail asked before yawning. He wanted to eat and get some sleep, not deal with idiots.

He looked past Geralhd at the dark shapes stretched out around campfire. Most of the bandits were already asleep. One smaller outline obviously belonged to Khita, and she was gently snoring. Blacknail was glad he didn't have to deal with her obnoxious personality right now.

"There's some stew. It's barely palatable though. We only had one pot and none of us had time to get proper rations, so we just threw in whatever we had," Geralhd explained as he pointed at a small iron pot that had been set on a stone beside the campfire.

"Fine," Blacknail grumbled as he walked over to it.

The stew didn't smell good, like boiled dried meat and grass. Although that wasn't surprising, since that was probably what it actually was. Blacknail picked up the pot, sat on the rock, and slurped down the stew.

As he ate, Geralhd continued talking. "There was a small cache of firewood under an overhang where it would stay dry, and we gathered a bit more from the forest before it got dark, but we will have to conserve it carefully if we want to keep the fire going all night."

Blacknail just kept eating. None of that sounded important. As soon as he was done eating, he planned on finding a spot next to the cliff, where it was safest, and curling up to sleep.

"Um, when you doubled back to check for pursuit, what did you find?" Geralhd asked.

Blacknail finally looked at him and blinked a few times as he sorted through events in his mind. He had no idea how to answer in a way that was truthful and which wouldn't invite a million more annoying questions, so he lied. "I didn't find anything worth talking about."

"So then… what was all the screaming we heard?" Geralhd asked.

Blacknail stared at the thin bandit for a second, then his gaze shifted to the man's tiny pink ears. Humans had such terrible hearing that the hobgoblin had assumed they hadn't heard anything.

"But then I ran into some of Werrick's men and killed them," Blacknail explained reluctantly. "You don't need to worry about them. We're safe now."

"And the bestial roars?" Geralhd asked.

"I stepped on a pinecone. It really hurt," Blacknail replied deadpan.

That answer clearly didn't satisfy Geralhd, but there was no way the hobgoblin was going to admit to even seeing a troll. It would bring up too many other questions he didn't want to answer, and the humans didn't need more reasons to be afraid and useless.

Blacknail told the man he was going to sleep. Reluctantly, Geralhd left the hobgoblin alone and went back to take his turn on watch. When he was gone, Blacknail found an empty spot and unpacked his blanket. The familiar softness of the cloth comforted and relaxed him. He yawned as he spread it over the hard ground then lay down. It smelled like home.

The stars shone brightly in the clear sky, but a lot of them weren't visible. The shadowy cliff loomed to one side, and a wall of trees rose on the other. It was almost like Blacknail was looking up from the bottom of a deep pit or well. The only sound to be heard was quiet human snoring and a faint rustling off in the forest somewhere. Blacknail stared at the stars as his body relaxed. However, for some reason, one corner of his mind couldn't let go of consciousness. It wasn't a problem he'd ever had before.

He was… troubled. He couldn't stop wondering about the future and thinking about the past. Blacknail was used to living in the present, so this feeling bothered him. It was like the illusion of the pit that surrounded him was real, instead of just in his mind. He had fallen into darkness. What did he do now that he had no master? What did he do without Saeter?

The howl of wolves echoed from off in the distance. Their sound was faint, even to his amazing ears, but easily recognizable. Blacknail listened, and a wave of memories washed over him. Saeter had found the sound beautiful. He had said it was the sound of the North. Blacknail didn't feel the same way. However, the howling reminded him of how vast the Green was and of all the strange things that lived within in it.

Wolves were just dogs though, and they were associated with his enemy. One day, Werrick would die at his hands. The hobgoblin focused on that thought until he drifted off to sleep.

Chapter 21

The early morning twitter of cheerful birds filled the air. Blacknail was repacking his bag and preparing to hike again, while contemplating the best way to murder as many of the birds as possible. All around him, the other remnants of Herad's band were getting ready to move as well. When one was being hunted by a hostile army, it was important to rise early and keep moving.

Over a quick breakfast, the bandits had decided to keep following the trail they were on as it paralleled the road north. They didn't have a lot of options. Heading back would be suicide, and there was nothing for them to the South. Most of them were wanted men, and the others didn't have the papers necessary to avoid being press-ganged into the army.

The plan was to use the trails for a few more days then slip back onto the main road. The forest path kept them hidden, but it was also less direct, so they moved much slower. Also, it made running into monsters more likely, which was bad.

The road would take them all the way to Daggerpoint. Once safely there, they would disband, disappear, and hopefully join up with other bands. Most bandit chieftains didn't ask their new recruits too many questions, and Werrick had no reason to put much effort into chasing down a few ragged and powerless survivors.

This plan didn't sit well with Blacknail, but he couldn't argue against it. It was frustrating, but he had no idea what he should do now. Would another tribe of humans take him in? Did he even want to join up with anyone else?

Well, if he didn't find a new tribe to join, he could always do what he'd done the last time he had gone to Daggerpoint. Living on the streets, stealing food, and killing people for fun and profit hadn't been so bad. A hobgoblin could do much worse.

Blacknail's idle thoughts were interrupted by Geralhd walking over. The man seemed to be muttering to himself. All morning, the thin bandit had been looking sickly and depressed. What a loser.

"Ah, Blacknail. How are you doing?" he asked. "We face a cruel new dawn today."

"I've been better," Blacknail replied as he eyed the young man critically. Did he want something?

"Those are my general feelings as well… I woke up expecting Vorscha to be lying next to me, then I realized that her presence would be ever denied me now," Geralhd mused sorrowfully.

That wasn't something Blacknail wanted to hear, or think, about. It brought to mind his own recent losses, among other things. No, he couldn't think about Saeter. Discipline, that was the key. Blacknail slipped on a vague smile, clenched his fists, and focused on doing sword drills in his head. He was used to using mental exercises to drive away bad thoughts.

"You should be getting ready to move," the hobgoblin pointed out as neutrally as he could.

"You're right, but I just felt like talking to someone, and no one else here seems like much of a listener," Geralhd admitted.

Blacknail wasn't sure why the quality of his hearing mattered. He was confused for a second, and his hesitation allowed Geralhd to keep talking uninterrupted.

"We had a complex relationship based on mutual self-interest, but I'm going to miss her deeply. She deserved better…"

Blacknail didn't care. Hopefully when they started moving, Geralhd would grow too tired to keep talking. Having conversations about your feelings was dumb. If you were happy, you should continue doing the things that made you happy, and if you were mad, then you should stab the person who had made you upset. That was the system that had always worked for Blacknail.

Admittedly, sadness was proving a little more complicated, but stabbing someone still seemed like a promising solution. It probably just had to be the right person, and if Geralhd didn't shut up, it might be him.

"Even Scamp looks melancholy." Geralhd pointed toward where the goblin was sitting. "He's probably missing Varhs. It's all rather distressing."

The motion drew Blacknail's attention to where the goblin was sitting on a rock. The little menace was wearing his usual shorts and had a large knapsack on his back. Blacknail immediately noticed one huge problem though.

"That's not Scamp," the hobgoblin observed warily.

"What?" Geralhd replied as Blacknail stalked over to the goblin.

It only took Blacknail a few moments to recognize the pale-skinned little creature with black hair. It was definitely Mahedium's pet, but what was it doing here?

The goblin calmly met Blacknail's suspicious gaze as the hobgoblin stomped his way. The relaxed look on its face annoyed Blacknail. How dare the little creep come into the hobgoblin's camp without asking permission or offering tribute!

"What are you doing here?" Blacknail asked as he snarled down at the goblin.

"Following you, great one," the creature replied politely.

His response startled Blacknail and threw him off track. He hadn't even known the goblin could talk! Still, it was being properly respectful at least.

"Where did you learn human speak?" he inquired in shock.

"I listen to people and talk to Scamp," the goblin answered.

That made sense… but it was also deeply suspicious! Blacknail didn't like the idea of the little goblin sitting in a dark corner while secretly listening to everything everyone said.

Worse, he had gone out of his way to learn things. On purpose. What kind of goblin did that? Learning was something you should only do when you had no other choice!

"Where is Scamp?" Geralhd asked as he walked up beside Blacknail. "Nothing happened to him, right?"

"Over there," the goblin replied as he pointed toward the forest.

Sure enough, a small green figure could be seen walking along the tree line. The goblin appeared to be rooting through the underbrush for bugs or other sources of food. That was normal behavior for Scamp, but there was something very odd about Mahedium's goblin, and Blacknail intended to put him in his place. He was the hobgoblin here, and this goblin was too arrogant.

"Fine, but what's in the sack?" Blacknail asked as he smiled smugly and nodded toward the bag on the goblin's back.

Something flickered behind the goblin's eyes for a second before he responded, like an incredibly fast thought. "I take shinies from Mahedium. You can have if you want, very tall stabber of humans, but it heavy."

Blacknail scowled in disappointment as he flipped open the sack and peered inside. He hadn't expected the goblin to offer him the bag. That took the fun out of taking it from him. However, he did like the titles the goblin was giving him. Blacknail knew his height was perfect for a hobgoblin.

"That certainly looks like equipment and materials from Mahedium's lab," Geralhd added as he leaned over Blacknail's shoulder. "The little goblin must have grabbed whatever caught his eye before fleeing the fire and following your scent. He must have thought it would be safer to follow a hobgoblin, since you're one of his kind."

Blacknail grunted in agreement. The bag was stuffed full of items that looked as if they had come from the mage's cabin. However, none of the junk at the top was all that interesting or useful during a long hike, and Blacknail didn't want to dig deeper in case something exploded.

"You can keep it," the hobgoblin announced as his scowl deepened.

Although it rang true, Geralhd's explanation didn't completely satisfy Blacknail. There was something off about this goblin and the way it acted. However, if the goblin wanted to drag heavy junk through the forest for who knows how long, then Blacknail wasn't going to stop him.

"Thanks, wise master," the goblin responded as he nodded respectfully.

"He needs a name. What should we call him?" Geralhd interjected happily.

What was this now? For some reason, the bandit's mood had picked up. Blacknail and the goblin turned toward Geralhd with confused expressions.

"Our new compatriot needs a name, like yours and Scamp's," the young man explained. "He doesn't have one yet, right?"

"Nope," the goblin confirmed as he sat there with an indecipherable expression.

After thinking it over for a few seconds, Blacknail realized that Geralhd was right. Naming the goblin would be useful. Unfortunately, the hobgoblin didn't really care all that much and no good names sprang to mind.

"I'll just call him Gob," Blacknail announced.

This name didn't appear to please anyone else. Geralhd winced as if in pain, and the goblin vigorously shook his head in denial.

"How about Imp, after the demon that punishes the arrogant who turn away from the gods?" Geralhd suggested.

As if a goblin needed a fancy name like that! Well, it didn't matter. Blacknail didn't feel like arguing about something so stupid, and at least it was short and easy to say.

"Whatever," he said before snorting and turning away.

Soon, everyone was ready to get going. With Blacknail leading the way, the surviving bandits entered the forest and made their way back to the path. As time went by, hiking grew monotonous. The trail was rough and narrow, so the going was difficult and tiring. Several of the humans talked quietly amongst themselves to pass the time, and their conversation drew Blacknail's interest.

"So the hobgoblin is our scout, but who is our leader? We should really have one in case we need someone to take charge in an emergency," a bandit pointed out.

Blacknail's ears perked up as he focused on the man's words. That was a good question! He had been too busy fighting and working to consider the fact that their group was currently leaderless. They obviously needed a chieftain, and it should obviously be him!

"I should be the new leader," Blacknail suggested as he came to a sudden stop and turned around.

There was silence as everyone stopped and considered this. For some reason, only he seemed to think it was good idea.

"Er, how do you figure?" a male bandit asked with surprise and doubt plain in his voice.

Blacknail's smile grew stiff as he let a small part of the vast ocean of cold rage he was suppressing show itself. "I'm the strongest and smartest person here. For example, I could kill you all or just leave you all to die in the forest. How could it be anyone else but me?"

"The person part is arguable," a blond bandit muttered.

Coolly, Blacknail turned and met the man's eyes.

"But he's still got my vote!" the man quickly added as he flinched.

"Blacknail should totally be the new boss!" Khita exclaimed with genuine excitement, but everyone ignored her.

"I'm not following a hobgoblin!" another man interjected.

"Just leave it," a woman told him. "What are you going to do? Fight him? That's not going to make anyone here think you're smart. We do need him more than he needs us."

As Blacknail watched and listened, the humans took several seconds to talk among themselves.

Surprisingly, it was Geralhd who took charge. “It’s not like we have any other plan but to follow him anyway. Why shouldn’t he be in charge?”

“Well, I’m not going to be the one to tell the murderous hobgoblin Slosher that he can’t be the leader,” a bearded bandit added.

“Er, can he even do the job? He’s undoubtedly a great fighter, but it takes more than that to lead,” someone else replied as he threw Blacknail a nervous look.

“I have a plan there,” Geralhd whispered conspiratorially before turning back to the hobgoblin. “We’ve agreed that you’re the best choice for leader, Blacknail.”

“Good,” Blacknail huffed impatiently. Had there ever been any doubt? Despite his sour mood, the hobgoblin felt a spark of cheerful pride worm its way into his heart. He was the leader! That meant he was better than everyone else and that they all knew it.

Geralhd coughed politely. “We also want to elect a sub-leader, in case you are too busy… doing important things… to take charge. You know, just in case.”

That made sense. Blacknail nodded, and the humans talked among themselves. Having a sub-leader would mean less work for him, and a real leader already did next to no work. This was going to be great!

“You seem to be the hobgoblin whisperer here, so it may as well be you,” the woman from earlier suggested to Geralhd.

After a brief but intense conversation, everyone else agreed. Some people looked angry and disappointed, but they didn’t argue. They were probably just jealous of Blacknail’s undeniable leadership skills.

“All right, that’s all settled then,” Geralhd concluded.

As everyone waited, Blacknail took a moment to plan his first move as the leader. He scanned the nearby people for a familiar face. Ah, there was Elyias! The young bandit was way at the back and Blacknail had almost forgotten he existed. How silly of him.

"Since I'm the leader, I shouldn't carry my own bags," Blacknail announced before pointing at Elyias. "You should take them."

"What? That's not fair!" the young man said in shock.

Elyias had been keeping to himself at the back of the party, but now he looked to the others for support. No one cared. They shrugged or even glared at him for trying to drag them into his problem.

"Just do it," the man next to him said mercilessly.

"Also, if you drop anything or steal from me, I'll kill you," Blacknail added as he passed the young man his bags.

"Damnation," Elyias swore as he took them. "How did I end up here?"

Free of the weight of his knapsacks, Blacknail's shoulders felt much looser. He nodded in approval as he rolled his shoulders and started leading his loyal tribe through the forest. He was the leader!

Travel was slow and uneventful over the next few days. They hiked through the day and took shelter during the night. Their movement through the forest was slow since they had little in the way of supplies and they had to forage for food. Luckily, Blacknail knew where to find edible plants. Saeter had taught him quite a lot, and he had a very good nose. The Green was dangerous, but also bountiful if you knew its ways. In the spring, quite a few young plant shoots could be eaten raw. Scamp and Imp were also skilled at gathering delicious bugs. They easily found more than they could eat and shared the rest with the humans. However, for some reason, the humans complained about the food. They were very spoiled.

"Would it be possible to find some real meat?" Geralhd eventually asked Blacknail.

Geralhd had just come from a brief huddle with most the other humans. They had thinned out a little and their eyes shone with hunger. Blacknail thought it was a good look on them. It made them more hobgoblin-like, and the loss of fat would allow them to run faster.

"Sure, it's out there," Blacknail replied as he pointed toward the forest.

"Er, I meant could you go get it? You're the best hunter here. The only hunter really," Geralhd clarified.

"You wanted to move quickly. Hunting takes time."

"We also need real food. Most of us are out of rations."

Blacknail considered that for a few moments. He didn't want to do it. However, since he was such a great leader, he would. "Fine, we'll stop early tonight and I'll set up some traps, which I'll empty in the morning."

That was good enough for Geralhd and the others. They continued hiking until it began to grow dark, then they set up camp. While the others foraged for plants, Blacknail sniffed out some rabbit trails and set up snares. That next morning, he checked them and found three rabbits. The excited humans turned them into a breakfast stew. Over the next few days of traveling, they kept up this pattern, even if it did slow them down.

Eventually, the trail they were on ended at the top of a cliff. Below them, they saw an expanse of trees and a wide roaring river. The river stretched down from a far-off mountain range and cut across the landscape. There was only one way to cross it, which meant they had to make their way back to the main road. Herad had destroyed the original bridge there, but it looked as though Werrick had repaired it. From atop the cliff, they could see it.

Some of the bandits thought it would be too risky to head back to the road. That was an obvious spot for an ambush. Blacknail explained that they had no choice. He knew of no other crossing, and trying to find one would be incredibly risky. Nervously, the harried group of survivors crept through the forest and back toward the main road. Blacknail led the way down the slope and through the trees. He moved carefully and kept his eyes open, just in case enemies were nearby. However, when Blacknail stepped out of the forest and under the sun, nothing happened. There was no ambush waiting for them on this side of the river. It was almost a disappointment. The rage within Blacknail hadn't died down, and it had been a while since he'd had a chance to kill some of the humans responsible for his loss.

"Maybe they don't care about us?" Geralhd remarked in relief. "I mean, why would they? With Herad dead, we're no threat to Werrick."

There was a chorus of agreements from the others, but Blacknail wasn't so sure. Why send rangers after them at all then? He intended to keep his eyes open. Cautiously, the hobgoblin made his way to the bridge. It was a slim, rickety-looking thing, but it was still much better than trying to swim. This early in the spring, the river was wide and its current was moving rapidly. Splashes of white water were constantly hitting the rocky banks.

After glancing across the river at the winding road and distant tree line for any sign of ambushers, and not seeing any, Blacknail crossed the bridge. The wooden planks creaked as he moved, and he was soon joined by the rest of his group.

They made it to the other side without anything dramatic or unexpected happening. Blacknail glanced back in the direction they had come before leading his party down the road. The mood of the group quickly picked up. Unlike on the forest trail, moving on the road was easy going and the trees weren't so oppressively close. Without branches hanging overhead and greenery blocking their sight, everyone felt much safer.

"We'll get to Daggerpoint within a few days at this rate!" someone cheered.

"If Werrick was chasing us, he would have guarded the bridge. That means we're in the clear!" another woman added happily.

"I'm just glad we don't have to walk through any more mud. I think my boot has sprung a leak," Khita announced.

Several other bandits joined in the celebration. Most of them seemed to believe that they had escaped their pursuers. However, Blacknail frowned, and Geralhd noticed his expression.

"What are you thinking about, Blacknail?" he asked.

"I don't think we are safe. I think they might think that we have a secret sneaky way across the river; this is our territory. That means they would ambush us anywhere but at the bridge," the hobgoblin explained.

"That's a little paranoid," one bandit suggested.

"Did that even make sense?" another asked.

There were murmurs of agreement from most of the humans, and that annoyed the hobgoblin more than a little. He turned to glare at them. He was the boss! How dare they question him!

"Shut up. You're all being too noisy. I'm the leader and I say be quiet," Blacknail ordered.

"Ya, he's the leader," Khita added.

Ignoring the annoying redhead, the hobgoblin's hand inched toward his sword hilt. If anyone challenged him, then he might have to make an example of one or two of them. It was important to keep minions in line.

"We should do as he says," Geralhd interjected. "There's no reason to attract unwanted attention."

There were nods of reluctant acknowledgment, and Blacknail let his hand fall away from his sword hilt. He snorted before turning back around. They still had a long journey ahead before they reached Daggerpoint, and anything could happen in the wilds. One thing was for sure though—Blacknail was going to have to muster all his considerable intelligence and natural leadership skills to get them there safely.

Chapter 22

Blacknail and his new subordinates made good time on the road before they had to stop for the night. The last time the hobgoblin had come this way, he'd stumbled upon a hidden cave the size of a small room. It had served as shelter from the elements and a hideaway, so he led the bandits to it.

As his minions were setting up camp inside the cave, and doing all the unimportant not-leader things, Blacknail went out to put up snares. It had become a nightly ritual, and his human followers depended on the food he caught. They were completely useless without him.

Once finished, the hobgoblin foraged for edible shoots and leaves. Several of his followers had already been through this area in their own search for food, but Blacknail had neglected to tell them that red cress leaves were edible. In fact, they were the tastiest treat around, which was why he hadn't told anyone about them. More for him!

When he got back to the cave, Geralhd was there to welcome him. Most the other bandits were seated around the cave and resting. Days of hiking had worn them down and given them more than a few aches. Most the bandits had bedrolls or blankets of some sort, even if they didn't have much more than that. Before fleeing the battle, they had grabbed what they could.

"It's a good thing you led us here. It looks like it might rain overnight, and we didn't find much in the way of firewood," Geralhd told the hobgoblin. "We're going to have to go most of the night without light, so I'm glad we're not out in the forest."

Blacknail nodded. He didn't really care, but that sounded like something important people talked about, and he was definitely important. "Of course, I'm the leader. I know of many secret hiding places, because I'm amazing."

After their brief conversation was over, Geralhd went to see if there was anything else that needed doing, and Blacknail let him. The humans could take care of themselves probably. In any case, most of them were expendable, so it didn't matter.

It quickly grew too dark to see outside. Even the inside of the cave was barely lit by a small flickering fire. As the leader, Blacknail didn't need to take a turn on watch, so he found somewhere comfortable to curl up and quickly fell asleep.

When he rose early the next morning, the hobgoblin yawned and started waking up everyone else. Several of the lazy humans tried to sleep in, but Blacknail didn't let them. They had things to do and a horde of murderous pursuers to evade.

"Ah, let me sleep just a little more!" Khita whined as she rolled over on her sleeping roll.

"No, I'm the leader. Get up!" Blacknail told her as he kicked her in the back.

"Ow, stop that!" the redhead snapped.

"No, I'm the leader. Get up!" Blacknail repeated as he kicked her again. He was enjoying this aspect of leadership quite a bit. Not only was physical discipline fun, but it was for their own good.

"Argh, fine! I'm getting you back for this later though," Khita growled as she sat up and turned to glare at him.

"You can't get back at me, I'm the leader," the hobgoblin explained. Didn't she know anything?

"We'll see about that," Khita responded as she got up and rolled up her blanket.

Blacknail left her and went to get the next lazy human moving. It only took one kick to wake Elyias. However, the still-drowsy young man took one look at the hobgoblin's face and yelped in terror. A second kick to the stomach shut him up. Minions were so funny.

After a quick breakfast, they were back on the road. Once the sun rose past the horizon, it became a bright day with little in the way of clouds. The bandits continued on their trek North for several hours. They saw no sign of pursuers, although a small flock of screeching harpies flew overhead at one point. However, they were long gone before Blacknail could string his bow and try to shoot one down. His minions were always complaining about being hungry, and a harpy had a fair bit of meat on it.

As he was walking, Blacknail tried to focus on his latest problem. The top of his head was itchy because his horns were growing. They were still only a pair of small bony nubs, but they were definitely getting bigger. It was annoying. All hobgoblins had horns—or at least Blacknail thought they did—but he kept his filed down so that they didn't get in the way of wearing hats and stuff. Unfortunately, Blacknail had forgotten his file, so he couldn't get rid of them. Even worse, none of his human minions had a file either. Blacknail had asked them, and then gone through their bags while they were sleeping, just to be sure they weren't holding out on him, but he still hadn't found one.

While Blacknail was scratching his scalp, an uneasy feeling came over him. It started with an itchy sensation like someone was watching him from out of sight, then his gut twisted slightly to the left. Since he hadn't recently eaten any strange mushrooms, that meant something else was wrong.

The hobgoblin stopped and scanned the tree line on both sides of the road. He didn't see anything, but the feeling didn't disappear, so he raised a hand and signaled for everyone to stop. Immediately, a surprised man walked right into Blacknail's back. The man apologized and backed off, but Blacknail was still annoyed. Most of the humans had completely ignored his signal and were still walking!

"When I have my hand up like this, it means you're supposed to stop!" an infuriated Blacknail explained as he tried to stare down everyone.

"Oh, sorry," the bandit right behind the hobgoblin replied nervously.

Everyone slowly came to an uneasy standstill as Blacknail glared at them. Who had trained these humans? They were terrible at everything! They must have been raised by awful masters.

Grumbling to himself, the hobgoblin turned back to the road up ahead and listened carefully. A branch snapped and birds sang, but he didn't hear anything too out of place or which explained his uneasy feeling.

"What is it?" Geralhd asked.

"Your great leader is not sure," Blacknail replied.

"We have a great leader?" someone muttered.

"It's probably nothing. The hobgoblin is just being paranoid again," a bearded bandit remarked.

"Really, you're going to question his instincts? Do you think your senses are better than his?" Geralhd countered with a voice full of ire.

The bearded man didn't reply. Everyone else was quiet as they waited for their hobgoblin leader to do or say something. After a few seconds of silence, Blacknail tilted his head back and sniffed the air. He smelled nothing unusual, so he walked forward. Once he had moved a few dozen feet ahead, the distracting scent of his stinky human followers disappeared. Blacknail sniffed the air again then crouched to press his nose against the dirt. He inhaled the scent of the road for a few seconds as he crawled around in a small circle.

"What is he doing?" someone inquired.

"Er, did you catch a scent?" Geralhd asked when the hobgoblin stood.

"Your glorious leader has found something important!" Blacknail replied as he brushed himself off.

"What?" Khita grumbled. The young redhead sounded tired and irritable. It was probably because she wasted so much energy being annoying. She should try to sleep a little more instead of talking so much.

"I found humans!" Blacknail announced gravely.

All the bandits glanced at each other. They frowned in confusion, and more than a few of them rolled their eyes.

"Er, we know we're humans…" Geralhd remarked.

"No, stupid minions, I mean different humans," Blacknail countered. "A large group of people was here less than an hour ago."

The bandits took several seconds to consider this, then they all tried to speak up at the same time.

"Damnation, that could mean anything!" someone said.

"What do we do?" a woman asked her fellows. "It's probably Werrick's men!"

"We need to know more before we do anything," the first person replied.

Before the humans could get too loud and waste his time, Blacknail shushed them. They all fell silent at the tone of his voice—and at the sound of his sword leaving its sheath.

"I'm the leader, so I decide what we do!" he told them as he brandished the blade.

"And what's that?" the woman asked.

The other bandits also seemed nervous and unsure of themselves. Luckily, they had a leader to tell them what to do! Blacknail considered his options before replying. Completely on his own, he concluded that he needed to know more before he could decide.

"You all stay here and try not to die. I'm going to look around," he ordered his minions.

There were murmurs of disagreement, but Blacknail ignored them. As the leader, his was the only opinion that mattered.

"I'll come with you!" Khita offered.

"No. If she tries to follow me, then stab her," Blacknail ordered Geralhd as he turned away from his followers.

"Er, sure," the thin man replied uncertainly.

"I'll do it for you, if you want," a bearded bandit offered.

Blacknail ignored them and headed for the edge of the forest. No one followed him as he slipped into the shadows cast by the branches overhead. Stealthily, the hobgoblin slipped around trees and bushes. All his senses were alert as he searched for signs of any watchers. When he didn't see anyone, he paralleled the road.

It was only after several minutes of walking that he detected someone. As Blacknail was climbing over an old rotting log, a rustling sound drew his eyes toward a tree next to the road. There was a black-haired man crouching in the shadows, where he couldn't be seen from the road but where he could still observe anyone approaching. Blacknail recognized him as a sentry. His gear was also too similar to what Werrick's men wore for it to be a coincidence.

Blacknail crept closer to get a better look. He circled around a thick green bush and hid behind the base of a particularly wide tree. Once there, he spotted a dozen other concealed humans near the road, and there were undoubtedly more that he couldn't see.

This was an ambush. Werrick's men were lying in wait, ready to pounce on Blacknail's party if they went down the road. They obviously knew that the survivors from Herad's band were nearby or they wouldn't be waiting like this. That meant Blacknail didn't have much time. It didn't look as if the first sentry Blacknail had seen was visible to any of the other ambushers. The hobgoblin weighed his options. It was best to retreat as quickly as possible, and killing the sentry might alert someone. However, on the other hand, he *really* enjoyed murdering people, and he was ever so angry at these human vermin.

Blacknail licked his lips as a shiver of bloodlust went up his spine. He was going to do it. He couldn't help himself.

Quickly, the hobgoblin slipped out from behind the tree and closed in on the man. Blacknail was absolutely silent as he glided up behind the bandit and drew a dagger. Once close enough, Blacknail lunged forward, cut the man's throat, then stabbed him under his ribs. The man barely had time to shiver and gasp before he bled to death in Blacknail's arms.

To avoid suspicion, Blacknail leaned the corpse against a tree in as natural a position as he could, then he hurried back the way he had come. The kill had barely sated his rage at all, but it would have to do for now. Soon, the enemy would realize that Blacknail's party wasn't going to walk into their ambush and they would give chase. The hobgoblin planned on not being around when that happened.

There was a small commotion when Blacknail stepped out of the bushes at the edge of the road. All his companions looked his way and started talking at once. Blacknail noticed that Khita was seated on the ground and sulking. The bearded bandit from before was standing behind her with a hand on his sword hilt.

The hobgoblin huffed in annoyance and signaled for Geralhd to speak. He was the sub-leader after all.

"You're back, Blacknail. What did you find?" the thin bandit asked nervously.

Blacknail filled everyone in. If they had been nervous before, they grew terrified as the hobgoblin told them what he had seen. By this point, their reaction didn't surprise the hobgoblin. Had every coward in Herad's band somehow made their way into this group? The only person who didn't look afraid was Khita, and that was because she was too dumb to feel proper emotions.

Before anyone could ask Blacknail the predictable and stupid questions he was always asked at time like this, the hobgoblin growled and stared everyone down. Then when he had their undivided attention, he explained his plan. It was a good plan.

"We're going to run away," he told them all.

"I think we should take their ambush from behind!" Khita suggested. "They're scum, and we'll easily cut them to pieces!"

"Shut up, nobody asked you," Blacknail replied.

"Where can we go?" the blond woman asked fearfully. "We can't go forward into the ambush, and there is nothing behind us but enemies!"

"We're already almost out of food! We can't afford a detour," another bandit added.

Their reactions annoyed Blacknail. It wasn't a minion's place to question the boss. "Shut up! I'm the leader, and I say we're running, so let's go."

The hobgoblin's angry tone made several people step away from him. They eyed each other nervously, but none of them moved.

"Let's go!" Blacknail repeated furiously. Why weren't they moving?

"Um, where are we running to? You haven't told us yet," Geralhd pointed out.

Oh, right. "We're going into the forest. I'll lead us around the ambush."

"Can you do that?" someone asked.

"Yes, easily," Blacknail replied. He wouldn't have any problem going around the ambush. It was everyone else who would have difficulty. They weren't nearly as sneaky as he was, and they were dumb. Half of them would probably fall into a hole or something. The same hole. All at once.

"I guess we don't have much of a choice," Geralhd admitted. "Every other option is worse."

"You really don't; I'm the leader."

The hobgoblin then got everyone moving. They didn't have much time, so he herded them toward the forest. Once they were all off the road, Blacknail took the lead again. No one spoke as they hiked through the woods. With all the overhanging branches and bushes nearby, everyone was afraid of being overheard by someone out of sight. Only Blacknail had any idea in which direction the enemy lay.

They had just walked into a small muddy gully when they heard shouting from back on the road. Everyone stopped and looked in that direction.

"They're on to us. Don't stand around like stupid toads! We need to move before they find our tracks or get our scent," Blacknail ordered his followers.

"They won't be able to track us by scent," Geralhd replied. "People can't do that."

"Not even if they put their noses really close to the ground and take deep breaths?" the hobgoblin asked.

"No."

"Humans are so useless," Blacknail remarked as he shook his head. "Why do you even have noses?"

No one replied, so the hobgoblin picked up his speed. Everyone struggled to follow him up the other side of the gully, but it didn't take them long to reach the top. Blacknail wanted to move at a faster pace, but some of the humans were frustratingly slow. He considered leaving them behind but decided against it for now. He could always abandon them later.

After fleeing through the forest for a bit, Blacknail heard sounds of pursuit. Someone had found their trail and was following it. The hobgoblin eyed his minions and considered his options. As he watched, one person near the back tripped over an exposed root and fell. Blacknail sighed as he quickly got back up. He was going to have to do something.

Why was it always him who had to take action? Chieftains weren't supposed to be the ones doing all the work. That was contrary to the entire point! He was obviously spoiling his minions rotten.

"We're being followed. Keep going forward and I'll deal with it," Blacknail explained as he turned and headed back.

"I'll go with you!" Khita suggested.

"No, you're slow," Blacknail replied.

"You're not letting me do anything!" she whined. "I want to fight."

Instead of replying, Blacknail turned to look meaningfully at the person behind her. It was the bearded bandit from before.

“Stab her if she tries to follow you?” the man guessed.

Blacknail nodded happily before walking away. It was possible to teach grown humans new tricks!

The rest of the survivors from Herad’s band headed deeper into the forest, and they soon were out of sight. Blacknail backtracked before spotting a hiding spot at the base of a large rock surrounded by bushes. As he moved toward it, he pulled his bow off his back and strung it. He then crouched, waiting. The enemy would be arriving soon, and the hobgoblin planned to be ready for them.

Chapter 23

It didn't take long for the sound of footsteps to reach Blacknail's pointy green ears. He listened with patient excitement as he crouched in his hiding spot between a boulder and a clump of bushes. It was almost time to attack. Soon, more of the foolish humans who had dared to take Blacknail's most precious things would be punished. That was what Blacknail desired above all else. Every second not spent killing these enemies was painful, though necessary. He'd worked on building self-discipline for too long to throw it away and get himself killed in a berserk rage now. That wasn't what his master would have wanted.

Blacknail stared out from behind a screen of leaves as three enemies walked into view. The trio was moving carefully and keeping an eye out for their quarry. At least one of them was a trained scout, because they were easily following the trail Blacknail's group had left.

All three of the men looked like Werrick's minions. They had rough, dirty armor and were armed to the teeth. Their faces were weathered and hard-looking. These were men who had seen more than their fair share of fighting and were looking for more. However, only one of them had a bow, and it wasn't strung. As he studied his prey, Blacknail heard more enemies approaching from behind. These first three men were just the enemy's vanguard.

"Have you noticed anything weird about some of the tracks?" one of the scouts asked.

"No, why?" the lead man replied as he looked at the ground.

"I, uh… I've heard that the Killer of Men might be among the group we're tracking," the first speaker admitted.

"The hobgoblin? He's just a tall tale meant to frighten townies. You don't really believe in magic talking hobgoblins, do you?" the third man interjected scornfully.

"No, of course not… I'm just telling you what I heard."

"Well, there's nothing strange about any of the signs I've seen. They all look human to me, although if the Killer of Men is wearing boots, then it might be hard to tell," the lead man joked.

All three of the enemy bandits chuckled, although the one man still looked more than a little anxious. Nearby, Blacknail joined in and cackled gleefully. It was funny because it was true.

"Um, who is that?" the nervous man asked. His eyes had gone wide with fear as soon as he realized someone else was there.

Before his companions could respond, Blacknail rose from his hiding place and shot the lead scout in the chest. There was a hollow thump as the arrow sank into flesh.As the other men jerked backward in shock, Blacknail swirled around and dashed away with startling speed. The hobgoblin used the bushes as cover and swerved behind a tree. Instead of trying to catch up with Geralhd and the others, he took off to the side.

The hobgoblin's plan was to distract and delay the enemy. He could run through the forest much faster than a bunch of clumsy humans, so he would lead them on a futile chase for a while before circling back.

Once out of sight, Blacknail couldn't help but laugh. The hunt was on! The thought sent excitement coursing through the hobgoblin, and it quickened his blood. The hobgoblin's laugh twisted into a chilling, inhuman howl. The dreadful sound echoed through the forest. Blacknail could only imagine the sweet fear it was stirring inside the hearts of the humans who thought they were chasing him. Soon, they would know how wrong they were.

After a few seconds, Blacknail grew red in the face. Unfortunately, it was hard to breathe and laugh at the same time. He had to stop and focus on running. To Blacknail's surprise, as he fell silent, an answering howl rose above the forest from off in the distance. Was it an echo, or had something answered his challenge? Well, whatever it was, it would have to wait. The angry humans chasing him were the priority.

After almost half an hour of running and stopping, the sound of his own heavy breathing filled Blacknail's ears as he grew tired. Somewhere close behind him, the enemy bandits were still in hot pursuit. That was the point though. He wanted them to chase him. He could have lost the enemy a long time ago if he had wanted to. They were only human.

Blacknail came to a stop again and looked over his shoulder. Off in the distance, he saw a small swarm of enemies running toward him through the trees. They looked sort of mad. Maybe it was because he had purposely led them through several thick clumps of thorn bushes and more than a few large mud pits?

After catching his breath, Blacknail decided that he was far enough away. It would be a bad idea to leave his minions leaderless for too long, so he should probably turn back. Who knew what trouble they would get into without him?

"Goodbye, smelly humans. Thanks for chasing me!" Blacknail yelled before dashing away.

Instead of goofing around like before, he went full-out. With startling speed, the hobgoblin ran toward his minions and left his pursuers behind. Trees zipped by as Blacknail sprinted through the forest. A small creek appeared in front of him, and he effortlessly jumped across it without slowing down. He kept up the hurried pace until he stumbled upon the first sign of his allies.

After stopping to make sure he was going in the right direction, he took off again and headed deeper into the woods. Hopefully his minions had kept going straight. He had specifically ordered them to, but then again, they were all a bunch of morons.

In front of Blacknail, the ground sloped upward and grew rockier. He had to swerve around several large grey rocks that jutted forth from the earth. Eventually, he spotted Geralhd and the others.

A rocky cliff face loomed up ahead. It was almost a hundred feet high and incredibly steep. Only a few stunted bushes grew on its face, but it was crowned by a line of trees where the forest continued up above. A single winding path ran up to the top. It looked like a difficult climb.

Geralhd and others had stopped near the base of the cliff and were arguing amongst each other. Scamp and Imp were sitting off to one side. They looked bored.

"We need to hurry up and start climbing. We have no time to waste!" Geralhd exclaimed.

"I'm not climbing that; we'd be easy targets, like frogs on a log! We should go around," a large bandit countered.

"Get climbing now!" Blacknail shouted as he jogged up behind them.

Everyone flinched and turned to look Blacknail's way. When they saw the angry look on his face, they all started moving. The hobgoblin took up the rear as they formed a line, so that he could punish any stragglers. They needed to hurry!

As they ascended, rocks were knocked loose by people's boots. The stones made a lot of noise as they rolled down the cliff. Blacknail looked down. It was already quite a ways to the ground. Falling would be bad.

Around two-thirds of the way to the top, the bandits' progress stopped. There was a break in the path that couldn't be walked over. The next section could be reached via a short climb, but only one person could do it at a time.

As Blacknail watched impatiently, Geralhd reached for a handhold and pulled himself up. Everyone else was forced to wait for him. Geralhd reached the top and Khita started climbing, but Blacknail grew frustrated by the sluggish pace. Even humans should be faster than this. They didn't have all day!

"Climb faster!" he hissed at the man in front of him.

"I can't. It's not even my turn yet," the man replied.

That statement of the obvious annoyed Blacknail. He knew that, but why did his minions have to make everything so complicated? They should just do as they were told.

Movement at the base of the incline drew the hobgoblin's attention. People were stepping out of the trees and gathering at the bottom of the cliff. There were at least three dozen of them, and they were obviously Werrick's men. Why would anyone else be out in this part of the woods?

"Slimy harpy spit," Blacknail swore.

His plan had been for his party to be on top of the cliff when the enemy showed up. That way they could just throw rocks down on anyone chasing them. The hobgoblin's lazy minions had ruined that great idea though.

Down below, a black-haired man with a goatee raised a hand and signaled toward Blacknail's location. A few seconds later, he shouted something and led a charge up the cliff path. Wait, Blacknail recognized him. It was Orvito. The man who'd killed Vorscha!

"Damnation, what do we do?" one of Blacknail's men asked.

A dozen men were still stuck on the lower part of the cliff path, and the enemy would be upon them in under a minute. There was nowhere they could escape to, and down below, three of Werrick's men held back and strung their bows.

"Don't just stand there. At least throw something at them!" Blacknail hissed as he pulled his own bow off his back.

A few of the bandits next to Blacknail leaped to obey. They grabbed large rocks from the ground and hurled them at the attackers charging up the path. It barely slowed the enemy, but it was better than nothing. Meanwhile, Blacknail had already nocked an arrow and let it loose. The projectile whirred through the air and into one of the unsuspecting archer's chests. He had been busy prepping his own weapon and hadn't even looked up.

As the wounded archer collapsed, Blacknail was already pulling another arrow from the quiver one of his minions was carrying. He nocked it and took aim again. He fired off his second shot as the enemy archers let loose. The arrows zoomed past each other through the air.

"Eep!" Blacknail yelled as he covered his head and ducked.

The ugly pink bastards had aimed at him! Their two projectiles buzzed over his head and slammed into the cliff face behind him. There was a loud cracking sound as one of them bounced off a rock and hit his leg. The impact stung, but it didn't draw blood.

Blacknail ignored the pain and glanced at the archers. The hobgoblin grinned when he saw that one of them had fallen on his ass and had an arrow sticking out of his arm. That left only one still standing, but the hobgoblin didn't have time to worry about him. He dropped his bow and drew his sword.

He was just in time. Orvito was approaching with startling speed, dashing ahead of his comrades with his blade raised above his head. Before anyone but Blacknail could react, he slashed at the bandit standing next to the hobgoblin. There was a loud metallic clang as Blacknail extended his weapon and blocked the attack. The hobgoblin's hands shook under the force of the blow, and he gritted his teeth. The man's strength and speed were too high for a normal human. He had to be a Slosher.

"Stinky troll piss," Blackail cursed as he eyed his opponent.

The man looked surprised for a second then smiled as he stepped back. His smug, taunting grin irritated Blacknail. The hobgoblin hated fighting Sloshers. In a fair fight, human swordsmen were already a pain to deal with, even when they didn't use Elixir.

"So you can talk. I hadn't thought that was true," the goateed man remarked as he raised his sword and took a defensive stance.

As he did so, the rest of the enemy fighters caught up to him. The cliff path they were standing on was only wide enough for three or four people and the footing was treacherous, so most of them held back. Only a few of them could engage the closest of Blacknail's minions.

"No, you're stupid," Blacknail replied as fighting broke out around him.

It was a terrible rebuttal, but it was the only thing that had come to mind. He was under a lot of pressure! The comment certainly didn't impress the enemy Slosher. Orvito smirked and gave the hobgoblin a condescending look. He looked as if he'd practiced it a lot.

When Blacknail hissed, Orvito attacked with a whip-like slash at his face. Blacknail was startled but managed to dodge to the side. The man attacked again, and as Blacknail blocked the blow with his own sword, he growled hatefully. Attacking while the enemy was distracted was his thing! The hobgoblin was going to enjoy killing this man. He was infuriating!

Blacknail snarled and slashed at his opponent. He wished he'd taken the time to drink some Elixir. He only had one vial left, but it wouldn't do him any good if he was dead.

The two fighters exchanged blows and maneuvered as much as their tight surroundings would allow. Neither one of them wanted to collide with the other bandits fighting nearby or to stumble and fall off the ledge. It was a long way down and the rocks looked pointy.

It soon became apparent that the goateed Slosher was stronger than Blacknail, even if their speed was almost the same. His blows were forcing the hobgoblin on the defensive, and there was nowhere to fall back to.

"Is this all you got? I'm disappointed!" the Slosher remarked as he pressed his advantage.

"Just wait. I've killed many Vessels like you," Blacknail hissed as he defended himself. This was true but ignored the fact that none of those men had been killed in fair fights, and this contest was looking to be way too even for the hobgoblin's comfort. He had to think up some way to cheat!

To Blacknail's left, one of the attackers fell off the ledge and rolled down the cliff. The man had been locked in a sword fight until he'd lost his balance. Now, he screamed as he hit jagged rocks and they tore into him.

Blacknail ducked under a slash aimed at his head and counterattacked. His blade sliced through the air toward his opponent's front foot, but the man stepped out of the way. Someone bumped into Blacknail from behind, and he was forced to take an awkward step forward to catch his balance. Orvito was quick to take advantage of this stumble. He lunged forward and slashed at Blacknail's exposed arm.

The hobgoblin could only lean clumsily out of the way, and it wasn't enough. The man's blade caught on Blacknail's sleeve and sliced through it. It cut into the flesh beneath and drew blood before coming free.

Hissing in pain, Blacknail flinched and stepped back. He forced his throbbing arm to keep a steady grip on his sword's hilt, and he raised his blade defensively again. He couldn't afford a moment of weakness. A single mistake would lead to his death.

To either side, other bandits were fighting, even if the thin pathway meant everyone was pressed tightly together. Most of Werrick's troops couldn't get near the melee. They formed several ranks as they waited for an opening. Behind Blacknail, around ten of his companions were still waiting to climb across the break in the path. Even when Blacknail's turn came, he couldn't climb while under attack. The next time anything like this happened, Blacknail was going to make sure the leader got to escape first!

"I'd heard you were a tricky fighter, but you don't seem like anything special," his opponent said condescendingly. "You're just an ugly green beast waving around a bit of metal in imitation of a person."

The man's tone made anger roar to life within Blacknail's guts. Screw escaping! He really wanted to kill this guy! He just needed an opening, a good one.

"At least I'm not pink and fat!" Blacknail hissed back.

The goateed Slosher attacked again with a flurry of strikes. Blacknail tried to slip past and get in a blow of his own, but he was forced to block an attack and was knocked back.

As he was scheming his next move, Blacknail noticed a green blur out of the corner of his eye. Both he and his opponent glanced down to see a goblin jump onto a nearby rock. It was Imp, and there was something in his hand.

"What's this?" the Slosher mumbled as he kept one eye on Blacknail.

As they watched, the goblin hurled something into the air over their heads. It was a crystal, and odd light flickered from it as it landed in the middle of the enemy's ranks.

"Oh, demon shit," Orvito remarked as he realized what he'd just seen.

Blacknail didn't bother to respond. He swirled around, crouched low, and pulled his cloak tightly about himself. The hobgoblin recognized magic when he saw it, and there was only one possible outcome of it when goblins were involved.

With a deafening boom, the crystal exploded. A wave of force washed over everyone, and a storm of dark crystal shards followed. The crystalline blades sliced into anyone in their path, and more than a dozen of Werrick's men were thrown over the ledge by the blast.

Screams filled the air as bodies fell and flesh was torn. Blood splattered against the rocks, and its tangy scent filled the air. In just over a second, the enemy formation had been smashed. Bodies littered the ground. Blacknail smiled as he climbed back to his feet.

"Ha, I always have a trick, even if I don't know about it yet," he bragged.

Smiling, Blacknail took in the sight before him. Who was laughing now? He had shown them! Imp had also helped a little.

"I always win!" The hobgoblin laughed.

However, the grin slipped from Blacknail's lips as Orvito stood back up and glared at him. What was this? The explosion hadn't done more than stun the man. That wasn't fair. Stupid magic.

The goateed man wasn't alone either; almost half the enemies on the ledge climbed to their feet. As impressive as the explosion and crystal shrapnel had been, the enemies closest to the blast had absorbed most of the damage. Blacknail's group was still outnumbered and cornered. Also, the enemy Vessel looked really mad now. Maybe Imp had another crystal?

The hobgoblin threw a look over his shoulder. Imp had taken advantage of the confusion to cut in line and climb over the break in the path. The little traitor had run away!

"What in all the burning hells was that? Never mind! You die now," the enemy Slosher spat as he leapt forward to cross swords with Blacknail again.

Chapter 24

As the fighting continued around him on the narrow path leading up the cliff, Blacknail raised his blade and lowered his center of gravity. He kept his weight balanced mostly on his back foot as the goateed Vessel lunged forward and slashed at him. There was a metallic ringing as the hobgoblin blocked the blow with a slash of his own. The impact almost knocked Blacknail over. His lips curled into a snarl as he struggled not to give ground. He had been hoping his enemy would still be too stunned to attack with his full force, but that was obviously not the case.

With a wordless cry full of determination, Orvito pressed forward. His weight and power pushed the hobgoblin back an arm's length. As Blacknail recovered, the man launched a brutal series of sword strikes from every direction. Each blow was stronger than the last and harder to stop. Blacknail's opponent was obviously burning Elixir without holding back. The clang of steel hitting steel rang out repeatedly, and Blacknail knew he was in trouble. He was fighting as hard as he could and using every ounce of power he could summon from within himself, but he couldn't keep this up. If only he'd taken the time to down some Elixir of his own!

"I'm going to carve my name in your hide!" the enemy Slosher roared.

The shout was quickly followed by a wide swing from the left that smashed Blacknail's guard aside. The hobgoblin stumbled, and Orvito raised his blade in preparation to strike again.

A cold feeling of inevitability filled Blacknail as he watched the blade descend, but then one of the hobgoblin's allies dove in from the side. The goateed man was forced to turn away from Blacknail and block the newcomer's attack.

A vicious toothy grin appeared on Blacknail's lips as he took advantage of the distraction. He stepped forward and stabbed at Orvito's exposed ribs. The enemy Slosher saw the blow coming, but instead of trying to block it, he took a deep breath and turned to look directly at Blacknail. Raw fury shone in the man's eyes as he exhaled a searing burst of red flames. The fireball shot toward Blacknail's head. Instinctively, the hobgoblin raised his arms to shield his face and fell backward. A wave of heat washed over him, and his ass hit the rocky ground with a painful thump.

Blacknail hissed in pain. His long experience with humans told him they didn't normally breathe fire. It must be a Vessel power. Why didn't he have a cool ability like that?The hobgoblin opened his eyes to see that his sleeves were on fire. Hurriedly, he smacked them against his pants until they went out.

"I hate doing that," Orvito admitted as he kicked aside Blacknail's surprised ally. "It burns far too much Elixir, and it tastes like ash."

The Slosher turned toward Blacknail and raised his sword again. That was when the hobgoblin realized he'd dropped his sword. Not good. The cliff edge to the hobgoblin's right prevented him from rolling that way, and there were people to his left and behind him.

With a victorious grin, Orvito slashed down at Blacknail. His blade cut through the air. Blacknail could only stare wide-eyed as… a rock fell from above and smashed into the man's head with a loud crack. Surprised, Blacknail blinked as the Slosher's eyes rolled up into his head until the whites showed. In slow motion, Orvito fell sideways and rolled off the ledge and out of sight.

"Huh, all right…" Blacknail said as he stared disbelievingly at the empty space his opponent had been occupying until a moment ago. He was alive. That was good.

Shaking his head, the hobgoblin looked up toward the source of the rock. The top of the cliff was empty. No one was there. None of Blacknail's companions were anywhere near the spot the rock had fallen from. They were in the opposite direction, on the far side of the pathway. Had the falling rock come loose on its own? That seemed unlikely…

The fall of their leader didn't go unnoticed by the other enemy bandits. Their lead elements stepped back and stopped fighting so that they could reevaluate the situation. Most of them looked stunned.

Sensing weakness, Blacknail grabbed his fallen sword and rose to his feet. He brandished the blade and growled as menacingly as he could. It was bluffing time.

The hobgoblin's aggressive move shook the remaining enemies' spirits. The closest ones flinched and instinctively stepped back. Fear and uncertainly was plain on their faces.

"Time to feast!" Blacknail cackled as two of his minions took up positions next to him and raised their blades.

"Let's finish these scum sacks," one of them suggested in a sinister tone.

Werrick's men wavered. They didn't know what to do. Nervously, one of the men at the front rank stepped back. It looked as though they were going to run, which was good since Blacknail was exhausted. Continuing the fight would be risky.

"Hold your ground! We still outnumber the freaks," a tall man said as he pushed his way to the front.

This new human was wearing chainmail shirt and holding a two-handed war axe. He was bald, and he looked particularly stupid when a rock dropped onto his head. With a hollow plunk, the man collapsed limply and dropped his weapon. Everyone looked up, but there was still no one there.

"Curse this mess!" one of Werrick's men swore as he turned away from the fight and pushed his way through his allies.

The rest of the enemies quickly did likewise, and their formation dissolved into chaos. They fought amongst themselves as they fled down the cliff and back toward the ground. Blacknail and his companions watched them go.

"Ha, I win!" the hobgoblin bragged as he puffed up his chest. He always won, even if he wasn't always sure how. He was amazing like that.

"What just happened?" a confused voice inquired.

"Did someone race ahead to the top of the cliff and drop that rock?" another bandit asked as he looked up.

"No, there hasn't been enough time. This side of the way is tough going," Geralhd yelled from the other side of the break in the path.

"That's weird. Maybe the gods are finally smiling down on us?" the man standing next to Blacknail suggested with a cheerfulness born of exhaustion.

"Well, if there's someone up there, we'll soon know," Geralhd speculated.

"I can't believe we made it out of that alive. Let's get the hells out of here!" Elyias suggested.

Blacknail grinned at the bodies of Werrick's fallen men. "We survived because I'm such a great leader. Look at all the foes we beat, and we didn't even lose anyone! I'm the best leader ever."

"We lost Marcus. He was cut down in the melee, and his corpse is right there," Geralhd responded as he pointed toward the man's body.

"Except for him," the hobgoblin corrected himself. "And one person barely counts anyway."

Every leader lost a minion here and there, even the best ones. Minions were like that, and Marcus hadn't been important. Blacknail didn't even remember him, since so many humans looked the same. Yes, Blacknail was a great leader.

Since it was possible that the enemy could return with reinforcements, Blacknail and the other bandits hurriedly climbed to the other side of the path. As Geralhd had pointed out, the way past it was rough going. They had to scramble over rocks and up inclines to reach the top. It was hard work, but they made their way to the top without any further incidents. This time, Blacknail went first, just in case. While he sat down and took a break, the person after him helped the others up.

The forest continued on at the top of the cliff. There was a thick line of bushes on the edge of the forest, where the sunlight got through, then row after row of trees after that. Down below the heights, the leaves of the trees looked like a green sea. Blacknail could see the river and the bridge they had used to cross it off in the distance. From up this high, he could see for miles.

"Let's take a break here," Geralhd suggested as the last man was pulled up to the top. It was Elyias, and he was still carrying Blacknail's bags.

Blacknail yawned. "Yep, sounds good, and that was my plan anyway, since I'm such an amazing leader."

Exhausted from the fight and the climb, everyone settled down to rest. Packs and bags were put down, and flasks of water were passed around. Most of the bandits looked over the cliff at the view that stretched out before them.

"Thank the gods we made it. I thought I was going to die!" Elyias remarked. "Do you think those bastards will chase us?"

One of the female bandits shook her head. "Eh, this cliff is easy to defend and it stretches a fair way in both directions. They'd be fools to try to go around it through the Green."

"True, but what do we do now?" Geralhd mused. "We can't go back to the road, and we're almost out of supplies."

There were a few seconds of silence as everyone digested that unwelcome bit of information. No one could think of a reply.

Eventually, Geralhd broke the silence again. "We'll have to find a trail and follow it North. It will be tough, but Blacknail should be able to keep us going in the right direction and find us enough food to get by."

"Of course Blacknail can. We have nothing to worry about," Khita exclaimed. "Blacknail's a hobgoblin and was trained by Saeter himself. He was, like, the best scout ever!"

"That will take weeks of hiking through the Green!" Elyias protested. "Trying that without real meals sounds like nothing but a slow death to me, and who knows what we'll run into out there!"

"We don't have much of a choice. You're welcome to choose a fast death though," a bearded bandit replied as he gestured significantly toward the cliff.

Elyias looked over the edge at the rocks below before stepping back away and slumping down into a sitting position in defeat.

"That's what I thought," the bearded man remarked disdainfully.

"Maybe we should ask Blacknail what he thinks," Khita said.

At her words, everyone turned to look toward Blacknail. The hobgoblin was lying on the ground and using a knapsack as a pillow, but he noticed the attention and perked up.

"We will find a trail and go North," he told his minions as he met their gazes. He had only vaguely been paying attention and he hadn't really been planning anything, but Geralhd's idea seemed fine.

No one had anything more to say to Blacknail, so after a few more minutes of rest, he got up to look at the nearby bushes. Staring at the view over the cliff had gotten boring. However, before he reached the shrubs at the edge of the woods, a rustling noise came from within them. Blacknail froze as a stone spear erupted from the undergrowth and came to a stop an inch from his face.

"Uh oh," the hobgoblin noted as he stared cross-eyed at the weapon's tip.

His voice drew his minions' attention and most of them looked his way—just in time to see a swarm of goblins launch themselves out of the bushes.

There was an outburst of inventive cursing as the bandits rose to their feet and reached for their weapons, but they were too slow. The goblins were upon them almost instantly. The green horde overran the humans, and a mass of stone-tipped spears prodded the unarmed bandits away from their gear and toward the cliff.

Blacknail took a careful step back from the weapon hovering in front of his eyes, just as the snarling hobgoblin holding it emerged from the undergrowth.

"Ah, this makes sense," Blacknail observed as he connected the mental dots. He had been wondering where those falling rocks had come from. Now he knew. Yeah!

"King's blood, we're all damned!" Elyias whined as he dodged the stab of a goblin spear.

"Everyone hold still and try not to provoke them," Geralhd ordered with uncharacteristic firmness before turning to Blacknail.

The humans had been pushed together by the swarm of gibbering goblins. They were surrounded except for where their backs were facing the empty air over the cliff ledge. Fear and desperation were plain on their faces.

The goblins were mostly nude, but a few of them worn loincloths. Primitive bracelets and necklaces made from bits of string, beads, and feathers were common decorations. The snarling hobgoblin leading them was also wearing a loincloth made of animal skin. Blacknail was reminded of the last hobgoblin he had fought. Like that one, this one had messy grey hair and two black horns. His horns were much smaller and didn't branch off like antlers though. He also looked younger and wasn't covered in scars.

"Are they hostile? What are they saying?" Geralhd asked Blacknail. He sounded terrified.

"How would I know? It sounds like stupid grunting to me," Blacknail responded. "I'm not from here."

That didn't cheer up anyone.

"I don't think they want to kill us," Khita remarked.

"It's a hobgoblin and a swarm of bloody goblins! Of course, they bloody want to murder us," another bandit countered. "I've heard this story. It ends with us in cook pot."

"Blacknail's a hobgoblin and he's not our enemy," Khita pointed out as she stared with great interest at the goblin poking at her with a spear.

"That's right, Blacknail! You're the leader, do something," Geralhd told him.

In response, Blacknail straightened up. Geralhd was right. He was the leader, so he had to do something. It was time for him to take charge and face danger head-on.

Blacknail stared at the hobgoblin in front of him. Uncowed, the hobgoblin returned the gaze and snarled. Blacknail didn't respond. Instead, as everyone watched, he slowly pushed aside the spear aimed at his face.

The feral hobgoblin continued to stare hatefully at Blacknail. Their eyes were locked as they regarded each other with careful consideration. Then Blacknail hissed and stepped forward. For a split second, the feral hobgoblin hesitated at the unexpected move.

Seizing his chance, Blacknail growled fearlessly as he raised a fist and smacked the hobgoblin over the head with it. There was a quiet thump, and the feral hobgoblin whined before collapsing onto the ground into a subordinate kneeling position. The goblins all went completely still.

Blacknail stood over his defeated opponent and bragged, "There, now I'm the goblin chief!"

No one said anything for several long seconds. They stared at the two hobgoblins with various mixed expressions. Disbelief was common. So was confusion.

"That's it?" Khita asked. "You're not going to fight?"

Blacknail gave the redhead a condescending look. "Why would we? Goblins aren't stupid like people, and anyway, I know him."

"What? How?" Geralhd asked as one of his eyes twitched.

"I just do. I ran into this tribe before and beat some sense into them. The hobgoblin was just a goblin then though," Blacknail replied as he suspiciously eyed the hobgoblin at his feet.He recognized this hobgoblin's scent. It was the same as a grey-haired goblin that had served as one of Blacknail's chief subordinates for a while.

What was he supposed to do with a hobgoblin minion? He had met one other hobgoblin before, and that encounter had ended in a duel to the death. Blacknail suspected that all hobgoblins were kind of jerks.

Well, this hobgoblin couldn't be worse than Khita, and he would undoubtedly be more useful. Blacknail would just have to keep an eye on him.

"So we're not going to die?" Elyias asked with desperate, unbelieving hope.

"Not unless you want to," Blacknail replied.

Elyias had gone totally white with fear, but color reappeared on his face. Blacknail ignored him and scratched his head where his horns were irritating his skin. He wasn't sure what his next move was.

"Er, could you do something about these goblins?" Geralhd politely interjected.

"Oh, right," Blacknail replied as he turned away from the kneeling hobgoblin.

The goblins holding Geralhd and the others hostage were dispersed with a little hand waving and angry yelling by Blacknail. They chattered senselessly as they scattered in all directions then reformed closer to their old leader. With curious expressions, they watched Blacknail interact with the humans.

Once no longer under immediate threat, the survivors of Herad's band moved to re-arm themselves and gather their gear. The humans then took up a defensive formation and talked amongst themselves.

"So… um, what do the goblins want?" Geralhd asked Blacknail.

It took Blacknail a few seconds to come up with an answer to that question, and he blinked in surprise. It was as if Geralhd was trying to be as confusing and stupid as possible.

"They want what I want them to want. I'm the chief now," Blacknail told him.

"Hmm, but why did they attack us?" Geralhd asked.

"They're goblins. This is their territory." Blacknail was losing patience.

Geralhd didn't look any less confused or afraid after Blacknail's answer. He opened his mouth to ask something else, but Blacknail ignored him and walked back to the other hobgoblin. He didn't want to answer any more pointless questions.

The feral hobgoblin had gotten off his knees, but his eyes shifted downward in submission when Blacknail looked his way. He clearly didn't want to fight. As Blacknail approached, the feral hobgoblin grumbled something incomprehensible. Blacknail had no idea what it meant, but it didn't really matter since he was in charge.

"I shall call you Gob. That's a great name," Blacknail remarked before motioning vaguely toward the forest and walking again.

The goblins fell in line behind him as he stepped into the trees.

"Hey, where are you going?" Geralhd called in surprise.

"To the goblins' den," Blacknail explained without turning around.

"What! You're just going to leave us here?" Khita asked.

Blacknail sighed in frustration before turning back to glare at the humans. Why were they so slow? “No, you have to follow me! I’m the leader.” How could they not understand this?

“I’m not going anywhere with a swarm of wild goblins!” one of the bandits exclaimed.

“The very idea is insane.” Elyias added hysterically. “We have to leave now!”

There was a general muttering of agreement from most of the other humans. They were still looking at the goblins with poorly disguised hostility and fear.

“They have food and a place to rest,” Blacknail pointed out.

There was silence as everyone considered this. Blacknail didn’t wait for a response. He walked again and pushed through the bushes into the forest proper. The grey-haired hobgoblin followed him, and so did the goblins. After a few minutes, Blacknail glanced over his shoulder. His human minions had decided to follow him after all, but they were keeping a generous distance between themselves and the goblins.

“This is the stupidest thing I’ve ever heard of,” a female bandit announced. “Even the morons you hear about in campfire horror stories weren’t dumb enough to follow two hobgoblins and a tribe of goblins into the Green. We’re so going to die horribly.”

“So stay here then, coward. I’m following Blacknail,” Khita remarked confidently.

“As long as they fatten us up before they eat us, then I’ll die happy,” the bearded bandit added.

“I’m sure Blacknail isn’t going to betray us. He’s always been a loyal and stalwart comrade,” Geralhd added in an obvious attempt to reassure the others. “I’m sure he has a plan.”

It took a few more minutes of walking for Blacknail to realize he had no idea where he was going, so he gestured for the feral hobgoblin to take the lead. That also gave Blacknail the advantage of placing Gob where he could be easily watched.

Being around him put Blacknail on edge. No one with a lick of sense would ever trust a hobgoblin.

Chapter 25

After the goblins' ambush, the trek through the forest was uneventful. The feral hobgoblin led the way, and they soon emerged from the trees into a clearing full of thick bushes and skinny saplings too tall to see over.

Blacknail instantly recognized the area. The main road wasn't too far away. Last year, during his trip to Daggerpoint, he had been attacked by the hobgoblin that had ruled this territory. After a long, brutal fight to the death, where Blacknail had been forced to use all his impressive cunning and skill, he'd had to stay here with the local tribe for a while to rest, before moving on.

Blacknail eyed Gob suspiciously out of the corner of his eye. The feral hobgoblin had been a mere goblin during Blacknail's last visit, and he'd only transformed into a hobgoblin after Blacknail had left to catch up with Herad and Saeter.

Gritting his teeth, Blacknail looked ahead and kept moving. The important thing was that the tribe should have plenty of food and a safe place for him to rest. As annoying as the goblins were, using them greatly increased the chances of his survival and that of his human minions. Blacknail had spent a fair amount of time teaching these goblins how to trap animals and smoke meat. If the stupid little critters had already forgotten his lessons, then Blacknail would be very mad. One way or another, they were going to provide him with as much food as he wanted.

A breeze swept through the trees as Blacknail pushed through the bushes in front of him. However, a sudden low growl from behind, followed by a fearful yelp, stopped his advance. He turned around to see what was happening and sighed. It was probably something dumb and annoying. His minions had problems with even the simplest instructions.

The people behind Blacknail had stopped moving. Gob was growling menacingly at Geralhd while standing in his way. The humans had backed away from the hostile hobgoblin and were looking nervous. Their posture was tense, and a few of them were reaching for their weapons. Scamp and Imp stood off to the side and watched.

"What now?" Blacknail mumbled as he walked back to see what all the commotion was about. It didn't look as though Gob was going to attack anyone, but he was obviously upset about something. "What did you do?"

"Nothing, he just won't let us pass!" Geralhd replied with obvious exasperation.

As if in response, Gob growled again and glared at Geralhd menacingly. The hobgoblin wasn't brandishing his weapon though, so Blacknail carefully observed the situation before a possible explanation occurred to him.

"Ah, you need to bow!" Blacknail declared as he met Geralhd's gaze.

"What?"

Blacknail rolled his eyes. How could anyone possibly survive long enough to reach adulthood without knowing this sort of thing? It was so basic. "Gob is angry because you're strangers. You need to join the tribe before he'll let you near his lair."

"And how do we do that?" Geralhd asked.

"Bow before me, your great leader, like Gob did before." Why did he have to explain this? It was obvious, and he had just answered this question a second ago.

"I'm not doing that," a blond woman replied as she grimaced.

Blacknail suppressed a growl as he glared at his ungrateful minions. The only reason they were alive was because he was trying to do what Saeter would have wanted him to. However, his master had been no fan of idiots, so a beating or two might be in order.

"There must be an easier way to show him we're not a threat," Geralhd remarked.

"There might be another way. Sometimes goblin leaders piss on their—"

"Bowing it is," the blonde cut in.

"What happens if we do neither?" a bearded bandit whose name Blacknail kept forgetting asked.

"Then you stay here while I go get something to eat," Blacknail replied.

After a lot of unhappy grumbling, all the bandits knelt in front of Blacknail, even if they did it reluctantly and as quickly as possible. As he watched with a satisfied smirk, the cold rage within him subsided a bit. It was so satisfying to see all his hard work and sacrifice pay off. He was finally being treated as he so rightly deserved to be, as the chief. In fact, for a moment, Blacknail felt even better than when he was slaughtering his enemies. Weird.

When the last human had finished bowing, Gob nodded and got out of the way. Blacknail felt a little better about having the hobgoblin around now. He was proving to be useful.

"Now that you have joined the tribe, you can enter," Blacknail told everyone before turning around and leading the way into the clearing. All the goblins except for Scamp and Imp had already gone ahead.

"I swear to the gods, there had better actually be food here or I'm going to kill someone," a bandit remarked bitterly as he followed Blacknail.

There was a bit more grumbling from some of the others, but none of them decided to stay behind. They all trailed after Blacknail as he headed toward the goblins' lair.

A few minutes later, a sense of nostalgia washed over Blacknail as he pushed aside the last bush. The goblins' lair had changed a lot since his last visit, but it was still recognizable. The tribe had built their home atop the ruins of a large human building. The worn-down remnants of the building's walls could be seen encircling their dwelling. The goblins had reinforced the breaks in the old brick wall with wooden stacks so that they had a defensive barrier. When Blacknail had been there before, there had only been a few small structures made of loosely piled branches leaning up against the walls, but now a new building was visible.

This new structure looked large enough to hold a dozen men, even if they had to slouch over because of the low roof. It was made of branches that had been carefully woven together and reinforced with twine. Layers of bark had been tied to the roof and walls to block out the wind and rain, although a few spots used tarp or bits of cloth that had obviously been stolen from humans.

The rest of the goblin camp was mostly packed dirt and a few tiny stick dwellings, except for where a large fire pit sat in the center of the site. Right where Blacknail remembered it, a huge old pot was hanging over the fire pit.

"Incredible! I didn't know goblins still made things like this," Geralhd remarked as he looked around.

"I showed them how to do stuff like that," Blacknail bragged.

"Ya, it's great if you love dirt and twigs," another bandit observed sarcastically.

"Where's the food?" Khita asked. Her priorities were clear.

"Just wait. Soon, we will have a feast to celebrate my great leadership!" Blacknail responded as he looked around.

The feral goblins were lurking around the edges of the camp, staring at the humans but giving them plenty of room. In sharp contrast, Gob was sticking close to the intruders. He slowly circled them while glaring their way, and his attitude clearly unnerved some of the bandits. Blacknail ignored all that. He walked over to the fire pit and examined the pot. He was intent on planning his victory celebration. A great chieftain deserved a great feast.

The first thing Blacknail needed to do was round up some goblins, so that was what he did. He stalked over to the closest one and grabbed it before it could escape. Then he hoisted it into the air and shook it a few times to get its attention. When he was sure the goblin knew who was the boss, he gestured toward the pot then in the direction where he knew a creek lay. The goblin seemed to understand because it nodded enthusiastically, so Blacknail dropped it.

Soon, Gob was leading a group of goblins to the creek to fetch water. Through various physical threats, complicated gestures, and bouts of hissing, Blacknail got a few more parties of goblins working on other jobs. Most importantly, he sent them out to gather food, or at least he hoped that was what they were doing. It was either that or they were going to set fire to the forest.

"You really should be trying to teach them some Elorian. It would make this much easier," Geralhd said as he observed Blacknail.

All the bandits who had come with Blacknail had found places to sit and rest at one end of the camp. They watched the goings-on with wary attention.

"What's Elorian?" Blacknail asked.

"It's the language we are speaking right now," Geralhd explained with a slight smirk.

"Oh, right, I knew that. I'm just too busy right now for more lessons," the hobgoblin replied.

"Then maybe I'll do it. Scamp learned it fairly quickly," the young man mused as he looked toward the large hut the goblins had built.

"Go ahead," Blacknail said as the first of the goblins filtered back in.

It wasn't long before the big pot was filled with water and hauled above the fire pit by Gob and a few goblins. Piles of leaves, roots, firewood, and small game where piled up off to one side. The goblin tribe was quite skilled at hunting rabbits, birds, and squirrels.

The feral tribe grew excited as Blacknail threw ingredients into the pot. He had cooked for them during his last visit, and apparently they had liked it. The goblins slipped past the nearby humans in order to peer over his shoulder, and he had to smack a few to keep them out of his way.

"It's done!" Blacknail announced a few minutes later.

The smell of the stew filled the air. As the feral goblins fought amongst themselves over the few bowls they possessed, the bandits served themselves. They were interrupted when a growling Gob forced his way to the front of the line. However, no one tried to fight the hobgoblin, so he took his food and withdrew peacefully.

"Huh, this isn't half bad," Elyias remarked after sitting down and tasting the food.

"It's the nectar of the gods compared to the stuff we were eating yesterday," another bandit added.

"Ya, if I went another day eating nothing but raw leaves and the occasional burnt squirrel, I was going to go crazy," a third agreed. "That and shit my brains out."

When all the humans had gotten out of the way, an unruly crowd of goblins ran over to get their own food. Scamp and Imp had been behind the last bandit, so they were in the swarm's way. Scamp had to fight his way through the mob. He hissed and scratched anyone who got too close to the bowl pressed protectively against his chest. In sharp contrast, none of the ferals bothered Imp. Whenever one got too close, he directed a cold stare their way and they scurried away.

Of course, Blacknail had taken the first bowl for himself. He'd just finished slurping down the meal when the feral goblins finished emptying the rest of the pot. However, since there were still plenty of ingredients left, it didn't take him long to get another batch going. He was almost finished when his cooking was interrupted by a loud screech that hurt his ears.

"Hey, that's mine!" Khita yelled as she jumped to her feet.

A goblin had somehow managed to get its hands on her knife. The little creature ran off into the bushes outside of the camp, and Khita disappeared after it. Blacknail snickered at the sight. What kind of idiot let her stuff get stolen by goblins?

After he had finished cooking, Blacknail yawned and decided to take a nap. He had stuffed himself, and his full stomach was making him more than a little sleepy, but before he could nod off, he was interrupted.

"Blacknail, what are we supposed to do now?" Geralhd asked after walking over.

"Sleep," the hobgoblin replied.

"Where should we do that?" Geralhd asked in a frustrated tone. "We need shelter, and I don't want to anger our… hosts."

"We also need some way to prevent the goblins from slitting our throats while we sleep," Elyias added. He sounded nervous and kept glancing around every time a goblin made the slightest of noises or movements.

Blacknail sighed and sat up. Couldn't the humans do anything for themselves? Did they really need him to tell them where to sleep?

After a brief conversation, Blacknail led Geralhd on a tour of the feral goblins' camp. The young bandit was surprised when Blacknail pulled open a makeshift trapdoor to reveal a staircase that led into the ground.

"Oh, this must be an old root cellar," Geralhd observed as they walked into a fair-sized room with stone walls.

A few goblins were lurking about, but Blacknail hissed and they quickly disappeared into a small tunnel in one of the walls. This was where the hobgoblin had slept the last time he was here. It was getting dark outside and there wasn't much light in the underground chamber, so Blacknail walked over to the fireplace he had dug into the wall during his last visit. There was already a tiny bit of dry wood and grass inside, so he got a fire going using sparks from a piece of flint and steel.

"Yes, it's a little dirty, but will work quite well," Geralhd remarked as he looked around. "We can seal that hole there easily enough, and then there is only one way in. I don't mean to offend your… friends, but I know we'll all sleep sounder in a secure location."

"I don't trust goblins either," Blacknail replied indifferently.

Why would you ever trust a goblin? Of course, humans were just as bad in their own way. Blacknail's heart twisted painfully as several memories overcame him. The only human he had ever really trusted was Saeter, and now his master was dead. That meant Blacknail was the only trustworthy person left. Being so loyal and incredibly amazing was a lonely burden.

"I'm going to sleep now. Don't bother me," Blacknail announced before getting his blanket out and curling up in one corner of the room.

The humans could sort everything out, and he didn't feel like interacting with feral goblins right now, not even the female ones. For some reason, he wasn't as interested in them as he had been before. They were kind of short and flat-chested… wait, why was he thinking about this?

It wasn't long before all the bandits came down into the cellar. Some of them brought wood to feed the fire. The flickering flames lit the room as everyone set up for the night.

Several hours after that, Khita finally showed up again. Blacknail awoke to the sound of her stomping down the stairs. Her clothes were covered with mud, and her exposed skin had scratches on it. She looked like she'd gotten into a fight with a thorn bush.

"Did you get your knife back?" he asked snidely.

"Damn you, you miserable bastard," she snarled before going to sit over by the fire. Blacknail was fairly sure that meant she hadn't gotten her knife back.

After an otherwise uneventful night, Blacknail led the bandits out of the root cellar and back up to the fire pit. He sighed as he observed how nervous and fearful they acted. Why were they so afraid of a few goblins and one hobgoblin? They were a bunch of big humans with steel weapons!

Gob greeted his new chieftain by kneeling before him, which pleased Blacknail greatly. Maybe the hobgoblin wasn't so bad after all, and that meant there was no reason to kill him and make it look like an accident. Blacknail had spent some time last night thinking about the best way to go about that. Goblin chiefs weren't supposed to kill their subordinates, but it happened all the time, especially when those subordinates got uppity.

"Hey, that's my knife!" Khita exclaimed when she noticed the item tucked into the side of the hobgoblin's loincloth.

She reached to take it, but Gob stepped back and hissed at her. The redhead and the hobgoblin stared at each other. Neither seemed likely to back down.

"Don't start anything," Geralhd warned her.

"Make him give it back," Khita told Blacknail.

"Get it back yourself," Blacknail replied. He didn't like her tone of voice. He was the leader and didn't take orders from anyone.

"Is this some sort of hobgoblin test? To see if I'm sneaky enough to steal it back and prove myself?" the redhead asked as her eyes narrowed.

"No, I just don't care," Blacknail remarked. If Khita couldn't hold onto her own stuff, then that wasn't his problem.

Khita huffed as she scowled at him. "You've become kind of an ass lately."

"Nope, wrong," the hobgoblin replied. He was completely sure he hadn't changed at all. There was just no one around to force him to do stupid things anymore, like care about Khita or take baths. Life was better when you were the leader.

Chapter 26

Blacknail ignored Khita and everyone else as he went to work on things that were actually important. The early morning sunshine shone on him as he got breakfast going. Sleeping—like everything else—made him hungry.

More meat was brought over by goblins and roasted over the fire. There was enough that all the humans got to eat their fill with lots left over for the goblins. During Blacknail's absence, the goblins had become skilled at hunting small game. Blacknail had shown them how to make slings and snares before he left. The tribe had certainly grown larger, and none of them looked hungry.

"I never thought I'd be so happy to eat a squirrel, or that they'd taste so good," Geralhd said after swallowing a bit of meat.

"They're pretty nice eating really. Much better than rats," Khita replied from where she was sitting on the ground by the fire.

Geralhd blinked and gave her a disbelieving frown.

Khita noticed his reaction and shrugged. "It's not like I've eaten a lot of rats, but when you're living on the streets and you're hungry, you eat whatever you can get."

Her explanation made Geralhd look more uncomfortable. He fidgeted and looked away.

"I used to live off rats and bugs, but now I prefer human food. It tastes less like dirt and it doesn't fight back," Blacknail added.

Khita threw Blacknail a friendly grin, which Blacknail returned, but there was silence as Geralhd and the other nearby humans considered this piece of hobgoblin wisdom.

"Er, that stew from yesterday… what was in it?" Elyias asked as he put down the rabbit on stick he had been eating.

A few of the others grimaced and looked queasy as well.

"Lots of stuff. Saeter taught me how to cook it," Blacknail replied.

The last part of his explanation seemed to reassure the humans a little. Most of them resumed eating. Blacknail smiled proudly. He was a great cook, and he was glad they had enjoyed his cooking, even if it hadn't been his best recipe. There had barely been any bugs in it at all! The next time he cooked, he was going to make sure he had the ingredients necessary to give the stew a proper crunch. That was the best part.

"This foray into goblin culinary habits has been fascinating, but we have some more important matters to discuss, like our next move," Geralhd said after he had finished eating.

There was agreement from the other bandits, and they talked about their plans. A few humans had grown tired of hiking through the forest, but they quickly decided that nothing had really changed. They still had no option but to try to find a trail that led North. After the confrontation with Werrick's men, there was no way there weren't enemies watching the main road.

"So we still have to walk through these gods deserted woods for what will probably be weeks," one of the women said. "We're lucky we made it this far without being eaten by something. Getting to Daggerpoint will be like trying to trek through one of the hells."

"At least we got to rest under a roof last night and eat our fill for once," said the bearded bandit whose Blacknail name kept forgetting. Maybe he should call the man Beardy. As the leader, he was allowed to change his minions' names, right?

It was still early in the morning when Blacknail led his troupe of humans and two goblins off into the woods. Several of the bandits visibly relaxed when the goblin camp was out of sight, which was stupid. Things were at their most dangerous when you couldn't see them.

The going was tough for the first few hours. The ground was uneven, and there were plenty of obstacles, such as rock and trees, to be avoided. Most of the trees were tall with long, slender needles instead of leaves, and sap oozed from breaks in their scaly bark. After a while though, the ground evened out, and smaller, leafier trees appeared. That was when Blacknail noticed something strange—their group had somehow picked up an extra human.

"Hmmm, how many people are we supposed to have?" he asked Geralhd, who was standing right behind him.

"What? Did we lose someone?" the bandit asked as he spun around to look.

"No, the opposite," Blacknail replied.

The bandits had all stopped walking and were gazing at Blacknail with confused expressions. None of them looked unfamiliar… but it was hard to say for sure. Blacknail couldn't always tell his humans apart. Of course, the hooded man at the back of the line was deeply suspicious. Blacknail walked past everyone until he got to the individual in question. He had a nagging suspicion about the hooded figure, which quickly proved correct.

Blacknail glared at the intruder. "What are you doing, Gob? That's my cloak trick. I did it first! Don't copy me!"

The feral hobgoblin froze for a second then made a shrug-like motion before pulling down his hood. The cloak had been doing a terrible job of concealing his horns anyway; the tips had been pushing up the fabric. Underneath the cloak, he was still dressed in a loincloth, but he was also wearing a brown shirt he had stolen from somewhere.

"By all that is holy!" Elyias cursed as he jerked away from the hobgoblin.

His reaction annoyed Blacknail. The hobgoblin wasn't much of a danger now that he had been exposed, and his disguise had been terrible anyway. Only an idiot like Elyias would have been fooled by it. Gob wasn't even wearing pants!

"Did he kill and replace one of us?" someone asked in horror.

"Everyone is still here. He just stole some clothes," Geralhd quickly explained to keep everyone calm.

The two hobgoblins stared at each for a few minutes. Gob hissed and barked, then Blacknail growled back. The humans watched the interplay nervously.

"Why is he following us?" Geralhd asked when they had both fallen silent.

"I don't know. He just keeps making weird noises," Blacknail explained.

Geralhd sighed. "Please make an educated guess then."

"He wants to stay with me because I'm such a great leader. I'm so handsome, strong, and wise that he will follow me anywhere," Blacknail observed with a fair bit of self-satisfaction. Now that he had said the words aloud, he realized they had to be true. What other explanation could there be?

"Well, he can't stay!" Beardy sputtered. He sounded angry and more than a little fearful.

"Oh? Are you the leader now?" Blacknail hissed as he rounded upon the man and leveled a cold stare his way. He hadn't actually wanted another hobgoblin around—they couldn't be trusted—but there was no way he was letting anyone else decide that! He was the leader, and now that Beardy was against it, Blacknail wanted Gob to stay.

"He's a wild hobgoblin!" another bandit protested.

"Which means he's way more useful than you, or anyone else here but me," Blacknail countered.

A few more bandits tried to argue with Blacknail's decision, but he didn't back down. Eventually, they had no choice but to accept Gob's presence. Blacknail was the leader and more than willing to stab a few people to make a point.

"Are the goblins going to be all right without their leader?" Geralhd asked with a level of concern that confused Blacknail. Why did he care?

"Yes," Blacknail replied. The goblins would probably be better off without the hobgoblin lazing about and stealing their food.

By this time, it was clear no one was going to try to chase him away, so Gob turned around and yelled something incomprehensible. Four goblins with spears and one carrying a large sack ambled out of the bushes and joined the hobgoblin.

"Bloody lovely," Beardy remarked.

"If they can bring in food, then I'd much rather have their company than yours," a woman remarked.

The addition of a few more goblins didn't bother Blacknail. He shrugged and walked back up to the front of the line. He then picked a direction at random and started hiking again. After a few suspicious glares, the bandits followed him, and behind them came the feral goblins. Scamp and Imp stuck with the bandits. If anything, they seemed more distrustful of the newcomers than the humans were. Scamp in particular gave them a few nasty looks and hugged his collection of pouches close.

The group walked for most of the day, with only a few breaks. The most interesting thing to happen was when they walked around a clump of bushes and spooked a herd of deer. The meeting was a surprise to both sides, but the animals were long gone before anyone could string a bow or try to bring one down.

When it began to grow dark and they stumbled upon a halfway decent campsite atop a rocky outcrop, Blacknail signaled for a stop. As they were setting up camp, the humans objected to sharing their space with the feral goblins, but Blacknail pointed out that he was the leader and they didn't get to decide anything. He also mentioned that it was better to keep the goblins close where they could be watched.

"They did share their camp with us earlier," Geralhd told the other bandits.

That bit of unasked-for truth earned him some angry mutters and glares, but it did seem to placate some of the dissenters. However, it was the goblins' ability to gather firewood, even when it got dark, that convinced the last of the objectors. When Gob built a fire for himself and the goblins, the bandits shut up and took a seat around it.

Geralhd even sat next to Gob and tried to communicate with him. It didn't take long for the feral hobgoblin to grow annoyed by the human. Gob threw Blacknail a suffering look that was clearly an attempt to ask for permission to gut the noisy human, but Blacknail shook his head, so the feral hobgoblin was forced to try to ignore the man instead.

In the morning, the ferals further impressed the humans by catching several rabbits and squirrels. As was proper, they offered them to their great chieftain Blacknail, and he in turn shared the spoils with everyone else—after he had finished eating his fill. It wasn't enough to fill everyone's bellies, except Blacknail's, but it was more than they would have had otherwise.

The early morning birds were out in full force, their singing filling the air. However, Blacknail grew tired of walking through the forest. It was nothing but the same mix of trees they had seen over the last few days. He was careful to avoid the older and darker areas where giant spiders might dwell, as well as the overgrown clearings mimics preferred. That was the safe thing to do, but it was also boring. Some excitement would almost be worth the risk of losing a few goblins or humans.

A loud cracking noise jerked Blacknail to attention. Everyone else heard it as well, but the sound echoed through the forest in a way that made it hard to guess where it had come from. The group stopped in their tracks and looked off in different directions.

There was another loud sound like wood shattering. This time, Blacknail zoned in on the origin. He saw only trees in that direction, but then he noticed a place where the ground dropped away. He couldn't see what lay at the bottom of the hill, but if there was something dangerous there, he needed to know about it. Plus it might be interesting.

Blacknail signaled for his followers to be quiet, then he stalked to the top of the hill. The incline was steep and muddy. At the bottom was a clearing full of long grass, and it was bristling with activity. Blacknail stared at the commotion below. The clearing was occupied by ogres. The herd was trampling through the grass along the edge of the clearing where the trees were, and they were using the huge claws on their front limbs to pull branches off the trees. The huge brown beasts then brought the foliage to their mouths and chowed down on the leaves before throwing most of the harder wood aside. That was the source of all the noise.

Several of the bandits, including Geralhd, joined Blacknail atop the hill. They let out quiet exclamations of surprise when they saw the ogres. Many of them had never seen the beasts before, so the group took a quick break to watch them.

"Wow, those are some huge hulking things." Khita's eyes were wide with surprise and awe as she watched the creatures.

"I've heard of ogres, but I didn't think anything got so large," Elyias remarked. "You don't scc anything like them down south. They must be twice as tall as a man when they stand up on their hind legs."

"Do you think they're dangerous? Are we safe up here?" Geralhd asked.

Blacknail took a moment to think the question over. He had only seen a herd of ogres once before, but because he was the leader, he wanted to sound as though he knew what he was talking about. "We're safe up here. Ogres don't chase people.

They will crush you if something scares them into stampeding, but they don't actually chase people."

"What could scare those giants?" Elyias asked with amused disbelief. He sounded as though he thought Blacknail was joking.

"Lots of stuff," Blacknail answered. "Trolls and drakes will hunt and eat ogres."

"Drakes are real? I thought they were just stories meant to frighten people…"

Geralhd chuckled. "Of course they're real. I mean, I've never seen one, but I've read about them."

"I saw one chase some ogres. It was way bigger than a house, and its teeth were longer than a man!" Blacknail held his arms out as far apart as possible to show everyone what he meant. "Its roar shook the trees and even Herad ran away from it."

Khita grinned and her eyes shone with glee. "If we wait here, do you think a drake will show up? They sound amazing!"

"I admit to a certain scholarly curiosity about the creatures as well, but that's not going to happen," Geralhd told her. "Our journey is dangerous enough without purposely trying to encounter a drake, and we don't have time to waste."

Blacknail had to agree with Geralhd. Waiting around would be stupid. He shooed a newly terrified Elyias back into line and quickly got everyone moving again. A long march still lay ahead of them, and they spent the rest of the day trying to shorten it as much as possible.

After another night in the forest and an early morning start to the day's hiking, Blacknail was forced to admit he had no idea where he was or how to get to Daggerpoint. Somehow, one of his minions had gotten them lost. Why were his minions so useless?

"Your plan isn't working," Blacknail accused Geralhd as he pulled him aside.

A confused expression appeared on the man's face. "My plan?"

"Yep, the one where we walk North until we find a trail to a human city. I haven't found any trails," Blacknail pointed out.

Geralhd winced as if in pain and sighed. He apparently didn't like being told the obvious. "Well, we can't turn back now. We'll just have to keep going and hope that we find a road, although I think we should head more toward the east now. That's the way Daggerpoint should be."

"Fine, whatever." Blacknail wasn't sure that was the greatest idea, but it didn't matter to him. He was fine with wandering the woods. It was as good a place to be as any, and he still wasn't certain what he would do when they got to Daggerpoint.

They resumed their march and stumbled into a swampy area. Soon, over half the standing green trees were replaced by white skeletal husks, and the firm ground gave way to mud. Pools of standing water blocked the way forward, and no one wanted to go for a swim. However, the real problem was the bugs. Swarms of buzzing insects descended on the bandits and goblins. The humans threw up their hoods, and the goblins rolled in the mud then made a run for it. Blacknail led the charge away from the swamp and up to drier ground. They only stopped running when they had reached a hill with enough wind to blow away all the insects chasing them.

"Now you've really gotten us lost," Blacknail accused Geralhd as he swatted a mosquito that had landed on his nose.

"I have? What did I do?" Geralhd replied indignantly.

"It's your plan, so everything is your fault," the hobgoblin explained.

"It hasn't failed us yet. Let's keep moving."

"Yes, let's keep walking off into the woods until we all fall over dead. That way the goblins get a free meal and don't even have to raise a hand against us," Beardy interjected. He didn't sound as if he actually liked Geralhd's plan.

"No, they just have to walk half a hundred miles. That's stupid. The goblins are the only ones here who aren't having any problems finding food," Geralhd replied.

“Ya, you’re stupid,” Blacknail added. He felt it was his duty as the leader to point that out.

A few more of the bandits grumbled, but they shut up when Blacknail glared their way. It wasn’t as though they had better ideas or anywhere they could escape to, so the long hike through the seemingly never-ending forest continued.

Chapter 27

The forest was darkening as dusk fell when Blacknail's band of misfits found themselves making their way up an unremarkable hill. A canopy of broad leaves towered above them, supported by scattered broad tree trunks that rose out of the earth. Dark soil was visible underneath the thin layer of plants that covered the ground.

They had been walking through the trees without stopping since they'd decided to head northeast in search of some sign of human civilization. Blacknail was about to admit defeat and look for somewhere to set up camp for the night when he stumbled across a nearly invisible game trail, where the earth had been flattened and no plants grew. It went almost straight North, so at first Blacknail didn't give it more than a brief glance. However, it was an unusually wide path, and that drew his interest. A lot of animals were obviously using it. Knowing what sort of creatures were nearby would be useful, in case any of them liked eating people. Blacknail only had so many spares.

A brief sniff revealed nothing more dangerous than some old wolf piss, but his eyes spotted something interesting. Saeter had taught the hobgoblin not to rely too much on smell and how to track by following physical signs. It wasn't usually that useful, but sometimes rain or time would wash away a weak scent.

Blacknail came to a stop and looked at his find. "Your great leader has found something, because he is the best scout ever."

"It's not another weird mushroom you want one of us to eat, is it? Elyias still looks a little out of it, but at least he's stopped mumbling to himself now," Beardy replied. He was third in line and he didn't sound too enthusiastic about Blacknail's discovery.

Elyias was holding up the rear of the bandits, and he looked more than a little green. Every once in a while, one of the feral goblins poked him and giggled before running away, but the young man barely reacted. He just plodded forward, staring ahead with unfocused eyes.

"No, it's a footprint, and Elyias will be fine. My minion's just feeling… relaxed now that his stomach is full and he's not so hungry. His skin color has never looked so good!"

"A footprint? Is it a human one?" Geralhd asked hopefully as everyone stopped walking and looked toward the hobgoblin scout.

"Yes, from a boot," Blacknail explained as he crouched and pointed at where the heel of a boot had left an imprint in the dirt. The smooth curved edge was clearly visible, and a quick inspection of the surroundings revealed a few more signs of passing humans.

"It's about bloody time! Gods, I hope this means we're near a town or something. I thought the Green would be more exciting than this. All we've done is walk and then walk some more." Khita sounded oddly bitter and disappointed that the worst thing they had run into was goblins.

"I'm fine with it being boring. It couldn't be Werrick's men who made those tracks, could it?" a woman asked nervously from near the back of the group of bandits.

"I can't think of any reason they'd be way the hells out here. They can't know where we're headed and it's a long walk," Geralhd replied.

"This trail looks like it goes back to the road, and it runs North the other way," Blacknail observed as he pointed one way then the other.

"Why would anyone travel up that way? There's nothing there but trees and then the mountains," Beardy asked. "Nobody has ever crossed the Iron Teeth mountains, and nobody lives there either."

No one had an answer, so after discussing their options for a bit, they decided on a course of action, which Geralhd then convinced Blacknail to take. Blacknail was the leader, so he got to decide everything important, even when he had no idea what was going on. Luckily, Geralhd was there to explain things to him and remind him of important stuff, like that humans needed to eat a certain amount or they would die.

Thus, Blacknail agreed that they should follow the trail North. His bandit minions hoped the path would eventually turn east toward civilization or at least lead somewhere where they could rest and resupply.

As they followed the trail, Blacknail noticed plenty of other signs of human passage. It seemed as though several different people were using the trail regularly. Even though the group made good time, they didn't reach the end of the trail before night started to fall. Everyone was subdued as they set up camp under a rocky ledge.

"Damnation, I want to keep going. The source of those tracks might be just out of sight, and that's going to bug me all night," a bandit said as he unrolled his blanket next to the fire.

"Go ahead, stupid, but I'm not going to track you down when you get lost in the dark," Blacknail replied as he supervised everyone else's work. He was the leader.

The only other person who did much talking was Geralhd. As had become routine over the past few days, he spent a while trying to communicate with Gob and teach him the human language. The goblins and the humans had gotten used to each other, but the bandits' long journey had worn them down. Most of them stared into the forest with fearful eyes, and even though they had been eating better they'd continued to lose weight. In the light cast by the campfire, their faces were thin and eyes sunken. Blacknail wasn't sure that some of them would last much longer. He didn't want to lose any minions, but if one of them did die, he hoped it would be the man with the nice red coat, or Khita.

The goblins were a little spooked, being in unfamiliar territory, but otherwise fine. If anything, the presence of so many large humans had come to reassure them.

When the sun had risen and everyone was up, they hiked again. The tantalizing prospect of stumbling onto the source of the tracks they were following energized the bandits. They moved more quickly than they had earlier, and soon the forest changed around them. The thicker leafy trees gave way to tall pine trees that were clustered tightly together. Their fallen needles covered the ground and smothered a lot of the underbrush, so there was little to block vision.

"Oh, benevolent goddess! I pray we reach succor soon. My feet are bloody killing me," Elyias whined. He was at the back of the group again, while Blacknail was leading the way up a shallow slope. He seemed to have recovered completely from the mushroom poisoning.

"Gods, you're a whiny brat. How the hells did you end up here and how have you survived this long?" Beardy responded. The large man spat contemptuously to the side.

A haunted look appeared on Elyias's face, and it took him a few moments to reply. "I don't know… but by all that is divine, I wish I did. I joined up with Herad in Daggerpoint because it seemed like a sure way to make some easy money." A miserable chuckle escaped his lips.

"Ha, how's that going for you?" Beardy asked as he grinned.

The large bearded man seemed to find Elyias's suffering amusing. That annoyed Blacknail a little because Elyias was his minion, so Elyias was supposed to amuse him! It was almost disloyal…

"It was going fine until that big street fight with those mercenaries in Daggerpoint." Elyias sighed deeply. "I hadn't signed up for that sort of shit. I'm a thief, not a soldier. Yet just when the fighting had all finished and I was starting to relax, Blacknail showed up."

"And then things became great! Because I made you my minion," Blacknail interjected happily.

"Something sort of like that," Elyias remarked bitterly.

The young man turned to stare off into the forest. He seemed depressed. Maybe he needed another mushroom to cheer him up? There had been some funny-looking purple ones a while back.

Before Blacknail could speak up, Khita called out in an unusually loud voice meant to get attention. It worked. "Hey, look over there!"

The group had just reached the top of the incline they had been climbing and could see beyond it. About a hundred feet up ahead, the tree line just stopped and gave way to a large clearing. The open area wasn't natural. Stumps littered the edge where the forest had been cut back not too long ago, and all the grass in the area had been trampled down. Nothing blocked their view of the settlement that stood in the middle of the clearing. Large wooden buildings could be seen behind a tall fence, and a pillar of smoke was rising from a chimney.

"It's a village or something," a bandit remarked as she stared past her companions. This pronouncement of the obvious earned her a few annoyed looks, including one from Blacknail.

"Everyone be quiet. Let's not give ourselves away until we've figured out who they are," Geralhd said as he looked around at the forest to make sure they weren't being observed.

"Ya, let's do that." Blacknail listened carefully, but all he heard were the usual forest noises, like the rustling of leaves. It didn't sound as if there were any strange people around. He would have heard them or smelled them unless they were waiting in ambush, and that was unlikely.

After a signal from their glorious leader, the bandits cautiously made their way to the edge of the forest and stared out into the clearing. The goblins followed them.

"Hmm, it's too big to be an outpost or a trapper's hut. You could fit a hundred people in there, maybe two. It must be village after all," Geralhd observed.

"Look at the ground here in front of us. Most of it has been worked in the past, and those areas closer to the wall look like they've already been planted," Elyias pointed out as he crouched and stared at the dirt in front of him. "You would only do that if you were living here."

Beardy scratched his head and scowled as he looked around. "They're farming out here? I thought all these little villages got raided and wiped out a long time ago."

"The bandits would have to find them first," Geralhd remarked. "This village is more than a little out of the way, and even bandits stick close to the main roads. I'm guessing they try to keep their location secret as well."

"So they're probably not too fond of visitors. Some small communities can get intense about that sort of thing," Elyias remarked warily.

Beardy glanced Blacknail's way. "Well, no matter who they are, they probably won't welcome a group of armed strangers in their hearth, and they definitely won't appreciate us bringing a pack of goblins with us."

"So what do we do now?" Khita asked. "I'm not staying out here when there's a nice comfy house right over there. I want to sleep on a bed. No, I *need* to sleep on a bed, and I have no problem with stabbing a few people to get it either."

"We should wait out of sight until nightfall and then find a way inside," Bready suggested. "They won't be expecting an attack. Those walls are for keeping beasts out, not people, and I'll eat my boots if they get travelers out here."

Everyone considered that plan for a few moments. Several people, including Geralhd, started to raise objections, but Khita cut them off. "What if we just grabbed some hostages? Then we could force them to let us in, and we wouldn't have to wait so long. Nightfall is a bloody long time from now!"

"Huh, you might be right. Waiting could be risky," Beardy admitted. "They know the area, and someone might stumble onto our trail and alert the village. So instead, we could have Blacknail climb over the wall and let us inside. He could probably manage that undetected, and then we could grab the first few people we find as bargaining chips."

"Why is every option you present so violent?" Geralhd asked as he glared at Beardy. "We have other alternatives, and not everything needs to end with drawn steel and bloodshed."

Beardy delivered his reply in a cold, dispassionate voice. "Because I'm a starving, murderous bandit who steals from people for a living, and because seeing my friends die bloodily and then taking a week-long trek through the damned Green has put me in a shitty mood."

"Fair enough, but let's not jump into anything," Geralhd replied in a carefully neutral voice. The other man's reply had clearly unsettled him. "Antagonizing these people could cost us a lot more than it would gain us. We should try to parley with them first."

"That would cost us the element of surprise, and we can't trust them. They live out in the deep Green! No one normal does that. They're probably all a bunch of cannibals or something worse," Elyias said as he stared nervously at the buildings.

"What in all the hells do you have against rural villages? Did one murder your parents?" a woman asked Elyias.

"What do you think we should do, Blacknail?" Khita threw the hobgoblin an excited grin.

It took a few moments for Blacknail to come up with a reply. He wasn't against sneaking into the village and killing some people—that was kind of what he did—but he wasn't sure what the point would be. In fact, what were they even after in the first place? The humans had different priorities than him, because they were so stupid.

"What do you want from the village?" Blacknail asked the group as he shrugged.

There was a quiet lull as the bandits considered the unexpected question.

"Food and rest?" Beardy replied uncertainly.

"Then we would need to kill them all or make nice," Blacknail remarked as he stared at the villages fortifications.

"He's right," Geralhd said. "Infuriating the natives won't get us anything. If we attack them, they will fight back, and we won't be able to trust them or drop our guards. We can't hope to kill them all either. Our only real way of securing a place to rest and recuperate is to talk to them and work out some sort of deal."

"But what if they're all a bunch of crazed, inbred cultists who worship some twisted forest god?" Elyias asked. "Maybe that's why they live way out here, and if we just walk up to their front door and announce ourselves, the bastards may run out and slaughter us for supper."

"Seriously, what is it with you?" the woman from before asked him.

"I've just had a few bad experiences with small towns, all right? They can be unfriendly places where the king's law isn't always upheld like it should be, and I've heard some things."

"Ha, let me guess. You tried to steal or cheat at gambling and the villagers ran you out of town because you were an outsider." Beardy chuckled.

"They didn't have a lick of evidence that I did anything wrong!" Elyias snapped. "I had to spend the night in an abandoned shed."

"We need to get back on topic," Geralhd told the others.

Blacknail nodded. "How about I take a person and ask them some questions before we talk to the village?"

"You mean kidnap," Geralhd corrected him. "You don't take or steal people; you kidnap them."

"I mean what I said."

"Fine, that plan could work, but where would you find this person?"

Blacknail grinned as he stared at the human settlement. "All prey must leave their lair to find food and water. We just need to watch and wait for an unsuspecting human to come to us."

"Creepy, but it's not a bad plan," Beardy replied. "However, if we don't want them dead set against us you'd better not let them know you're a hobgoblin. That means one of us should do most of the talking and the actual grabbing."

"Fine," Blacknail answered. He was never against doing less work.

"Someone leaving the village might not come out in this direction. There might even be villagers over in the forest on the other side," Geralhd said.

"I'll go look over there then," Blacknail replied as he stood.

"It's a big forest. Maybe you should take help. I'm sure the goblins could track down a villager for us."

Blacknail turned to observe the pack of goblins. They were all clustered off to the side at the edge of the forest where they could hide among some stumps and bushes. Like the humans, they were mostly staring at the village. As Blacknail watched, two of the goblins hissed at each other and began fighting. They wrestled for a second before Gob pulled them apart. The growling hobgoblin grabbed both of the goblins' necks and pressed them down into the dirt until they shut up. He then let them go, and they quickly scampered away.

"I don't think they're smart enough for that," Blacknail said as he scowled at the scene.

"You had them doing more complex tasks than this before," Geralhd pointed out.

"Yes, but not important things, just stuff that didn't affect me if they messed up. Also, I can't explain the details to them because they don't talk well."

"I think they understand more than you think, and I've been teaching Gob. He can give them the details."

This idea didn't sit well with Blacknail for some reason, but if it worked, then he would have less work to do, so it was worth a shot. He sighed. "Fine, but if this goes badly, it's all your fault."

Part Four:

The Suffering Souls

Chapter 28

Blacknail walked away from the village that stood in the clearing behind him and headed toward Gob and the feral goblins lounging about among some bushes and tree stumps at the edge of the forest.

Geralhd trailed after Blacknail. "I'm surprised you didn't talk to Gob more on the way here. You've barely said two words to him since your reunion."

Blacknail sniffed in annoyance. "Why would I want to speak to him? He's a hobgoblin, so he has nothing interesting to say."

"Well, if he learns a few more words—"

Blacknail snorted rudely and cut him off. "No, wrong. I mean Gob has nothing to say because he lives out in a forest with a bunch of goblins. I've seen the forest and I know all about goblins. Talking about those things would be dumb."

Geralhd wasn't able to come up with a reply before they reached Gob's side. The hobgoblin looked their way and bowed his head submissively toward Blacknail. Blacknail snorted again; however, Geralhd greeted Gob with a cheerful wave and a smile. The two then communicated through hand gestures and a few human words as Blacknail watched. Most of it was confusing nonsense, but it certainly seemed like Geralhd was asking Gob to send out goblins to help scout the forest.

"Yes. Yes," Gob replied in a scratchy voice after Geralhd had finished speaking. The hobgoblin's head bobbed up and down enthusiastically, then he looked toward Blacknail. There was a questioning look in his eyes, obviously seeking Blacknail's approval to do whatever Geralhd had asked of him.

He didn't get it right away. Blacknail stared at Gob suspiciously for a second before nodding. He had no reason to go against the plan, but he couldn't resist ending the nod with a haughty growl. Blacknail wanted to remind Gob who the boss was. It was him. He was the boss.

Gob turned around and made a barking sound. The goblins loitering all around him perked up and looked his way. When he had their attention, Gob hissed and grunted a few times before motioning toward the forest.

Blacknail watched intently. He had no idea what any of those stupid sounds were supposed to mean. When he tried to command the goblins, it usually took him much longer. Gob was certainly useful to have around, which unfortunately meant Blacknail couldn't kill him yet. The goblins muttered amongst themselves for a few moments before running off into the woods. One of them tried to stay behind, but Blacknail gave the lazy critter a swift kick that sent him scampering into the bushes. The little pest was probably going to sit down somewhere out of sight, but there was nothing Blacknail could do about it.

Soon, all the goblins had left except for Scamp and Imp, who were still sitting over by the bandits. Blacknail considered giving them both a kick and forcing them out into the forest as well, but Scamp was useless and Imp was still wearing his backpack. Blacknail was afraid an impact might cause something in the sack to explode.

"I hope you know what you're doing," Beardy remarked as he walked up next to Geralhd.

Blacknail shrugged. "It's Geralhd's idea, so everything that goes badly is his fault."

The bandits fell into quiet conversation as they watched the village from afar and waited for the goblins to return. It took a little over half an hour for the first of the green critters to come back. The goblin scampered out of the bushes and ran over to Gob with an excited gleam in his eyes. The hobgoblin and the goblin grunted at each other a few times, then Gob turned toward Blacknail and pointed out into the forest.

"It looks like they've found someone," Geralhd remarked.

"Let's see who it is," Blacknail replied as he motioned for the rest of the humans to join him.

The hobgoblin had gotten sick of waiting around. Recently, when he stayed still, he couldn't help but reflect on his memories. This wasn't something he enjoyed. Whenever Saeter's face came to mind, cold rage flared to life in his chest. It was only by keeping busy that he'd managed to stay calm, and there hadn't been any acceptable targets for his rage around lately.

When they were ready to move, Blacknail signaled Gob. The feral hobgoblin hissed at the goblin that had come back, and the pair walked off into the forest. Blacknail and his human minions followed silently. They circled through the thick greenery around the edge of the clearing for a few minutes. The goblin then sniffed an exposed tree root and veered off deeper into the woods. Blacknail eyed the surroundings carefully. It was faint, but the dirt here had been beaten down and hardened into a trail that led from the village off into the woods. People were obviously using this path frequently.

The goblin and the bandits followed the trail until the sound of voices reached Blacknail's ears. Gob noticed them at the same time, and both the hobgoblins stared ahead toward the noises' source. As he listened, Blacknail raised a hand to signal for silence and slowed his pace. He took extra effort to move quietly as he walked forward. It sounded as though only two people were talking: a man and a woman. Blacknail smiled. That was a perfect size group for the bandits to target, so he crept closer through the underbrush, and soon he spotted his quarry.

There were three humans, not two. One of them had simply been staying quiet. The first two were standing right next to each other. A blond girl and the other was a brown-haired boy were a few feet from the path and looking at something on the ground.

Several branches and bushes were in the way, so the details were hard to make out, but that much was visible.

Blacknail crept up beside a tree and peered around the trunk to get a better look, but he didn't have any luck, so he switched to studying the third person. A second young man was leaning against a tree a few feet from his companions. He was blond, and he had an expression that betrayed a mix of annoyance and disgust as he watched the other two.

Apparently Blacknail wasn't the only one who noticed the boy's expression. The other young man did as well, and he spoke up. "Why did you come with us if you're just going to glare and make stupid faces at my back?"

"You know the reason. Anyone going out into the woods needs to be in groups of at least three," the blond young man replied.

"But we're only a few minutes away from home. This is practically our yard!"

"The rules still stand. You never know what's out here. The forest is a dangerous place, and I wasn't going to let my sister come out here without any real protection, especially with you."

"What the hells is that supposed to mean?" the brunet boy replied indignantly. There was a rustling as he rose to his feet, but the other boy smiled.

"It means I don't think you can take care of yourself, let alone others, and if you trip over a root and crack your skull, then I don't want her to have to carry you back herself."

There was a second of angry silence before the girl said, "Come on boys, stop arguing, it's just silly. Let's have a good time."

After that, their voices grew quieter, so Blacknail retreated back to the rest of his party. He had heard and seen enough anyway. These people would make great hostages and be easy to capture. They were clearly idiots with little in the way of survival skills.

"What did you see?" Geralhd asked Blacknail when he got back. His voice was quiet and nervous. Behind him stood the other bandits and Gob.

"Three scrawny and weak-looking humans. Two males and a female," Blacknail replied.

"Great, let's grab them!" Beardy said as he stepped forward. He didn't get far though, because Blacknail sniffed disdainfully and got in his way.

"No, that's stupid. You can't just rush in there or they will escape, stupid."

"Then what should we do?"

"It's obvious. You need to cut them off and encircle them," Blacknail explained as he raised a finger and drew a circle in the air.

As everyone listened, the hobgoblin laid out his plan. If there was one thing Blacknail was an expert at, it was hunting prey, especially human prey. They were very predictable.

When they were done planning, the humans split into two groups and headed off in different directions. Blacknail told Gob and the goblins to stay put, then he followed Geralhd's group. A second later, he spun back around and hissed at the goblins shadowing him until they ran back to Gob. The stupid creatures really needed to take some initiative and learn a real language so he could yell at them properly.

Geralhd led his half of the group through the forest until they were well away from their quarry, then they stepped onto the path and leisurely followed it back. Blacknail pulled up his hood and kept behind his human minions. He was supposed to stay out of sight so that his fearsome greatness didn't scare the humans too much, or something. He had forgotten the exact reason, but it wasn't important. Probably.

Before closing the last stretch and approaching the three youths, Blacknail raised two fingers to his lips and whistled to signal their approach. The sound was almost indistinguishable from that of a real bird, and from off in the forest, there was a quick reply from the other party, so they kept moving. It hadn't been a good reply, unless the signaler had been trying to imitate a bird that had died halfway through its song, but it served its purpose. Both groups were in position as the three youths came into sight.

"I'm telling you that last birdcall was weird. We should head back. What if it was a harpy or something?" the shorter brown-haired boy told the other. The blond woman was pressed up against him, and all three of them were standing on the path together and talking.

"There would have to be more than one harpy to threaten us, and they know better than to come near here. Every time one of those things shows their ugly face, a hunting party is sent out to exterminate them. Our father still has a skull he got from the last hunt," the blond young man replied. He didn't sound too concerned.

"What about goblins?"

"Those stunted wretches? What about them? I know the old folks like to tell horror stories about them, but that's all they are. Stories. We're in no danger from goblins. You're just being jumpy."

The girl looked past her companions and spotted the bandits walking their way. She flinched, and her mouth fell open slightly in shock. The two boys noticed and turned to see what she was looking at.

"Oh, hello there!" Geralhd's voice was pleasant as he waved in their direction.

The men behind him also smiled, but in a far less friendly way. They were about thirty feet away now.

The blond boy was the one who replied. He stuttered as he spoke, and he'd gone pale. He was clearly terrified but trying not to show it. "W-who are you?"

Geralhd smiled reassuringly. "I'm just a harmless traveler who has gotten lost and is looking to get some directions and maybe some shelter for the night."

The girl stepped closer to the other boy and hugged his arm tightly. She didn't seem convinced.

"And what about all the men behind you with the weapons?" the blond boy asked as he stuck out an arm and pushed the other two behind him. All three of the youths took a few steps away from the bandits.

"They are my associates. The forest is a dangerous place for a lone traveler. You don't need to be afraid of them," Geralhd replied in the same calm voice.

It looked as though the young humans were going to bolt off into the forest, but they didn't get a chance. With a rustling sound, the other group of bandits stepped out of the bushes and onto the path behind the youths. The youngsters paled even more when they saw the newcomers. They were surrounded, and they knew it.

"Those are also some of my associates," Geralhd said as the young woman trembled.

"What do you want?" the shorter boy asked as he held the girl and glared defiantly at Geralhd.

"I already told you. I just want to ask you some questions, that's all. We can all be friends, so why don't you sit down so we can talk," Geralhd answered. This time, his cold tone made it clear he wasn't really making a suggestion.

All three of the youths stepped closer together. With a desperate look in their eyes, they searched for an escape route.

"Sit," Geralhd ordered as both groups of bandits closed in.

All three of the youths sat down on the ground. The rough-looking and dirty bandits took the opportunity to encircle them.

"If you harm us, our parents and the others will hunt you down," the blond boy explained.

There were amused chuckles from a lot of the bandits. Khita's laugh was one of the loudest, and her voice drew the tall blond boy's attention. He clearly had no idea what to make of her, because he frowned in confusion.

"I don't want to harm you," Geralhd reassured them as he crouched so that their faces were almost level. "I just want to ask you some questions and then maybe you can do us a quick favor and introduce us to your village."

The three youths exchanged glances before the girl replied. "What do you want to know, sir?"

The question took Geralhd by surprise. He hesitated as he tried to come up with an answer. They hadn't actually planned this part. "Um… we just want to know about your village."

There was no immediate reply, so Elyias took the opportunity to lean down and ask his own question. "Do you worship any strange gods that command you to murder outsiders or eat human flesh?"

"No… um, we have a small shrine to Ter-vur," the blond boy answered slowly. He had obviously been taken aback by the question, and everyone was looking at Elyias weirdly.

"What kind of stupid question was that?" Beardy asked.

"An important one," Elyias replied defensively. "Do you want to be eaten by cannibals?"

Before anyone else could speak up, Blacknail stepped forward. "Do you have cheese?" The bandits had run out days ago and Blacknail dearly missed the taste.

This time, the girl replied. "A little? We have a few goats, although the last cow died a couple years back."

There was an exasperated sigh from Beardy, and before the hobgoblin could respond to the girl, Geralhd glared at him. Oh right, he wasn't supposed to be talking. Why had he agreed to that again?

Without any more interruptions, Geralhd interrogated the captives about their village. They were reluctant to talk about certain things, but soon a clear picture of the fortified community appeared.

"It seems like a half-decent place to get some supplies and maybe spend a night," Geralhd observed. "They have empty homes, and they don't sound like a bunch of paranoid bastards we can't trust."

Most the other bandits agreed, and they soon came to a decision. They would risk trying to contact the village and seeing if they could spend the night there. Blacknail went along with it mostly because it sounded much more exciting than staying out in the forest. Plus they had cheese.

"Let's grab these younglings and get moving then," Beardy said.

"I volunteer to guard the girl on the way over," Elyias said as he leered her way.

"As if, greenhorn. I'll do that," an older bandit remarked.

"I'll watch her," Blacknail said as he stepped closer to the blonde.

"Er, why? I thought you weren't into that…"

"Into what?" Blacknail asked as he blinked in confusion. Why couldn't the humans make sense?

"You know…" the older bandit replied as he made several crude finger gestures.

Blacknail stared blankly at him. He had no idea what the bandit was trying to get at, so he just clarified his own thoughts. "I'm much faster and a better guard than any of you, and the other two little people smell horrible."

"Ah, that makes sense," the bandit said as the two boys gave Blacknail hostile looks.

Humans could be weirdly sensitive about their smell even though their noses were barely functional. The girl looked frightened by all the sudden attention. The captives had calmed down somewhat once it became apparent they weren't about to be assaulted and murdered, but they were still on edge.

"You should probably stay back and keep watch. You're our best scout after all," Geralhd interjected before lowering his voice to a whisper. "And you promised to stay away from the captives! They can't learn that you're a hobgoblin."

That made Blacknail snort in annoyance, but he didn't argue the point. Without a word, he moved to the back of the group as they got moving. The captives were in the middle of the party as they made their way back up the trail and toward the village.

The three youths weren't the only nervous ones though. Most the bandits looked uncertain and moved stiffly. Approaching the village was something they had to do, but it was also dangerous. They didn't know exactly what they would find there. Soon enough, they reached the edge of the woods and crossed the clearing and the worked earth within it. Ahead of them loomed the settlement wall made up of wooden stakes. Its hostile presence informed everyone that the village was prepared to defend itself from outsiders.

Chapter 29

Before approaching the walls of the remote village, the bandits took pains to make themselves as presentable and harmless-looking as possible. Unfortunately, after spending so long hiking through the forest, that was pretty much impossible. They still looked exactly like what they were—a pack of desperate bandits that sane people should avoid.

The captured youths being herded by the bandits had said that there wasn't usually a lookout on duty at the gate, just a guard, and that seemed to be true. Blacknail's group got right to the entrance before they were noticed. Geralhd opened his mouth to shout for attention when he was interrupted by a spiel of swearing from the other side. That was quickly followed by the hidden man there yelling for backup and crying for the village to take up arms.

"This already could have gone better," Beardy commented.

"Let's run while we still have the chance," Elyias muttered fearfully.

"Just let me do all the talking and we'll be fine," Geralhd said as they waited for someone in the village to take charge. He didn't sound too convincing.

Eventually a gruff voice addressed them from the other side of the gate. "Who are you and what are you doing with those children?"

"Greeting, good man! We're just some lost travelers who happened to stumble upon your humble abode and thought to introduce ourselves," Geralhd replied politely. "We mean you no harm, and we certainly wouldn't harm any children. It's just that we encountered them in the woods and thought maybe we could ask them some questions about your village. They're here with us now because I thought you'd want them to come home after all this commotion."

There was a disbelieving huff from the hidden man. "So you'll let them go at any time?"

"Of course, although they can't exactly go inside as long as this gate is closed," Geralhd pointed out.

"Then how about you back up and leave them here?"

Geralhd smiled at the wall. "That would hardly be very gracious on your part, and speaking of manners, you haven't introduced yourself."

"I'm Tannin, the headsman of this village. Other than a silver-tongued liar, who are you supposed to be?"

"My name is Geralhd Rhodeius, and it's a pleasure to meet you, Tannin. Why don't you open this gate so that we can talk properly? I assure you that we mean you no harm."

There was no reply for a few seconds, then Geralhd had to step back as the wooden gate swung open. On the other side were about two dozen burly men armed with various improvised weapons, including axes and pitchforks. All of them were wearing the rough homespun clothing of peasants. Standing out front was an older man with thick arms and a long grey beard. His head was balding and thin of hair, but his eyes were full of fierce energy.

"Now, Geralhd, how about you let the children come over and you tell us what is it that you really want?" the man asked in Tannin's voice.

The bandits glanced at each other nervously but didn't draw their weapons.

"We weren't holding them, so of course they can leave," Geralhd replied as he signaled to the men behind him, who stepped aside.

The three youths ran away from the bandits and joined the villagers. The headsman relaxed slightly when they reached him, but he quickly shushed them and pushed them back behind his men so they were out of the way.

"See, we aren't here to hurt anyone." Geralhd smiled politely. "We only want to have a friendly conversation."

"We don't get many visitors here and I have a low tolerance for bullshit, so why don't you get right to the point and tell me exactly what you want," Tannin replied.

"Fair enough. My companions and I are traveling east, but we need to avoid the main road. Thus, we want to buy supplies, get directions, and rest here for the night."

Tannin's eyes narrowed as he studied Geralhd. "And why should we let you in or deal with your kind at all? We could just close this gate and you'd be forced to leave."

"It's a nice wall, but it's hardly a real guarantee of protection. Besides, if you're going to be that inhospitable to everyone who passes by, then eventually you'll anger someone. Such a person or group might stick around to cause problems for you, and I really doubt you would want them spreading news of your community around when they do leave. You'd be better off staying on their good side and getting something out of dealing with them."

"Ha, how do you propose to pay us for our goods?"

"We have coin and a few extra small blades we could trade. Isolated as you are, I doubt you have much in the way of spare iron here."

Tannin huffed. "I might be able to arrange the things you want, but if we did let you inside, what guarantee do I have that you'll behave? You all seem to be armed to the teeth, and that concerns me more than a little."

"There aren't enough of us to attack this settlement, so making enemies out of you would only come back to bite us. We have every reason to stay friendly."

As the armed villagers watched the bandits, Geralhd and the village headsman continued to talk for several long minutes. A dozen more armed villagers arrived, but Tannin's expression grew less hostile and angry over time. He eventually decided to let the bandits in, so they began to bargain about the price. Things grew slightly heated when Tannin ordered the bandits to hand over their weapons.

Geralhd didn't back down. "Even armed, we are still far too outnumbered to take this village, but without our blades, we stand no chance at all of defending ourselves if you decide to rob us instead of sticking to your word."

Tannin was obviously unhappy with that line of reasoning but eventually conceded the point. "Fine, I'll show where you can bunk up and I'll arrange to see what we can sell you. You'll be under guard though, so don't wander around or cause trouble."

Blacknail thought he detected a sly slant to Tannin's smile but didn't know what to make of it.

Geralhd nodded and grinned triumphantly. With sighs of relief, the bandits followed the villagers deeper into the settlement. It seemed as though a fight had been avoided.

As Blacknail fell in behind the bandits, Geralhd turned and whispered, "You should sneak away now, Blacknail. The goblins shouldn't be left alone, and you can meet up with us after dark. I'm sure you can make it into the village and find us without being detected."

His words sounded a bit too much like orders, so the hobgoblin scowled. "I'm the leader and think I should stay here and instead you should go meet up with the goblins."

Geralhd grimaced. "Yes, you're the leader… but they're still suspicious of us, and with your hood up, you stand out. You can't hide your skin color from them, and if the villagers do turn against us, then you're the only one who could sneak in and free us."

That argument didn't sit well with Blacknail. He wanted to stay closer to the cheese, but he had to admit Geralhd had several good points. He grunted in aggravation then spun around. Blacknail was only a few steps from the gate, so it took him but a moment to slip back outside the wall. Several bandits were between him and the villagers, so none of them noticed him leave. The cloaked hobgoblin crept around the outside of the wall for a bit—to avoid any watchers—before sprinting toward the forest. He would be back when it got darker.

Singing birds could be heard as Blacknail trudged through the bush. It was a fair walk back to where he had left the goblins, but after a few minutes, some of the bushes up ahead shook and a familiar pair of goblins ran out. It was Scamp and Imp, and Imp was still hauling around his heavy backpack. They must have been waiting for Blacknail to leave the village.

"Where are the others?" Blacknail asked. None of the feral goblins had appeared.

Scamp threw a look over his shoulder, and a confused frown appeared on his ugly green face. It seemed as though he hadn't even noticed that the ferals weren't around. On the other hand, Imp gave the hobgoblin a calm, knowing look that irritated Blacknail.

"They left to follow a smell. Gob looked angry." Imp didn't seem too concerned, but then again, he never did.

"They're not very nice, so we stayed to wait for you, boss. You're much better than them," Scamp added helpfully.

This news didn't please Blacknail. Not only was he supposed to keep a watch on the goblins, but Gob had acted without permission. That was what Blacknail had been afraid of and why hobgoblins couldn't be trusted! He could only hope Gob wasn't leading a raid on the human settlement at this very moment. He should have dealt with the other hobgoblin days ago.

"What way did they go?" the hobgoblin asked.

Both the goblins pointed in completely different directions. Blacknail groaned and rubbed his eyes. This was dumb. Was he going to have to go all the way back to the place he'd last seen Gob and track him from there? That would be a waste of his time, and he probably didn't have much left.

“They went off into the forest away from the humans,” Imp added, which made Scamp nod. Both the goblins dropped their arms.

That was an important bit of news. Imp was undoubtedly the smarter of the pair…

“Which way did they go again?” Blacknail asked as he got ready to move.

Unsurprisingly, the goblins pointed in different directions again, but this time Scamp was clearly pointing far to the left of his last choice, while Imp’s orientation hadn’t changed.

“That way it is,” Blacknail grumbled as he broke into a quick jog in the direction Imp had indicated.

The goblins followed him as he cut through the forest and headed deeper into the woods. It took the hobgoblin a few minutes to stumble upon the feral goblins’ trail. Imp had apparently been right. They had made a lot of tracks and disturbed the forest. Blacknail picked up speed as he followed the signs, but even then it took him a while to find anything.

As the hobgoblin jumped over a fallen log, he spotted the missing goblins. They were all crouched behind a clump of bushes and peering through the branches. Blacknail snarled as he saw Gob in the center of the group. He drew his sword and stalked toward the other hobgoblin. How dare he disobey an order!

The noise drew Gob’s attention. He looked over his shoulder and flinched in terror at the sight of Blacknail closing in on him.

“What are you doing?” Blacknail hissed. He didn’t appreciate having to run so much.

“Enemy goblin,” Gob replied as he lurched to his feet. There was an uncertain look on his face as he met Blacknail’s gaze, then he turned away to look through the bush again.

Blacknail followed his stare. Whatever was there must be important, or this was some sort of trick.

Up ahead, the forest ended and gave way to a series of low rocky hills. Only a few scraggly trees spotted their desolate surface. The terrain on the way here had been uneven and steep, so the area they were in now was hidden within a low valley surrounded by tall peaks covered in greenery.

At first, Blacknail didn't notice anything special about the place, other than all the rocks, but then something caught his eye. At the bottom of one of the rocky hills was a post, and a human skull had been placed atop of it. Its empty eye sockets stared into the forest. Colored feathers had been jammed into gaps in the wood, and weird symbols had been carved into the post below the bleached bones. Half the symbols looked like crudely drawn genitalia, so this was probably the work of feral goblins.

"Goblins attack goblin. Follow here," Gob explained.

"I see," Blacknail mumbled before glancing back at his hobgoblin minion.

He now understood what had happened. One of the goblins he had sent out to scout must have stumbled upon a goblin from another pack. The two had fought and things had naturally escalated until Gob had decided to raid the enemy and slaughter them all.

That left Blacknail with only one real option—total war. These goblins were his minions—even if he didn't really want them—so an attack on them was an attack on him, as well as a good excuse to have some fun. Besides, it was only a bit past noon now. It wouldn't be dark for hours, and Blacknail didn't want to sit around and wait. Geralhd had wanted Blacknail to keep the goblins out of trouble, but he probably wouldn't care about something like a small tribal war, or ever even know about it. Who would tell him? Most of the goblins couldn't talk, and Scamp was an idiot who rarely remembered anything that wasn't literally beaten into him.

The problem was that post. It wasn't something a small tribe would make, and Gob only had half a dozen goblins with him. The post was also too tall for a goblin to have placed that skull there alone, and teamwork was unlikely. Thus, it was most likely the work of a hobgoblin, which would explain Gob's aggressive behavior. The scent of the other hobgoblin must have enraged him.

"You're lucky I showed up," Blacknail told Gob as he sheathed his sword. "You're kind of runty for a hobgoblin, and it's stupid to attack an enemy in their own territory without a plan."

Blacknail grinned as he stepped through the bushes and walked over to the post. He was still angry, but now he had a new target to focus on, one he didn't have to hold back against. His hood was down and his hobgoblin features were plainly visible as he strode into the clearing. The rule about walking into enemy territory didn't apply to him. He was special, and these were just goblins. They were far less dangerous than the humans he'd been slaughtering lately.

Almost immediately, two dozen goblins rose from hiding places atop the nearby hills and behind rocks. They growled, their ugly green faces scrunched up into vicious snarls as they grabbed stones and raised them in preparation to throw. Blacknail watched as a single stony projectile zoomed his way, but it fell short and rolled harmlessly to a stop at his feet. With a grin, he scooped up the rock and pulled out his sling. A twirl of the weapon sent the projectile straight back at its original thrower. It hit the surprised goblin right between eyes with a loud thud and knocked it unconscious. The other goblins fell silent as they watched their companion roll down the side of the hill.

"Now what will you do?" Blacknail looked around for the enemy leader. He still hadn't shown himself.

Gob and his goblins stepped out of the bushes and took up position behind Blacknail. The enemy goblins looked afraid now. Nothing happened for several long moments as the two groups stared at each other, and Blacknail grew impatient. If the enemy wasn't going to show himself, then Blacknail would force his hand. The hobgoblin drew a deep breath and bellowed as loudly as he could. The unexpected blast of sound startled everyone, but as soon as Blacknail fell silent, an answering roar rose from the enemy hobgoblin stepping out from behind a jagged boulder.

Striking yellow eyes filled with hate glared at Blacknail from atop a crooked nose. The hobgoblin was bulky and taller than any other hobgoblin Blacknail had seen, but his two horns were short and straight. Several long pale scars decorated his skin. He was dressed in dirty rags that could only have once been human clothing, and he was holding a rusty axe. It was clearly a woodsman's tool and its edge had dulled from neglect, but it still looked dangerous.

The hobgoblin's appearance made Blacknail smile hungrily. Blacknail was still outnumbered and in hostile territory, but it had been a while since he'd had an opportunity to let loose. This looked as if it was going to be fun and deliciously bloody. Oh, yes.

Chapter 30

The swarm of feral goblins glared at Blacknail with hate-filled eyes. More and more of them were slipping into sight from behind rocky hills and grey boulders, until there were almost forty of them. Most of them gathered behind their leader, the yellow-eyed hobgoblin. They shook and fidgeted as they worked themselves into a fury. In the center of the group, their hobgoblin chieftain watched Blacknail confidently but seemed willing to wait.

"Let's run away," Scamp said as he cowered behind Blacknail. He clearly regretted coming out of the bushes that bordered the forest.

"Run and I'll make you into a loincloth," Blacknail hissed as he studied the enemy.

This wasn't a small tribe at all, and they far outnumbered Blacknail's paltry force. Although it was two hobgoblins against one, they would quickly be swarmed by the goblin mob in a straight-up fight. Even a good sword wouldn't stop such an angry green wave. Blacknail wasn't too worried though. It wouldn't come to that, because that wasn't how goblins acted. None of them would risk being near the front of a mob, and without a leader, none of them would charge. Still, it was a terrible idea to let the enemy have time to plan or build up their confidence.

"We're going to charge. Follow me or I'll rip your guts out," Blacknail ordered his followers. He eyed Gob and made an aggressive gesture that he hoped conveyed his meaning. The other hobgoblin didn't have a great understanding of how to talk.

“What?” Scamp asked disbelievingly.

Instead of responding, Blacknail drew his sword and launched himself forward. Another roar echoed from his throat as he closed the distance between himself and his target. “Die, you snotty runts!”

The enemy goblins flinched in surprise. Instinctively, they huddled closer together for a moment for safety. The yellow-eyed hobgoblin froze then quickly raised his axe. This didn’t faze Blacknail. He grinned savagely as he dove forward. Meanwhile, the massed goblins realized who Blacknail’s target was. The sudden noise and the attack startled them, so they didn’t have time to do anything but react. Screeching filled the air as the goblins dove away from the charging hobgoblin. It was one thing for them to seek safety in numbers from an enemy, but it was something completely different to place themselves directly between two fighting hobgoblins.

Blacknail didn’t waste this opportunity. He attacked the exposed enemy leader. However, one of the fleeing goblins was too slow and didn’t manage to get out of the way in time. Blacknail kicked him aside before slashing at the yellow-eyed hobgoblin. There was a loud thud as the hobgoblin pivoted away from the attack and knocked the sword blade aside with a swing of his axe. The blade bit into the wooden shaft but didn’t do much damage.

The startled mass of goblins flinched away from the fighting like rippling water and dissolved into chaos. They didn’t know what to do. Their leader tried to step back and strike at Blacknail, but he was too slow. Blacknail growled and lunged forward at the same moment. Their weapons were still locked together. A shimmer of fear flashed in the hobgoblin’s yellow eyes, and he was forced to step back as Blacknail leaned forward and snapped at him. Blacknail’s teeth closed on empty air, but the action had startled his opponent.

"You're a big fish in a small pond, very small," Blacknail growled at his surprised opponent.

A few enemy goblins that Blacknail had scattered decided to act despite their fear. Three of them jumped at him from the side, but that was when Gob joined the fight. With fists swinging wildly, he assaulted any of the goblins that tried to get close to Blacknail. The smaller fighters screeched as they were pushed aside by this new threat, and Gob's own minions rushed in to support him.

One goblin did manage to get through, and Blacknail had to take a second to kick it away. That gave the enemy hobgoblin time to recover, but Blacknail didn't care.

Blacknail laughed as he raised his blade. "Poor stupid hobgoblin. You have no idea what I am, and you don't know how afraid you should be!"

The cloak draped over Blacknail's shoulders rippled as he moved. Letting his emotions run wild after controlling himself around humans for so long felt good. Out here, their rules no longer applied to him. He was free.

The uncomprehending feral hobgoblin hissed and sputtered angrily. He didn't know what Blacknail had said, but the confidence his opponent was projecting appeared to worry him. A shimmer of fear appeared in his yellow eyes, but instead of trying to retreat, he attacked again. The feral hobgoblin raised his axe and swung it straight at Blacknail.

The blow didn't connect. Instead, a metallic noise rang out as Blacknail parried the attack. He stepped forward and slugged his yellow-eyed opponent in the face. With a wet crack, the hobgoblin fell over backward. His long green nose was bent at an awkward angle, and his eyes were wide with pain and surprise.

A nearby goblin saw an opportunity and jumped at Blacknail from behind. He was gripping a large sharp rock in one hand. Blacknail saw him coming, turned, grabbed his arm, and used the goblin's momentum to toss him over a nearby pile of rock.

Several other nearby goblins watched with impressed looks on their faces.

The yellow-eyed hobgoblin once again tried to catch Blacknail off guard. From where he had fallen, he whistled sharply, and a goblin that had been hanging back out of the fight rushed forward and tossed something his way. The yellow-eyed hobgoblin caught the javelin out of the air, then he whipped it at Blacknail's head as he jumped to his feet.

The projectile zoomed past Blacknail's face as he leaned out of the way. It all happened in a single instant, but Blacknail noticed that something had been smeared across the tip of the weapon. It was probably some sort of poison, and Blacknail made a mental note to watch out for such tricks. The enemy hobgoblin hissed in disappointment when his surprise attack failed. He picked up his fallen axe, but Blacknail didn't give him time to take a defensive stance. He extended the momentum of his dodge into a quick spin and slashed at his enemy.

"I'm bloody magic!" Blacknail hissed as his blade sliced into his opponent's shoulder. "I have killed beasts and men far more dangerous than you!"

The cut wasn't deep, but the pain made the enemy hobgoblin gasp and waver. Blacknail had no mercy. It was time to end this farce of a fight. He unleashed a flurry of attacks that leapt past his enemy's defenses and drew blood. His opponent stumbled again, so Blacknail slashed at his eyes. The enemy ducked down out of the way, but the attack had been a feint. As the yellow-eyed hobgoblin dropped, Blacknail's booted foot smashed into his groin.

There was a shrill squeak and a pop as the enemy hobgoblin's eyes crossed and he collapsed. He looked as though he was in a lot of pain, so Blacknail helped him out. Before the hobgoblin had even hit the ground, Blacknail swung his sword in an arc and the tip of his blade ripped open the hobgoblin's throat.

"Ouchie," Scamp remarked from the edge of the fighting.

There were groans and gasps of shock from many of the other goblins. All of them stopped fighting and stared uncertainly at the victor of the duel. As they watched, Blacknail stomped on his fallen opponent's body a few times. When the feral hobgoblin stopped gurgling and twitching, he turned to meet the gazes of the onlookers.

"All of you, big goblins and small ones, you have no idea what lurks outside your territory, the things I have seen. You are all so petty and stupid, just beasts that live in the dirt," Blacknail said as he sneered at the nearby goblins.

They cowered and shifted under his vicious gaze. Their fear amused Blacknail, but also angered him. What did they know about anything? What did they have to lose?

"That's kind of mean," Scamp remarked.

Blacknail ignored him since he was too far away to kick. The joy of victory had lifted Blacknail's spirits. All his previous doubts were as nothing. Why had he even cared about such stupid things? He was full of confidence and energy. He could do anything.

"I am the greatest of hobgoblins! A chief among chiefs!" Blacknail screamed as he stomped on his fallen foe's body a few more times. Conquest felt good. A lot of Herad's old actions made more sense now. He should do this more often.

No one interrupted Blacknail, but after a few minutes, standing around and gloating to a bunch of goblins got boring, so Blacknail stepped away from the yellow-eyed goblin's corpse. An eager Gob walked over to Blacknail and gibbered something before motioning toward the nearby hills. He was practically vibrating with energy, and his eyes were wide with excitement.

"You're right, Gob. Let's go see what I've conquered," Blacknail replied as he walked toward the nearest hill. There had to be a lair around here somewhere.

As he searched the hills for a cave or crevice, the defeated goblins dispersed. Since it was clear that Blacknail wasn't going to try to slaughter them all right that instant, they had things to do. One smallish goblin with a bluish tint to her skin wandered over to one hill and called out to Blacknail. When the hobgoblin looked over, she pointed toward an opening. She was obviously trying to get on Blacknail's good side by being his guide, and that was fine with him.

Closer inspection of the opening revealed a dark crevice that the yellow-eyed hobgoblin had apparently been using as his personal chamber. It was big enough to hold a dozen goblins, but it looked and smelled as though only the hobgoblin had slept here. A few items stashed were around the place, but nothing all that interesting.

Once he was done looking over that cavern, Blacknail's guide led him to several other small caves being used by the goblins. None of them caught Blacknail's attention, but as they were walking, other local goblins approached him to offer tribute. Blacknail took most of the berries and fresh meat for himself but passed the shiny stones and other such things to Gob. He had enough of that sort of stuff already.

The last cave he was led to was different from the others. The entrance was at the bottom of a hole near the post, and it took a second to climb down. This cave was much larger than all the others and didn't look as if the goblins had used it much. It was wide and extended deep into the ground until it ended at a pile of rubble. It looked as though there had been a cave-in at some point. Unfortunately, it was hard to make out the details since it was too dark even for goblin eyes to see clearly inside. One small section of the wall did contain a bit of the yellow metal that humans liked though.

Once Blacknail had completed his inspection, he walked over to the tallest hill and sat atop it. From there he could see everything in the rocky area and the forest beyond it. He was no longer quite so euphoric, but his mind felt clearer than it had during the march North. Gob and several goblins waited for him at the bottom. Gob knelt reverently and a few of the goblins copied him, although most of them just sat down.

Now Blacknail was the chieftain of another bunch of goblins. Did that matter? Was that what he wanted? The joy of shedding blood and destroying his enemies was fading. Taking this place had been fun, but staying here seemed boring. It couldn't compare to being part of Herad's band. These were just goblins. There was no Saeter here, and no sense of home. Blacknail's memories tugged at his heart. The problem with everything was there was no Saeter anywhere anymore…

The sky darkened as the sun fell toward the western horizon, and Blacknail sighed. It was time to get back to the human village and the bandits. Who knew what sort of trouble they had gotten themselves into without him around? Blacknail took a few moments to explain to Gob that he was in charge of everything while Blacknail was gone and that he didn't want to be followed. Gob appeared to reluctantly accept this command, so Blacknail left everyone and sprinted off into the woods.

The lone hobgoblin ran at a pace that soon left him out of breath, because he didn't want to take too long or be out in the forest when darkness fell. That was when things got truly dangerous. As he ran, Blacknail realized that he could just leave Gob and the others behind and they would never bother him again. That was an idea worth considering. The goblins were more than a little annoying.

After a bit, the hobgoblin reached the village and its tall wooden walls. No ravenous beasts or monsters blocked his way. After waiting a few more aggravating minutes for the sun to set and for the night to grow darker, Blacknail crept out of the bushes at the edge of the clearing and stalked across the empty fields. He reached the wall without incident and listened carefully for any sign of watchers before choosing a deserted-looking section of the wall to climb over. He took off his boots, and his claws made the ascent simple. They dug into the soft wood and easily found purchase.

The village was largely quiet. Before proceeding, Blacknail took a moment to pull up his hood and put his boots back on. There didn't seem to be much in the way of late afternoon activity here, unlike in larger human settlements such as Daggerpoint. Blacknail moved cautiously and kept to the shadows as he searched for Geralhd and the others. He hoped they hadn't all been killed. He already had enough dead humans to avenge.

The village only had thirty or forty buildings of various sizes, so it didn't take the hobgoblin too long to find his first clue to his friends' location. Several armed villagers were standing in the middle of one section of the street and watching three nearby homes. Blacknail was pretty sure he knew what that meant, so he slipped into an alley and circled around to the back of the buildings. Once in the dark, tight space between the homes where no one could see him, the sound of conversation drew Blacknail's attention. He sneaked up to a first-floor window and listened.

"Thank you again for your hospitality, Master Tannin," Geralhd said.

"Ha, there is no need for stuffy titles out here, lad. I'm just another villager, and not a master of anything but myself," Tannin replied.

"Still, I'm grateful."

"Feel free. Graciousness is never unwanted, however let's talk about something more important. You seem like a bright young man, so I bet you're wondering why I let you all in. You're clearly not just a bunch of lost travelers, not armed like that, you're not."

"We have no intention of causing trouble." Geralhd sounded slightly concerned now.

"I'm not saying you do. The truth of the matter is that you're hardly the first bunch of miscreants to wander by, although you're the largest yet."

Blacknail took a chance and peered through the window for a second. In the small room on the other side, no one was looking his way. Tannin and Geralhd were seated at a small table across from each other.

"Er… and what happened to those people, may I ask?" Geralhd asked.

Tannin laughed loudly and slapped his thighs. "Nothing too terrible, lad. I'm one of them. Anyone who wanders out in this direction has reasons to want to stay out of sight, and this settlement is always looking for more manpower."

"If that's an invitation to take up residence here, we will have to decline. Several of our group are looking forward to getting back to civilization."

"Ah, that's too bad. You seem like a useful person to have around. I'll let you think about it overnight and discuss it with your companions," Tannin replied jovially as he stood and pushed his chair aside.

As Blacknail squatted in the alley and listened, a realization crystallized in his head. It had been nagging at him for weeks, but only now was it clear. He didn't want to go to Daggerpoint. There was nothing for him there. Events had been forcing Blacknail to react and do what other people wanted. That was going to end. Instead, he would find out what he truly wanted and seize it! In the shadows, the hobgoblin began to plan…

Chapter 31

Of course, the problem was all the humans. Their weird mental issues really complicated Blacknail's plans. The tight alley was dark and shadowy as the hobgoblin leaned against the side of the building he'd been spying into. It seemed unlikely that anyone would stumble his way, so he had plenty of time to think.

What did Blacknail want for himself? Food? Shiny things? No, he wanted to kill Werrick. Blacknail's mouth watered whenever he thought about it. The memories of Saeter's last moments were still fresh in Blacknail's mind, and they demanded action. Blood had to be paid with blood, but killing Werrick would be difficult and dangerous.

None of the survivors of Herad's camp were anything like Saeter. Not even Geralhd, and especially not Khita. Blacknail had traveled with them for a while now, but it hadn't filled the hole in his chest Going to Daggerpoint wouldn't satisfy him either. His master couldn't be replaced by anyone else. It was pointless to try. Only vengeance was left.

Werrick would be difficult to kill though. He was a powerful Vessel, and he had a horde of minions. Being sneaky wouldn't be enough, which meant Blacknail needed more power, and the easiest way to get that was by increasing the size of his tribe. Werrick had a large army, so Blacknail needed one too. Unfortunately, while that idea was appealing, it would be hard to accomplish.

After having observed his human minions for a while, Blacknail had come to the troubling conclusion that most of them didn't like having him in charge. Even though he'd done such a great job as their leader, and saved their lives too many times to count, they didn't trust him. It was obviously because he was a hobgoblin. What a bunch of stupid herd animals.

Blacknail sighed as doubt clouded his mind. He couldn't build a human army the way Herad or Werrick had. Being the strongest fighter wasn't enough. Did that mean his goal was impossible? Maybe he was just thinking about this the wrong way. What if he thought about this as though it was… a hunt? Yes, that could work. He had certain tools available, and it was all about using them correctly in order to corner his quarry. Most of the tools were humans, and they were defined by their fear and their greed. Controlling them was simply a matter of introducing the right motivation at the right time. He had some other tools available, like the goblins, even if they were useless for anything that required an attention span of over a minute.

After going over his options for a while, Blacknail was forced to take a break. The pieces weren't falling into place. He'd hit a mental wall, and while he had been thinking, night had fallen around him. It was almost pitch black now. The only noise was from far-off night birds and the occasional rustle of a rat moving through the garbage behind the hobgoblin.

"Time to sleep. I can think later." Blacknail yawned, then turned and climbed through the window that led into the home Geralhd was using.

The room on the other side was lit by a single flickering candle. Geralhd was still sitting in his chair at the table, but it looked as if he had fallen asleep. He was slumped over, and his chest rose and fell slowly as a quiet whistling sound issued from his mouth. Blacknail poked him on the cheek.

"Ah, what?" the man exclaimed in surprise as his now wide-open eyes looked around the room before focusing on Blacknail.

"It's just me, be quiet," the hobgoblin replied as Geralhd visibly relaxed.

"Oh, Blacknail, it's you. I was waiting for you, but I was beginning to wonder if you were ever going to show up tonight."

"I had stuff to do." Blacknail looked around the room then peered through a doorway into the bedroom beyond.

"Well, I was talking to Tannin, this village's headsman, and it doesn't seem like they're going to trick or attack us."

"Yes, I heard."

Geralhd gave the hobgoblin a questioning look. "If you were there, then why didn't you come in earlier?"

"There was someone coming, so I had to leave," Blacknail lied as he walked into the bedroom and stared at the bed up against the far wall. He ruffled up the blankets.

"Actually, I was planning on sleeping there…" Geralhd muttered after getting up.

Blacknail ignored him and sat on the bed. The hobgoblin's mouth stretched wide open as he yawned.

"I guess I'll just use the smaller bed in the next room." Geralhd sounded quite annoyed, but Blacknail didn't care.

"Did anything important happen while I was gone? You humans keep getting into trouble."

"Nothing much, except what I already told you. The plan is to take day tomorrow to buy what we need and rest our feet. We can leave for Daggerpoint the next day."

There was a creaking noise from the bed as Blacknail leaned over sideways. He kept his eyes on Geralhd and scowled slightly. He was still the leader, sohe was the one who got to decide when they would leave, although another day to think up his own plan would probably be enough.

While Geralhd was here, Blacknail decided to ask him some questions. He had heard the man discuss something interesting with Tannin, and maybe a human's point of view would help the hobgoblin. Geralhd was the most human-like human Blacknail knew. He was slow to react, confused about everything, and loved saying pointless things that barely made sense.

Blacknail coughed and straightened his posture so that he looked more leader-like. “I give you permission to do all that stuff you said, but I have some questions.”

Geralhd frowned. “Oh, what do you want to know?”

“Tannin asked you if you wanted to stay here in this village.”

“Ah, that. You don’t have to worry about any of us wanting to stay out here. Remaining in the wilds isn’t an appealing option to most of us. This place is just a bunch of dirty shacks. I’m a city man myself, and I can’t wait to get back to civilization, where people bathe and women have less facial hair.”

“Hmm, what’s the first thing you want to do when you get to the city?” Blacknail asked. He wanted to understand the humans’ motivations a little better.

“Ha, that’s easy. I want to hit up a tavern and purchase a hot meal. Next, I’ll take a hot bath. It will cost more than few coins, but it will be worth it. That’s probably what most of the band will do. We still have a fair bit of silver between us, but we can’t spend it out here.” Geralhd laughed.

That answer greatly interested Blacknail. There was a cheery new shine to his eyes as he replied. “Which minions do you think want to get back to a human city the most?”

Geralhd laughed again before replying. He seemed to enjoy discussing the topic and thinking about civilization. While he was talking, Blacknail took a second to match names to faces and remember how much he liked those people. Most of them were disposable.

The hobgoblin and the man talked for a few more minutes before Blacknail yawned again and let Geralhd go. By that time, Blacknail had gotten the inspiration he’d wanted. When he was alone, Blacknail took off his boots and coat. He curled up on his bed and smiled before closing his eyes. He had a plan now. The hunt was on.

The next morning, Blacknail was up before the sunrise. First, he got dressed and slipped out of the house before Geralhd was awake. Next, he found a file someone had misplaced in a drawer and borrowed it permanently. His plan called for being around humans a lot, thus he had to file his horns down, so he could disguise himself. Then, while the other bandits were exploring the village and getting ready to leave the next day, he ran through the forest and back to the goblins' lair, where Gob was.

When the rocky hills that concealed the caves came into sight, several goblins climbing over them noticed Blacknail, and one of them let out a trumpeting screech. A few seconds later, Gob hurried into sight and approached Blacknail.

"You are back, great chief! Command me," Gob said as he gave a quick respectful bow.

"Yes, your amazing leader is here," Blacknail replied as he stared at Gob. Having another hobgoblin around had originally annoyed Blacknail to no end. There was just something wrong and dangerous about it. But after careful consideration, he had decided that the advantages outweighed the disadvantages.

Blacknail looked at the nearby goblins wandering around the clearing. This tribe was a lot bigger than Gob's old one. Blacknail wasn't even sure how many goblins lived here, but there were at least fifty. Several different groups of various sizes lived in the nearby caves. The plan Blacknail had come up with last night would only work if he could somehow turn this chaotic goblin tribe into a useful force that would follow orders. It would be hard, but Blacknail had a few ideas that might work. He was the smartest hobgoblin in the entire world, after all.

After collecting his thoughts for a moment, Blacknail gave orders to Gob. A primitive camp like the one here wouldn't do. A more secure base had to be built and provided with a steady supply of food. In order for that to happen, the goblins had to be brought to heel, so the first thing Blacknail ordered Gob to do was to select a group of loyal followers he could stalk and force into obedience. Once they'd been beaten into submission, they were to be taught how to use traps and stone tools. From their ranks, loyal lieutenants could be selected, which in turn would bring more goblins under Blacknail's control, even if Blacknail was too busy and important to do that himself.

"Can I rejoin the humans now? I want to see Geralhd," Scamp whined as he interrupted Blacknail's conversation.

Imp was right behind Scamp, but he just watched the proceedings with his usual inscrutable expression.

"No, they don't want you," Blacknail replied.

"That's not true. They pet me and give me tons of treats!"

"They are with other humans who don't like goblins, so you have to stay here."

"Not fair!"

Blacknail glared at the goblin. "Shut up before I throw a rock at you."

"I hate it here. Everyone is so mean and the food sucks," Scamp muttered as he turned to leave.

"I didn't say you could go," Blacknail added as he grabbed Scamp's shoulder.

"Eh?" the surprised goblin said as he stared at Blacknail in confusion.

"You know a lot of human tricks, so help out or I'll string your puny body up from a tree by your slobbery little tongue."

Herding goblins was a difficult task, and before Blacknail had accomplished all that much, the day was approaching its end. That meant it was time to get back to Geralhd and the others. Blacknail took a moment to stretch before heading back into the forest. As he ran, the hobgoblin considered the next step of his plan.

About an hour later, he arrived at the village and sneaked back inside. Going over the wall was easy in the dark. However, instead of visiting Geralhd again, Blacknail sneaked around the town and met up with a few of the other bandits. He talked to them for several hours before slipping back into the house Geralhd was using and going to sleep.

When morning came, Blacknail was leading the way back toward Daggerpoint. The sky was still dark, and the forest was a maze of shadows. His group had left the village at the break of dawn to avoid unnecessary attention. There was no wind, but the early morning storm of bird song was at full force.

"Ha, I can't wait to get to Daggerpoint. I know we still have a long way to go, but it seems like we're almost there to me," a short bandit with dark hair and a moustache announced. He was following right behind Blacknail.

A taller bandit with fair hair sighed. "Don't say that. Now you just know some horrible beast is going to jump out of the bushes and attack."

"Oh, don't worry. That's not going to happen," Blacknail replied before chuckling.

There was a brief pause before the fair-haired bandit spoke up. "You're unusually talkative today, Blacknail."

"It's a good day. Don't you agree?" the hobgoblin asked as he smiled at the man.

"I can't argue against that. It's certainly seems like it's going to be better than I thought it would. I'm definitely richer than yesterday."

There were only four men and Blacknail within sight. The hobgoblin was leading the way between a maze of tall trees. The earth was dark and soft where it was visible between the short, broad-leaved plants dotting the ground.

"Are you sure no one is going to catch up to us?" Elyias asked nervously as he looked over his shoulder.

"Yes, we aren't following the same path as before, and none of them are trackers," Blacknail answered with a dismissive wave.

"Some of the villagers could be half-decent woodsmen," the mustached bandit pointed out.

Blacknail shook his head. "They're just humans, and I would hear them if they got close. As long as you're with me, you don't need to worry about anything else."

The fair-haired bandit smiled smugly. “That’s right, they’re just a dumb bunch of peasants. The inbred dirt famers probably never leave their shacks, and we’ve got Blacknail with us. He has proven that he knows what he’s doing.”

“I definitely have a plan,” Blacknail agreed. It was nice to finally get some proper appreciation.

The group hiked through the forest for several hours. The sun rose until its light shone straight down through the branches overhead. Up ahead, Blacknail spotted a hill through the trees. It wasn’t a particularly tall mound, but there was plenty of room to sit on top of it and it was nice and dry. A small creek with a rocky bottom ran through the trees and passed by the bottom of the hill. The bubbling water looked clear and clean.

“This looks like a good place to stop. There’s a creek right there. I’ll make stew,” Blacknail announced as he put down his pack.

“Do we have time for that? We should probably keep moving,” the mustached bandit replied.

“It will be quick. I have everything already prepared. I just need to heat the water.”

“Still, we should save the large meal for supper. We can just eat a quick bite of dried trail food right now.”

“I wasn’t asking for your advice,” Blacknail hissed. He stopped unpacking his bag so that he could glare at the man. “I’m stopping to make stew. You can walk off into the woods by yourself if you want. Are you going to do that?”

“No… I’m not. You’re the boss, so let’s eat,” the man admitted. He looked more than a little angry at being forced to concede. Normally this would have annoyed Blacknail, but the hobgoblin was in a forgiving mood.

“Yep, that’s me. I’m the leader,” the hobgoblin agreed cheerfully as he got a fire started. He had brought a bit of dried firewood with him for this exact purpose.

The other bandits settled down to rest as Blacknail cooked. The hobgoblin took his time and enjoyed the process. He liked the process of throwing ingredients into a pot and boiling it.

"I have to admit that I was skeptical of your plan when you met with me last night, but it's going perfectly," the fair-haired bandit said. "We might actually come out of this horrible trek through the woods with some real gains. I thought that when Herad fell, we were doomed."

"Damn right," another bandit agreed. "I just regret not being there to see that whiny wimp Geralhd's face when he realized that we'd run off with everyone's coin and valuables!"

"Split between the five of us, we have enough coin to have a proper good time when we get to Daggerpoint. This is a plan worthy of a hobgoblin. It's cunning and merciless! I like it," the mustached man added as he grinned.

"I'm very smart, and I didn't get anything out of guiding a bunch of idiots to Daggerpoint. So why would I do it?" Blacknail said as he returned their smiles. He was practically blushing now from the unexpected compliments.

Elyias was silent as Blacknail passed out bowls of stew. He looked uncomfortable but too nervous to talk. When Blacknail had recruited him for this betrayal, it had been less of an offer and more of a threat to disembowel him and choke him to death with his own guts. It was only when Blacknail went back to stirring the pot without handing him any food that Elyias finally spoke up. "Um, where's my bowl?"

"You don't get any," Blacknail replied as one of the other bandits coughed.

"What? Why not?"

"Because I poisoned it, you pink idiot," Blacknail answered as he stood.

The other two bandits were coughing as well now. All three were struggling to breathe, and their eyes were wide with fear. They grasped at their necks in a vain attempt to gasp down some air. One of them managed to struggle to his feet, but the other two were writhing on the ground. Blacknail drew a knife and walked over to the man who was standing. The bandit desperately flailed in a pathetic attempt to keep Blacknail away, but the hobgoblin dodged the blow and cut the man's throat.

"That's part one of the plan complete. Now for part two," Blacknail exclaimed happily as the bandits died and Elyias watched with horror.

Chapter 32

The corpse of the man Blacknail had killed lay on the ground in front of him. Blood leaked from its torn open throat. The other two men he'd poisoned had also stopped choking and gone still. A mere minute ago, they had been talking with Blacknail in a friendly manner, then the hobgoblin had killed them without mercy or warning.

There was a look of complete, horrified shock on Elyias's face. His eyes were wide with terror as he took a fumbling step away from Blacknail. "Oh gods! What the hells? Have you gone crazy? Are you going to kill me now? I knew this was going to happen, but no one listened to me. Oh gods, why didn't they listen?"

"You're fine," Blacknail reassured his minion. "Didn't I tell you about this part of the plan? I thought I'd told you…"

"Plan? You can't just kill people!"

"They betrayed the rest of the band, so it's fine. That's the kind of people you're supposed to kill. Herad did it all the time."

"You're the one who convinced them to do that! You led them out here, so you're just as responsible as them."

"Don't be silly. I'm the leader; I can't be a traitor. It was a test and they failed," Blacknail replied as he rolled his eyes in a condescending manner. Humans sure could convince themselves of some crazy things.

Elyias stared slack-jawed at Blacknail. He didn't seem to know what to say. "Why did you bring us out here if you were just planning on killing them? It makes no sense. You're insane!"

"It makes lots of sense, too much sense for a minion like you," Blacknail answered. "You're here to help me carry things, and I brought them because they were in the way of my plan."

"What plan? To see how many humans you can lure out into the woods and murder?" Elyias's voice echoed through the trees.

"No, that's dumb. The answer is almost all of them, and I don't want to kill you humans. You're part of my tribe, so I'm trying to help you."

"By lying to us and poisoning our food?"

"Phh, I'm trying to help *most* of you, the ones who deserve it. Like you. You're a good minion. Aren't you?" Blacknail asked as he stared meaningfully at Elyias.

The human minion got the message. "Er, yes?" he responded in a much lower voice.

"Good. Going to Daggerpoint through the forest was a stupid idea. We all would have died," Blacknail replied. Elyias was always fun to have around. His reactions were so amusing, and he was easy to control with threats.

"You still haven't explained your plan at all."

"And I'm not going to right now. There's a lot to do, and you need to get to work."

Despite the man's obvious reluctance and residual fear, Blacknail ordered Elyias to help him move the bodies and gather up their valuables, including all the coins they had stolen from the other bandits.

"What do you even want all this money for?" Elyias asked as he picked up the last coin purse.

"Nothing. I just don't want other people to have it," Blacknail replied.

When they were done, the hobgoblin led the way back. Elyias had no option but to follow him. They were in the middle of the forest and Elyias wasn't anything remotely like a woodsman.

"Shouldn't we have gotten back by now?" Elyias asked after a few hours of hiking at a steady pace. He had a large pack on his back, and the effort of carrying it had obviously tired him out. His brow was sweaty and he was breathing heavily.

"We would have reached the village if that was where we were going," Blacknail answered without slowing or turning around.

"Where are we going?" Elyias asked. He didn't sound happy.

"You'll see soon," Blacknail replied.

After only a few more minutes of walking, the pair arrived at the caves where the goblins lived. Gob was standing at the base of one of the hills and supervising a group of goblins. He noticed Blacknail right away and hurried over to meet him.

"Where did all these goblins come from?" Elyias asked Blacknail as he looked around. "There are a lot more of them here than before. Even goblins don't breed this quickly."

"I conquered them. It was a great battle! I had to fight a ten-foot-tall hobgoblin with a poison spear," Blacknail replied proudly.

Elyias looked doubtful. "Do hobgoblins get that large?"

"Of course. I think I know more about hobgoblins than you."

"All right, but what are we doing here? Why didn't we go back to the village?"

"I'm not doing anything here. I'm leaving. You're going to stay here though," the hobgoblin explained.

"What? I'm not staying out here with a bunch of goblins!"

"I'm the leader, so you don't have much of a choice."

"You can't just imprison me!"

"Yes, I can. I'm the leader, and you betrayed the tribe. If you try to run, I'll hunt you down and skin you alive."

Elyias was overwhelmed by indignant horror. He could only gape as Blacknail turned toward the other hobgoblin.

"Guard this human. Make sure he doesn't go anywhere and keep this gear safe. I don't want any goblins stealing anything," Blacknail told Gob as he shoved Elyias his way.

"Yes, chief," Gob replied as he nodded and grabbed Elyias' shoulder.

Nothing appeared about to explode or catch fire, so Blacknail saw no reason to stick around. It was already late in the afternoon. He dropped all the stuff he had taken from the bandits he'd killed and got ready to leave. The grey-skinned hobgoblin was being his usual obedient self, but Elyias still seemed to find him threatening.

"Hey, where are you going? Gods damn it all. You can't leave me here! What if they eat me?" Elyias wailed.

"Don't let anyone eat him," Blacknail yelled at Gob as he jogged away.

There was a wordless scream of frustration from behind him, but he ignored it.

The next stage of plan was to talk to Geralhd again. Blacknail ran back to the village. He was really doing this way too much lately. All the running back and forth was getting tiresome. Hmm, could he find a way to make his minions do his running for him?

When the hobgoblin reached the clearing that contained the village, he pushed aside the bushes and saw something unexpected. A figure was sitting on a chair by the gate. After peering at the man for a few seconds, Blacknail realized it was Geralhd. He didn't appear to be injured or in distress, so why was he sitting there?

This wasn't something Blacknail had predicted would happen, and it certainly wasn't part of his plan. Blacknail had been planning to sneak back in, but somehow a stupid human had already managed to mess things up. Irately, the hobgoblin stared at Geralhd for a few seconds before shrugging, pulling up his hood, and stepping out of the forest. He didn't really have any option but to go talk to the man.

Tentatively, Blacknail walked over the barren fields. Before he got halfway to the wall, there was a sudden jerk of movement from Geralhd as the man noticed Blacknail.

He jumped to his feet. "There you are! Thank the gods. I was afraid you had disappeared as well. I've been out here for hours. I didn't know what else to do. I'm sorry I missed the meeting this morning, but some rather unfortunate events occurred."

Geralhd had missed the meeting this morning as well? That was convenient. Blacknail had been planning on claiming he'd been distracted by a crisis.

"You answer my questions first. What are you doing out here?" the hobgoblin asked as he threw a suspicious glance toward the village walls. Someone was probably watching from there.

"I had to get your attention somehow. There are things you need to know, and I didn't want you trying to sneak into the village."

Blacknail stared at Geralhd. The man didn't seem suspicious at all, and he even sounded apologetic. "What's going on?" There was no point incriminating himself.

"Four of our compatriots disappeared this morning. We think they stole some things and ran off. As if that wasn't bad enough, the whole mess has made Tannin unduly suspicious of our group. He has the entire village on lock-down, which is why sneaking in would be a terrible idea."

Blacknail tried to look surprised and outraged. "They took stuff and headed off into the forest by themselves? Those dirty thieves!"

"Rhgalt, Marag, Elyias, and Adalk are gone. Those sons of whores must be headed back to civilization by themselves! I don't know what they could possibly be thinking, but they couldn't have gone anywhere else."

"Elyias? That traitor! I thought he was loyal. I have been betrayed!" Blacknail hissed.

"I thought they all were. Have you seen any sign of them?" Geralhd asked.

"No, but I can check for their trail. If they left toward Daggerpoint, there will be signs. Do you want me to hunt them down, or will we all go after them together when we leave?"

"We need to talk to Tannin first," Gerald told him. "He's suspicious of us now and needs some reassurance. Also, I don't think our entire party will be heading South anytime soon."

"What?" Blacknail asked with fake outrage. That actually sounded exactly like what he'd been aiming for.

Geralhd grimaced and looked uncomfortable. "On top of the stealing, the deserters also destroyed quite a few pairs of boots and other gear. We only have enough for three people, and getting through the untamed Green without good boots is nigh impossible."

Blacknail had to hide his smirk. He had enjoyed cutting that stuff up. He pretended to glower. "How long of a wait?"

"That's the thing… we will need to replace quite a few pieces of gear, and the people here aren't going to give anything up for free. Most likely it will take quite a while to earn their value in trade. Also, if we can reassure Tannin, he will probably let us stay here indefinitely. The men who left were some of the most vocal advocates of leaving, and without any coin, even if we get to a city, we would basically be on the streets. Thus, laying low here for a while sounds pretty tempting to some of the men and women."

"So we aren't leaving?"

"Probably not any time soon, no."

"You don't get to decide that! I'm the leader, and I don't want to stay here," Blacknail hissed with fake fury.

"I, uh… don't think we have much choice. I certainly don't enjoy the thought of dwelling out here in these boonies for a second longer than we must. They don't even have an inn! It's nothing but a collection of shacks, but what's the other option?"

The first solution that popped into Blacknail's head was that they could rob someone. That was an activity they had some experience with. However, bringing that up wouldn't serve Blacknail's purposes, so instead he stepped forward until his face was only a few inches from Geralhd's and growled. "Fine, but you all owe me. This is a debt that must be paid."

Geralhd flinched as the hobgoblin's hot breath hit his face. There was a hint of fear in his eyes. "Um, what do you want?"

"Cheese," Blacknail whispered as he stared into Geralhd's eyes. "The village has cheese, so as long as we are here, you and the others will bring it to me."

"Not a problem. I'm sure I can get that for you," Geralhd replied nervously as he stepped back.

A smile appeared on the hobgoblin's lips. His plan was coming along perfectly, and his cheese supply had been acquired. "You'd better. Now explain why you want me to talk to Tannin."

"Like I said, Mister Tannin is feeling paranoid. I had to negotiate to leave the village at all. He thinks we might have allies hiding out in the forest and that we're planning to attack the village from within and without at the same time. I had to reassure him that we only have one person out in the forest and that I needed to talk to him."

"You told him about me?" Blacknail asked. Geralhd had been the one telling the hobgoblin to keep his presence a secret.

"I told him you're a ranger who hates being around people and didn't want to stay in the village. The story is that your face was mutilated by a run-in with a bear and that's why your voice is so… unique. You can keep your hood up and wrap a scarf around your jaw when you meet him."

"Meet him? Why would I do that?"

"Um, yes… I had to promise him a quick conversation with you so that he would know I was telling the truth. It shouldn't be big deal. We'll just head to the gate and you can say a word or two."

This wasn't part of Blacknail's plan. He didn't think it would be too big of a problem though. He'd been hoping to talk to Tannin eventually. "Fine."

The hobgoblin pulled on a pair of gloves. Geralhd handed him a scarf which he then wrapped around his face. That done, the pair headed over to the gate, which opened as they approached. Someone had indeed been watching. When the gate swung open, Tannin stepped out. The bearded older man had a smoke pipe in his mouth, and with a hard look on his face, he studied Blacknail's hooded form.

"See, there's no reason to be concerned. It's just as I explained. There is no one out here but our scout, and he's no threat to you or yours," Geralhd said with false cheer as they came to a stop in front of Tannin.

"That remains to be seen," the older man replied before turning to Blacknail. "So you're this mysterious ranger of theirs. I thought I noticed one of you slipping away yesterday, and the young ones mentioned a creepy cloaked fellow."

"Yes," Blacknail replied in his best imitation of a human voice. Its high hiss-like tone still left something to be desired.

"You're not exactly talkative, are you?"

"No."

Tannin grunted in dissatisfaction. "I hear you're a sodomite."

Geralhd let out a startled cough. Blacknail didn't react. He wasn't familiar with that word, but it sounded like an insult. Normally he would have responded violently to such a display of disrespect, but he was trying to lay low, and killing or injuring Tannin would probably ruin his plans. Cheese was worth a few unkind words.

"What? Preposterous. Why do think that?" Geralhd asked.

"The young lassie you kidnapped before, Joan, mentioned some of the things your bunch said around her. Like how this one here wasn't interested in women."

"That's a misunderstanding, and a large one. Like I said, Blacknail just isn't social at all. His injuries were rather extensive..."

"Blacknail, that's an interesting name. I don't believe you've mentioned it before." Tannin said with a sly smile.

"Yes," the hobgoblin responded deadpan. Tannin was clearly trying to annoy him so that he would talk, but that wouldn't work because Blacknail was too smart. Also, he still had no idea what they were talking about. Every time Blacknail thought he had learned every human word, they came up with a new one.

"Blacknail is but a silly nickname. We all have them," Geralhd said as he shrugged. He had obviously intended for the gesture to look nonchalant, but he couldn't disguise his nervousness.

"Oh, it sounds like there is an interesting story there. Care to share it?"

"I have a black toenail," Blacknail explained slowly.

"I see…" Tannin responded as he puffed on his pipe. He seemed to have been expecting more.

For a few seconds, Tannin and Blacknail stared at each other. Neither of them spoke, and a hostile atmosphere began to build. Their staring competition was interrupted by an unexpected yell from someone within the village.

"Blacknail, there you are!" Khita shouted as she ran over.

The young redhead was smiling. Blacknail felt a shiver of dread work its way up his spine, and Tannin frowned at the intrusion. He clearly didn't know how to handle the young woman.

"I was beginning to think you were avoiding me," Khita said as she came to stop in front of the hobgoblin.

Blacknail's grimace was hidden by his scarf. He *had* been avoiding her.

"So you and this man are friendly, are you?" Tannin asked with obvious interest.

"Of course, we go way back," Khita replied cheerfully. "We've fought together a dozen times, and his master used to train me as well."

"No," Blacknail said.

"His master?" Tannin blew some smoke from his pipe. He looked thoughtful.

"She means Saeter, the ranger who trained him," Geralhd interjected.

"Was this before or after he was maimed by the bear?"

"Before," Geralhd responded just as Khita said, "After."

There was an awkward moment of silence, and Tannin grinned smugly. He obviously wasn't convinced by Geralhd's cover story.

"This is all beside the point. Khita shouldn't be here," Geralhd argued.

"She's half the reason I'm inclined to trust your group. If you truly meant me and mine harm, then I doubt she could keep it a secret," Tannin replied.

"Well, then you should extend that same trust to Blacknail. He really is just a ranger who likes to keep to himself. You've met him and had a nice little chat, so he probably wants to leave now," Geralhd argued.

"Yes," Blacknail said.

Tannin shook his head. "We haven't even gotten down to business yet. There's a reason I wanted to see you, beyond just measuring your character."

"Oh, what do you need?" Geralhd asked.

"Shelter has only remained safe because we've remained secret and hidden from the bandits that plague this land. Your recently departed companions have shown that they're unworthy of trust, and thus they've become a direct threat to my folk. I need a ranger to lead a group South and deal with them before they blab to anyone they shouldn't."

"Not a problem. I hate traitors," Blacknail told the village elder. He'd been planning on using the bandits' disappearance as an excuse to go South anyway.

This earned Blacknail a stiff nod from Tannin. Geralhd grimaced but didn't object.

"Ya, let's go," Khita interjected herself into the conversation.

"We?" the hobgoblin asked as he experienced a sudden sense of unease.

"Well, I'm not staying here while you have adventures. That stupid kid Hassiol keeps bugging me, and these dirty bumpkins want me to do chores."

"We *are* giving you a house. How do you expect to earn a living without working?" Tannin pointed out in exasperation.

"It's not my fault this stupid mud heap isn't large enough to support a proper gang."

"Why would we want a street gang?" Tannin glowered at Khita.

"It doesn't matter, because I'm joining Blacknail. I can be a forest ranger with him and scout out secret trails while we find hidden treasure." That idea didn't seem to impress any of the people listening to her. The young redhead had managed to annoy and drive everyone else to exasperation in under a minute.

"You're not coming," Blacknail told Khita. There was no way he was going to let her accompany him South.

Chapter 33

"So what are you looking for?" Khita asked as Blacknail leaned over to examine the branches of a bush with lush green leaves.

The hobgoblin groaned loudly from frustration. "Signs that humans have been by this way. We're trying to track down the deserters, remember?"

Blacknail wasn't expecting to find any though. He knew where the deserters were, because he'd killed them and dumped their bodies in the Green. However, since he was the only tracker around, he could basically say whatever he wanted and everyone would believe him.

That was why he was now leading a small party of five people South. Blacknail had dragged Geralhd along for his own reasons, and Beardy had come because he didn't trust Blacknail. Khita had somehow managed to invite herself. Their last member was a man from Shelter who Tannin had selected to keep an eye on the others. His name was Kenid, and Blacknail had a whole bunch of fun things in store for him. The other bandits who had traveled North with Blacknail had remained behind since they were lazy and they'd let their gear be destroyed.

After staring at the bush for several more seconds, Blacknail walked deeper into the Green. Everyone else assumed he'd found something and followed without complaint.

It was only when they were setting up camp for the night that anyone asked him about their quarry.

"So are we on the right track?" Kenid asked as they sat down to eat.

"Oh, yes. The others went this way. I'm sure of it," Blacknail lied before biting into a piece of dried meat.

"How much of a head start do they have?" Geralhd asked.

Blacknail shrugged before resuming his chewing. "A few days."

Beardy seemed less than impressed, but the others accepted Blacknail's response without question. Soon after that, they all hit the sack.

The next day, as they traveled, Blacknail amused himself by suggesting that every tree Kenid went near was actually a hungry mimic. He even tied some string to a branch and pulled on it when Kenid got close. Much to Blacknail's glee, that freaked out the man, and he soon became paranoid about every tree and bush they passed. It was great fun.

The day after that, Blacknail stumbled upon a rare small but harmless snake. When the party stopped for lunch, the hobgoblin sneaked the snake into Kenid's pack, and it bit him on the shoulder when it slithered out. As Kenid was swearing and jumping around in pain, Blacknail informed him that the snake had a strong venom that drove people mad. Luckily, the venom could be counteracted by a rare plant. As Blacknail hid his grin behind his scarf, Kenid spent the next few hours sweating and mumbling to himself as they hiked through the thick forest. It was only right before dinner time that Blacknail miraculously happened to stumble upon the antidote—stinkweed. Convinced that he was dying, Kenid ate as many leaves as he could, despite their terrible smell and rancid taste. As everyone else was eating supper, he spent his time vomiting up the leaves. Looking on with satisfaction, Blacknail pronounced the man cured of the venom.

On the third day, Beardy pulled Blacknail aside. “I think you need to give our pal Kenid a break. You’ve had your fun, but we can’t have him slowing us down. He’s looking pretty terrible.”

Blacknail sighed but nodded. He still had quite a few funny jokes left, but Beardy was right. Kenid looked quite sick. His face was red, his eyes were unfocused, and he swayed noticeably as he walked. He needed to toughen up if he wanted to survive out in the Green. Blacknail could help him with that after he’d recovered a bit. There was one plant that made anyone who touched it super itchy. Elyias and Khita had eventually become immune, but Kenid was probably still susceptible.

Now that he was headed back South to seek his master’s enemies, Blacknail’s mood was much lighter. Being the hunter again felt wonderful, and it was much easier to ignore the pain of loss now that he wasn’t siting around and brooding.

“I really don’t think I’m cut out for traveling through the Green,” Kenid observed when they stopped for a quick lunch. “I thought I was tougher than this, but I guess I was wrong.”

“Practice makes perfect. I’m glad you’re here, and you’ll improve given time,” Blacknail said in a friendly tone.

“Ya, look at me. I was born and raised a city girl, but here I am, practically a master ranger!” Khita pointed out. That earned her a glare from Blacknail.

A few hours later, Kenid almost walked into a real mimic, but Blacknail pulled him back at the last second. After that, the man needed a few minutes to recover his wits and change his pants before they could continue on their way.

The next morning, they finally stumbled upon a major road. Everyone, including Blacknail, was quite happy to be out of the forest. Truthfully, he’d been a little lost. Even hobgoblins could lose their bearings, and he probably should have focused more on actual tracking and less on practical jokes. Obviously, the problem was he cared too much about others and helping them grow used to the Green.

“Did the others come this way?” Geralhd asked as he examined the road.

Blacknail hesitated. "Um, I'm not sure. I lost them a while back."

"Well, we'll just have to ask around and find out if anyone has seen them," Geralhd told him.

No one had any better ideas, so Blacknail chose a random direction and they followed the road that way. Thankfully, they quickly ran into a pair of grizzled trappers heading out to check their traps. Like all smart travelers in the North, the pair were wary at first, but Geralhd soon got them talking.

Unsurprisingly, neither of them had seen any sign of the runaways, but they were able to give Blacknail's party basic directions. There were two walled towns in the area: one up the road they were on and the other down the other way. Blacknail had more questions for them though.

"Are there any bandits around this area we should look out for? I hear Werrick sent some of his minions through here a while ago," he asked the trappers.

The lead trapper, a scruffy man with a long black beard and a fur vest, scratched his head. "Aye, you always need to keep an eye out for deserters and thugs in these parts, but I did hear that a new chief had claimed this territory. I believe he sent a representative to Pinecap. He's supposedly staying in town, but I haven't heard too much about him. He seems to be keeping to himself. Which is fine with me, you know."

"Was his name Orvito or something?" Blacknail asked.

"Ya, that sounds familiar. Why do you ask?"

A shiver of hungry excitement went up Blacknail's spine. "No reason. I just heard he might be around." Blacknail thanked the man and turned to talk to his allies as the trappers walked away. "All right, let's get moving. Pinecap is our new destination."

"What? Why would we want to go to the same place as the bandit we were just warned about?" Kenid asked.

Blacknail immediately made something up. “Because that’s where the runaways would go. They’d want to sell him the information about your village obviously.”

Skeptical looks appeared on Geralhd and Beardy’s faces, but Kenid seemed to buy Blacknail’s explanation. He nodded thoughtfully and walked that way.

“Why are we really going to this Pinecap place? Orvito was hunting us, remember?” Geralhd asked when Kenid was out of earshot.

Beardy and Khita leaned in to eavesdrop.

“To make sure the runaways don’t sell us out. I’ll tell you the rest when we get there,” Blacknail replied as he walked. He could tell his words hadn’t satisfied them, but they would just have to wait. He was the leader, so they had no choice.

It didn’t take them long to reach the town of Pinecap. It looked almost exactly the same as all the other walled towns Blacknail had seen scattered around the North. Its grey stone walls were about twelve feet tall and ringed it completely. Only a few of the taller buildings could be seen rising above the stone barrier. Pinecap’s walls had obviously been designed to resist attack by organized humans and not just beasts from the forest. They were also the only reason the town still existed. Blacknail had seen plenty of ruins of human towns. The North was infested with bands of deserters, and every target without a strong defense had been raided and torn apart as the outlaws searched for loot.

“A pair of guards are stationed outside, and they’re checking everyone who wants to enter,” Beardy said as he pointed toward the gate.

Blacknail looked over and saw that he was right.

“Do you want to separate from us and sneak in by yourself?” Geralhd asked.

Blacknail shook his head. “No, I don’t think it will be problem. Let’s just go talk to them.”

Beardy gave the hobgoblin a skeptical look, but Blacknail ignored it. The guards saw them coming but didn’t react until they were almost to the gate. Both guards were wearing steel skull caps and chainmail. They also had truncheons hanging at their hips.

"Halt and state your names and intentions!" one of them yelled as he raised a hand.

Geralhd stepped forward to talk to them. "Greetings, good sirs. It's great to finally arrive here at Pinecap. If I may introduce myself, my name is Geralhd Rhodeius. Behind me, you will find my companions. We're simple travelers who have been visiting friends and are now headed home. We plan on staying the night here and maybe taking a day or two to rest, because we've heard of your excellent inns."

One of the guards snorted in disgust at Geralhd's honied tone, but he motioned for them to move on through the gate. It was only when Blacknail passed that he signaled for them to stop.

"Hey, what's with the hood, traveler? Are you hiding something from us?" he asked as he glared at Blacknail.

Unworried, Blacknail raised both hands in a friendly gesture and stepped closer to the guard. Instead of dropping his hood though, he reached into his coat and pulled out several silver coins. "I'm very ugly. You don't want to see my face."

The guard hesitated then nodded sagely. "Aye, I'd probably lose my lunch or something. Move one." He took the coins and waved Blacknail onward.

Blacknail and his companions didn't face any more difficulties getting into the town. They walked through the gate and found themselves standing in the middle of a wide dirt street that ran through the center of the town. Ramshackle buildings of various sizes and shapes ran along both sides of the street. They all used wood and similar grey stone, but few of them had the same style. A few people were walking around, but not that many. The town had survived while others had died, but it was far from prosperous.

“My feet aren’t used to so much walking,” Kenid remarked sourly. “Let’s find an inn and rest a bit.”

No one had any problems with that idea, so they walked deeper into Pinecap. They soon found an establishment that suited their needs—the Horse’s Mouth. It was neither too rundown and dirty, nor too fancy and expensive. It was the type of place that the better-off workmen or apprentice craftsmen might visit. Most importantly, the innkeeper didn’t ask questions and had several rooms available.

After renting their rooms with coin supplied by Blacknail—he’d steal it back later— the group settled down to eat in the common room. They chose a table in the corner. The place was almost empty, so it was easy to avoid other people and get a little privacy. They drank for a few minutes—Blacknail got water—then the innkeeper himself brought over their food. It was chicken and potato stew.

“So, what do you fellows want to do now?” Kenid asked after taking another swig of ale from his mug. “We need to find those pals of yours that ran off.”

“I’ll find them if they’re in town. I just need to look around. That might even be them there,” Blacknail said as he pointed toward the door. It had just swung open.

As everyone turned to see who he was pointing at, Blacknail took the opportunity to sprinkle some dried leaves onto Kenid’s stew. Upon seeing a middle-aged woman walk through the door and go over to talk to the innkeeper, everyone turned back around, and Blacknail grinned as he leaned back nonchalantly.

“Let’s eat. It’s getting cold and we have stuff to do,” the hobgoblin said as he raised his spoon suggestively.

The others nodded and slurped down their stew. Soon, it was all gone, and most of them had satisfied looks on their faces.

“That was quite good. I feel ready to get to work!” Geralhd remarked as he put down his empty bowl.

There was a queasy grumble from Kenid’s belly in reply. The man’s face had gone pale, and he was grimacing as if in pain. “I think I'm going to use the chamberpot, and then maybe I'll take a quick nap. You fellows should head on without me."

Kenid pushed his chair back and got to his feet. A moment later, he was staggering toward the back of the inn.

"Now we can talk," Blacknail told his companions.

"Um, what did you do to Kenid? Is he going to be all right?" Geralhd asked.

Blacknail made a dismissive gesture. "He'll be fine. He's simply going to be spending the next few hours shitting."

Khita chuckled, but Beardy wasn't amused. He glared at Blacknail. "You poisoned him? That's dangerous."

"It's more of a medicine. Some people do this to themselves on purpose, to clean themselves out," Blacknail countered. Humans did a lot of dumb things to their bodies. Blacknail still remembered his only experiment with alcohol. Never again.

"We needed to get rid of him anyway, and at least he'll survive this. I was thinking of just stabbing him." Khita giggled. "So what's the rest of the plan, Blacknail? You always come up with great stuff!"

"We're going to hunt down and kill Orvito," Blacknail explained.

Beardy jumped to his feet and glared at the hobgoblin. "What! Why in all the hells would we do that?"

"It does seem like a risky move without much in the way of reward," Geralhd added neutrally.

"Nuh uh," Blacknail disagreed with shake of his head. "Orvito knows too much. He's hanging around here looking for us, and the deserters will probably head this way. I lost their scent in the woods, but we can't let them meet Orvito. Really, we have no choice. We have to kill him."

"Maybe…" Geralhd admitted. "However, it still seems like a risky endeavor. It was only due to good fates that Orvito didn't get us the last time we met. He is a dangerous man."

"Don't worry. I'll do all the hard work. Leave it to me," Blacknail replied with a confident smile.

Beardy groaned and massaged his forehead. "You know what? Do what you want. I'm going to take a nap and maybe make sure Kenid doesn't shit himself to death. This isn't my problem anymore."

The grumpy former bandit walked away from the table and made his way over to the stairs leading to the second floor of the inn.

"He's going to miss out on all the fun. Well, there will be more for us now," Khita said happily.

"I don't think I'll be helping you with this." Geralhd looked doubtful about the plan.

That wasn't good. His involvement was important. In fact, Blacknail had planned on using this opportunity to twist the man to his will. Really, it was for his own good. He'd been very sad lately, and Blacknail knew only one cure for that.

"Orvito was the one who killed Vorscha," Blacknail pointed out. "Did you forget that? I saw it happen. He was very nasty about it. He stabbed her several times."

"I-I'm aware of that, Blacknail. I don't believe she would have wanted me to risk myself to get vengeance though. Not after she gave her life to protect us," Geralhd replied sadly.

Blacknail snorted and leaned across the table to meet Geralhd's gaze, and Geralhd froze. "But you want it. Revenge. I see smell it in you. You're hurt, like me. They took something precious from you, and you can never get it back." Geralhd opened his mouth, but Blacknail cut him off. "Words will not fill the emptiness in your chest. Nothing but action will. You ran in fear once. Will you do that again? Or will you challenge yourself and rise above? You want happiness? Take it, as it was taken from you!"

Geralhd didn't look away from Blacknail for several long seconds. Then he leaned back and let out a deep breath. He looked weary. "Demons below and gods above, maybe you're right." He grimaced as if in pain. "I must admit to finding myself lacking. I would give much to cure my sullen heart. Perhaps this is a risk I must take, and it's not like I haven't killed in vengeance before. It was blood spilled during a duel that got me exiled to the frozen North in the first place."

Khita had been sitting silently and grinning as the other two talked, but upon Geralhd's agreement, the redhead raised a fist and gave a happy little shout. "Right, so let's go kill this damned bastard!"

Chapter 34

Having secured help from Geralhd, Blacknail headed out of the inn and onto the streets of Pinecap. He'd left Khita and Geralhd behind because they wouldn't be of much use until later. Blacknail needed to find his target, but he didn't think it would be too hard. Orvito was somewhere in Pinecap, and it wasn't that big of a town.

Blacknail wandered aimlessly at first. He wanted to get a feel for the town and its people. Only after he'd made a complete circuit of the place did he look for his target in earnest. Pinecap was a relatively tame settlement. The people seemed like rough-mannered hard workers. For the most part, they wore simple but serviceable clothes that looked as though they'd seen better days. However, there was a hint of nervousness in the air, and Blacknail almost instantly figured out the cause. This place didn't normally have a large criminal element, if only because there wasn't all that much to steal, but now the town was playing host to a group of bandits. Pinecap was used to fighting to keep bandits out, but Werrick's minions were too powerful to fight, and the Wolf had a history of sparing those who surrendered.

Blacknail could probably have asked anyone he passed for Orvito's location, but he had an itch he needed to scratch. His speech to Geralhd had gotten him riled up, and his spirit was hungry for action. After turning down a side street, Blacknail found himself walking past some smaller homes and buildings. They were made of weathered wood and quite cramped looking. Their walls practically pressed up against each other.

Out front of one of the buildings was a statue of a man, a small flower garden around it. It caught Blacknail's eye because that was far more decoration than the other buildings had, then he spotted a real human sitting on the brickwork around the garden. He was an older man with a bald head and a white robe. The man looked up as Blacknail walked by, and he gave Blacknail a warm smile. That was an unusual reaction to Blacknail's presence, and it made him hesitate.

Sensing weakness, the man stood and moved to intercept Blacknail. "Hello there! It's a nice day, isn't it? Perhaps you'd like talk for a moment and unburden yourself. Or if you seek solace, I invite you to pray in my garden. I'm Hayt, a priest of Tera-Nan."

Uh oh, a priest. Blacknail had been warned about them by Saeter several times. According to him, they were always trying to pry into matters that didn't concern them, and that was the last thing Blacknail wanted to deal with right now.

"I'm busy right now, and like my master, I don't pray much. He said his god preferred action," Blacknail explained as he kept walking.

"It sounds like your master is a wise man," the priest replied with a polite nod.

"The wisest ever," Blacknail replied as he came to a sudden stop. He couldn't resist the opportunity to brag about how wonderful Saeter had been.

"Like your master, do you happen to follow the way of any of the gods?"

"No, I don't know much about them. I haven't had time for big spirits. I've been busy staying alive and plotting. I've been doing a lot plotting lately."

The priest sighed. "The gods are more than big spirits. I can see you need to learn more about them, but you're in luck. I can teach you everything you need to know, including all the right prayers."

Blacknail grimaced. He wasn't looking to learn anything right now. He knew plenty already. "Hmm, I'm a little busy. How about I copy my master and please the gods through my actions?"

"That's better than nothing. What task are you about to undertake? You should at least know which god to dedicate your service to."

"Is there a murder god?" Blacknail asked with genuine interest. Saeter had never mentioned one, but he'd never talked about a lot of things.

The priest frowned. "Not really, no."

"That means there sort of is one," Blacknail pointed out.

The priest glared at Blacknail. "I can see that you're not being serious. Please leave if you aren't genuine in your desire to know divinity."

"All right, bye!" Blacknail exclaimed as he turned to leave. He could ask Khita about possible murder gods later. She would undoubtedly know more than this priest. He looked as though he'd never murdered anyone in his life!

Deciding not to waste any more time, Blacknail hurried down the street and out of sight. He stepped into an alley and looked around. When he was sure no people were nearby, he raised his fingers to his lips and whistled shrilly. The harsh sound echoed through the alley and out into the streets, and within moments, there were several replying whistles. Blacknail nodded.

As he waited, there was movement all around him and the sound of skittering footsteps. Shadowy shapes appeared at the edges of his vision and scuttled over. They were all shapes and sizes. Some were covered in fur while others were bundles of rags. As they gathered, they first seemed like an odd and rather disturbing collection of dirty animals and small urchins, but their true nature quickly became apparent. They were goblins. Every one of them was wearing some sort of disguise that covered almost all their green skin.

Some of the goblins had tanned animal skins draped over their bodies and stared out at the world though the dead creatures' eyeholes. At a distance, they might be mistaken for dogs or groundhogs, and they were stealthy and spry enough that few humans would ever catch more than a glimpse of them. Closer up, the goblins looked like misshapen parodies of animals and would probably be mistaken for evil spirits by any human that got a good look at them. The goblins wearing rags weren't much better. Most of them didn't understand human clothing and had simply thrown patched cloaks over themselves. They might be mistaken for urchins at first, but their proportions were all wrong and the way they moved was far too animalistic.

Blacknail studied his minions for a moment. At his command, they'd followed him here all the way from Shelter. It was no problem for them to avoid the notice of humans and slip over or under the walls of the town. They could also track him by scent. He smelled a lot better than any human.

Now, Blacknail was going to use those abilities. He issued his goblin minions a new set of orders. They were to disperse and find a single human. A large male who looked dangerous and was somewhere isolated.

The goblins signaled their assent and ran off to obey. They slipped back into the shadows and scurried onto the nearby roofs. Blacknail watched them leave then headed back to the mouth of the alley to wait.

He didn't have to wait long. After only a few minutes, he heard the shrill whistle again. Smiling, Blacknail went to investigate. The sound led him down the street and into another alley. There, a tall man in rough clothing was stumbling through the shadows. Blacknail assessed that he was indeed a bandit and also very drunk. His clothes were too shabby yet thick to belong to a villager. This was a man who traveled a lot and wanted to look tough. Grinning in anticipation, Blacknail crept into the alley and silently approached the man's back.

"Gonna find me a good whore. That's what I'll do," the man muttered as he stopped and straightened a little. He didn't glance backward and see Blacknail though.

The hobgoblin was thus able to reach the man's back undetected. Still smiling, he reached around and placed the blade of a knife against the man's throat. The thug froze, and Blacknail felt his heart beat like crazy.

"I have questions," Blacknail announced.

"Oh, let me help you then," the man replied. He sounded fairly sober now. Terror sometimes did that.

Blacknail started with something easy. "You work for Orvito?"

The man hesitated as if considering lying. "Aye, I do."

"And he has a base, right?"

"He does. It's a tavern that he took over. Only his men are allowed inside now."

"And where is this place and how many men are usually there?" Blacknail asked. The man quickly answered, and the hobgoblin asked him a few more questions before he became satisfied. "That's all I need to know. Thank you for your help."

"I don't suppose you're going to let me go now, eh?" the man asked with brittle hope.

"No." Blacknail cut the man's throat. He didn't have anything against the thug, except that he worked for Werrick, but he couldn't have the man talking about this encounter, and he didn't have any other way of keeping him silent.

As blood spurted from the thug's throat, Blacknail grabbed his collar and dragged him to a nearby empty barrel. It was easy enough to stuff the corpse inside, and it would be a while before anyone found it there. Feeling a little calmer now that his bloodlust had been sated, Blacknail headed back out into the street to find Orvito's base of operations.

It turned out that the dead bandit had given him terrible directions. It took Blacknail almost half an hour to find the tavern he'd described. Annoyed at the man's thoughtlessness, Blacknail studied the building from outside. There wasn't anything special about it. It was just another two-story tavern with a stone foundation and wooden walls. Obviously Orvito wasn't expecting an attack, or he would have chosen a more defensible building. Snorting in disgust, Blacknail shook his head and left before someone took note of the suspicious hooded man standing on the street.

Blacknail didn't go far though. He veered off the road and into another alley. Once there, he whistled and waited for his minions to gather. Blacknail then ordered several of them to watch the area and report any large movements of people. Communicating anything but the vaguest commands to the goblins was difficult, but most of them had been around humans long enough to pick up a few words. It was also frustrating that he didn't have anything with Orvito's scent on it, but he ordered his goblins to sniff the trail of everyone who left the tavern and pay particular attention to anyone who smelled strange. Some Vessels were easy to detect by smell. Others weren't.

That done, Blacknail hurried back to the inn where he'd left his allies. It probably wasn't a good idea to leave them alone for too long. Geralhd might convince himself that he didn't want revenge after all, and Khita might wander off somewhere and get into trouble. Blacknail knew Kenid wasn't going anywhere.

When he got back to the inn, Blacknail found his companions up in their rooms. It seemed as though they were all taking naps. What a bunch of slackers. There was work to be done! Well, whatever. He'd give them a small break, even if it was slightly annoying. Blacknail was the leader. That meant he was supposed to do the least amount of work, but it never seemed to work out that way.

Feeling sort of hungry, Blacknail went to find some food. He could have bought something at the inn, but that wasn't any fun. Instead, he went to find street vendors. They always had the greasiest food, and he liked the challenge of tricking them out of their wares, which was very different from stealing. Food was at its tastiest when you'd taken it right out from under someone's nose. Besides, if everything went as planned, Blacknail would be spending a lot of time out in the Green soon, and then he wouldn't get many chances to indulge himself.

Once Blacknail had acquired some unidentifiable meat on a stick from a very fat man, Blacknail found some shadows next to an empty wagon and settled down to eat. It was rather impressive that even with his sensitive nose, he couldn't figure out what he was eating. The fat man was obviously a master at his craft.

As Blacknail was finishing his succulent meal, a goblin wearing a shirt far too large for him and a straw hat crawled out from under a cart and bowed at his feet. Sighing, Blacknail asked him to report in. The goblin quickly spoke, and Blacknail became interested. It seemed as though a large force of enemies had left the tavern they'd appropriated, and the goblins were sure that Orvito wasn't among them. He was still inside. That brought a smile to Blacknail's lips. He smelled opportunity.

Blacknail dismissed the goblin and headed back to the inn where he'd left Khita and Geralhd. He would need them for this. Rushing down the streets, Blacknail weaved around the occasional pedestrian or cart. No one gave him more than brief look. Except for their priests, the people of Pinecap weren't social or friendly, and Blacknail made sure to avoid anyone who looked like a priest.

A few minutes later, Blacknail reached the inn and entered through the front door. He passed several people eating at the tables in the common room before heading upstairs. The innkeeper glanced his way but recognized him as a paying customer, and that was all he cared about.

When he got upstairs, Blacknail knocked on Khita's door. It only took her a few seconds to open the door, but she blinked at him as though she'd just woken up.

"Come on, it's time to go." Blacknail grabbed her shoulder and dragged her into the hallway.

"Ouch, what? Where are we going and what are we going to do?" she asked.

"We need to get Geralhd, then we need to do the other thing we talked about earlier," Blacknail replied as they approached Geralhd's door.

When Blacknail knocked, instead of opening, there was a shout from within. "Who is it?"

Blacknail snorted impatiently. "It's me. Open up."

"All right, one moment. There's no need to rush," Geralhd told him.

A few seconds later, the door swung open. Geralhd also looked tired and unsteady. But judging by his rather strong odor, he'd been drinking rather than napping. He blinked at the hobgoblin and stumbled back as his visitors pushed their way into the room.

"What's all this about?" Geralhd asked.

"I located Orvito, and he might be vulnerable right now. We need to move," Blacknail explained after he closed the door. He didn't want anyone listening, for obvious reasons.

Geralhd looked surprised. "Right now? I thought we'd at least wait until tomorrow or something."

Blacknail shrugged. "He's weak now. Why wait?"

Khita sighed and turned to give Blacknail a level stare. "I think we need to wait. Us humans need a break and a little bit of forewarning next time. Anyway, we'd need to leave after we killed our guy, and there's no way Kenid could go. Also, I don't think Geralhd is in fighting shape, and you seem to want to bring him for some reason."

Geralhd huffed. "Oh, I've killed people while deeper into my cups than this."

Khita threw him a condescending sneer. "Was it on purpose?"

Groaning, Blacknail took a moment to think. The redhead had a point. Perhaps he was rushing things. "Fine, but you need to be ready to move at my order tomorrow."

"Sure thing," Khita replied as Geralhd nodded.

Shaking his head in frustration, Blacknail went to his own room. It was getting late, so he'd hit the sack early. Tomorrow, he'd get his chance at Orvito. The man still had no idea what was coming for him.

Chapter 35

Blacknail's eyes flew open as he detected a shuffling sound from nearby and instincts gained from sleeping countless nights in the wild kicked in. The room was dark and shadowy. Only a hint of light came in through the window, which was where the noise was coming from, but Blacknail couldn't see it. He was looking in the wrong direction.

So Blacknail slowly grabbed the dagger he kept sheathed on his leg when he slept. At the same time, he stealthily turned his head until he was looking at the window. As he moved, he was ready to spring and attack. However, what he saw calmed him down. A goblin had just pulled itself up into the windowsill. Once there, it hesitated, as if afraid to enter the room and unsure of what else to do.

"Why are you here?" Blacknail asked.

The goblin jumped at the unexpected noise but quickly answered his boss with a series of crude grunts, hisses, and mispronounced human words.

A jolt of excitement went through Blacknail as he listened, and he sat up in bed. "Good job. Where are they now?"

It turned out that the men who had left Orvito's hideout earlier had gone out to party. They'd been up all night at a whorehouse, and the last one had finally nodded off. Two goblins had heard them talking about partying some more before they were sent out on the road tomorrow. Apparently they had a long patrol coming up and were under orders to look for certain unidentified people. Blacknail could guess who they were after.

After dismissing the goblin, Blacknail got dressed and went to the window. He then climbed out and made his way over to Khita's chamber. Knocking and waiting at her door would be loud and a waste of time, so he went through her window instead.

When he got inside, Blacknail strode over to Khita's snoring form and gave her a strong shake. She came awake with a load groan and tried to push Blacknail away. When that didn't work, she turned away from him in an attempt to go back to sleep. Blacknail didn't let her get away with that. He shook her again until she sat up and looked around with an angry scowl.

"Ugh, it's not even dawn yet. Why in all the hells have you woken me up?" Khita remarked as she stared out the dark window behind Blacknail.

"It's time to go attack Orvito."

"What? You promised that we were going to wait until tomorrow."

"That was last night. *Yesterday*," Blacknail pointed out. He didn't see the problem here.

Khita tried to argue some more, but Blacknail pulled her out of bed, forced her to get dressed, and pushed her toward the door. When they got to Geralhd's room, Blacknail knocked politely. A moment later, the door was opened by a smiling goblin who then walked to the window and climbed outside. Khita watched the critter with a startled and confused expression. She then blinked and stared at the now-empty window as if she wasn't sure if she was awake or dreaming. The redhead was obviously still a little out of it.

Blacknail marched over to Geralhd. A few words whispered in his ear were enough to jolt him awake. He gasped and stared at Blacknail with obvious shock until he recognized the hobgoblin and calmed down.

"Dear heavenly gods, what are you doing here?" he asked.

"Blacknail thinks now is a great time to go after Werrick's guy," Khita grumbled.

"What?" Geralhd replied as his eyes went wide. He seemed horrified by the thought.

Despite both humans' vocal protests, Blacknail managed to get them moving. They required some time and thick tea to fully wake up, but Blacknail was soon pushing them outside. He didn't even need to threaten to stab them much.

It was still dark out, but the sun was peaking above the horizon. Its glow gave the humans enough light to navigate by. When they had trouble, like when Geralhd walked into a post, Blacknail stepped in to help. He had great night vision, and since no one else was out on the streets, the three of them were able to make good time. As they neared their goal, Blacknail led his allies into a nearby alley.

Geralhd turned to Blacknail and scowled. "Okay, this is far enough. You dragged us out of bed without warning, and now we're the gods only know where. Do you have a real plan to kill Orvito? Or are you just planning on running in and getting us all killed?"

"I have a plan, and it's a great one, because I'm a genius," Blacknail replied as he gave the ignorant human a pitying look. He then raised his fingers to his lips and whistled sharply.

"Why'd you do that? There isn't anyone around to signal to," Khita asked as Geralhd threw Blacknail a confused look. The redhead had recognized the whistle as a sign rangers sometimes used.

Blacknail didn't answer right away, so Khita opened her mouth to ask again. However, before she could speak, she was startled by a rattling noise coming from the dark alleyway behind her. Flinching, she threw a glance over her shoulder. There, a goblin wearing a fur hide and a deer skull on its head had just walked out from behind a rain barrel.

Yelping from fright, Khita jumped backward. Her reaction made Geralhd draw his sword and raise his guard. Blacknail laughed as several more goblins slipped out of the shadows and surrounded the group. In the dark, the two humans had failed to recognize what they were seeing. Geralhd actually shook as Khita clumsily pulled out her own blade.

"You're afraid of goblins." Blacknail laughed as he pointed at them. Pathetic.

"What?" Khita responded indignantly as she peered again at the critters surrounding them. Her frightened posture only relaxed when she realized what she was seeing.

"They're goblins," Geralhd remarked with obvious surprise. "But how did they get here?"

"I ordered them to follow us from Shelter. You're just blind and stuffed, so you didn't notice," Blacknail told him.

"Stuffed? What does that mean?"

"It's like blind, but for your nose. You humans didn't have a word for that, because you're all stuffed, so I made one myself. All the goblins use it. I'm a wordsmith!"

As they talked, more and more poorly disguised goblins gathered. Soon, there were over thirty of them. That number even surprised Blacknail, although he kept his face neutral. Was it possible they'd picked up some feral goblins on the way? Well, whatever. As long as they followed orders, it was fine.

Geralhd blinked and looked around. "Gob isn't here, is he?"

"No, I needed to leave someone smart in charge," Blacknail replied. Elyias also needed someone to watch over him and keep him from doing dumb things.

"What are you going to do with all these goblins?" Khita asked.

"Humans don't look for goblins. You don't see them even when you look right at them. So these ones have already scouted the enemy's hideout and counted his minions," Blacknail replied. Although, most of them had given him wildly different numbers. Goblins weren't great at counting.

Blacknail outlined the basics of his strategy. He had it all planned out. They were going to charge in and murder everyone, saving Orvito for last so they could take their time and enjoy killing him. It was a perfect plan.

"And you don't think you might be a little too confident? Last time you fought Orvito, he kicked you all over the place," Geralhd pointed out.

"No, this time I get to start the fight, and I plan on cheating, like, a lot." In Blacknail's experience, if you weren't cheating, then you were probably too lazy to live long.

Without giving the humans any more chance to delay, Blacknail sent the goblins forward. They gibbered among themselves as they swarmed toward the inn across the street.

"Come on. Follow me," Blacknail told the humans as he headed for the target's front door.

Blacknail downed a few drops of Elixir as he glided through the darkness. There was no one standing near the door, but there was a window off to one side, so he peered through the shutters. As the goblins had reported, three men were inside. Two of them were seated at a table, while the third was standing nearby. All of them were big men in dirty clothing, and they were all armed. Nodding, Blacknail moved back to the door and pressed his ear against it. That was when Khita and Geralhd caught up to him.

"You two take the man on the left. I got the others," Blacknail told them.

Confused expressions appeared on their faces, but before they could whisper any questions, Blacknail heard a commotion from inside.

"Hey, I think there's a huge rat or something over there!" one of the men exclaimed in disgust.

"Where?" one of his companions asked.

That was what Blacknail had been waiting for. Moving quickly, he pulled the door open and dashed inside. The entire chamber was lit by two candles. As their flames flickered, Blacknail ran silently toward the human guards. Unfortunately for them, they were all looking in the wrong direction. A goblin wearing an animal skin had distracted them before slipping away into the darkness.

With startling speed, Blacknail drew his blade and stabbed the exposed back of the man to the right of the table. Before anyone even knew he was there, his blade pierced the man's leather jerkin and sliced deep into his chest. It slid past bone and tore into his lungs, silencing him before he knew what was happening. After tugging the blade out with a quick jerk, Blacknail turned and slashed at the next man's neck. Fueled by wild instinct and Elixir, the hobgoblin moved with inhuman speed and his target barely had time to react. The man tried to stand up out of his chair and raise his arms defensively, but he was too slow. Blacknail's sword cleaved into his neck, unleashing a fatal spray of life blood.

"What the damned hells!" the third man yelled as he got to his feet.

That was when Khita and Geralhd crashed into the third guard. He managed to scream once before their swords skewered him. He coughed up a splatter of blood and collapsed onto the table. When he was clearly dead, Blacknail's companions freed their weapons and stepped back away from their victim.

"You messed up," Blacknail told his human allies with a disappointed sigh. "You had one job."

"You didn't give us enough time!" Khita shot back with a furious glare.

The floorboards above their heads creaked as the people on the second floor reacted to the noise the third man had made. Khita was so useless. Why had he even brought her?

"Go guard that door. It leads to the kitchen, and there are servants inside," Blacknail told Khita as he pointed at the door in question. "I'm taking Geralhd and going up."

"I want to go with you," the redhead replied petulantly.

"This is something Geralhd needs to do. It's for Vorscha," Blacknail told her.

"Urgh, fine," she grunted before doing as she was told. Humans were so easy to manipulate.

"Umm, are you sure you want me along? I might just hold you back…" Geralhd remarked as Khita walked away.

"You're coming." Blacknail huffed as he grabbed the man's shirt and pulled him toward the stairs. "Don't worry. The plan can still work! I assumed you and Khita would mess up."

"Wonderful," Geralhd replied sarcastically.

He didn't resist Blacknail's pull too hard though, so they were soon running up to the next floor. Ahead of them, there was shouting and the creak of floorboards as people rushed around. Leaping up to the second floor, Blacknail scanned the shadows of the hallway. Three enemy bandits were in sight: two in the hallway up ahead and one stepping out of a room to the left. Hmm, that was good enough odds.

"I got these ones!" Blacknail yelled as he charged the two men ahead of him. Both of them already had their weapons out. One was wielding a club, while the other had a long dagger in hand, but there was barely room enough for them to stand side-by-side in the tight hallway.

Burning a hint of Elixir, Blacknail whirled into the bandits. His blade slashed at the man on the right. The man managed to block the blow, but Blacknail was already spinning around and slashing at his leg. The hobgoblin's blade cut into the man's thigh, leaving an inch-deep wound, then Blacknail was forced to jump back. The second man had swung his club at Blacknail's head. Behind him, Blacknail heard the ringing clash of blades as Geralhd engaged the third man.

As the man with the dagger stumbled from the pain of his leg wound, his ally hesitated. Blacknail took advantage of that and surged forward. The man with the club swung at him, but Blacknail dodged sideways and used his momentum to power a kick at the wounded man's gut. It connected with a crack, and the man sprawled over backward. Blacknail then dodged under another wild club swing and stabbed its wielder in the gut. The man jerked in surprise as his internal organs were destroyed, then he fell over. Mercilessly, Blacknail moved on to the wounded knife-wielder and hacked him apart. Both the bandits were soon dead.

When that was done, Blacknail turned to see how Geralhd was doing. He was just in time to see his ally sidestep a sword strike aimed at his chest and respond by slashing at his opponent's face. The attack only left a shallow cut, but crimson blood gushed from the wound and poured into the thug's eyes. Blinded, he was easy pickings for Geralhd, who finished him off with a carefully aimed slash to the neck.

Unfortunately, Blacknail and Geralhd barely had time to catch their breath before another group of three enemies stepped into the hallway, and this time, Orvito was with them. The bandit Vessel had managed to find the time to pull on a chainmail shirt and a steel helm. He was also holding a long sword, and although he was still clean-shaven and disciplined-looking, there was a furious look on his usually stern face.

"What have we here? The quarry has decided to turn on the hounds, has it?" Orvito observed as he surveyed the hallway and the people in it. "Well, thank you for sparing me the effort of having to track you down. I was getting very sick of this dirty village, but Werrick ordered me to stay and keep an eye out for you."

As the enemy thugs stepped forward, Blacknail pushed Geralhd back. "Stay out of my way." It would ruin Blacknail's plan if Geralhd died now. He'd brought him for a reason.

Orvito's two subordinates hesitated to engage the hobgoblin that had taken out their companions. They let their boss take the lead, but they couldn't stay out of the fight completely. One of them grimaced as he was forced to step up and support Orvito.

"You can't breathe fire in here. Lots of dry wood," Blacknail observed as he smirked at the enemy Vessel and glanced toward thc hallway's wooden walls.

“I don’t think that will be necessary. No flying rocks from nowhere will save you this time,” Orvito replied. “You are not my match. Only pure fortune saved you last time.”

Blacknail laughed. With hungry delight, he charged forward to face the enemy. It was time to test himself. He’d come all this way to meet Orvito blade-to-blade. He needed to prove to himself that he was the predator, not the prey. He’d run from this man before, but now things were different. He would run from him no more. He might die here, but so be it. If he succeeded, then he would have purpose again. A path would be set out before him. He would set his will against that of the world and he would fear no man, not even Werrick.

Chapter 36

Orvito met Blacknail's charge with a heavy downward slash. Blacknail sidestepped it and countered with a swift stab to the chest, but the enemy Vessel swayed out of the way and attacked again. A furious exchange of blows followed as the hobgoblin and the man fought within the tight confines of the tavern's hallway.

The thug standing next to Orvito largely stayed out of the fight as Blacknail and his boss clashed. There was room for him to attack, but he knew he was outmatched and chose to hang back instead. Meanwhile, the Vessels hacked and slashed at each other without restraint. Blacknail moved with speed and grace, but he found himself being pushed back by Orvito's power and confidence. They were both pushed beyond the limits of normal human strength and speed by the magic flowing though their blood.

Thus, Blacknail decided to cheat and use one of the tricks he'd prepared beforehand. As he stepped back, he reached into his coat and pulled out a small bag that he tossed at Orvito. The Vessel saw the object coming and moved with supernatural quickness. He jumped back out of the way as the pouch hit the floor and released a cloud of dust. His ally wasn't so quick. He barely had time to flinch before Blacknail lunged forward through the harmless dust and cut him down with a strike to his groin that would soon bleed him out. The hobgoblin whirled around and raised his guard as he gave Orvito a smug grin. On the ground, the fallen man screamed and rolled into a ball as he went into shock.

The enemy Vessel returned the hobgoblin's look with a furious one of his own. "You're a disgusting creature."

"I'm not the one that's pink and smells like dog breath," Blacknail replied.

Face red with anger, Orvito stepped forward to attack again. Yes, that was it. Blacknail wanted his enemy angry. It made humans so predictable. The remaining bandit that had been hanging back stepped up to help. He sure looked unhappy about it though.

Instead of facing them, Blacknail jumped backward and yelled for Geralhd. "Come over here and help now!"

"Why now?" the former bandit asked as he took up position beside his hobgoblin ally.

"It's all part of the plan. Trust the plan," Blacknail replied as they prepared for combat.

The four combatants faced each other with grim expressions and swords in hand, except for Blacknail, who was still grinning. It was two against two now, but the narrow hallway meant they had to watch what they were doing lest they stumble into their ally.

"You can't win. More of my men will be joining us soon," Orvito told them.

"Ya, maybe," Blacknail replied with a roll of his eyes. "Let's fight and see."

"As you wish, creature," the Vessel barked as he lunged forward. He was really angry now.

Blacknail stepped forward into the attack. Their blades met with a loud clang then bounced apart. At the same time, Geralhd and the thug exchanged blows. At first, both sides seemed even. Fighting in the tight corridor was difficult. However, Blacknail was soon forced back by Orvito's heavy blows, and that meant Geralhd had to retreat as well.

As Blacknail stepped back, he misplaced his foot slightly and stumbled for the briefest moment. That was all Orvito needed.

His blade came around in a violent arc as it sought the hobgoblin's blood. Blacknail jerked sideways to dodge the attack, which was only partially successful. The tip of Orvito's sword sliced into Blacknail's arm, drawing blood. Wincing, but not seriously wounded, the hobgoblin retreated.

"We're losing!" Geralhd remarked in alarm as Blacknail dodged another slash that almost took off his nose.

"Yep," the hobgoblin said with a nod. It was time to fix that. His nose was too important to risk.

Ducking under a cut aimed at his eyes, Blacknail raised his fingers to his lips and whistled. He was forced to jump back to avoid being stabbed though the chest, and he grabbed Geralhd and pulled him back as well.

As the still-enraged Orvito stepped forward to continue his attack, there was movement behind him down the hall. A dozen goblins spilled out of the nearby rooms and formed up in the corridor. As Blacknail warded off Orvito with a wild swing of his sword, the goblins pulled out slings and twirled them.

"Get down," Blacknail hissed as he grabbed Geralhd and pulled him to the floor.

Orvito hesitated at the unexpected movement and noise, but his fury kept him focused on Blacknail. He stepped forward to attack again while the hobgoblin's guard was down. However, that was when the goblins unleashed their volley of stones at Orvito and his companion. The rocky projectiles slammed into the two humans' backs. There was a loud crack as a rock ricocheted off the head of Orvito's ally and several muted thuds as rocks hit fleshier parts of his body. Orvito was hit twice. His chainmail blocked one strike, but another rock hit his leg. The man grimaced and staggered as his companion fell to the floor. A blow from a sling was strong enough to break bone.

Meanwhile, those shots that had missed and zipped past the two humans flew harmlessly over Blacknail and Geralhd's heads. Taking advantage of his foe's pain, Blacknail slashed at Orvito's head, but the blow was blocked at the last moment when Orvito gritted his teeth and raised his weapon. That didn't stop

Blacknail. Holding nothing back, he burned Elixir and unleashed a furious flurry of strikes. The first few were blocked, then Blacknail knocked aside the Vessel's blade and stabbed him in the stomach. The feeling of steel sliding through blood and meat was deeply satisfying to the hobgoblin. At last, sweet vengeance and the end of the hunt!

Orvito's eyes went wide with shock as he stumbled backward. But as Blacknail tugged his blade out and stepped in closer, the man's gaze focused on the hobgoblin. His eyes shone with hate and fury as he took a deep breath. Blacknail was fairly sure he knew where this was going. Orvito opened his mouth and a burst of fire appeared, but Blacknail was already in motion. Before the Vessel could exhale, Blacknail kicked him in the gut, right where he'd been stabbed. Instantly, Orvito choked and his mouth snapped shut from the pain. Wisps of black smoke shot out of his nose as he was forced to swallow his own flames. The hobgoblin thought that looked hilarious.

Mercilessly, Blacknail didn't give Orvito any time to recover. He ripped off the man's helmet, grabbed his hair, and smashed his head into the closest wall as hard as he could. Then he did it five more times until Orvito stopped moving. That left several blood-stained holes in the wall.

"Is he still alive?" Geralhd asked as he walked over. He sounded a little shocked, as though he was still trying to catch up.

Blacknail nodded but didn't take his eyes off his prey. "He's still breathing. I was going to let you finish him off, for Vorscha."

"Well, I may as well get it over with so we can get the hells out of here," Geralhd replied as he raised his weapon to strike.

"Try to sound happier about it. It took a lot of hard work and super-smart scheming to make this happen." Blacknail was quite pleased. There was a huge grin on his face, and he felt he was practically glowing with self-satisfaction. He'd won. Werrick's lieutenant had fallen before his amazing cunning and strength, and this was just the start! There would be more to come.

With a wet thump, Geralhd's blade bit deep into Orvito's neck. He didn't come close to decapitating the man, but halfway was still completely fatal.

"How do you feel?" Blacknail asked as his ally withdrew his bloody sword from his fallen foe.

Geralhd looked thoughtful as he wiped his blade clean on Orvito's shirt. "Much better actually, thank you. It might just be the thrill of the fight, but facing the cause of my sorrow has certainly lifted my spirits. I'd let my own supposed helplessness stifle me and prevent me from moving on."

"Don't forget the revenge for Vorscha. It feels good, doesn't it?" Geralhd needed to be pushed in the right direction. He was already the vengeful type, but he was also a bit of coward when he wasn't angry.

Geralhd sighed as he sheathed his sword. "Ah, Vorscha… she was a wonderful woman and I didn't deserve her love. Truly, her death has lessened both me and the world forever. Hers was a light that brightened my very soul! I will miss her forever and ever."

Amused, Blacknail rolled his eyes. That wasn't how he remembered Geralhd and Vorscha's relationship. Hadn't they both agreed it was a temporary thing? Well, this served his purpose, so he wasn't going to question it. He'd put it down as another stupid human thing. "You know, Orvito wasn't the only one responsible for Vorscha's death. He was just following Werrick's orders. "

"This isn't the best place for a conversation. For now, let's get out of here. We can discuss this somewhere safer," Geralhd remarked with a frown.

"Sure," Blacknail replied with a nod. He'd planted the seed, and with some careful tending, it would grow the way he wanted it.

The goblins were already gone, so they headed down the stairs. Back on the first floor, they met up with Khita. She had actually stayed near the door she'd been ordered to guard. That was unusual considering her short attention span. Blacknail was almost impressed.

"Did we win? Is Orvito dead?" the redhead asked as she ran over to join them.

"Yep, your leader's plan worked perfectly. I'm super smart after all," Blacknail told her proudly.

"Well, you're definitely the person I'd ask if I wanted help killing someone," Khita replied with a smirk.

Since they were in a hurry to leave, they didn't have time for any more conversation. Instead, they ran past the dead thugs and through the door that led out of the tavern. Morning had officially begun. A few villagers were walking around outside under the dawn light, but no one tried to stop them as they ran across the street and into an alley. They got a few looks, but it was still very early and no one wanted to get involved in a problem that they hadn't even witnessed between outsiders.

With a huge grin, Blacknail led the others back to their inn. They'd done it! One of the men directly responsible for Saeter's death had been dealt with. Many others were still alive, but Blacknail felt new confidence and purpose. He could bring them down. He wasn't lost in the Green any longer, and he had a real plan. The next part was already underway. Orvito's death was a message that Werrick couldn't ignore. Out in the Deep Green, Blacknail was beyond the Wolf's reach, but he needed to remain a threat that lurked in his enemy's thoughts. Blacknail knew well the minds of humans. He had to make sure that Werrick perceived him a certain way, then the man would become predictable. When the time was ripe, that illusion would lure the Wolf to his doom. Orvito had been a mere minion. Only the death of the man who had ultimately been responsible for the death of Saeter would satisfy Blacknail and fill the painful hole in his chest.

Anyhow, Kenid was probably feeling better by now. That meant they could head back to Shelter. They could simply lie to the man and say they'd killed the deserters and had to leave town in a hurry. Yes, that would work. The sudden commotion would make Beardy grumpy and miserable, but he always was anyway. He'd complain, but he'd follow them back to Shelter. He was too lazy and set in his ways to do otherwise.

"It's barely past dawn and I already need a bath," Geralhd remarked in disgust as he hurried after his hobgoblin ally.

Blacknail chuckled as he swerved around an empty cart. Once he was back at the goblin camp near Shelter, he could begin the next phase of his scheme. His goblin minions had proven quite useful here. Having a small squad of hobgoblins would be even more useful. All he had to do was build up the goblin camp and teach them some new tricks. Then they would prosper under his rule, and when goblins grew fat and secure, they became hobgoblins.

With a squad of hobgoblins at his back, Blacknail could take control of enough humans to challenge Werrick. Plenty of bandits hadn't accepted the Wolf's rule. All he had to do was hunt them down and force them into line. Humans seemed to dislike serving a hobgoblin though, which was why Blacknail needed to slowly manipulate Geralhd and the other former members of Herad's band into becoming his minions. Once loyal, they would serve as his lieutenants and figureheads. At the very least, he could show them off as proof that he didn't eat people. Why were humans so against being eaten anyway? Dead was dead.

Yes, things were going great for Blacknail. The future looked bright and bloody! However, even though he was the best leader ever, there were a few things even he had to watch out for. For instance, trolls. He needed to avoid those better in the future. He also didn't want too many hobgoblins around. That would be annoying and unbelievable chaotic. Blacknail shuddered just thinking about it. They would be too difficult to control, and you couldn't trust them. Gob might be the only exception to that.

Well, whatever. How hard could it be to keep some goblins in line? Blacknail was sure he could keep his new goblin tribe under control long enough to train the minions he needed. Then they could do all the work for him and he could concentrate on murder! That was what minions were for after all. What could go wrong?

Epilogue: A Difference of Perspective

The morning sun was rising. The sky was blue and clear of clouds, so the sunlight was bright and strong as it shone down on the goblin settlement near Shelter. The hobgoblin that had been given the name Gob was standing among the rocky hills that lay within the settlement. In front of him, two dozen goblins were making primitive tools in the shade. Gob watched over them with as close to complete focus and unyielding determination as he could manage. If any of them slacked off for more than a second or made even a tiny mistake, he rebuked them and corrected their mistake. Anything less than perfect was unacceptable. This was the job he'd been entrusted with by his god-king, Blacknail.

Gob had been at this for days—since his master had left—and was weary, but he didn't stop. Taking a deep breath, he steeled his resolve and focused on what needed done. He had orders, and he would not fail his god king. The work must be completed. It was his duty to instruct the goblins and train them. Some of the goblins were making twine from plant husks, while others used that twine to make tools. This was not make-work. Primitive as they were, each of those tools was invaluable. Snares for hunting would allow goblins to catch small prey with ease, slings would allow them to hunt birds and protect themselves from predators, and stone axes would make it much easier to cut down young trees to build shelter. All these items had the power to transform the lives of the goblins, but they were just the beginning.

Right now, that settlement was little more than a few caves in some rocky hills. It was unworthy of his lord, but Gob knew that would soon change. He'd already seen it happen once, and he knew that had been but a small taste of the things to come.

His god king held much greater secrets that he would share upon his return. Blacknail had lived with humans and knew their ways. Limited as he was, even Gob could see that there was much more to be learned from the humans. They built complex structures and tools far beyond what Gob could comprehend. They did this by working together and disciplining themselves. Those concepts had once been alien to Gob, as they were to all feral goblins, but now he saw their worth. Blacknail had taught him much, and he saw the world through different eyes now.

Gob had been a mere goblin the first time he'd met Blacknail, and he'd thought the hobgoblin a fool. How blind he'd been. The god king had proven his might by crushing the horned hobgoblin that had challenged him and then taken over his vanquished foe's tribe. After that, he'd taken a few days to teach Gob and his small tribe some of his knowledge. It had transformed them and allowed them to flourish unlike ever before. Unfortunately, the god king had left, but Gob had known he would return. That was why he'd seized control of the tribe and become a hobgoblin. Someone had to make sure the others obeyed the will of the god king, and Gob's faith had been rewarded. Not only had the tribe grown and prospered, but Blacknail had returned to the tribe with several human minions. A hobgoblin with tame humans! That was beyond even Gob's lofty expectations.

Upon his grand return, the god king had led the most loyal goblins to this new settlement. Here, there was much more room to grow and the humans were less dangerous. Yes, this was a much better spot than the old one. It would allow the tribe to flourish and grow strong.

The life of goblins in the Green was harsh. They scrabbled and fought among themselves for scraps. Countless were the beasts that would chase them down and devour them. They were forced to dig into the dirt for fleeting safety. When they came up to find food, danger lurked behind every tree and up in every branch. That was changing, but it wasn't just because of the tools. Gob could see how his master's tribe was different from any other. The goblins in it had learned and been changed.

Usually, goblins and hobgoblins worked together only reluctantly and never trusted each other. They didn't even understand what trust was. They turned on one another for the slightest advantage and preyed on the weak. Blacknail didn't act that way, and he enforced that behavior in others. Every goblin in the tribe knew that he had to offer the god king their personal loyalty, but they did more than that. The god king ruled the tribe and enforced rules that allowed the goblins to coexist in a way they couldn't in the wild. Without such an unquestionable authority to punish rulebreakers and thieves, they would swiftly turn on each other. Now though, every goblin in the tribe fought their nature in exchange for all the benefits that serving the god king brought.

That was the true gift Blacknail had brought to his tribe. Discipline. That was why Gob served him without question and why the tribe could grow and learn from the humans. Oh, yes. The knowledge and skill of humans would allow the goblin settlement to grow beyond even Gob's wildest dreams. Drawn by abundant shelter and food, the swarms of feral goblins that sulked and hid throughout the Green would flock to the settlement in massive numbers. Goblins lurked in the shadow of every tree.

However, everything had to be done one step at a time, and thus Gob had to make sure he taught the goblins already here how to work properly and contribute to the tribe. Unending were the wonders that his god king could bestow upon his subjects, but they had to be earned.

A crack split the air, and Gob glanced toward the source of the noise. A log had been burning in a fire pit and cracked open to release a shower of sparks. The fire was burning in a shallow pit ringed by stones, and two goblins, Imp and Ferrar, were tending it. Gob studied them for a moment. They were just goblins, but they were far from ordinary. Ferrar was shrewd and the most skilled maker of tools in the tribe already, even if he did like to burn things a little too much and occasionally muttered about building the biggest fire ever. The other goblin, Imp, was a mage. Mages did magic. Gob had no idea what magic was, but its ability to blow things up impressed him. Imp could definitely contribute to the tribe. The god king had been wise, as he always was, to bring him along.

Grinning, Gob watched the goblin workers again, but was losing focus. He couldn't help but dream of the future that was coming. The tribe would swell in numbers and expand their territory out into the forest. Feeding such a horde would usually be a concern, but the god king knew ways to preserve food, as he knew everything. Thus, the tribe would soon control everything within several days of walking. After that, who knew how far their reach would extend? How wide was the world?

Of course, the tribe would contain more than goblins. As a hobgoblin, Gob knew this well. With so many goblins around, some of them would transform into hobgoblins. Keeping them from killing each other and getting them to obey orders would be challenging, but without a doubt, the god king could do it somehow. There was nothing he couldn't do, after all!

Thus, Gob planned on supplying his master with as many hobgoblin minions as possible. He would raise swarms of them—an uncountable horde!—so they could serve the tribe and do what mere goblins couldn't, which was a lot.

Obviously this was what the god king desired as well. Anything less than an unprecedented horde of hobgoblin minions was an insult to his greatness. Gob closed his eyes and took a moment to bask in the glory of the tribe's potential. Soon, with Blacknail at their head, they would spill across the North and everything would change. The harpies would fall to their slings, the not-trees would be burned, and even the trolls would be held at bay by spears and walls. All the beasts that fed on goblins would find themselves fighting not to be consumed in turn. It was impossible to stop now. Yes, soon all the North would belong to the god-king and his tribe.

About The Author

I'm just a normal everyday guy by the name of Scott Straughan. I also go by the moniker Clearmadness sometimes. Like a surprising number of authors, I'm Canadian. These days I live in the province of Ontario, and contrary to the rumors, I am not actually a goblin.

I started writing because I love world building and reading. I started reading at a young age and never ever stopped. My teachers had to confiscate my books. Eventually, all those ideas and characters took root in my brain and I had to start writing, so here we are.

Visit the Author's Website

at www.ironteethserial.com

You can find the further adventures of my characters at my website. You can also get information on future releases and a bonus side story by signing up for my mailing list.

Support my Patreon at www.patreon.com/Clearmadness

Get access to special chapters and content by signing up to be a patron. Your support helps me put my all into writing and produce more content for all you readers. I love writing and want to write as much as possible.

Coming Soon!

The Iron Teeth: Book Four

More Information at:

www.ironteethserial.com

Made in the USA
Coppell, TX
11 November 2019